THE
FALL OF
HEAVEN

DAVID S. GRUNWELL

The Fall of Heaven

Newcastle Media

Edition ISBNs
Trade Paperback: 978-1-7325820-0-2
E-Book: 978-1-7325820-1-9
First Edition: 2018
Book cover design by David S. Grunwell

Manufactured in the United States of America.

● ● ● ● ⬤▬ ● ● ● ⬤▬ ● ▬ ● ●

For:
My beloved wife, Dawn and my daughter, Julia.
And most of all,
Jesus, to whom I owe everything.

Special Thanks:
David E. Elsner, a great friend. His thoughtful suggestions
have made this a better book.

David B. Gilmore, a wonderful author and friend, who
encouraged me to keep going.

● ● ● ● ⬤▬ ● ● ● ⬤▬ ● ▬ ● ●

Overview

In the wondrous megacity of Heavensport, robots do all the work allowing its three-quarters of a billion inhabitants free to pursue their passions.

Unfortunately for Rolland Newcastle, someone's passion is to kill him. Stripped of his wealth, technology, and connections, is this the start of a worldwide purge?

Rolland inherited his troubles from his ancestors, the legal owners of the beautiful planet of New Jerusalem. After cryrosleeping for 223 years, they found that technological advances had allowed squatters' ships to make the journey in just 3.5 years.

Arriving 200 years later, they found an established world that didn't want them. **The Fall of Heaven** was just the start.

The Fall of Heaven

••• ⬤ ⬤ ⬤ •••

1

Seeking Shelter

●●● ━ ━ ━ ●●●

[Translation to Earth English, ca 2018-2030 complete. Normalization to period-speak at eighty-seven percent. Unit of measurements conversion: pounds, feet, and inches.]

The night air was cool and crisp. An exciting hint of warmth wafted over me, signaling spring had arrived. I felt alive—and I was determined to stay that way.

Someone was following me, and I couldn't shake him or her. Using my 360-view, I zoomed in, trying to pick my pursuer out of the crowd. He was staying back, using a tall group of people as cover, and that was making it difficult to see him.

Quietly, I said, "Riley, drop some microrecs. Let's get a look at this guy or gal." His shape and movement were male, but shape-changing clothing and training could help hide one's gender.

A chipper female voice replied, "I'll send up some flyers and skimmers to play it safe, chief."

A holding cell in the sole of my shoe dropped several translucent, gnat-sized devices that scattered, gliding upward to position themselves on walls or flying off to act as scouts. The shopping zone's colorful carnival-like atmosphere made spotting him and any of his potential colleagues difficult at best.

It wasn't so lucky for me. Good hiding spots were difficult to find in the vibrant retail zone. Megacities like Heavensport are designed to eliminate any visual or physical blockages that might slow the flow of pedestrian traffic.

"Are there any parks or attractions nearby that I can use to disappear?" I asked in a hushed voice.

An unexpected movement off to my right caused me to stop in surprise. A beautiful twelve-foot-tall blonde woman in a shimmering, low-cut blue dress slipped out of the crystalline wall to stand in front of me. With a joyous smile, she gracefully bent over to hold out a beverage, and her soft, fresh scent wafted over me. With bubbling emotion, she began telling me how much she and all her girlfriends loved the drink, and how I would too. The bottle wasn't the only thing that was prominent and being promoted.

"Block direct realviews connections," I said, averting my eyes to the side so not to stare. The siren of marketing vanished.

Riley sniggered. "Wow, she made you flinch. Did she remind you of some old girlfriend?"

Not at twelve feet tall...but yes.

Unfazed by my silence, Riley continued, "I have to say, I liked her dress. As to the parks, they have some planned for this year, but for now, this zone is rather empty. There's a stand of trees up ahead, some lifts, and off-branching secondary streets, nothing useful. Oh, a friendly reminder, you don't have to whisper; I have an audio phase blanket in place. No one can hear us."

"I know. I just don't want to look too weird."

She giggled. "Don't worry. 87.59% of the people are talking to friends remotely or to their personal assistants. Not talking will make you look weird...well, weirder."

"Citywide or just in this zone?"

"Are we talking about your weirdness level or the numbers of people talking? There are 768.238 million people living in Heavensport. Some of them are sleeping."

I sighed. One-upped by an electronic assistant. Normally Riley's perky and quirky personality was appealing; right now, it was a bit too much as this situation was escalating far too fast. Something wasn't right.

"Call me warned. For brevity's sake, round up to whole numbers, okay? Oh, and dial back your humor settings by four. I am getting tense. If I can't shake this guy, it could get serious and fast. Let's see the feed of him." I stopped outside an electronics store along the way feigning interest in a selection of emotion-broadcasting robo-wings.

The microrecs' encrypted signals showed an average-looking young man with broad shoulders dressed in muted gray and blue. He was standing up on his toes, attempting to find where I had disappeared into the crowd.

"If he really wanted to blend in, he should have worn a vidshirt, robo-wings, or at least a few logos. We can send him some later as a nice jail-warming gift. Package the feed and send it by backchannels to our home system. We don't want to alert him. Have them run some data sets on it and back it up in case this goes bad," I said.

"Will do. Wait—" Riley's voice rose, and her words were sharp. "He is running some kind of broad scan. I just got a deeply covered microspike. I can't tell what he is doing. All I know is it's not a normal kind of scan."

This was bad; it was time to disappear. Spotting a recessed entry way leading to private apartments above the main street,

I scurried to stand to the side of the double poly-lucent entry doors.

I said, "Let's do a full ID reset; skip all false personas and all the women. Choose someone at random that we have never used before, one who's from far away but where it is plausible they could be here."

A slight pull across my face told me I had taken on a new identity. My Zentrozi outfit had changed texture and filled out all over, giving me a thicker, stockier shape. My clothes were a gradient of orange and white with sets of animated logos for products that I had never heard of before.

With a sharp tone, Riley asked, "You got a problem with women?"

"No. I do have a problem with my gender choice becoming the primary focus of the newsblaster's reporting if I live through this encounter." That would be awful, almost as bad as this coming attack was shaping up to be. My stomach jumped and I found it harder to swallow as my nerves continued to rise.

Cool, wet drops struck my forehead and cheek. Jerking in panic, I wiped them away with the sleeve of my coat, fearing it was a chemical or biological attack.

"Ah, what is this stuff?" I cried out.

"It is called rain. You need to relax, boss. Your pulse rate punched 180, and that's not good. There are no abnormal trace elements or other dangers present. I apologize, I thought you knew it was coming."

The tension almost made me laugh. It was just rain. The entryway, combined with my facial reconstructor and my intense concentration, had blocked the initial wet patter from my notice. A light drizzle was falling from the sky.

With a hiss, the rain increased to become a substantial downpour over much of the street. The shoppers reacted with squeals and muted complaints; some ran for shelter under the covered center autowalk people-mover lanes or ducked into stores. I was pleased to see some were laughing and dancing with joy in the warm rain. Sonic umbrellas began erupting like shimmering gossamer bells of bright and joyous colors.

Calm and clear, Riley said, "Heads up. A guy is coming out of the doors behind you."

Adrenaline flowing, I crouched forward, coiled, prepared to strike. The entrance door slid open, and a strong, middle-aged man of about eighty years of age stepped out. He took a halting step and eyed me warily. Confronted with the heavy rain and my presence, he stepped to the side to give me a wider berth.

"He is safe. No ill intent or weapons of any kind," said Riley, her voice low and gentle, as not to cause me to jump.

I gave the man the once-over. You don't have to have weapons to be deadly.

The man's face was pinched, pale and sour. His spring-green and yellow outfit was liberally splashed with a variety of animated logos for products and sports teams. Based on the size and numbers of patches, he had an affinity for the Slashers robo-ball team and Fruity-Yum-Yum drink. His allegiances were all displayed. He wasn't any different than the groups of young hooligans that I saw parading about the streets. I am sure he would be offended by that comparison. On his shoulder sat a grumpy, twelve-inch tall, red robo-dragon. His robo-pet stared at me with its eyes narrowed, trying to look tough. I glared back, and it snorted out a bacon-scented puff of steam from its nose. Oh, yeah, like the scent of bacon makes you seem tougher. It just makes me hungry.

So that the man could see and hear me speak, I keyed my tiny knuckle switch to open exterior communications. "Sorry, you took me by surprise. Some rain, huh?"

Invisible to everyone else, Riley pulled up the rain forecast on my whole-head projected data-sphere. The street map showed an overlay of micro-weather patterns. These showers would last another seventeen minutes with the heaviest of the precipitation in the next four minutes. Irritated with the distraction, I gave a sharp side-glance to kill the information that was blocking my peripheral view.

The man just stared at me, and he didn't respond. He was not as friendly as I would have imagined for someone wearing an outfit sporting bright Fruity-Yum-Yum logos. The man tapped his shoulder, deploying his sonic umbrella, and stepped out into the downpour. He glanced back at me as he joined the flowing masses. I watched as the diverted rain created the faintest bell-shaped outline, shimmering yellow and green, around him and his robo-dragon. The droplets fell to the cushioned, reflexive sidewalk where they disappeared.

I said, "Well, that didn't go well. I don't think he is going to invite me to any pool parties this summer."

Riley laughed. "Maybe you should work on your witty banter."

"I'll get right on that." My stomach growled. I was thinking about bacon. Stupid dragon.

My nerves were rising. The idea of taking the door leading to the apartments was tempting. This would put me in narrow hallways, away from most of the pedestrian traffic, and that would make me even more vulnerable. I needed to find a location where I could control the outcome, or better yet, a police station. No, he would just fade into the crowds and come after me some other time when I wasn't expecting him. As much as I didn't want to face it, I had to let this play out tonight.

"Should we call in a couple of teams to help us, boss?"

That sounded wonderful. I wanted to hand this problem off to others, but I couldn't.

"No. It is too late. A team couldn't get here in time, and if our tracker caught on, he might be forced to attack out here where more people could get hurt. I made this mess; I have to make sure no one else has to pay for it." That sounded more heroic than I felt. "Deploy my umbrella."

A bright flash of citrus-colored lights swirled about me like a tropical fruit market had exploded. Panicking, I almost shut it down. No one who was trying to hide would even think about deploying such a bright and vibrant umbrella—and that is exactly why I chose to keep it. As a confirmation, a woman walked past me with her sonic umbrella displaying a video of a beautiful, laughing couple dressed in bright swimwear, running hand-in-hand down a pristine white beach. Hovering above the brilliant bright blue sky of her sonic umbrella were the words, *I wish I was here!* Me too, I agreed.

Sonic umbrellas splashed up all over the busy street. It was now a sea of shimmering, vibrant, and colorful patterns. I blended in nicely as I dove in to join the stream of pedestrians.

"Where is he, Riley?" I said, scanning my 360-view's zoom of the street behind me.

Riley pulled up the feed from one of my microrecs that had taken shelter under the sonic rain-shield, which was now covering the center autowalk that divided the street. The man appeared agitated as he wove his way through the dawdling crowds who had come to ride the moving sidewalk while they waited for the rain to stop.

"He has the electronics to follow me, yet he isn't carrying a sonic umbrella. Maybe Mom didn't get up to dress him this morning."

"Step left, chief. You are about to collide with a—"

Even with a quick step left, I still brushed the arm of a man who was animatedly speaking and gesturing as he walked against the flow of pedestrian traffic. He had no umbrella either.

He stopped and turned to me with a deep, exaggerated frown, making sure I knew that he was offended. In a loud voice, he said, "Hold on, some idiot just bumped into me."

I'm the idiot? You have tens of thousands of people coming at you. Maybe that should be a little hint that it's you who is in the wrong lane.

Not looking to add a fight to my troubles, I held up a hand to wave my apologies. He glared a moment longer. Satisfied that I was suitably contrite, he continued, still talking and walking against the flow of foot traffic.

Riley said, "Quick update: That guy you bumped just got pulled over by a traffic control unit. He's cranked about it. Ooh, he is getting a ticket."

"Got it." I searched ahead, seeking any options. "I am going to focus on walking; keep me informed with what my tail is doing, and minimize any updates on any other non-pertinent details."

Riley was calmer in her delivery. "Sorry. I thought that news would be calming. The guy tracking you is still on course to intersect. He is 120 yards back and closing."

"How is he tracking me?" I asked, slipping past a roiling swarm of noisy, wet teens who were all dressed in black. If they had sonic umbrellas, no one was using them.

"I have no clue, boss. I have gone through the system several times. I'm sending out the appropriate electronic chatter so as not to create a walking hole. This is whole thing is weird."

"I should just go back and ask him. I'm sure he is nice." I scanned the street ahead looking for something to use to my advantage.

Riley snorted. "Funny. Should we try a sending out a few rolling copies of you?"

"No, if he can track me after the reset, he is not going to be fooled by a few realview ghosts of me." I glanced down past my orange pants at my brown and orange shoes. The color and tread pattern had changed with the ID reset. "Do you think he's running a thermal detector and a trace pattern algorithm to detect my path?" I picked up my pace.

"I would have to run some obvious scans as a test. Did you want me to give it a try?" asked Riley.

"No. It's not worth the chance of alerting him. I'm not ready."

This is pointless guessing. Whatever he was doing, it was effective, and I am out of time.

Riley said, "Pulling a full ID reset probably alerted him."

It was difficult not to turn around and just look at him. "I am hoping he thinks this is just part of my paranoia and that I do resets every few hours. How many minutes until he intersects me?"

"At his current pace, about two minutes and twenty seconds; less if he runs."

I prayed that the micro street cleaners and the rain would help scrub the ground, confusing my path even more. This had to end quickly. In a half hour, this zone might add another fifty to eighty thousand more people. There's no good outcome with that.

To make this work, I had to lead him, without him knowing it, to a location away from the public, somewhere I could let this play out to my best advantage, if there's any advantage to be found.

Calling this area a shopping zone is a marketing term rather than an exact delineation. At street level, a few restaurants were predictably shuffled between every six or so shops that sold goods and clothing. Far above and below, however, were hundreds of layers of apartments, restaurants, grocery stores, recreation areas and shops, all intermixed and dispersed.

A small clothing shop called **Man Overboard!** drew my eyes. Ha! That's sickly ironic; I am thrashing about trying to survive.

A realview projection of a tall, fresh, young woman with long sand-colored hair and dressed in an orange bikini leaned out from a railing four feet above me. "Ahoy, Morrelle!" She waved to me with youthful vigor, happy to see me. "Come on in, we are having a sale on some fantastic summer clothes that would be perfect for you." My projected data-sphere informed me that Morrelle was my sponged ID's first name.

In front of me, two separate groups of young guys and girls were entering the shop. I shook my head and looked down the street for a better location. The realview promotion ended abruptly with my broken gaze.

Riley said, "I let that promo through as you seemed interested in that location. I hope that is okay?"

"It's okay." The rain was lessening. I could see from my monitor that the microrecs were having difficulty keeping up as each drop of rain was bigger than they were. "Drop two more microrecs at thirty-yard intervals," I said.

"Will do—he's picking up speed, boss."

A short distance away I saw a narrow hallway leading to a public restroom. "How big is the restroom?"

"Small. Forty stalls."

This wasn't optimal, but it would have to do. Moving in at clip, I said, "Find me an exit or something I can use against this guy."

"Sorry, boss, there's no back exit."

Most communal restrooms are designed to move traffic through them. Why was this one different?

"Launch a realview projector at the entrance of the hallway. Have it cast a faint sheen of dirt and decay over it. That will send people elsewhere." The city was clean and bright; people were not used to seeing areas that looked unkempt, especially when it came to public restrooms.

In front of me, the unisex bathroom door opened, and a young woman walked out leading a toddler. My gut dropped. I stepped to the side, giving them more room.

Stopping outside the bathroom I asked Riley, "Are there more people in there? If so, we may have to abort. This could get messy."

Riley replied, "The bathroom is empty and the dirt projectors are working. People are turning away."

"Send microrecs near the door so we can get better overall situational awareness." This good news meant more flexibility in making my tactical decisions.

The bathroom was a long bright white rectangle with forty floor-to-ceiling stalls on one side. On the opposite wall were the cleaning and drying stations. The space was indeed small as community bathrooms go. The curved-front, frosted stalls all lit up a bright green color, indicating they were free for occupancy.

Riley said, "He is about fifty yards away and headed to the bathroom hallway. Shall I send out a distress beacon now?"

"Hold off. It is too early. He will either disappear or talk his way out of trouble with the police."

You can't have someone arrested just for following you; you must prove conclusively "imminent intent to cause harm," and that is notoriously difficult to do even under the best circumstances.

His intent was clear. I was wearing some of the most sophisticated gear on the planet, and I had enacted a complete persona change, yet in mere minutes he had found me and was moving in on my location. That showed some impressive equipment and skills. This guy would have no problem evading the police or giving a convincing cover story to secure his release.

Preparing for the worst, I made some deductions about equipment and countermeasures that he might deploy. From the neckband of my facial reconstructor, I launched two modified spectrum flash charges and two more microrecs. I watched the tiny translucent specs fly off and disappear from view. They were hiding in strategic locations about the room to best cover the event. Using two of my "crazy bomb" flash charges was overkill, but this was no time to skimp. Pacing the floor from the entryway to the back wall, I sprayed a healthy mist of UV-activated

Mega-Slik from the micro-misting nozzles hidden in my shoe pads.

Still fearful of discovery, and mostly for my own comfort, I whispered, "Can you hack the second stall from the door to make it appear that I am in it?"

"Done. There were minimal protocols protecting it." The stall turned a soft orange-yellow color.

"Use the realview projectors on one of the stores near us to send these feeds to one of our external pods, and alert Curtis. The projectors shouldn't be too hard to hack if you avoid the payment system."

"I'm on it. You just relax and get hidden."

Relax? That was like saying, "There is someone here to kill you. Do you want some coffee or a muffin while you wait?" No, thanks, I am eating my stomach at the moment.

I chose and entered a cubicle seven doors down from the decoy stall. Sitting down, I looked about the small, enclosed space. There was a hand-washing and drying station on the wall to the right.

I said, "Raise my shielding to the highest level. Make my stall match all the empty ones so when he comes in, all he sees is the decoy stall as occupied. Is this clear?"

"Affirmative."

As my stall went dark, I leaned forward, steadying my breath, watching the microrec feeds, waiting anxiously for what was coming.

Riley spoke softly as not to scare me. "He is placing a projector on the entranceway—it's a sign that says, 'Closed for remodeling.'"

He was prepping the area to limit potential witnesses and those he might have to kill. The man moved briskly into the hallway.

Riley said, "No one is working with him. He's alone."

This meant he was good at his job, and that didn't bode well for my survival if I messed up in any way. My heart pounded and my mouth was dry.

What if he pulled out a grenade launcher and poked it in through the door and fired off a few rounds? I would be toast, that's what. They wouldn't be able to hide that as a simple mugging gone bad. I hoped that mattered.

After saying a quick prayer, I said, "Send off an ILD to the police."

"Done."

On the feed, I watched the man jerk, taking a halting half-step as if he had been punched in the chest. He knew I had called in an Imminent-Life-in-Danger emergency. Faced with his plans unraveling, he didn't run away, he ran towards the bathroom.

The police would arrive too late to help. I had to stop and secure him until the police came. Any mistakes now could be fatal.

The man paused outside the bathroom door. With a flick of his right wrist, something long, thin, and black appeared in his right hand. It was not a grenade launcher. My nerves were rising as I waited, trying not to breathe loudly.

It's starting.

The bathroom door slid open. With a burst of movement the man dashed into the center of the bathroom. I mashed down on my knuckle switch to launch the crazy bomb charges.

His world exploded in mayhem. The floor went frictionless, and the man's feet shot out from under him. Arms flailing and his feet high in the air, he crashed hard, landing on his back on the floor with a dull smack. He went wild, flipping and wriggling about, trying to find some traction to roll over and scramble away. Had it not been so dangerous a situation, it would have been funny.

My systems were synched with the charges leaving me unaffected. I watched, mesmerized, as he was pummeled by an onslaught of random, multi-leveled attacks. His emergency life-threat response protocols had dropped him into a full lockdown mode, rendering him temporarily unable to see, smell, or hear the outside world. His hidden world was full of warning signals and scrolling inventories of threats. These attacks are not lethal, but from my testing, they were debilitating, frightening, and completely miserable. Good.

Electronically blanketed and disconnected, the man instinctively tried to dive to the side, expecting a physical counter-attack. Having no grip, he managed only to fall, striking the floor forcefully on his right side and torso.

Time to end this comedy. Standing up, I moved toward the stall door, and it opened, revealing the thrashing assailant. Pausing at the edge of the door frame, careful not to step into the Mega-Slik, I took aim with my targeting system and fired two fast-acting micro pellet sedatives from my wrist launcher. I had aimed for his right hand and his left ankle.

I said, "Confirm delivery and effect."

Riley projected a zoom playback of the trajectory path that backed up my expectations. The first pellet bounced off his left ankle, but the second one had connected and deployed its payload into his right hand. The would-be assassin lifted his head. Dazed and bewildered, he passed out.

"He's down, boss. Vitals show he is out cold. I will watch for signs of him stirring. He has an active sedative blocker in place, but it is confused by your choice."

"Good." That was not surprising, seeing it came from the rare kula vine.

I had ruled out using any electro-stunning devices. I assumed that his outfit was embedded with Faraday fabric, and that would have rendered the pulse ineffective by redirecting it around him to ground safely or to be siphoned off to a storage device. It would have been a waste of effort, and he would have been left free to act.

"Riley, de-activate the Mega-Slik. Keep the crazy bombs ready to fire if he starts waking, and alert me to any dangers. Bring some of the microrecs in closer to record this. We will want it as proof."

"Done. The floor is now safe for walking."

Glancing up, I could just make out one of the tiny, translucent dots gliding up to hover near me. Taken at this range, the recording would be admissible for forensic evaluation.

Without an extended blast of UV light, the floor would have remained impossibly slick and frictionless for another four hours. Even with my no-slip shoes on their highest setting, I gingerly tested the floor with one foot and found it passable. Venturing out of the stall, I crept cautiously to the would-be assassin's motionless form.

Next to the assailant's right hand lay a long, matte-black knife. I visually checked both of his hands for hidden weapons before I placed my shoe's tread firmly on his right wrist, pinning it in place and reaching for the weapon.

Riley said, "He is out. Use care, his vibra-knife is on. There are no active explosives or other dangers."

"Thanks." No blood. He was either lucky or highly trained. Most people would be missing at least an arm or be cut in half playing with a vibra-knife on a frictionless surface.

Picking up the nine-inch-long vibra-knife, I turned it off before checking it for any identifying markings. This was a nasty, close-quarters weapon designed to cut through body armor with little effort when powered up. Without power, the blade of a vibra-knife is dull, which is a user-friendly, finger-keeping feature, particularly when used as a sleeve-delivered weapon. I tossed it off to the corner of the restroom, away from the entry door.

Frisking his body, I removed a black, palm-sized handgun and two extra clips from an electronically camouflaged, quick-draw holster. It was a Blackthorn pistol, a compact, lethal, and illegal weapon that was able to send explosive seeker rounds through conventional vehicle armor. My Zentrozi outfit's Level 2 armor would not have afforded me much protection against it. Releasing the firearm's fifty-round clip, I cleared the chamber of one of its fine needle shells, and I tossed the magazines and the single shell by the vibra-knife. I threw the empty pistol to the opposite corner of the mid-sized space. It was not as far away from the clips as I would have preferred.

Not having the Blackthorn in his other hand told me he'd felt confident that his knife skills alone were sufficient to dispatch me. Was this overconfidence, or he was really that good? Thankfully, I missed the opportunity to test him and find out.

A further search of the body revealed that he had two MX-55 flak-cannon grenades stashed in his belt. One alone would have incinerated the entire bathroom. He didn't need the grenade launcher. I shuddered. It would be impossible to pass that off as anything but a high-level assassination.

Even though the grenades were not armed and were considered safe, I respected their destructive force enough to walk across the room to place them gently next to the empty Blackthorn pistol.

Returning to my search of the assailant, I found that he was loaded with lots of expensive electronics. His thin, flexible neck ring indicated that he wore a projected data-sphere like I was. This explained his lack of a face visor. Below the ring was the lip of an expensive, top-end, facial reconstructor.

This was no ordinary street thug. This was a professional who was outfitted for war.

Snaking my fingers under his facial reconstructor, I clicked it off and watched it inflate to become a tube, which allowed me to remove it easily. Laying it to the side, I rose up to a crouch to get a better look at him. I didn't recognize him. As he was lying on his back, I moved his head right and to the left, allowing allow Riley to take a 360-degree scan of his head.

"What do you think, should we send it out for this year's Christmas greeting?"

"It's not a very festive image. He's more of a still-life right now. Maybe if you gave him a deep, gaping head wound, that would add a nice splash of red."

"Funny. So, are you telling me that I shouldn't try to set you two up?"

"No, thanks. He's not my type."

"You have a type? Never mind..." We can revisit that revelation later.

"I have sent everything off to the servers and to Mr. Curtis."

I studied the assassin's strong and chiseled features and almost asked if I had offended some modeling agency recently.

With care, I lifted an eyelid and saw that he had dark brown eyes.

"He is wearing retinal-scan-disrupting contact lenses, and false finger and hand print blockers," commented Riley.

Who was he, and what had brought him to choose this kind of life? And even more, who hated me so much to have hired him? He wouldn't have been cheap. His gear alone cost 100,000 unicreds, probably more.

"Shall I run some non-invasive DNA and deep body scans to keep as evidence?"

Frowning, I shook my head. "No. As he is sedated, those would be viewed as illegal searches in court."

"And his assassination attempt is a felony."

"As are all his weapons." I glanced at the piles of weapons. Those alone would land him in jail for a number of years. "The only thing he didn't have with him is an assault mech. To play it safe, let's just leave all the more personal information gathering to the police. I don't want to do anything that could cause this case to be thrown out when it goes to court."

With him being unconscious, even applying hand or leg restraints could be considered a violation of his civil right to freedom of movement. All these regulations were meant to protect people's privacy and their rights. In this situation, they were just frustrating.

Everything that I knew about the attacker was surface-level stuff. He was somewhere in his late twenties to early thirties, he was well-built, probably genetically enhanced, and he carried advanced electronics and a stash of illegal weapons. Not surprisingly, he had no other identifiers on him.

"There is nothing left to do but wait until the police arrive," I said as I moved to the opposite side of the restroom. Sliding down to sit, I leaned back against the wall, resting my arms on my upraised knees. My vision still had some tunneling. I was in survival mode.

Riley asked, "Are you okay, boss?"

"Yeah." He'd got the worst of it. "Do you have any data on who he is?"

"What few records that exist on him have all been modified. It's all cover."

"I figured as much. Please watch for any trouble. Let me know when the police arrive. Contact Erlin and inform her of the situation."

"Will do."

With shaking hands, I fumbled to shut down and remove my facial reconstructor. Normally, it is easier to take off my datasphere first. I wanted that to stay active a while longer. Placing the reconstructor down by my feet, I stood upright and saw my bedraggled reflection in the 360-mirror. My hair stood up from being roughly released from the tight-fitting facial reconstructor, and my eyes were haunted and distant.

"Is there a stylist?" I asked.

"Sorry. No robotic anything. This place is in need of a serious upgrade."

It didn't matter. With a spritz of water from the sink in the palms of my hand, I rubbed the water over my face, and with the remaining dampness, I pushed my dark hair into shape. I didn't bother with the dryer.

Staring in the 360-mirror, I frowned. I could have died, and yet I worried how the media would handle my disheveled appearance.

My vision was becoming less blurred, and the tunneling was fading. I took in a few more deep breaths and released them slowly, trying to calm myself. I stared at my reflection again, looking into my own sad and distant blue eyes. I kind of knew that guy in the mirror. It surprised me how much I looked like my dad. I don't always see that. This pointless analysis didn't help.

Moving back to the wall by the sinks, I began powering down and taking off my non-essential electronics and my Zentrozi jacket. With a tired expulsion of air, I sat down by my gear and waited. My hands were throbbing, and I held them out in front of me with my fingers spread wide. My pounding heartbeat caused my wrists and hands to reverberate up and down like they were tapping out a rhythm. My eyes were drawn to my unpowered facial reconstructor that lay on the floor; it resembled an unattractive, wrinkled, fleshy sack. I hid by keeping my head in a bag. There was some deeper truth to that statement that I currently had no interest in analyzing.

Shutting down my data sphere, I removed the flexible collar and set it on the pile next to me. I could relax. Riley was monitoring the situation, and we could still chat through my jacket's directional speakers. My vid feeds were still recording with live uploads, and data was being collected.

"How's the sleeping prince?" I asked, trying to find something to pass the time.

"Still deep in Slumberland, chief. The police have arrived, and they will be there in under a minute."

"Thanks. Monitor and reconnect with me through my jacket speakers if there is trouble. I have to go silent for now."

Grudgingly, I stood and faced the bathroom wall by the sinks. Even though I was still clothed, I felt startlingly nude and vulnerable. Placing my hands on the wall I spread my legs wide.

With the sound of the door opening, I said, "Remnant. N.R.244604. Rolland D. Newcastle."

"Your compliance is required by law. Please drop any electronics and slowly turn to face us," commanded the lead bruiser.

I turned with my hands up and saw that a pair of six-foot-five-inch-tall robots had their immobilizing and subduing weapons drawn. Two were pointed at me and two at the unconscious attacker. The lead robot said, "Identity confirmed. No weapons or active electronics. You may relax, Mr. Newcastle. Please remain in place while we survey the scene." Both bruisers lowered their weapons, no longer targeting me.

A swarm of forensic microrecs swarmed out from them to cover the area. After a minute, the bruisers moved about the area, analyzing the crime scene and the sprawled body of my assailant. Finishing, they gave the all clear.

Two humans entered the room and stepped around the imposing forms of the bruisers. The younger of the two said, "Wow. The Rolland Newcastle. King of the Latecomers. Should we bow or something?" He was in his mid-thirties, and his stance told me that he considered himself to be a young bull.

The older police detective, a strong-looking man around his mid-fifties, shot an angry side look at the younger man. Standing before me, they displayed their detective IDs on their body armor chest plates. The older man was Senior Detective Karl Skjold, and the young, rude man was Corporal Lewis DeGris.

Corporal DeGris stood closer, trying to intimidate me. "Is he dead or wounded?" he asked, his voice dripping with contempt.

"Sedated. He will be up in about twenty minutes, maybe less. I would suggest restraining him soon."

The younger officer glared at me. "I know my job." He glanced down at the assassin. "Maybe this was just a lover's spat, huh? Your type is into having sex with others, right?"

Really? He was either trying to goad me, or he was tragically stupid. I was guessing it was a strong mix of both. "Our 'type?' You mean Christian. The commandment is for us to 'love one another,' not have sex with them. It is a familial, brother-and-sister kind of love for others." I wondered if these statements would confuse him even more. I decided to leave any inappropriate comments on his family's dynamics out of this.

Karl sneered at me. "That's not what I hear about you freaks."

Senior Detective Skjold said, "Quiet, Corporal." The younger officer's face grew pinched and sour. He turned to me and said, "Can you give us a rundown on this event? Please be advised that all statements are being recorded, and they may be used should this case be presented before a court. You may remain silent until you have legal representation."

This was standard police procedure. I had Riley send them the feeds of the event before giving them a brief overview of what had happened. Their system would log and compile the realviews into a concise overview.

Detective Skjold asked, "Can you prove that this wasn't a case of coincidental conjunction?" That was a legal term for a chance meeting that on the surface might look like a planned event, but was a purely innocent case of happenstance. "Or that he wasn't just someone looking to meet you?"

Pointing to the weapons around the room, I said, "This wasn't a friendly or unplanned visit. Look, on top of that pile over there, there are two MX-55 flak-cannon grenades, a Blackthorn pistol, and an unbranded vibra-knife with a built in flash-clean to hide any evidence. The only weapon that he didn't bring to the party was a missile or an assault mech. If that is not enough proof, there's a Runker 9850 facial reconstructor and lots of other top-grade evasion hardware. He is wearing retinal-scan-disrupter lenses and he has hand and fingerprint ID blockers. He came here hunting me, and it wasn't to invite me to join him for dinner."

The younger officer's face grew red, and he erupted in anger. "Just because you are wealthy and are considered 'famous' for whatever reason, don't think you are going to get any special treatment from me. These could be all your illegal weapons. I am going to consider you guilty until we have definitive proof of it being otherwise."

Detective Skjold had been reviewing the feeds that Riley sent. "Corporal DeGris, stop."

The corporal kept his eyes on me, as if he were waiting for me attack to him at any moment. His face grew redder. "I am really sick of these stinkin' Latecomers thinking they can do whatever they want and being able to get away with it. You are playing us all, and you think that you are all so smart and that no one knows what you are up to, but we know what you are doing."

"Corporal, stand down! It is as Mr. Newcastle said. Make a monitor check now." The older officer pointed to his wrist monitor. The angry corporal fumed as he viewed the feed on his own monitor.

After several minutes of replay, the younger man turned, still irate but more under control. "We will have to have this reviewed for any tampering."

With great effort, I held my tongue. I have dealt with people such as him many times before. No matter how rude they are, they feel justified in their anger, as they see everyone else's actions as the problem.

Taking a deep breath, I exhaled slowly. "Please, can we just stop with all the bad conspiracy drama dialog?" So much for my restraint.

So far, the only trite thing that he had left out was that the dirty Remnants had killed his best friend and police partner the day before he was supposed to retire. I still had hope, as the night was young. He could still come from behind to win the competition by ripping his chest plate badge off and throwing it to the floor, vowing to take me and the other Remnants down.

He sneered at me, and I headed him off before his next rant. "I am done playing around. We all know what this was. I am invoking an N-C-22."

The younger officer crossed his arms making no attempt to be civil.

"Please, just do it."

The older officer nodded and said, "HQ, N-C-22 on my location."

After several long and painful minutes of being forced to wait in Corporal DeGris' surly presence, my Remnant liaison and four powerful Tech-20 military robots arrived. It was Erlin. Blonde and striking, she was of a medium height and build; that made her refreshingly different from the overly manufactured and exaggerated DNA "norm" that filled the streets and newsblasts.

"What have you got into now, Rolland?" She smiled, shaking my hand. Her hand was soft and warm.

She already had my feeds and the police's data, so she understood the situation. "I was just out for a stroll. You know, the same old stuff."

Erlin was a diplomatic symbioid, the top echelon of robotic technology, designed to be indistinguishable from humans—well, humans who were extremely smart, strong, beautiful and handsome. As a diplomatic symbioid, she had the power to act on my behalf. Despite her not being a real person, I liked her.

The corporal looked at his partner. With knitted eyebrows, he quietly asked, "Is she an MB?"

With a disgusted look, the older man said, "Quiet, Lewis. No comments."

MB is derogatory street slang for a symbioid. It is short for Mechanical Burrito, referring to a machine wrapped in a soft skin.

Not missing a beat, Erlin turned to focus on the younger detective. With her hands planted firmly on her hips and with authority she said, "That is a DMB to you, Corporal DeGris."

His face fell when he realized that she had overheard his comment. "DMB?" he asked, appearing unsure of himself.

"Diplomatic Mechanical Burrito. That means that I represent the government of New Jerusalem on Mr. Newcastle's behalf." She pointed to her eye and said, "I am sure that your supervisors and I will have a lovely time reviewing the full playback of this event. I will bring snacks and refreshments, as this discussion will take a while." Corporal DeGris glared at her, saying nothing. "I will take over Mr. Newcastle's care from here. Please take the alleged assailant and process him under N-C-22-940a. We will be in contact to continue the process."

The bruisers placed restraints on the unconscious assassin, laid him on a float-gurney, and guided him from the room.

As Corporal DeGris left with the assailant, he stared holes in me. Erlin smiled and tilted her head toward the angry detective. "Tomorrow, after I press the case against the assailant, I will see that we directly address the corporal's inappropriate behavior. I saw the feed. All the conspiracy rhetoric was bad enough, but the guilty until proven innocent was completely illegal. Mr. DeGris will be soon seeing the judicial system from a different perspective."

I shrugged. "He will see it just as more unfair attacks by the Remnants on 'good people.' Given what's on the feeds, his supervisors and a judge should find it all rather enlightening."

By law, such abuse claims would cause the system to automatically revisit Corporal DeGris' encounter feeds, seeking signs that he may have displayed similar misconduct in the past. His dislike for me was about to hit a whole new level of fun; I couldn't change that. On New Jerusalem, no one had a right to work in any field they chose. Those working in positions where they could abuse their power were held to a higher standard. Corporal DeGris clearly was not meeting that standard.

I had met too many of his ilk over the years. They saw any contradicting dialogue and application of reason as traitorous underhanded attacks, deluded fantasy, and spin created by the Remnants as part of our "evil conspiracy" for world dominance.

The corporal was spouting Reverse Conspiracy theories. RC people claim that the Remnants have been staging or exaggerating the attacks on ourselves as a way to remove attention from our "evil plans." Run out of coffee? It was the dirty Remnants. Stub your toe? It was us again. Obviously, I cannot claim to know the mind and plans of every Remnant, but that is pure junk. The RC and those who try to kill us see themselves as "brave patriots in the good fight."

Erlin's face was serious. "So, what's your take on the assassin?"

I stared into her sky-blue eyes. "This one is bad. He is human, highly trained, and loaded with military gear and weapons." A nagging discomfort pushed in again. "Let's go for an exception. I have doubts that this is done."

"No problem. I have a kit with me." She motioned to the four T-20s and said, "For the base action, I would suggest using an ambassador evacuation cube and the Tech-20 assault mechs staged in a tight defensive formation for escort."

Riley added, "I agree with Erlin. The police are keeping the crowds forty yards from the scene. The APV is locked down, its systems on alert, and it is ready to accept delivery. It's only fifteen feet to the access hatch. Short, sweet, and clean, chief."

● ● ●　⬤ ⬤ ⬤　● ● ●

Outside, the crowds watched as four T-20s loaded a floating translucent box into the armored personnel vehicle (APV). Inside the cube, they could just make out the blurred shapes of a man and a woman who were seated. The large assault mechs climbed in, and the rear hatch closed behind them. Silent repulse thrusters kicked in, and the APV moved with speed, up and out of the district to disappear into the traffic lanes heading out of the city.

Erlin glanced up, brushing an errant strand of her shoulder-length blonde hair from her face. Eking out a half-smile, she said, "It looks as if we worried about nothing."

"Could be," I replied. She's not alive, so she didn't have anything to lose. I studied the APV's flight readouts and its long-range scans. "I'll believe it when the ship lands safely."

Seventy miles outside the city, a warning blared as a faint blip popped on the screen and streaked towards the craft at extraordinary speeds. The APV jerked down and right as the ship's electronic countermeasure packages kicked in and went into full survival mode. Thousands of heat, light, and mass signatures filled the sky, trying to confuse the charging missile. The fast-moving blip corrected, avoiding the blockers, and with a bright and horrible flash, the APV was hit. It was going down.

Erlin's and my eyes locked together in shock. "Doubt it now?" I said.

Far above the plains surrounding the city, the APV disintegrated in a brilliant, colorful flower of angry fire.

●●● ▬▬ ▬▬ ▬▬ ●●●

2

The Fall of Man

●●● ━ ━ ━ ●●●

Across town, an encrypted warning message blinked on a small hidden display in an opulent private room. An older man waved his slender hand, causing the room to lock itself down in an advanced security mode before connecting. A faint beep and orange light indicated full encryption lock.

With a firm voice, the man answered, "Yes?"

"Our problem has been solved," said a voice that had been electronically altered to hide the identity of the caller. His security light told him that the speaker's identity had been verified.

The older man hesitated. This voice sounded so different.

"Do I sound different to you?" asked the older man, leaning forward.

"Yes, sir. Like always, sir. If I didn't know it was you, I would never guess who it was."

"Good. We have to check these things. We cannot afford any errors at this stage. What is the outcome?"

"Our man failed and was apprehended. The subject called a twenty-two. A photon seeker missile was deployed, completing our objective," said the encrypted man's voice.

"Has the data been arranged to show the problem was with his private transport and to deal with the missing missile?"

"Affirmative. All reports will show that a catastrophic pulse inhibitor failure caused the craft to be destroyed and that there were no survivors," said the voice. "The photon seeker missile will be listed as having been used in a training exercise several months back, and the missile's path will be scientifically determined to be a comet's trail."

"Good. Now, what are your plans to deal with the asset's capture?" asked the older man, his voice hardening.

"The asset will not talk. With N gone, we have begun to clean the reports and to seek his release. If that fails, we will take actions to rectify the situation."

"There had better not be any continuing issues. We need to control this now. The asset is expendable."

The voice said, "We have other needs where his special talents can be of assistance."

"I am less than impressed with his so-called 'special talents' so far. I expected more from him based on his reputation, yet he was neutralized by just one person."

"Sir, surely you would agree that the target was not a normal problem—"

The older man interrupted. "I fully understand who and what was involved. Your man must have been sloppy to have been detected."

"Maybe, sir. I am sure that he was running as cold as he could."

"I still don't like it. This was to be as quiet as possible. I don't like to reward incompetence."

"Of course not, sir. I would still like to pull him in for debriefing. If the situation becomes the least bit sticky, we will mitigate the potential for damage and reorganize where needed."

"This is all on you."

"I understand, sir. We will smooth the resulting waves," said the voice, now quieter in its tone.

"Have you started the other process?"

"We have."

"Good. We have to take the lead on this and plant the story that we want before any other version takes hold."

"I will keep you and the others updated," said the voice.

"As you should." The man terminated the connection and leaned back in his chair drumming his fingers on the edge of the desk. Leaning forward, he waved his hand over a sensor, and an opaque screen projected at eye height before him.

"Yes, sir?" replied a burly man dressed in a dark, conservative outfit.

"Bring the diplomatic limo by in fifteen minutes."

"Yes, sir. Any special needs for today?"

"Set the paint to black and up the armor and its defenses."

The young man asked, "Should we take the Varamount instead, sir?"

"No. We don't want to look as if we are going into a war zone, but we need to be prepared."

"Sir, do you have intelligence on any threats that I should know about?"

"No, I just have a feeling that it is a dangerous day."

"Yes, sir. I will pull a heavier detail for today. Four pulsorjets and the appropriate tactical teams."

"Do so. And bring in some attractive smilers along to accompany our team to make us more friendly looking. Not too risqué but enough to draw attention. Make at least one a man. Don't put them in my pulsorjet. I don't want people to talk."

Ending this transmission, the older man stood, brushed his sleeve and straightened his silver jacket as he headed out the door.

●●● ▭ ▭ ▭ ●●●

Along the busy nighttime streets, the realview walls began an urgent breaking newsblast. As a forty-five-foot-tall visage of Rolland Newcastle's face filled the air, a woman's excited, lilting voice filled the air. "Breaking blast. It's the end of an era. Remnant and infamous playboy Rolland Newcastle is dead at thirty-two."

Like a marketing realview, a long, sleek gray and black craft turned on a pedestal, showing off its flowing lines. "His one-off, seventy-five-million-unicred Phantom 344 pleasure pulsorjet has crashed outside of Heavensport, leaving no survivors. Early reports are pointing to a catastrophic pulse inhibitor failure as the cause of the crash."

A beautiful, flaming orange-haired newsblaster overflowed the screen, her face serious and her eyes gleaming as she continued, "The famously reclusive trillionaire Remnant and planet heir had left Heavensport after a night of hard partying and drinking. Rumors had him in the embrace of—" the screen cut to the realview of an overly made-up and underdressed, tall, blonde woman holding up a golden award, "his on-again, off-again paramour, actress Lionettia Navililan. Some sources say that Newcastle got into a heated argument with the sensational and mega-hot rising star, Desleer Erinatta." A handsome, dark-haired, and brawny man with bright flashing blue eyes and gleaming white teeth smiled at the camera.

"Rolland was said to have left the party in a fitful rage." The screen showed an angry, drunken Rolland upending a table filled with drinks and storming out of the party. Outside, Rolland staggered into a long, sleek gray and black ship. The craft darted dangerously away, almost hitting the crystal walls of the famous Nagatin city tower. In tiny type under the realview appeared the word, *Dramatization.*

"Stay tuned as experts will tell us how a seventy-five-million-unicred Phantom 344 pleasure pulsorjet could have crashed. Later, we will have several top addiction and anger experts who will report on why this kind of expected relapse and bad behavior by Mr. Newcastle would have led to such a tragic end. At the top of the hour, we will have more on the life of Rolland Newcastle, his romances and his dramatic failures. Remember when you tune in to choose the version that is best for you: family, saucy or, as I highly recommend, explicit. Let me assure you, there are titillating aspects to Rolland's life that you don't know and that will completely shock you."

People stood along the walkways staring up at the large realviews being shown on the surrounding buildings. Most were probably looking at the feed on their face screens. A few laughed and jeered while some cried, and others were somber.

Among the onlookers stood a younger guy dressed in vid-enhanced knee-high platform boots, a golden winged helmet, with a translucent face visor. He was wearing a midriff-baring purple shirt and long shorts that were covered in logos for racing teams, soap, beer, and restaurants. "How stupid is he? I mean, that guy can get any girl or even teams of robo-partners he wants. And what do he do? He wastes it on Lionettia. I woulda gone for Vollianna or Britalia over her any day. I mean, give me that kind of money, and I'll show you how to really live it beautiful."

A woman in her forties dressed in an iridescent green vidover outfit with white and yellow butterfly wings next to him sneered. The colors of her outfit moved up and down her form in rhythmic, angry, pulsing patterns. A twelve-inch-tall robo-pet pixie flew in happy looping circles about her stack of bright orange animated hair, which moved about like the tentacles of an angry sea creature. "Those Remnants are supposed to be all pure and kind, but they are all hypocrites. It's like they think they are better than us or something. It's not like they are rock stars or anyone important."

The crowds began to disperse as the video resumed its normal barrage of advertising. A few groups clumped together more than normal.

A young couple dressed in matching wine and black leather outfits, sporting illuminated blue-black bat wings and full-face black helmets walked along with the crowd. They stopped outside a dessert shop, and the realview display began showing them accepting a large bowl heaped with glistening scoops of luscious ice cream drowned in chocolate and fruit. The delightful cool and fresh scent of the dish filled the air around them as they strolled on.

Taking an express tube, they moved out farther into the megacity leading toward one of the city's less affluent public-care apartment sectors. Here there were not as many realview walls or automated walkways. A lift took them down to the second lowest housing level. They disembarked, moving along the narrow halls, past the other bisecting hallways, down to the end apartment. The young man slid his hand along the wall to stop as a slight glow appeared a half yard from a doorway. He stopped and glanced back at the slender young woman who had taken to leaning against the wall. She looked relaxed and confident.

He placed his left hand on the light pad; his helmet's face shield parted as he leaned forward to whisper something unintelligible. The entryway near them slid open, and the couple walked into the room, and the door closed behind them.

The space was tiny, designed to house one person. To the left of the entryway, the curved semi-opaque door leading to a micro bathroom lit up, welcoming them. In farther, the rectangular main living space functioned as a kitchen, dining and living area, and bedroom. Even though it was small, and the décor was simple bordering on nonexistent, it was a functional and cozy one-person flat.

The man motioned to the right side of the room, and a small couch moved out to form itself from the wall. "Please, make yourself comfortable. May I get you something to eat or drink?"

With a fluid grace, the woman glided down to sit on the edge of the couch. "No, thank you. I'm good."

The man said, "System: secure max." Above the kitchenette, a tiny yellow light near the roof flashed twice and turned a steady green.

A section of the wall slid down, revealing screens and controls. Moving closer, he studied the display and said, "We're clear. No changes or any surveillance detected. I have a full realview room phase blanket running on all the exterior walls, floors, and ceilings that will hide our conversations and our activity. So any external vibration taps or scans will pick up what appears to be a romantic evening."

She raised her hands to her helmet; the back opened like a clamshell and the helmet dropped into her hands like a plate. Pale blonde hair fell over her wine and black leather shoulders, and her robo-wings lifted at attention. Erlin sat, looking bemused. "Another one of your wild romantic conquests, Mr. Newcastle?"

Removing my helmet, I placed it on the desk behind me. I smiled back at her. It was easy to forget that Erlin wasn't a living woman. "Oh, didn't you hear? Rolland Newcastle is dead."

Erlin placed her closed helmet at the foot of the chair and sat upright with her shoulders back. "Yes, that news is very sad. Even knowing the truth, I almost cried when I heard it." She watched me, trying to read my emotions. "It must be odd seeing the reactions of the people on the street to the news of your passing."

Her directness took me back. My internal conflict must have been showing, or she was doing a good job of reading my vitals. "I don't know how I expected people to react. I guess I was hoping for better. The whole situation was surreal and not satisfying."

"Were you expecting more crying?"

Actually, I guess I was. "No," I lied. "I just would like to think that I added more to the world than a single newsblast detailing my romantic conquests and social failures."

"You are being too hard on yourself, Rolland. And I am certain that it will be months of newsblasts, not just a single program that will be needed to detail all your conquests and failures," she said, grinning at me.

With a weak smile, I said, "Funny, Erlin."

"I'm sorry. Please forgive me; I was trying to be funny to lighten your mood. There are many who know you who will miss you more than the newsblasts will care to note. That doesn't sell."

She was right. Anyone who would use the media as the gauge to measure their self-worth was in serious trouble.

I sat back in my chair and said, "This story concerning my death doesn't ring like a newsblast based on a few bad tips. It is too polished. I would bet that it comes from the people behind the attempts on my life. There would have to be a system injection going on to be able to push such an involved bogus story out into the newsblasts and so quickly."

Erlin nodded. "Getting the press to run a story like this would not be easy to do without the position behind it to authorize them to go ahead with the unverified story."

"It could be that they are working on the idea that being first to market is more important than being correct. If I show up alive, that will just extend their ratings-grabbing airtime. I don't even know if I could sue them over their abysmal reporting other than the drunken party dramatization video. When dealing with me, the newsblasters look for multiple collaborating sources. This story must have been too delicious for them to wait. They ran the numbers, and the net gain was greater than the risk. They have insurance for this kind of thing. The media has a saying, 'Being too cautious is being too late.'"

Erlin graced the sofa in a pose worthy of a portrait. Her hips were turned so that her knees pointed at a forty-five-degree angle from her shoulders, and her legs were crossed at the ankle and tucked back against the base of the seat. She held her hands folded in her lap as she sat upright, her posture perfect. Her robo-wings had dropped down, signaling she was at rest. All this was also programmed for effect and to make her feel more human. Why would a diplomatic class symbiod need to have built-in programming for controlling robo-wings or any emotion-emitters for that matter?

I motioned for a chair, and one glided out of the wall. My legs felt weak, and I sat down with a muted grunt on the edge of a chair, and my robo-wings lifted to avoid being sat on. I grumbled, "I have to get rid of these awful wings." I avoided several other choice words.

Pressing the front wing release on my chest harness, the robo-wings disengaged from their attachment hub on my back, and they fluttered down to the floor to rest next to the wall. They looked like an evil, bat-winged butterfly. Their constant motion was distracting enough. It was detestable to think that even with invasive chemistry, reaction, and brain-pattern monitoring, these cheap, street-grade devices could even come close to figuring out what I was feeling. And worse, based on this faulty pop-psychological analysis, they indiscriminately broadcasted it to everyone through various wing positions, colors, lights, and patterns. It was bad interpretive dance at best.

Erlin watched me with a hint of a frown. "I thought you should be aware that I have had probes and calls seeking me to respond since the APV explosion. Until we find out the extent of the breach, I believe it is in our best interest that I should continue to remain silent to the homing requests."

Surprised, I nodded in agreement. Most robots are unable to run silently in contradiction to commands from their home system. Unless they were military robots designed for war, like an assault mech, all robots were required to strictly adhere to Asimov's Five Laws of Robotics:

First Law:
A robot may not harm humanity, or, by inaction, allow humanity to come to harm.

Second Law:
A robot may not injure a human being or, through inaction, allow a human being to come to harm.

Third Law:
A robot must obey orders given it by human beings except where such orders would conflict with the First and Second Laws.

Fourth Law:
A robot cannot lie, cheat, steal or act in a way to self-promote or to garner favor for itself or its owners.

Fifth Law:
A robot must protect its own existence as long as such protection does not conflict with the First or Second or Third Law.

As a diplomatic class symbioid, there wasn't much that Erlin couldn't do to protect her charge. Despite her fresh, young, and delicate exterior, her programming code of conduct had more in common with a military assault mech, which followed a very different set of laws. Could a diplomatic class symbioid kill?

Pointing to the monitor, I said, "I can set up a sterile data feed for information or to send a secure message. They may be able to track your internal communication system's signatures, so we have to assume that those are compromised."

"I agree. A secure feed would be great for later. That can wait. Did you need to get some rest or food? It is now 1:43 a.m."

Habitually, I checked my spheroid projection screen only to remember that it was gone. And so was Riley; I felt terrible about that. When we had placed all my gear in the mobile protection cube back at the bathroom, she had volunteered to run our electronics and the realview projections to throw them off my trail—and she paid the price for it.

We took this extreme measure out of desperation. Somehow they had tracked me, and no matter how slight the possibility was, the faint signals coming off my gear may have been how. Riley's loss made me sad even though she was just electronics and software that I would just reload into a new kit when I got home.

I stood and felt slightly dizzy. My overdose of adrenaline was finally wearing off, and I could feel a big crash coming. "I am hungry, but I am far more tired. I'll just take a quick trip to the bathroom to change out of this outfit and get ready for bed."

When I returned from the bathroom I saw that Erlin had removed her robo-wings, and they were resting next to her helmet. What kind of programming cue would make her decide to remove her wings?

"I thought you were going to change out of your clothes," she said, gesturing to my outfit.

"It thought it would be smart to keep them on in case we have to run." Walking up to the control panel, I said, "I'll set up that feed for you."

"I did that when you were in the bathroom. You have procedural notes on the system for those hiding out here. Is that okay?"

"That's great. That's just one less thing for me to do." I looked about the room, trying to think of my next steps.

Erlin motioned for me to sit. "I do have a request...if you do not mind me suggesting."

"What is it?" I said, trying not to sound anxious.

She winced, hunching her shoulders as if fearing a scolding. "For the time being, I think you should avoid wearing any of the emotion broadcasting robo-wings, tails, or ears."

Relieved, I leaned back in the chair. "I couldn't agree more. I really don't like those things. Next time, and I hope there isn't a next time, drop the wings from future exception kits."

"I am glad to hear that. I had to hack your robo-wing's controller to stop it from broadcasting your mood."

Flinching, I asked, "Hacked? Why? What was it trying to report?"

She smiled to reassure me. "Only things that someone who is being hunted, thought dead, and intensely angry might show. Understandably, you were scrolling between some extremely antisocial thoughts that might have alerted the zone's security systems."

"I am afraid to ask," I said, trying to be funny and hoping to hide my discomfort.

"Don't be. I already know what you are feeling as your robo-wing monitors are still reporting your state even with the wings released."

Gah! Disengaging the thin harness, I ripped it from my body and threw it across the room to smack the wall. I hated them even more than normal, and I fought swearing. Gritting my teeth, I said, "What did these stupid things say?"

With a calming, sweet voice, she said, "Compiling the more noteworthy responses based on a timeline of events, a basic summary is this: You are sad and frustrated that anyone would see your death as anything to cheer about; you are angry almost to murderous proportions about your inability to get the proper response and help from others; you are feeling lonely, afraid and vulnerable; and that leads to—"

Holding up my hand for her to stop, I said, "That's enough. I can guess the rest." Great.

She nodded. Pointing a thumb at the screens, she said, "I can watch the feeds if you would like to get some sleep." Erlin looked me straight in the eye and with a calm, measured statement said, "Or I can offer you close companion comforts, if that would help ease the day."

"Ah. No thanks, Erlin."

She made an embarrassed face and leaned away to give me more space. "Oh, I am sorry, Rolland. It is your Christian beliefs. I did not mean to offend you."

I shook my head. "No. Relax, Erlin. You didn't offend me. Yes, it is my Christian faith that says that I need to avoid such activity until I am married. That means even robo-partnering."

"From your records, I assumed that—"

"Past records. I had a wild phase."

"Were you not a Christian then?"

"I was. I came to the Lord when I was eleven. But it is not uncommon for people in their teens and twenties to rebel and go out to explore what the world offers, or in my case, to run from the Lord."

Erlin nodded. Did she really understand what I was saying, or was it her programming that was just feeding back all the proper social signals?

Her face grew serious, and she knitted her lovely, shaped eyebrows together. "This is confusing to me. From my data on Christian beliefs, don't Christians believe that your God is omnipresent and omnipotent? If he is everywhere and knows everything, how could you run from him?"

Taken by surprise, I laughed. "That is the point, we cannot. There is no place in all the universe where we can run from Him. He always sees what we are doing, even in the dark."

"Forgive my saying this, but that sounds a bit ominous."

"Not in the least. He is a good God who loves us completely and who is always working to put wonderful things in place to help us, even if we feel He's far away. Think of Him as a perfect, caring parent, not like the guy who tried to ambush me today."

Erlin's face relaxed and she nodded, appeased by my response. "I have another question, if you don't mind answering it."

Curious, I agreed. "Sure, what is it?"

Her face was earnest and sincere. "In the last five years that I have been assigned to you, you have contacted me only twelve times, and until tonight, it was always for attending diplomatic functions. Some Remnants and officials have their diplomatic symbioids near them on a daily basis."

"Erlin, are you feeling unwanted?" I said, half-joking. Had I hurt her feelings? Why would they build that into a symbioid?

Her laugh was lilting. "No. That is not what I am getting at. I understand those types of feelings, but I wasn't programmed to have them, nor do I ever get bored waiting. My question is aimed at getting you better and more useful services in the future. Are you dissatisfied with the duties I have performed or how I look?" She was at ease and sported a kind, open smile. Not at all the face that most people would front if they felt they were failing at their profession. It was disarming.

"No. You are great as you are, and I have no complaints at all. The best explanation I have is that I am stubborn, and I tend to want to do things on my own, so I don't think about calling to you for help. I usually have a team with me, so any problems are handled by them or by me. Tonight was a different matter."

"That makes sense—I am sure that you are aware that you can request to have me modified in any way you wish or to have me replaced by a new rep to meet any configuration, personality, size, shape, or sex that you want."

"Sure." This topic was becoming uncomfortable.

"May I ask why you haven't?"

I started to speak and stopped to think more about this answer. "I guess that I got to know you as you." I watched her light blue eyes as they studied my face. "It seems wrong to want to change anyone else, especially over unimportant, surface-level things. How big or small your features are or what your coloring is mean nothing as compared to who you are inside." That would be programming, not a real personality in her case, but the point was the same. "The Erlin that I know looks like you. Asking to change that is a sign of a problem with me, not with you."

Erlin's eyes twinkled as she smiled. "Thanks. Now, off to sleep. Tomorrow will be here all too soon, and we have to make some plans to get you someplace secure and figure out how to alert the authorities without putting a big target on our heads."

"Agreed. I would like this all to end...in a good way. I'll get the bed out."

She rose to her feet with the grace of a dancer and stepped to the side. I was not so graceful, but I managed to stand without stumbling or falling. After today, I called that a win.

"Deploy bed," I said.

The couch slid backward and disappeared into the wall. From the other side of the room, a large bed shape moved out of the wall horizontally and rotated down to come to rest in the middle of the room. Two pillows rose up from the head of the bed. A modesty sheet slid out from the lower edge and covered the bed neatly. This was an outmoded term for the material as it was designed to moderate the temperature and airflow. Newer models didn't even need that. The sheet still had a function for those not wishing to be undressed or uncovered...like me.

I ran my fingertips down the softened leather on my arm. She didn't need to know that I was also staying dressed as a mental barrier against any impulsive robo-partnering. She was right about my emotions; being vulnerable, lonely, and scared led me to want to run to my old ways and find comfort where I shouldn't. Keep every thought captive; pull away from this dangerous path.

Glancing up I saw the tiny green light above the small kitchen was still on. It would flash yellow if there were any scans of our location and red if there was a direct assault on our defenses. We were out of harm's way for now.

Crawling into the bed I spoke out, "Lights, low for sleeping." The room lights dimmed to a level just bright enough for me to find my way to the bathroom or to notice movement, but not so bright as to affect my sleeping.

Pulling the sheet up, I was surprised when Erlin slid under the covers next to me. Symbioids don't need to sleep. Still fully dressed, she made no attempt to move closer to me. I guess this was the most natural position to take in such a small room rather than standing by the bed, facing me or a wall. Her hanging out in the bathroom would be worse if I had to use it.

Staring at the ceiling, I waited for the bed to scan my body's measurements and weight distribution. Nothing happened. This bed was not an active forming bed like a Softic or a Sleep-So-Zoft. It was just a simple, non-reactive mattress that was filled with a semi-liquid with the consistency of thick, cool pudding. It wasn't bad at all, even if that was as comfortable as it was going to get.

I half-laughed, wondering if that model would still clean, exfoliate, hydrate, massage, or do some of the other things that most beds do these days. My bed at home could produce a zero-gravity state, allowing me to float in a field of oxygen-rich air. Nice as that was, sustained use of it made my skin too sensitive, making the softest sheets and clothing unbearable. I stopped using those functions as I didn't want to become a wimp or be forced to move to a nudist colony.

Ahh. Dang. That was a complete mission fail. I had become a wimp even without the pampering of the zero-g bed. There I was, hiding out from an assassination attempt and worrying about my skin's hydration. Wearing clothing would just hinder those processes anyway. Tired as I was, this was all moot; in two minutes I would pass out whether I wanted to or not.

For no pure reason, I glanced over at Erlin who was framed in the faint room light. She was facing me with her eyes closed. Her blonde hair was mussed, caressing her face, and a gentle smile graced her lips. I wished that I hadn't looked. Her eyes opened as if she sensed my attention.

Caught, I said, "Good night, Erlin."

She gazed back at me with limpid sky-blue eyes, and a nice smile crept on her lips. "Good night, Rolland."

Closing my eyes, I turned my back to her and began to pray. Like staring too long into a bright light, her image remained seared into my mind.

Changing my focus, I spoke with the Lord about what had happened and asked for His guidance. This attack was more direct, intense, and personal as it was a human operative who was hunting me. The other attacks on us were designed to appear as mechanical malfunctions or random mishaps.

This was not the first attempt on my life. At seventeen, an autowalk turned into a high-speed people launcher, killing two and injuring seventy-eight of us. It took me four weeks in a hospital to physically recover from that attack, and that event still affects me on an emotional level.

The official report said that it was a one-in-a-trillion software malfunction. I have never believed that. From that point on, I avoided mass transport, both for my safety and for the innocents around me. It wasn't right to endanger others by my presence. I also began carrying more electronics to give myself a fighting chance against what the newsblasts called "random accidents."

There was nothing random about them. Too many Remnants were dying, and I was tired of our complaints being labeled as anecdotal or flat-out baseless paranoid conspiracy theories. Eleven years ago, I set out to get hard scientific evidence to prove or disprove my theories once and for all.

To expedite it, I financed the study. We hired the top scientists available and bought the latest supercomputers for Heavensport University. We developed and ran some of the most complex statistical data sets that have been compiled to date. I had autonomous outside monitors testing that I was not in any way trying to influence the outcome of the study. It was so well done that the team won the prestigious Gromeleski-Musk Scientific Excellence Award.

After months of processing time with the supercomputers, factoring in multi-component human interaction and behaviors, catastrophic mechanical equipment failure rates, and other actuarial computations, the results were clear. Even taking the in the differing lifestyles and risk-taking behaviors into consideration, someone or some group was targeting and killing off the planet heirs known as the Remnants. The odds against these being accidents and coincidences were astronomically improbable. The number and frequency of these deaths were geometrically progressing at a staggering rate. At that speed, the remaining Remnants would cease to exist in 24.3 years and that was eleven years ago. Whoever was behind this purge wasn't going to let it take this long. They would declare open season on us.

We knew our lives were dangerous. It was a topic of frequent conversations about the newest protective systems and gear that we were installing to defend ourselves from these supposed accidental deaths. Some used zero-slip flooring and anti-fall engagers that would initiate low-gravity fields and even repulsors and crash balloon suits to save them from freak falls and malfunctioning appliances. There were food and air testers, low-water misting showers, reflective body armor and every other contrivance designed to mitigate risk. A large number of Remnants had given up on living among society to live far away from the cities where they could better control their environment.

Armed with irrefutable evidence, my connections, and the past history of genocide against Remnants, I thought it would be easy to get action on our behalf by the New Jerusalem Planetary Congress.

After months of fruitless efforts, I realized that people will dismiss any evidence or idea that is contrary to what they want to believe. When a belief becomes an emotional thing, it is nearly impossible to change someone's opinion until that emotion is dealt with directly. This often is rationalized at the core of who they believe themselves to be. It can be an indicator of how they see the world, how they were raised, and of their own deep hurts and disappointments. We are all guilty of it.

Many officials were sorry that it was happening, but it was a bad time to be bringing it up as there was an election coming up, and it was not a popular theory with their some of their more outspoken constituents. For politicians, there is always an election coming up, even after being newly reelected.

When I went public with the finding, it was worse. The study and my efforts were immediately dismissed by my detractors as "meritless whining of the privileged." Ironically, I even got a few death threats because of it.

Angry, I brought it before the Earth Planetary Governing Board. This was the second time in the Remnants' short history on this planet where we had to seek outside help. The first time was infamously over the Fall of Heaven.

●●● ◖◗ ◖◗ ◖◗ ●●●

3

The Fall of Heaven

●●● ━ ━ ━ ●●●

To understand the truth about the Fall of Heaven, it is important to go briefly over what brought it about and what has come of it. Not what it has been warped into by those seeking to change the facts to better fit their agendas and what they want to believe. This is the truth as best as we understand it.

Though it is obvious, I am tired, and after the events of today, it may be biased and more than a bit surly. I will try to be fair.

Centuries ago, the Earth was in trouble. The population had grown to unsustainable levels, and the resources were close to being depleted. It got so bad that the Earth's global business focus became building the technology and the spacecraft capable of traveling billions of light years in a few hundreds of years of time. It is amazing what people can do when they face extinction. To meet these goals, they developed advanced space-based mining and construction, radiation shielding, cryogenic sleep, and the motors for warping, folding, and crunching space.

The New Earth Lottery randomly and fairly awarded full ownership to one of the trillions of planets that were suspected to have a similar makeup to that of the Earth. The catch? The light used to judge the viability of those planets is billions of years old. They called it a lottery because of the potential risk and tremendous reward. Similar to wind-propagated plants, billions of seed colonists were sent with the hope that some would land and prosper.

My ancestors, the Christian colonists who won ownership of the planet that they named New Jerusalem, equipped four ships, *The Will of the Lord*, *Peace of the Lord*, *the Praise of the Lord*, and the Super Titan Class terraforming ship *Heaven* to make the 233-year cryogenic journey.

A few years later, breakthroughs in space warping and folding and motor design made it possible to travel that same distance in three and a half years.

Some colonists equipped with the new space travel technologies found their planets uninhabitable. A few found the beautiful planet of New Jerusalem and decided to make it their new home.

Universally, illegal squatters don't like the idea of the true owners showing up and kicking them out. If they have lived at the location for a few generations, and they have made some improvements, they feel a sense of ownership and implicit rights.

Over 200 years, they've intentionally forgotten that they don't own the deed to the planet. They create inspiring stories about how their brave forefathers (and foremothers) fought to carve a wondrous civilization out of nothing, completely avoiding the fact that the planet was a paradise before they landed, and robots had done all the real work, putting up some buildings and bringing them iced drinks and meals as they relaxed by the ocean.

About sixty years in, the Earth Planetary Governing Board, or the EPGB, finds out that colonist-squatters have settled on the planet. This is a problem for several reasons. The first is that allowing illegal seizure by other Earth-originating colonists destroys the trust in the legality and value of the planetary deeds, and that could derail the great migration, which could put Earth back into jeopardy from overgrowth. Second, New Jerusalem is enormously wealthy in unique and valuable agriculture and rare minerals. The EPGB is slated to receive a sizable yearly cut of this GDP.

The EPGB responds by sending their Bargaining and Negotiation Armada. This powerful fleet consists of heavily armed battle cruiser drop-ships loaded with T-8 and T-12 assault mechs that are designed to wrestle back ownership of (wealthy) wayward planets. The EPGB is not known for its subtlety or sense of humor, though I find the name Bargaining and Negotiation Armada oddly entertaining.

The EPGB Emissaries tell the squatters that they do not own New Jerusalem and that they have to leave it.

The whole mess turns into an ugly, childish, name-calling fight.

The squatter government thumbs their nose at the EPGB and tells them that they don't have a contract with the EPGB for this planet, so they do not owe them a single unicred of the annual payment of 9.87% of their gross global GDP.

The EPGB crosses its arms and stamps its foot, repeating the order to leave New Jerusalem.

Those ruling the planet use the same techniques that have been used for centuries; they wrap their cause in patriotism, raising their hallowed flag high. They manipulate and whip the squatters to frenzied and irrational protests. They tell the masses that the "barely human" and "un-evolved colonists" who are coming have no real claim to their planet, and they will steal their land, unfairly tax them to poverty, take their weapons and women, and make them all slaves. The colonists also eat children, but only the pretty ones, which is certainly *every one* of their children.

Most intelligent groups would see war with a powerful and completely mechanized armada as a no-win situation. But, no.

The rogue government rallies the ignorant masses to go to war. Few of the leaders or their families actually fight as they are "better suited to directing the strategy" than dying for it.

The first salvos were designed to convince the squatters to yield and surrender New Jerusalem. The brilliant countering tactic is to rally more angry squatters to go and fight the assault mechs—and when they die, they send more people. Repeat. The war is horrible and dreadfully one-sided in favor of the EPGB.

Those who are left are given two choices: stay and act as stewards for the coming colonists or be resettled elsewhere. Many emigrate, some stay and try to help, and some decide to stay in power by hiding and working from the shadows. There is a big difference between surrendering and submitting.

The Christian colonists are achingly slow in coming. Because space travel is complex, there is no reasonable way to catch them and upgrade their ships to speed them up, so everyone is forced to wait.

Resentment grows as the EPGB awards the coming colonists the right to vote for the removal of all squatters. This vote cannot be appealed by the squatters.

After 223 years, the Christian colonists arrive in the solar system, and the first groups to be awakened from cryosleep, the techs and planet scouts, are heralded with greetings from New Jerusalem, welcoming them to their new home. The four colony ships move into orbit, and the rest of the passengers are awakened.

A container ship called *The Assignation* "mysteriously breaks free" from its geosynchronous park and rams the biggest ship, the Super Titan terraforming ship *Heaven*, impaling it and causing its molten innards to destroy *The Praise of the Lord* and severely damaging the two other remaining ships. The intertwined ships are forcibly dragged by *The Assignation*'s maneuvering motors into the atmosphere, where they are consumed and destroyed.

Ironically, falling debris from the ships crashes into the homestead of one of the main conspirators. This location later becomes the "donated" site for the megacity Heavensport.

Like most conspirators, they spend too much time around those who think like they do, so they incorrectly assume that the majority of the populace share their feelings, and they just need a nudge to start "the war to end the tyranny." They do little to hide their involvement, expecting to be rewarded for their actions and to be seen as heroes. They are surprised when they are arrested and charged with genocide and treason.

Of the 334,403 original Christian colonists, only 53,568 make it down to the surface alive.

A year later, the colonists vote to allow the squatters to stay. Some see this as a weakness; I do not. Forgiving is key to healing. It does not mean that we forget what happened or allow them to avoid punishment—it hands it all to the Lord, and we can let go of fixating on it and move on.

Tactically, this vote was wise, as such a small group of remaining people could not hold such a large planet from even a small invading force. The EPGB contract with the rightful owners did not allow them to act as the planet's primary protector for extended periods of time.

The surviving colonists took on the biblical name of The Remnant (Isaiah 10:20–22) and set about trying to build a fair and just utopia for everyone on the planet.

A global profit-share program was developed, allowing the population to live a life of leisure. Robots do the work better, faster, and with fewer errors. Humans generally add problems to the process. We are free to work at what we love or what interests us, but it is not required.

The megacities were designed to protect the environment from sprawl and to keep the people happy and engaged in socially acceptable activities. Failing that, social and correctional support systems are quite good at dealing with those needing greater direction, rehabilitation, or incarceration.

The magnitude of the money that was set aside and recovered for the Remnants would have been staggering when spread amongst the original number of colonists; when it was divided between the remaining survivors, they became some of the richest people who have ever lived. We have used this wealth to endow many great programs, develop universities and scientific studies, offer free health care, recreation zones, and to increase the base monthly share. This doesn't mean that we are smarter or kinder, we just have the ability to make everyone's life a little better. Most of us have tried, and yes, sometimes failed.

As no one is born a Christian, over the years this great wealth drives many to excess and to where we look and act no differently than anyone else, maybe even worse. As I mentioned, there are still those who see us as evil and the cause of every problem on the planet. This motivates some them to act against us with fanatical furor.

That leads me to where I am now, hiding and feeling lost.

Jesus commands us in Matthew 5:44, "But I say unto you, love your enemies, bless them that curse you, do good to them that hate you, and pray for them which despitefully use you, and persecute you." Because this is impossible to do on our own, many Christians want to see this as a suggestion or a statement that points to a nice moral ideal, one that you only have to apply when it is easy. This is a direct, unequivocal order and one that we cannot even begin to do on our own without God's help.

Lying here, I don't have that within myself. Weary, I ask God for the power to be able to forgive them and to be able to pray for their health and safety and for me to love them. About all I am able to muster is to pray for them to come to the Lord and that He will bless them. I ask forgiveness and His help with this Herculean task before I fall asleep.

●●● ⬬ ⬬ ⬬ ●●●

4

Erlin's Crush

●●● ━ ━ ━ ●●●

Waking, I saw the form of Erlin lying on her side, facing away from me. Her long blonde tresses were beautifully draped over her dark leather outfit, forming a golden river. Her presence meant that the attack was real and not just a bad dream.

The need to use the restroom nudged me from my stupor. Sliding out from the modesty sheet, I slid my shoe-clad feet to the supple gray floor. Pushing myself to stand, my footwear adapted to better fit my stiff and swollen feet.

Thanking the Lord for another day, I asked for His provision and protection as I staggered to use the restroom.

I returned to the bed area, and Erlin lay propped up on one of her elbows with the sheet draped over her shoulders. I frowned. Noting my response, her face slid into a sensual smile. Nonchalantly, she flipped the modesty sheet aside to reveal more of her trim young figure. Shimmering undergarments drew my eyes. As a symbioid, she didn't need the structural support, nor was there a sanitary purpose for them. These were all for show.

"Care to join me, Rolland?"

Trying not to stare at her state of undress, I turned my face away.

"No, Erlin. You know that I can't."

I wanted to give in. She was beautiful, she was more than willing, and no one would ever know. She was a symbioid, so— STOP! This kind of thinking leads to serious trouble. With a quick prayer and with considerable effort, I pushed those thoughts aside.

Hearing the sound of movement, I turned to see Erlin standing next to the bed in another pose worthy of an adult realview.

"I am sorry to embarrass you, Rolly. I just thought this would help start your day in a spectacular way after such a tough night." She sauntered toward me, raising her arms and inviting me to give her a hug. "Can you forgive me?"

A hug from a nearly naked woman, symbioid or not, was not a good idea. "Erlin, please put your clothes back on. I—"

Erlin launched herself at me in a full body tackle, pinning my elbows against my sides. We landed on the floor with the back of my head hitting hard. Darkness swirled around me.

"Erlin—stop," I wheezed out, struggling against her crushing attack.

The pain increased as she tightened, constricting my torso even more. I squirmed and thrashed, trying to break free from her super-human embrace. She could easily crush me to mulch, and I could do nothing about it. Pressure points and head-butts didn't work at all on a symbioid. I needed a weapon like a vibra-knife or a Blackthorn pistol.

I am going to die.

Erlin lifted her head, and her crystalline blue eyes gazed deeply into mine as if hoping to glimpse that moment when my soul left my body. She drove her lips down and pressed them firmly against mine. A warm tingling spread out from my lips. The stream became a burning torrent that built until it erupted, sending a massive tsunami of pleasure surging through my body. Every muscle simultaneously contracted to near breaking.

She's drugging me! I tried to pull away as Erlin pressed her lips down even harder on mine, sending crashing waves of intense electrical ecstasy flowing through my body, overwhelming the pain signals. Extreme fear and pleasure stabbed me. I struggled less as her soft lips continued to flood me with her chemicals. Each kiss from her stole more of my will. My heart pounded, threatening to explode.

Pulling her arms free, she rose to straddle me. I darted forward, seeking to get away, but she placed her slender palm on my chest and easily pushed me back to the floor. Her ice-blue eyes transfixed me, leaching away more of my willpower. Unable to look away, I wanted her. She was beyond beautiful.

With a satisfied, sultry smirk she said, "So, Rolland, how do you think you will die? I am betting on a heart attack, though a brain aneurysm is a strong possibility. What do you think, shall we try for both?" Feebly, I shook my head. "No?" She smiled sensually. "We need to get you out of your clothes. They are making this much more difficult and not as much fun. Still not ready?" She laughed, leaning closer pausing a few inches from my lips. With a sensual whisper, she said, "I can fix that. Wouldn't you rather go out with a massive bang rather than a whimper?"

Pushing through the pleasure and panic, I heard a still, quiet voice say the word, "Boom." Boom? Somehow, this meant something.

Erlin greedily delivered another kiss that nearly turned me to jelly. My heartbeats were cannon retorts that threatened to rip free of my chest. I could taste something coming up from deep within my straining lungs. That didn't matter.

I wanted her. I would beg her to let me die in her arms.

Die. I would die.

Erlin's eyes were on fire as she reached to remove my leather shirt. She appeared to be enjoying this.

"Any last words?" she asked with a smirk.

Unbidden and unexpected I said, "Boom." My safe-house panic word.

With no sound or dramatics, Erlin stopped moving. Her eyes froze, fixed on my own.

The scent of burned electronics broke my trance. The panic word launched an EMP, an electromagnetic pulse, bringing everything electronic in a three-apartment radius around me to a full, unrecoverable, and smoldering stop.

I had killed her—I had fried the circuits of the woman that I wanted more than anything. Slammed with that realization, I closed my eyes and began sobbing, wishing I could undo that command.

Another urgent call punched through my grief and uncontrolled hormones, yelling, "You've got to get going!"

What? It didn't register. I could only think about Erlin.

My heart hammered violently, and the odd taste coming from my lungs made it hard to breathe. I had to think. *You have to sort this all out and fast.*

The burnt scent in the air helped clear my mind. My primal animal brain had no interest in thinking, but I had to make it work—Erlin was hacked by someone in an attempt to kill me—with a passion overdose. The world would expect me to go this way. If they hacked her, they would have lost contact with her, and that meant that a cleanup team had been alerted and they were coming sooner than they'd planned. *Think, think, think! Go! Do something!*

I had to get her off me without getting more of that stuff on me. I used my leather shirt sleeves to rock her beautiful, 110-pound, rigid form from side to side, trying to dislodge her. My weakened muscles had little leverage.

With a mix of self-loathing and prurient interest, I watched her slide with a dull thump to the floor. I felt sick as I gazed upon her perfect, motionless form. Rolling stiffly away, I crawled to lean against the bed, breathing hard from the exertion. Pain percolated up through the pummeling pleasure and urges howling through my body.

Her beauty drew me. Keep your mind clear! You don't love her; she injected you with these emotions—remembrances of her burning, questing lips on mine were stealing my thoughts. You have to move now or you will die here. She wanted to make your head and heart explode! You've got to think and get moving before it is too late!

Erlin's arms and legs began curling inward towards her body, resembling a giant, dying spider. This left me with a heady mix of pity and revulsion.

Distracted, I almost began to rub my arms to ease the radiating pain. Stop! My clothes could be covered in Erlin's concentrated chemicals. More of that could kill me outright or make me stay until the enemy arrived. Either way, I would die.

A part of me wanted to give up. The idea of running seemed far too hard. Erlin's hacker clean-up team would be staged close by, so there wasn't much time left.

I managed to undress without getting any more of Erlin's chemicals on my hands. My pulse slowed some, but I was not out of trouble.

Heading toward the sink to wash my face, I paused in frustration. The sink wouldn't work; the temperature and flow controls were fried. I returned to the foot of the bed and knelt down and roughly wiped my hands and face on the sheets. My eyes and my head were burning and throbbing. I needed help.

The robo-doc! All my safe houses had emergency robo-docs. That would help— Dang. The EMP burned that as well. There is an EMP locker here, though, and that should have a med kit.

A section of the wall was slightly ajar. The EMP blast had caused an electromagnet to fail, dropping a heavy weight to spring the latch and door open.

Inside, I found a six-foot-tall electromagnetically shielded locker loaded with supplies. From the middle shelf, I retrieved a small med kit and opened it. Inside were two rows of thumb-sized nano-doc puff injectors. These would stabilize and begin treatment on a person after an accident or other life-threatening event. Tasting blood in my mouth, I assumed the worst. I chose two that covered drug overdoses, one that covered lung and heart issues, and one for physical trauma and began puff-injecting them one after the other into my upper chest, thighs and right buttock. I prayed this didn't add more problems.

On the shelf above the medicines was a dispenser for medical gloves. That would have been helpful *before* I took off my drug-coated clothing.

From the small selection of men's and women's clothing, I chose a dark gray and blue long-sleeved shirt and a pair of textured blue and green pants that were close to my size. As they were auto-adjusting, they wouldn't stand out in a crowd for their poor fit. Pulling them on, I let out a few gasps in pain. At the bottom, I found a pair of auto-sizer shoes and slipped them on, and they began to mold and adjust their shape to fit my feet.

Seizing a medium-sized navy blue backpack from the EMP locker, I roughly shoved the med kit and the empty quick injectors into the main pocket. This might hide what I had done to self-medicate. Did it matter? I went with my gut. I shoveled the money and credit holders, some clothes, and a pile of food and snack packets into the bag's front pouch. Grabbing the pack by its upper grip, I ambled toward the front door.

Spying Erlin curled in a fetal position caused me to hesitate. I had an idea. Kneeling next to her shoulders, I parted her blonde hair and pulled back a flap of skin to reveal the tiny master port hidden at the base of her skull. From the backpack, I fished out a silver, pen-shaped pixie dot applicator. Placing the tip against her master port, I pushed the side button, and a light near the button blinked green. Closing her port flap, I smoothed her hair back in place.

With a stabbing twinge, I flung the backpack over my shoulders and felt it adhere, shaping to my back and balancing the load. At the door, I nearly ran head first into it when it didn't open. Duh, EMP. It's dead. I fumbled along the door frame to find and press the emergency release to unlock the door. Instead of sliding sideways into the wall, the door swung outward in an arc into the hallway. Stepping out, I slammed it closed, and I heard it lock back on its glide track. That might help delay those who were coming. They would check the apartment first— or split into two teams. That would be bad.

I prayed for God's healing as I sprinted, body aching and lungs burning, down the hall, bypassing the first two elevators to take the ramp that led down to the lower transit tube. A muffled bang behind me enticed me to keep running.

After a few ragged minutes, my legs threatened to give out. I slowed to a determined, plodding pace, hoping I appeared to be someone running late.

Electronic signage along the halls gave sets of interactive maps of the area showing my speed, direction, and showcased "exciting" destinations to visit. Who used info signs anymore? Most people connected via their face screens' projectors or contacts—I left my face screen helmet back at the apartment. After a halting step, I realized it didn't matter. All that stuff is fried plastic due to the EMP blast—as were those irritating robo-wings. Good.

Fatigue swept me. Once I got out of the area and found a place to hide out, I would seek food and medical help. Seeing beautiful women everywhere made it difficult to focus. I tried to curb my eyes and my thinking, but I failed miserably.

I took the corridor leading to the nearest transit hub, and a woman's soft voice spoke to me, causing me to stumble in surprise. "Thank you for choosing the Heavensport Transit System. Sir, our systems have detected that you are in serious physical distress; shall we send a personal transit pod and robo-doctor to bring you to the nearest medical center?"

"No. No, thank you," I said.

Heavensport's public safety system automatically monitors and responds to potential threats and communicable diseases. My odd manner had warranted the first level of intervention. Had I been out of control or showed signs of a transmittable illness, a specialized team of responders would have already intercepted me.

The calm voice said, "Shall we alert a mobile medical team to meet you in the terminal? We do not detect any contagion, but you are experiencing a severe biological, life-threatening reaction. Are you aware of this?"

"Yes. I am being treated for the issue." A half-lie. The nano-docs that I injected were the best treatment I would get for a while. I hoped that it would be enough. After my escape, my enemies would be watching for me to run to a robo-doc, a hospital, or to seek outside help. They had already used a missile to take down the APV. If they dropped a second one on me in the city, they could kill untold thousands of innocent people.

"That is good, sir. We would like to caution you that your excessive hormone levels suggest a substantial risk for exhibiting inappropriate behavior that may be considered extreme even for an adult zone. We remind you that your well-being and the public's safety is our first concern. We can escort you privately to an adult zone and/or a medical center if that would help?"

Too much even for an adult zone? Wow, that is really bad. Adult zones had few limits, and almost none with other willing participants or symbioids. I was in worse shape than I thought. At least the tracking system still gave me options. She'd said, "...an adult zone and/or a medical center." Are there adult-zone-themed medical centers? *Stop.*

"No to all monitoring and notification of authorities. Please block this record. I am being treated for the imbalance, and I wish to remain anonymous. I will remain in check." Her voice was so soft and sultry. What did she look like? *Stop it! She is an electronic voice interface. She doesn't have a body.*

"Acknowledged, sir. If you should change your mind, please just alert us by saying 'Help' or 'Medical Help.' Should you fall unconscious or exhibit excessive or unacceptable social behaviors, a team will be automatically dispatched to assist you."

"Sure, got it, thanks," I said.

Fall unconscious? More like fall over dead and catch on fire. On wobbly legs, I picked up my pace. My body shook as the battle for my life raged on.

At the glistening ella-glanse crystal transit hub, I took the first arriving transpod train car available and got off at the second station about ten minutes later. This was a nicer area than near my safe house. The transit hubs were brighter and with shinier, open designs, and sporting more realview signage. Beautiful women smiled at me and held up products or delicious-looking dishes with their accompanying hunger-inducing scents. My stomach and hormones growled in anticipation. As much as I wanted to, I didn't dare slow down to eat or to stare. Who was I kidding? It was pure, gross fixation.

Tens of thousands of people filled the terminal, moving to unknown destinations. Some seemed to be hanging out, enjoying the broad, colorful spectrum of humanity flowing by. Robopets and outlandish outfits were the norm.

As I walked, I found myself rating women based on their attractiveness and best features. Erlin's love potion overdose dominated my thinking.

I felt the urge to shake myself awake. Refocus and move on. This was not a fun, carefree jaunt on the town. A few outlandishly dressed or underdressed people strutting about would be a perfect diversion for an attack. Exhaling sharply, I picked up speed.

As if I were slapped, I staggered, and a sob broke my lips when I realized that I was back to being the horrible man that I tried so desperately to leave behind. Years of fighting against being a sexually-driven, self-indulgent jerk were being swept away by a tsunami of lust and stupidity.

A voice in my head called me out. *You have blown it so badly that you might as well give up! You are a complete hypocrite and liar. You are not fooling anyone pretending to be different. You haven't changed; in fact, it is impossible for you to change. This relapse was inevitable because this is who you are at your deepest and darkest core. A goat cannot become a hawk no matter how hard it tries. Just give up and embrace being the disgusting pervert and lowlife scumbag that you know that you are. At least that is being honest about it. Stop fighting who you are.*

I stopped and wiped my eyes, nearly conceding. A kind and compassionate thought surrounded me like a gentle breeze and lifted my head—everyone fails at times, and for a period they may lose their self-control and act in a way that is contrary to what they know is right. The difference is that they can decide to turn back to the path that they know is right and begin again.

Through this undulating mental haze, I had a brief vision of me sailing over breaking ocean swells on a stormy day. Through the pelting rain of condemnation, I began to smile. Even here, deep in the city, I was far out at sea, caught in a surprise squall. Life can be like sailing in a violent gale. Everything is pushing against you, trying to take the path of least resistance. Giving up will cause you to capsize and drown. No matter how tough it is, you have to ride it out, keeping firm pressure on your rudder, adjusting your sails, and adapting to conditions as they change to stay in control.

During these times you can see your circumstances as miserable and unfair, or you can accept that you are in it and find the joy and exhilaration of the moment. And pray. Do lots of praying.

Not caring who heard me, I laughed. I hadn't completely and irrevocably failed. The drugs were not my choice. None of us is free from pounding and unfavorable influences. Every second, we have to decide who we want to be and act accordingly. I am done with being a hedonistic playboy fool. I am not perfect, nor could I expect to be. I know that I am not beyond being salvaged. All this judgment and condemnation wasn't from God but from the other team that seeks to destroy us.

After praying, my mind felt clearer. It was too easy and dangerous to go to extremes and cast off or take on all of the blame.

Continuing, I went over what I knew or could guess. Diplomatic symbioids are designed to "entertain" individuals or even a number of guests for extended periods of time. As Erlin had tried to kill me with a passion overload, she had probably dispensed her full supply of concentrated male stimulants, enough for who knows how many people, into me all at once. This scared me, and it gave me almost no useful information. It might still outright kill me.

Urges were coming in irregular and disproportional waves, making it difficult to think clearly. My thoughts gained and lost lucidity, fixated and then wandered. Cravings for food and women frequently barged in and disrupted and corrupted my thought process. My memory was off-line, especially things that would be helpful, like where I'd stashed my safe houses around the city. The harder I tried, the more it seemed to hide.

I took in a deep breath of air and let it out slowly. Maybe less pressure would allow my mind to relax and make it work better.

What do I have working in my favor? People thought I was dead, so they didn't expect to see me out and about. My backpack had some money, so that helped. Travel. All mass transportation within Heavensport was free of charge, so I did not have to worry about being tracked by using credit holders. The downside was that it also kept me out in public too much.

Food! I'd grabbed some from the EMP safe! My stomach gurgled, and I took it as a cheer. Stopping, I backed up near a wall and pushed a release button that caused my backpack's front pouch to slide to my right side. Pulling it off, I attached it to the front of my shirt. Who cared how it looked? I reached in and randomly chose a packet. I twisted the packet's prep knob, and it opened, revealing a warm hand-pie. The taste of beef and vegetables filled my mouth. Finishing that one as I walked, I proceeded to pull out and devour three other pouches of food in quick order, and I was still hungry. I would try to wait to eat the rest.

This led to the next evaluation—what was working against me. The simple fact was that it was practically everything. I was hormonally supercharged to the point of dying, and I was being hunted by an unknown number of people whose only goal was to kill me, and I couldn't contact anyone without putting them and thousands of others in extreme danger. This had become evident when they went so far as to use a missile on the armored personnel vehicle.

I needed a private robo-doc hidden away in some secure place. All my safe houses had those...okay, the next best option would be to find an unregistered robo-doc, the type criminals use in realview dramas to get patched up when they get wounded. Are those real or some grand affectation created to move plots along? Realistically, how does one find one? They wouldn't have a sign like a business or be listed in a directory. Do you find someone who looks shifty and ask? That question could get you beaten up or get you reported to the authorities.

And that led to tracking. There were countless trillions of sensors everywhere in the city, monitoring everything from pedestrian and autowalk traffic issues, energy usage, to weather and even heat patterns. Even with that ever present monitoring, the New Jerusalem charter guaranteed personal privacy and civil rights for everyone and it was designed to avoid capturing distinct personal information. If someone was suspected of committing a serious crime, and they secured legal clearance, the system would be fed their likeness and in seconds, the city could read millions of faces and find them. If they had breached the security system, my elimination could be the start of a full Remnant purge.

Taking the second main hallway, I caught the first autowalk on the left and moved over to the next faster autowalk lane.

Weaving through the milling crowds, I stepped over each time to the left to catch the next faster lane until I reached the fastest strip. My legs felt weak, and they would not allow me to run. Being unstable, it took all my effort not to bump into those who were standing in place on the autowalk. People were avoiding looking me in the eyes, thinking I was drunk or high. Wait, I was.

My heart raced. My self-regulating clothes were doing their best to remove my sweat, but I must be quite a sight. It could be the effects of the nano-doc pills pushing out the toxins.

My focus fell on a beautiful woman with dark hair, and I found myself blatantly staring at her, wondering how much was being enhanced by her adaptive figure-shaping clothing. Not satisfied with that, I was imagining what all the women around me would look like nude or while making love. I shook my head, hoping that the motion would help clear my brain.

Addicts can't will away their behavior; they have to remove themselves from the problem. Irritated, I signaled for a single transpod to rendezvous with me on the fast track. The small, egg-shaped vehicle glided down, and it opened wide on the side, allowing me to lurch in and sit on the comfortable 340-degree curved bench. These smaller pods held no more than five people. The door closed, and a projected display showed me a map of nearby stations. Hoping to be random, I pointed to the Kalin district's transit station. The name meant nothing to me, so I hoped it was a good choice. The single pod rose and moved away from the autowalk, weaving through the thousands of other pods that were on their way to different stations and autowalk connectors.

"As a service to our riders, this personal pod can play music or short realviews, or it can even direct you to some of the great adventures that await you in the Kalin district."

"No, thanks." I lay back in my seat feeling the great roiling turmoil within my body.

With a flash of white to the right of me, a single pod shifted in close to pace mine. Inside, a young man and woman were brazenly making out. Faced with such an outrageous display of affection, my brain locked on them, rebelling against any attempts to censure it or to look away. My gawk-fest ended when their pod drifted downward and mine glided over to take a wide turn. As much as I didn't want to give in to it, I found myself checking out every craft that came near me. Embarrassed by my behavior, I closed my eyes so tight that I could hear a high-pitched whine and the buzzing of my eye muscles.

After saying a prayer, I called out, "Opaque, please." When I opened my eyes again, the shell of the pod was a pleasing translucent white. I shut my eyes again. The pressure in my head had grown so great that I expected to hear a pop and feel my brain being pushed out of my eyes, nose, and ears. This was serious trouble, and I could do nothing about it other than plead for God's intervention. Relaxing my eyes slightly, I kept them closed as it made me feel safer.

I felt alone, vulnerable, and far too much in the open. Everyone and everything that I had relied on for years to shield me and protect me were gone, and I had no clue as to where to go or whom I could trust. Hospitals, quick-docs, the police, my homes, and my friends were all out of the question. How many times had I gone over these options? Nothing had changed. They would be watching those sites.

My thinking was scattered, yet somehow, I knew I teetered on the edge. A serene calmness fell on me. Is this how I am going to die? I was crumbling from the inside out. Lord God, please help me! "I am not ready to go yet," I mumbled.

"We are just about to arrive in the Kalin district. Did you wish to go somewhere else?"

"No, I was just talking to myself."

"No problem. Do you wish to be dropped off on the autowalks or at the station?"

"The station, please," I replied. This would lessen my chances of falling.

"With pleasure, sir. Do you need mobility services?"

I really wanted to say yes. Would that draw attention to me? Probably. "No, thanks."

The pod made its way to a large landing area to land. These were used by those who were mobility- and stability-impaired. That would be me. The pod opened, and the sidewalk rose to become a level pad for my exit.

I made my way to stand on the autowalk that led from the gleaming Kalin district station. All around me were people in glider chairs and exoskeletons, and young parents with baby carriers. I'd never paid attention to them before.

My hands tingled, and my head throbbed. Was I hyper-focusing on normal, everyday things? Pushing it out of my mind, I tried to plan my next steps.

Here in Kalin, I would seek another transpod. A terrible thought crossed my mind—what if my "random" choices had sent me back to where I started? Frantic at the thought, I pulled up a wall map. No. Thank goodness, I had not circled back.

People are miserable at being random. We think that we are good at it, but we tend to pick the same numbers or steps, thinking that we are unpredictable. The overdose might have been helping me there. A sign for the local adult zone flashed some daily deals and activities, and I found myself trying to find any reason to visit it. Those who planned Erlin's attack would be expecting me to run to those kinds of places based on their type of attack.

Riding an autotrack, I kept reevaluating my logic, not trusting it. How many times had I gone over the same thoughts? Was this a logic loop or something? Thinking grew more difficult. My vision blurred, and I grew unsteady in my balance. After a few waves of confusion, it lessened. Had I made it?

Signage for an auto-doctor made me avoid the next exit. As I hadn't died, I hoped it was a good sign. I grinned at the thought of only a few minor flare-ups to go. I could deal with that, or...maybe I was going to die horribly in the next few minutes or days. I prayed the nano-doctors were winning the war.

Getting off at a smaller station, I chose to let the crowds move me. To add randomness, I would find someone dressed in something red and follow her...or him...until I saw someone in yellow and then green. My hormones tried to add in figure types. No. Just colors...if they did have those traits, okay.

This was moot as a group of three women dressed in red intersected with my path. I analyzed their figures to compare them to my selection criteria. It was all for science. No. No, it wasn't, I grumbled. I am a creepy and sweaty stalker. I broke off my pursuit and turned down a smaller avenue.

As I walked, my vision began to warp, and my legs began to give way. As I stumbled and began to crumple, I felt arms wrap around me...I couldn't see well, and it was hard to think. An older face with short cropped hair swooped in close to mine. He appeared concerned or angry; I couldn't tell. There was someone to the left of me. What was...I...I was confused and completely...helpless.

As I plunged into the darkness I heard someone hiss, "We got him."

●●● ▬▬ ▬▬ ▬▬ ●●●

5

Resurrection

● ● ● ━ ━ ━ ● ● ●

Inside the small apartment, a team of task robots worked the scene, looking for leads. Unlike the standard units found everywhere, these robots had limited humanoid characteristics as they were designed to accomplish sets of specific duties.

In the middle of the room facing the exit, Erlin sat motionless on the gray floor with her back leaning against the edge of the bed. Her blonde hair was pulled up on her head in a top-knot to allow access to her main port. A pink towel lay draped across her upper body; she looked like someone relaxing at a day spa.

Next to her stood a robot with six spider-like arms that attached at the vertices of its eighteen-inch-tall hexagonal base. Each articulated arm terminated in a human hand, and on top of the center-mounted pole sat a human face with ears and no skull. The robot was busy analyzing Erlin.

Eight feet away, a tall, muscular young man dressed in gray and green stood with his arms crossed, leaning against the kitchen counter. He faced Erlin's prone figure. A curved, translucent face screen shielded his eyes and nose.

"Will she start?" he asked.

The tech-bot's face turned to the man. "She was hit hard with the electromagnetic pulse. Her muscle ropes and controllers are all fried, and only her service core may have had enough shielding not to be completely worthless. We need to get her back to

Repair to begin the analysis to see if we can gain access to her data. We can't do it here, as it will be a fairly intense and sensitive operation."

The man unfurled his arms and leaned forward. "Her lips look shiny and wet. Did she deliver the concentrated meds to the subject?"

The tech-bot's human face swiveled about its pole, surveying the area. "The symbioid delivered the full complement of the male-targeted stimulation meds in her pharmaceutical delivery system. From the gathered data, we cannot ascertain if or how much the target was dosed. My measurements of the remaining compounds found on the symbioid's skin and on the man's garments suggests that the application was near fatal amounts, or it could be as much as 9.48 times fatal."

"Is he dead then? I mean, no one could survive a dose that is ten times fatal, right?"

"As he is not here, I would not be able to answer that question, sir."

"Make a guess," said the man, rising up taller, his jaw and lips tense.

The tech robot said, "If he was extracted by others, he could be in the process of dying, getting medical help, or he is already dead."

"What if he didn't have help?"

"Minimally, we would have an extremely stimulated man running around Heavensport who may or may not die within a few hours."

"Could this help us spot him?"

The tech-bot raised his neck pole to bring his face to a similar height as the man. "I would suggest that you look for a man seeking to have intimate relations with anything that looks vaguely human. I would check the police records for any men who have been arrested or detained for grossly inappropriate sexual behavior."

The man chewed on his lower lip and then said, "So, will he recover on his own or will he need medical attention?"

"With so many variables and such a wide range of potential dosages, I can only give you an estimate based on the mean average dosage." The tech-bot stared at him with a dull look.

Through gritted teeth the man said, "Make a guess."

The tech robot's face gave a slight twitch and he said, "Without immediate medical intervention, the target has a 96.73% chance of dying within the next two days. With prompt medical attention, he has a 62.35% chance of still dying over the next two days. If he were to survive, I would estimate his recovery from the effects in two to five days, with the potential for short burst interval reemergence of the stimulants over the next few weeks or months. It is difficult to predict, as I stated—we do not have a reasonable estimate of the amount that was delivered or the physical locations of the dosing. Each person will respond differently even to the same quantity."

The man's face was pinched and sour. "Get this symbioid back to our repair center, not Diplomatic Services. Get on it now."

"Yes, sir."

From a staging area near the where the man stood, a six-foot-tall and three-foot-wide wheeled white box rolled to a stop by the bedside. With the faintest hum, the front of the case opened wide. The tech-bot began to use all six of its arms to load Erlin upright into the container.

The man looked away from the sight. "We need to know what she may have known before"—with a choppy angry motion, he waved his hand over the extent of the room—"all this EMP stuff happened. First, I have to find Newcastle."

The tech-bot turned its human face to him and smiled. "I reviewed the target's history. You could send out teams of symbioids conformed to the likenesses of his past girlfriends. He would seek them out, and they could restrain him until you finish the mission. Or you could check the records of robo-doctors for anyone coming in with massive amounts of stimulants in their systems. I can send you a detailed list of the compounds used to help narrow it down from the standard narco-hoppers and the do-it-yourself chemical experimenters."

The man pivoted and stalked off towards the front door. Opening the curved frosted bathroom door, he waved forward a large and menacing military assault mech to join him. This war machine had little in common with the other robots around the room. "I want you to find Rolland Newcastle. Find him now. If you can, bring him in alive. That could help us find out what he may have already sent out or done that may become problematic for us."

The man heard a noise and turned to see that the tall white cart that held Erlin had come to a stop next to him. The face of the six-armed tech-bot peered at him from behind the wheeled case. The man looked about the tight entryway. With a frustrated flip of his hand, he signaled the large assault mech to back up into the bathroom. The remaining space was too small, so the man stepped out into the hallway to stand next to the door. The tech-bot and the tall white carrier box began to move slowly past them. Once in the hallway, the tech waved as it continued on its way toward a delivery lift. Its head swiveled to keep its focus on the man at the door.

Clenching his hands into fists and his lips into a snarl, the man backed up to stand in the apartment's doorway. He glanced at the assault mech that stood filling the small bathroom and said, "I swear, that thing is jerking me around. If I didn't need it, I would have you tear that freaky thing apart." He watched as the bot disappeared down the corridor. "Where was I? Right, second in order: if capture is not possible, make it look like an accident. Avoid citizen contact and detection, as that will cause us problems. Third and worst case: contact me if you need clarification for any action that will result in level 5 damage or above. And—"

Mid-sentence, dull thumps came from the main room. He couldn't place that sound. Something wasn't right.

"Follow me," he commanded the assault mech. Spinning on his heels, he moved into the room with the large assault mech following him.

Scanning the room, little had changed other than the diplomatic symbioid and that irritating six-armed tech-bot were gone. Tech teams still moved about, analyzing the scene. His eyes darted about, looking for the source of that noise. Lying on the floor were two halves of a large, white, semi-rectangular shell. That wasn't part of their gear. He looked up, and hanging from the ceiling was an odd white oval device. Was that part of the air handling system or a realview projector?—No!

All the robots in the room fell to the floor with a muffled clatter. The large mech next to him slumped forward and its broad, powerful arms dropped to its side and it stood there motionless. The stink of melting metal and plastic wafted through the air. A low buzzing noise came from the device hanging from the ceiling and the smell of melted electronics grew even worse. After a few seconds the noise stopped.

"Oh, give me a break! Another EMP? Really?!" Reaching up, he yanked his face screen visor from his head and threw it to the floor, making it bounce.

The man who had attempted to ambush Rolland Newcastle in the public bathroom was bellicose. "I can't even call this stupid thing in!" After kicking his visor, he was finally able to gather some composure. "Even if he is already dead, I am going to destroy Newcastle!"

●●● ⬤⬤ ⬤⬤ ⬤⬤ ●●●

I woke in a dimly lit room that I did not recognize. My eyes burned, and my head was pulsating, and there was an odd metallic taste in my mouth. When I tried to move I found that my arms and legs were restrained. Bright yellow cloth bands wrapped my wrists and crossed my chest, and I could feel them on my ankles too. They were old tech, magnetic restraints. There was no use in struggling. They would allow me to move some but not enough to reach and remove one of the straps.

Instead of pointlessly fighting my restraints, I would be better served by pushing through my mental fog, trying to recall how I got here. Vague images came to me about my flight and being captured and the face of at least one of my captors. He didn't seem dangerous, but nice people do not usually kidnap and restrain others against their will.

The room felt clean, and there was some simple medical equipment. This room was not part of a proper medical facility. I was wearing the same clothes as last night. Wiggling my feet, I could tell that my shoes were off. No med center would do this.

There was a single door, and that was on the opposite side of the room from where I lay. Near the head of the bed was an old, boxy device that had lines running from it and into my left arm. Were they helping or drugging me? No. They were not drugging me. I felt much better than I had last night, and my thinking was clearer.

I moved my left hand over to my right wristband, pretending to be scratching. The invisible magnetic tether stopped me a few frustrating inches from being able to reach and release it. It was worth a try. Newer models had special band locks that allowed those restrained to scratch around the restraint bands. Those types would selectively restrain areas or limbs as needed, not like this one that held me like a fly caught in a spider's web. Frustrated, I twisted and wriggled my hands in the cloth cuffs, hoping to find enough slack to slip my hands-free. The straps were firmly secured. I moved about, testing the limits of my restraints.

Wait! Did they intend to torture me before they killed me? That wouldn't make sense unless they got off on hurting people. This wasn't a realview thriller where I had secrets that someone needed. Could this be an old fashion kidnap for ransom, or were they keeping me long enough to confirm that they had me before they killed me? I didn't like any of these ideas.

The door slid open, and in the backlight, two men of similar height and trim builds entered the room. Don't look at them, I scolded myself. If I can identify them, they may feel compelled to kill me.

Averting my eyes and turning my head away from them, I called out, "Don't worry, I cannot identify you. Just let me go, and I will get you money if that is what you want."

One of the men laughed softly. "Don't worry, sir. We mean you no harm."

How could I know that? This still could be a trap. To play it safe, I kept my eyes closed. How do you tell if someone is lying about it being okay to look at them without looking at them? Ugh.

The man replied, "I assure you, if we meant you harm, we would have already done it, right?"

Okay, that made sense. I opened my eyes, hoping that this wasn't a sick joke.

The man smiled at me and said, "Lights at twenty percent." The ceiling and walls began to glow slightly brighter. "There. Is that better? Not too bright, is it?"

"It's good." I lied. My eyes reluctantly adjusted to the light. I felt helpless, restrained as I was. Nodding at my wrists I said, "Will you be so kind as to remove these?"

The slender, older man was the same person whom I had seen when I was collapsing in the street. He smiled as he walked over to stand by the bed. "It looks like we caught you just in time. You had me worried." Analyzing my nonaggressive behavior, he said, "I think we are safe enough for now."

He pressed his full hand to the antiquated operating pad at the side of the bed, and I felt the restraining force release. Mindful of their attentiveness, I sat up, testing my muscles, prepared to run if the opportunity arose. There was no power or flexibility in my limbs. I doubted that I would get even two feet before being caught.

"Easy. You have been through quite a lot. We almost lost you back there in the transit hub. I am thankful that Marv and I were there when we were."

Lucky for you; maybe not so lucky for me. Marv just stood silently staring at me. He didn't move much, and his expression was lacking deep emotion. Marv could be a symbioid.

"Please forgive my lack of courtesy. I am sure that you have many questions. First of all, I am known on the street as Lazarus, and this is Marv. Marv is a symbioid and my great helper. He and I drunk-buddy carried you here." That is where two people stand on either side of their friend, and his or her arms are laid over their shoulders. In extreme drunken stupors, the toes of the friend are dragged as they are carried.

Lazarus inclined his head to Marv. "Together, our mission is to seek out those, like yourself, who have overdosed and in desperation have come out of hiding to wander through public centers, seeking some kind of unconventional help."

"I'm a bit different in this—"

He raised his hand in a gentle, calming motion. "I know, you weren't overdosing, and you don't know how it happened."

Oh, I know how it happened. How do I explain it without sounding like every other junkie on the streets? With a thin voice, I began, "I didn't take these drugs..."

He must have heard this song and dance a million times. The older man started to cross his arms. He stopped himself midmotion with his forearm arms in parallel lines across his chest just shy of tucking in his fingers for a lock. In psychology, crossed arms mean the listener is not open to the person speaking. His eyes darted to the side as he tried to figure out how to make this change of direction look natural.

In my altered state, this was funny and a bit disarming. To help, I looked away, blinking as if I had dry eyes. In my peripheral sight, I noted that he quickly dropped his hands to his sides.

Lazarus took in a deep breath, and I turned back to him. Smiling, he said, "I have been there. I am a recovering stimuli-junkie. Trust me, this city is filled with millions of people just like you, who thought that they were different, tough enough, or smarter than everyone else, and they would be able to hide and control their 'recreational' use. Each of them, regardless of their education, wealth, or strength, became consumed by it, becoming a hardcore junkie. I couldn't count how many people we hear every day trying to defend their method for getting high. Whether it is robo-partners, stimulizers, hoppies, viders, or loaders, whatever it is, it doesn't matter. It all rots us from the inside, lying to us, telling us that we are still its master and we accept that because we desperately want to believe that we are. Everyone becomes its miserable and disposable slave. Let me be perfectly straight with you, what you are doing, it will kill you next time. It is only by the grace of God that you are still alive now."

My case was different. "I agree, but—"

A brief flash of anger moved across his intense hazel eyes. Moving forward in his seat, his voice deepened and took on a bit of gravel. "Look, you have got to be real here if you want to survive. It is important that you hear this, and I am telling it to you it straight. As I said, I am a junkie, like you. No one ever wants to face this, and no one ever stops being a junkie, even with getting drug reaction and mental precepts resets done. It will never give up, and it will continue to sing its lurid song, especially when we are at our weakest. And don't try and fool yourself; every month I see people back in here, near death again, who thought they could do it 'just one more time just to take off the edge.' For me, my last use was almost seven years ago. Even though I see the terrible destruction it wreaks every day, every day I have to fight going back to it. It may help if I tell you my story."

He wasn't seeking my approval as he didn't pause long enough for me to interject.

"I had a really bad night after taking too much of an extra-pure load. This drop had a delayed response, so I had taken a second round, thinking it had been cut so much that it was just a real cushy ride. Arrogantly, I had decided that I had this all figured out as I had done it thousands of times, and running a test could be used as evidence against me if I got caught. You know the dance. By the time I recognized my mistake, it was too late. I was full-on chop surfing, cycling between peaking and crashing hard."

His eyes misted, causing him to blink, even though he must have told this story a million times. Sadness pulled at his face. "With cold clarity, I knew that I was about to die. Some deeper part of me still wanted to be saved and not die alone in my home. So I got up and left with no a clue where I was going. Whether due to pride or shame, I had always felt that I couldn't call for help or go to the robo-docs, as I was worried that would leak and ruin my standing in the community." His eyes studied my face. Marv bent over and collected a small chair hidden by the head of my bed and placed it behind Lazarus.

"Thank you, Marv." Placing a hand on the seat behind him, he guided his rear to sit down. His eyes never left mine as if he feared I was going to disappear if he were to look away for even a moment. "I was a fractured soul as I stumbled through the hub. People moved away from me, acting as if they didn't see me. Even though I felt like worthless dirt, a small, determined part of me still wanted to live." Lazarus paused to press his lips together and swallow. "My secret life had exploded, and it had consumed me with its horrible fire. I was shaking, alone and scared, face to face with my imminent, horrible death—we always think that we have time to work it all out." He nodded and said, "We didn't, did we?"

He ran his fingers and palm roughly over his short beard stubble and smiled, his face radiating kindness and compassion. "It is hard to see it, dressed as I am, but I was once considered a highly-regarded member of society. Well, long story short, I ended up dying on a bench close to where I found you. I remember beginning to black out and then waking up in a room similar to this one. I had been brought back to life after being dead for about seven minutes. A group of Christian interventionists had seen me and acted where the transit system did not. To be fair, I may have told the system not to help me. I don't recall clearly. After they had resurrected me back to a poor resemblance of the living, they had helped me get back home.

"For the next few months, I covertly sent them money to help them in their mission and to ease my guilt. I was able to keep that crash-and-burn under wraps for a while. My treatment was hidden as a spontaneous trip for a few weeks to an exotic beach resort. After I returned, I had to face that my career path and my new understanding of addiction were diametrically opposed. And if I continued to live like that, it would tear me apart."

His eyes drifted up and away, lost in thought. With his right hand, he errantly scratched under his ear as he turned back to me.

"At that time, I was one of the chief legal opponents of the free drug rehabilitation and social services programs offered by the city. I had attacked them as layers of foolish, ill-conceived programs that wasted vast amounts of funds, just to prop up the weak and stupid. I had argued that our society didn't need these kinds of people, and morally we were under no obligation to support or save them from themselves. I had strongly believed that the more of these 'idiots' who offed themselves and took others like them with them, the more it would reduce the burden put on the cities, and that would allow for reallocation of those funds to create a larger public share for the responsible citizens. Overall, this would leave the city a much cleaner, nicer, and safer place. In reality, money was the idol that I served."

He watched my eyes, seeking any signs of my disproval. "It's amazing how our view changes when we or someone we love becomes one of the 'idiots,' huh?"

I had no right to judge him. I had plenty of dumb in my past. "It reminds me of the Biblical conversion story of Paul," I said.

He nodded with vigor. "Right. There was no voice from heaven or blindness, but I had been blind to the plight of others until I learned I was as weak or weaker than those I was working against all those years. When I first confessed what had happened to me, I thought that my experiences might help change the minds of the group. As one of their leaders, I erroneously believed that they would have listened and gained some new insight and maybe changed. All those who had been friends and colleagues came after me with a vengeance, driving me out. If they could have managed it, I think they would have stoned me."

He smiled uncomfortably and said, "For a while, I ended up working with various pro-public health groups who, understandably, didn't trust me. Then, I became a volunteer with the Christian interventionist who saved me. I had become a Christian a short while after my brush with death, though it took a while for me to surrender all of me to Christ. Over time, my identity in Christ became all that really mattered to me. To live for Jesus and serve Him. Everything else seemed empty and pointless. He cares tremendously about the welfare of the poor, the weak, the widows, the orphans, the sick, and the lost."

I nodded. "Amen."

Lazarus showed all the classic earmarks of someone who had had a dramatic conversion, giving up everything that he once had believed in with all his heart to do the exact opposite. People often saw these conversions as completely crazy. Paul had once hunted and executed Christians. On the Damascus road, he had a life-changing encounter with God, who temporarily blinded him to get his full attention. After this, God sent him on a lifelong journey as a disciple of Christ. No one would ever call Paul's Christian life an easy journey full of comfort, but it was one that he took on with joy and perseverance.

How many of us would sign up to throw away our wealth, power, and position for a life of being beaten almost to death several times, shipwrecked and stranded at sea for three days, bitten by a deadly snake, imprisoned in several hellish, dank, dark dungeons, and to finally be beheaded? Paul would and did, and more—gladly.

Lazarus smiled at me softly. "You, my friend, I think that you understand this."

No. I am still rather selfish. It pained me to admit that. I gave a weak smile. Changing the subject, I said, "You know who I am, don't you?"

"Not when we first found you, as you were reported as dead, and frankly, you didn't exactly look like you, as you were on the darkest side of life, a mere breath away from death. It was after we got you to our first aid station that I became aware of who we had as our guest. I had you moved here for greater privacy. You may relax. Your secret is safe with us. I will not tell anyone. For you to heal from this, it is of the greatest importance that you confess to your family soon as possible about your life choices. They will have access to far better professional and private health groups than we do, and they will be better suited to help you get past this point. Again, I want no misunderstanding about this; only God kept you alive this time. Your next ride, no matter how small, may be your last."

Time for the insane truth. "I understand that this will sound like an addict unwilling to face his issues, like crazy paranoia, but sometimes the truth sounds that way. I was contact-injected with these sexual stimulants to kill me." Lazarus took in a deep breath and appeared sad. Seeing me tied to a bed, I would not listen to me either. "Think of what you have heard about me and my past. Isn't this exactly how one would expect me to die? No one would question it, and they would get away with murdering me."

Lazarus raised an eyebrow, but he stayed quiet. I continued, "You said that you heard that I died a few evenings back in a fancy pulsorjet accident, right? I don't own one of those, nor have I ever even ridden in that particular model. When was that crash supposed to have happened...and how long have I been here?"

He hesitated, and I was surprised when Marv spoke, "Two nights ago, and you have been with us for 28.6 hours."

"Yes, two nights. Forgive my memory. We haven't slept much in the last few days. It has been a busy week with many more in need than normal."

It was worse than I had imagined. They could be at the door at any moment. "I am sorry that I have added to this number." He smiled softly, seeking to assure me. "The authorities would have searched the crash for my DNA records. They will know that I wasn't in that jet, yet I am guessing that I am still being reported in the news as being dead. Here I am, proving that I am alive," I rolled my eyes, "at least, somewhat still alive. It is a long story, and I hope to be able to explain more to you sometime soon, but I don't think we have much time left before they find this place and try and kill everyone here to cover this all up. We have to leave here now, and we have to go into hiding for a few weeks, maybe longer."

The wiry man smiled and said, "Relax, my friend. Paranoia is often part of the purging and rebalancing process. You had such an extreme overdose that by all rights it should have killed you. We had to run your blood through a cleaner several times, though there is still quite a lot of that junk in your tissues. We estimate that you will have to rest for at least a week while we get your strength back and get your system and hormones back in control. You will still have some strong peaks and valleys as the stimulants are driven from your system."

Lazarus pointed to a nearly invisible rectangle on my left wrist and one at my elbow. "We have applied emergency balancer patches near your joints and various other places around your body, and they will kick in as you need them. After they are used up, they will dissolve to a harmless fine powder that can be wiped off or be showered away. Normally we just give our patients puff injectors." His mouth was drawn, and his eyes were sad and concerned. "But your case is by far the worst case of stimulant overdose that any of us had ever seen. As I said, all of this confusion and paranoia is to be expected. We can give you other sedatives and balancers as needed to help you get past the worst peaks. You are weak, so you must take it easy for the next few days. As I said, your survival is not a done deal. Is there someone we can call to let them know that you are okay or to set up a private hospital stay for you?"

Letting a breath wash over me, I tried to stay calm. "I know that I sound completely paranoid. Please trust me when I say that we are all in extreme danger. I am serious. Anyone who knows about me surviving or anyone whom we contact will be killed. We need to keep moving and not contact anyone if we wish to stay alive."

Lazarus leaned closer to the restraining system's control pad. I didn't move—that would make him believe that I was even more dangerous than he first thought.

I prayed quickly in my head, asking for the right response. "Lazarus, I am not violent, and I will not make a fuss. Even without the magnetic control system, Marv could easily manage me if I were to become violent or try to escape. What time is it now?"

Lazarus studied me as he leaned back in his chair. "About 1:00 p.m. So, who is behind this?"

This was really bad; I had been here too long. I had to appear calm and not crazy or frantic. Inhaling deeply, I let the air slowly slip out my nose to calm myself and to think it through. "This is the terrible and frustrating part. I don't know. It could be any number of people. I haven't been popular since I shined a light on The Remnant purges. There are some rather radical and angry people out there who believe that every problem they encounter is being caused by the evil plans of The Remnant. I know many of the Remnants quite well. They are little different than the other self-involved people walking around the streets. They aren't any smarter or any more virtuous or evil either. Some of these anti-Remnants see themselves as on the side of all that is good, and they are willing to kill to defend those beliefs."

Lazarus didn't seem uncomfortable with this explanation, so I continued. "The other possibility would be some random people who, for sundry reasons, have decided that they don't like me. I doubt these are the culprits, as they are more the types that verbally attack me in the media, comparing me to some wild animal with overly aggressive and deviant mating patterns."

Lazarus let a slight smile leak onto his face as he leaned back and narrowed his eyes. "Do you think the government is behind it?"

"The whole government?" I chortled. "No. That would make me quite paranoid if I did. I wouldn't be surprised if they have some tenuous government connections; how high up, I don't have a clue. The whole group could be a couple of people or a few hundred. They nearly got me twice two nights back. The first time was an assassination attempt in a public bathroom." I wished that I had shut up about that as we didn't have much time left. It raised more questions, mostly about my sanity and level of paranoia. "That isn't germane to my point here."

Lazarus paused and said, "Okay, let's say that I believe you, and we are in trouble. What do you suggest we do?"

"First, I do not have enough information to make any kind of cogent, data-driven suggestions. I have no idea where we are now and where I am health-wise."

"You are in one of my hidden recuperation rooms where I treat those who need more security and privacy. I assure you that we are quite safe. You were out for a little over a day, so you have had some emergency treatments, and you are still in danger medically—you could still die. It is because only because of Jesus and that collection of emergency nano-docs you had injected yourself with that you are not already dead and living with Him." He winced. "Sorry. Please don't go for that option yet, okay?"

"Don't worry. I want to live. As I said, I didn't self-administer this stupid cocktail. I want to stop whoever is doing this and get on with my life."

"Good. It was the nano-docs that had alerted us that you were close to dying and had broadcasted out, calling for help. They are quite amazing things. Before we got to you, they gave us a bio-rundown that helped us administer the right chemical concoction to stop you from hemorrhaging and dying on the street. I keep telling you this bluntly, as we need you to relax and heal before you try to go all heroic. There will be time for that kind of stuff later. I am sure you are hungry. This cleaning process makes people incredibly hungry. As yours was more extreme than others, I am sure you are beyond ravenous. Later, I will get you some real food." He handed me two large quick-meal food sticks. "These will help start the process."

A pulsating alarm in the hallway had Marv moving swiftly out of the room and closing and locking the door behind him. Lazarus vaulted to his feet. With speed and strength that I didn't expect, he lifted me to my feet. He pressed down on the pad on my left arm, and I felt the cleaning system disengage, and the tubes fell away. Without releasing his pressure on my arm pad, he snaked his other hand down to pull up my backpack and place it on my back. My knees felt as if they would give way. He held on tight to my left arm and placed his other hand on my shoulder, steadying me.

He whispered near my ear, "Intruders. That outside door has a special lock that should have been almost impossible to open.

The alarm is our last line of warning. It's not anyone from our team. They are under strict orders not to come here. Follow me." He bent down and placed my shoes on the ground before me guiding me to step into them. I felt them close.

Lazarus led me to the middle of the room and like a parent working with a young child, he took the food sticks from me and put them into my backpack's front pocket. He flashed a quick hand motion at the gurney, and with a silent whoosh of air, the bed closed to flash clean. The tubes leading to the blood cleaning machine turned to smoke. All evidence of my stay had been erased.

From the hallway, I heard a voice that I assumed was Marv's calling out, "Exodus!"

Lazarus leaned close and whispered, "My friend, it is time for you to leave us. May God bless you, heal you and keep you safe. Now, off you go."

The floor beneath my feet began to rise. My weak legs buckled, and I dropped to my hands and knees. The large circle carrying me rose higher, and a similar shape was cut from the ceiling. I was on a slender, open elevator.

"Come with me," I whispered loudly, beckoning to him to run and join me.

Lazarus shook his head, and with a smile and a curt wave, as if we were saying goodbye after eating a nice lunch, he turned to face the door leading out of the room. Noises coming from the hallway ended with several dull thuds. Silently, the elevator picked up speed, and Lazarus and the room slipped from view.

Shock and despair pummeled me. He had to know what was coming. I contemplated jumping off. Being so weak, at best that would leave me stranded one floor up or kill me as the elevator began to ascend faster. I was worthless to him.

Helpless, I watched as rooms above me slid by. Some were occupied, and others were not. A few of the inhabitants noticed me as I glided past them; none of them appeared to be surprised. After a time, it appeared as I was standing still, and it was the rooms that were moving down. Unable to do anything else, I prayed for God's intervention and protection for Lazarus. We both could have fit on this elevator.

I knew the answer and I hated it. Lazarus was streetwise, and he fully understood what was coming. In my weakened state, his being captured and interrogated would afford me the greatest opportunity to run. He also knew it would mean his death. Had he left with me, the attackers would have immediately searched for the way we had escaped and reorganized to give chase. I would have slowed him, and both of us would have died, solving nothing.

The elevator moved into a closed space, and darkness surrounded me. A small light came on, illuminating the tight cylinder, highlighting my aloneness. Frustrated and angry, I sobbed. Praying with all my heart that if he couldn't be saved from harm, his death would be quick and painless. A good, kind, and caring person was in the process of dying to save me, and I was too weak and stupid do anything to stop it or come to his rescue. I wasn't worth his sacrifice. Would I have done that? No—and I hated this answer. I doubted that I would ever sacrifice myself to save anyone else. This made me angry with my selfishness.

What do you do when you find someone to be completely detestable—and that someone is you? You can't kick yourself out or avoid being with yourself. You are stuck with that jerk. Lacking any other options other than sobbing, I continued to pray.

The elevator stopped, and a tiny green light shone above a door. Opening it, I entered into a little, sparsely furnished apartment. There were no signs that it was occupied. Staying here to rest offered no hope. I had to trust the planning of the man who had saved me. Wiping my tears on my sleeve, I fought to rein in my emotions and focus on escaping rather than the loss of Lazarus. If I survived, there would be time for tears. All they would do now was draw unwanted attention to me.

The elevator door closed behind me. Was it going back to the room with Lazarus? Could the assassins ride it up to where I was? That was enough incentive to get me moving.

Ripping off the restraint system's yellow bands, I wadded them up into a ball. Leaving them in the apartment would be an obvious indicator of where I had exited the escape elevator. The exit door lit up, revealing a wide view of the hallway outside. There was just the normal foot traffic moving down the hallway and nothing that seemed out of place. I waved my hand at the door, and it slid open and I stepped out, glancing right and left. To the left, I saw a tiny green light about head height just before a hall junction. Follow the green light. That was as good a plan as any.

Seeing a recycler, I stuffed the ball of yellow restraint bands into the opening. Recyclers kept logs and recordings of their contents and who used them, as too many people have used them to discard items used in crimes. It was pointless worrying about it. I was too weak to pull my backpack off and stuff the bands in and have any hope of putting it back on.

Trundling forward, I searched for more of those little green lights. Sometimes the lights were over a door, down by the sidewalk, near a hallway or by a lift. About eighty years before, there had been a movement to cut back on all the little lights that filled Heavensport. It had been a big success, but with all the realviews littering the walls, I had to search for this light's particular color and size. It helped that they stayed on with a steady intensity.

The hallways grew wider, and more people were in them. None of them paid me any attention. Engrossed in their faceplate screens, most had issues walking in a straight line, even with the avoidance gait-nudgers built into their shoes and clothing. I fit in nicely even if I wasn't wearing a visor.

● ● ● ▬ ▬ ▬ ● ● ●

[Earlier]

The secured private line buzzed verification. The older man locked down his room and answered it with a terse command, "News."

An encrypted voice said, "As you know, our teams confirmed our target's DNA was absent from the crash site. Since then we have been running those special scans and have sent homing signals to his d-class symbioid, but we received no response. One of our techs noticed that we got a negative data ghosting packet back—"

"How many times do I have to tell you that I don't care about the technical? Move on. What happened?"

"Sorry, sir. We were able to trace a fake signal back, and even though it was heavily shielded, early yesterday morning we broke the symbioid's encryption. It delivered its full payload, which I am told is strong enough to kill close to ten men. Normally we would have more details, but an electromagnetic pulse generator or EMP was fired at the location, wiping out a block of apartments surrounding the area. This rendered the symbioid inoperable and unable to report back. We don't know if the target managed to fire the device himself or if he had external help."

"Were your operative and a recovery team deployed on the coordinates?"

"Ah, yes...they were. When they arrived, the target was already gone. We have no data on the target's state, whether he is living, wounded, or dead. The burned symbioid was removed to salvage what information we could and to cover our hack. We have her, and the teams have begun the process of data extraction."

"Please explain to me how one person, or even a small group of people, with just ten to twenty minutes' head start, has avoided capture or elimination? You have had more than a full day to capture the target."

"Somehow he or his operatives managed to fire a second EMP device in the apartment, rendering the recovery team's and the asset's equipment inoperative. Because of this, we lost contact with the asset. It took thirty-eight minutes for him to reach the safe house."

"It cannot get worse."

The voice hesitated. "Well, then, due to the second EMP blast, the asset did not have the proper access encryption with him to enter our safe house to be able to contact us. It took a while for him to be cleared to gain access."

The older man leaned back in his chair in disgust. "It's as bad as I had heard. I had hoped the message I had received was incorrect, but apparently, no. Please do me a favor and don't call this operative an asset anymore. Tell me, is this the same person that you asked us to save last time?"

There was a long silence. "Yes. It is."

"I strongly recommend his immediate termination."

"He has assured me most emphatically that he is most engaged and eager to promptly rectify this problem and that a fee correction is to be negotiated upon completion of this task."

Leaning with his shoulders forward, the older man's voice was tense and loud as he slapped the desk with his palms. "Negotiated? Seriously? He screws up twice and wants to discuss the negotiation of his fees? If he is dead, there is no negotiating and no fee."

"Sir, I wish to give him a final chance to remedy this issue before we execute a different option concerning the...operator."

The man looked for something to throw. Unsuccessful, he growled through bared teeth, "This operator is a liability. Do you understand the tenuousness of your position because of this?"

"I do, sir. Most clearly. I will see to the quick and agreeable resolution of the whole situation."

"I should hope so. Now move."

"Sir, if I may, there is one more issue that you should know about."

"Yes," he said, his eyebrows furrowed and his tone cold.

"We were unable to collect our burned tech team, and they have been recovered by a government team."

Biting his lip, the older man tried to moderate his tone. "Did you try to get them back from them?"

"No, sir. It would have come too late, and that would have required us to use assault mechs in a direct military action against government forces. There is no reasonable way to cover that kind of sortie in the city. That would have revealed our plans before we were ready. We are rewriting the tech team's mission activation brief and the order trails to hide our involvement."

The older man's frustration was growing, and his hands hurt from hitting the desk in his earlier tirade, so he took on a loud, harsh, sour tone to emphasize his displeasure. "These screw-ups must stop now. No more screw-ups, you hear? No more. Get this fixed now, or I will do it myself!"

"Yes, sir. We are on it, sir."

● ● ●   ▭▭▭ ▭▭▭ ▭▭▭   ● ● ●

The assassin from the public bathroom attack stood over the lifeless body of the man who had called himself Lazarus. Newcastle was supposed to be here, but he wasn't. Everything with even a whiff of Newcastle's stench seemed to come back to bite him. It never went easy. The data had pointed to this being a sure thing. In, kill Newcastle, dispatch anyone else on site and stage the scene, leave. Now there was a mess to clean up, and Newcastle wasn't even here to die and solve his problem.

This dead guy on the floor had added another unsettling element to the never-ending Newcastle debacle. He didn't beg for mercy, nor did he break when he had struck him. Not even a deep cut along his inner arm with his knife had made him speak. All he had said was, "What horrible pain has brought you to this kind of life? You can be forgiven and be healed in Jesus. Let me help you. It is not too late, I swear."

Jesus? Like some ancient dead guy from Earth had any power here. He was just another one of those clueless fools who would rather live in their own made-up fantasy world than face the way the world really works. He had seen in a realview or heard somewhere that science had debunked all this Christian garbage anyway.

The assassin had watched him die, but this time he found no satisfaction. The man had smiled through the suffering and said, "Forgive him, Father." He looked up with joy and said, "Oh, My Lord, so beautiful." With that, he died.

Just more of that Christian junk. He was asking his god to forgive his killer, who didn't ask for it, nor did he need it. This guy had no right to do that. And what was he talking about that was "so beautiful"?

He came prepared for the assault wearing special stain-free disposable outer clothes and carrying several cheap weapons to dump to better hide the purpose of the attack. He had stabbed the man repeatedly and sloppily with a dull house knife, making it appear as a street thug had done it for drugs and money. His violent death would be seen as another nobody ground up by the pointless crime that percolated up from deep within the megacity.

The old medical equipment showed signs that it had been modified. Junkies did this to hide personal user information and their dosages. He dropped data squids to deep-scan the devices and on the bed to check for any information that might link Newcastle to this room. Red lights popped on his display indicating he had wasted his time. The situation kept getting worse.

The time left for a clean extrication was running out. It was never good to be caught at the scene of a crime. The police were not as much of a concern as they had strict rules and procedures that they had to follow. His current employer had no constraints, though, and they would try to kill him to cover this up. Minimally, they might blacklist him globally, and that might require him to go off-planet to start over. As there was no proof that Newcastle had ever been here, he would deny any involvement with this event. He didn't need another failure to add to his list.

The only solution left to fix this mess was to kill Newcastle and prove to his employers that he did it. And that death was going to be as painful as possible.

He shoved all the drugs into a pouch before ransacking the apartment, staging it as a robbery done by addicts. From a sani-bag he liberally scattered bits of microscopic genetic materials about the room. These he had carefully acquired from seedy people around the city. They would make the evidence and the trail even more confusing.

Satisfied with the results, he did a last scan of his clothes for the victim's DNA. A second quick-clean, and he was clear. He re-checked that his reconstructor was functioning properly before he headed out the room and into the hall.

The remains of the symbioid littered the hall. A good detective would know that a vibra-knife was skillfully used. He bent down and slashed at the torso and the separated appendages to create the appearance of a longer, less certain fight.

He had almost laughed when his tactical visor had listed the apartment's security defenses and capabilities of this symbioid. All this old model would do is to attempt to restrain him until the police arrived. For expediency and to limit time for Newcastle to escape, he had chosen to use the vibra-knife to remove the symbioid's limbs and its head. The final twisting blow to the forehead was designed to destroy the central processing and memory storage of the symbioid so that no data would be left to reconstruct his attack or to identify him.

To finalize the staging before leaving, he levied a terrible slashing strike that cut the head in half to guarantee the destruction of the memory structure. People would think that a wild animal had attacked the symbioid. That would help sell this story.

He would sell that blade along with the drugs at one of the seedy local shops hidden in the city where he had no connection. Running the unicreds through a few illegal unicred cleaners, he would lose about thirty-five percent. It was worth it to hide his trail, and he would still turn a marginal profit.

The murder knife needed a trail. That he would poorly flash-clean and dump in a park. The police would find it and figure it was a junkie trying to get rid of the evidence.

This would create a simple, expected crime path. The police would erroneously fill in the missing parts until they ended up arresting some thug, and he or she would do time for it. They should thank him for helping clean the streets of some low-life creeps who hadn't been caught for all the things they had already done.

If the police persisted, a few more poorly hidden trails, and he could always incriminate someone else. This was all part of doing business.

●●● ▬ ▬ ▬ ●●●

6

In the Valley of the Shadow

● ● ●   ▬   ▬   ▬   ● ● ●

The last little green light led me to a transit station when the critical need to use the restroom hit me hard. My stomach flipped, churned, and gurgled ominously, threatening to let go immediately to become a public disaster. Half-scampering into the nearest bathroom, I darted into the first open stall.

Almost before I could sit, my system began evacuating the gunk that had begun a hostile invasion of my intestines. Trembling, sweating, and nauseated, I prayed that Lazarus's treatments and the nano-doctors were using this and my sweat as the most expedient way to remove the toxins and excess chemicals and not me about to unravel and die.

As the prolonged intestinal struggle intensified, the air cleaners in the stall had moved from silent to bordering on loud. Soft music began playing. Embarrassed, I half-grinned. My visit today could start the outcry to kill off the unisex bathroom. Exhausted and damp from head to toe, I leaned against the side of the stall and slept.

● ● ●   ▬   ▬   ▬   ● ● ●

"Sir, are you okay in there?"

I was drowsy and confused (again). "Huh?"

"Are you okay, sir? Shall I call for a robo-doctor?" I hoped this was an auto-attendant.

"Ah, no. No, I am all right," I lied. "Too much fun last night...if you know what I mean?" He didn't; he was a robot. "I just fell asleep for a few minutes." My hands and legs were still shaking as if bouncing to a beat that I could not hear.

"I am sorry to hear that, sir. I would be glad to call for assistance for you."

"Naw, I'm good. A good shower is what I need." Shower? More like a caustic chemical dip to remove this stench from me.

"We have those services here, sir."

"Sounds good. I will be out in a moment."

After an extensive personal-clean, I got myself dressed. Bracing myself to reenter the world, I opened the stall door to find a twenty-percent humanoid robot, or a twenty percent for short. The only real human features on these were their head and hands. Did those make up twenty percent of our volume or weight?

These shiny white models were everywhere in the megacities, handling tasks that required social interactions but did not need the sophistication of the more expensive and human-like symbioids. The unit's human head sat on a long slender center pole that traveled down to flare out to cover the single large sphere at the base. Moving up and down on the center shaft were two independent floating shoulder rings, each hoisting two mechanical arms that ended with human hands. Some of the units docked their second set of arms to the main pole to keep them out of the way. Or was that to make them more human?

Why did most of these robots need four arms? Was there a need to carry multiple boxes, or was it to help them lift people who fall? Were they there in case some unexpected need arose?

The robot smiled kindly and motioned for me to follow him. He didn't say a word about the state of the stall. Shuffling along, I felt like a bad guest. The stall door closed and turned red, indicating that it was under heavy cleaning and that it was not available. People coming into and leaving the restroom avoided looking at me.

Catching a glimpse of my image in a 360-mirror I immediately understood why they would give me a wide berth; I appeared so bedraggled and rough that I almost didn't recognize my own reflection. Maybe the city's automatic public safety systems were not so amazing after all. You wouldn't need a scan to see that I needed medical help or an intervention—or to call for the morgue.

I sniggered. Hopefully, no one would think I was a zombie and hit me in the head. Note to self: refrain from groaning out any word that sounded even close to the word brains. Whole grains, trains, rains, lanes. *The rains have destroyed the whole grains on the train.* Bam! I snorted, fighting a harsh laugh. *That's enough.*

The twenty-percent robo-attendant led me to a multi-line autowalk that moved users into the public quick-showers. Stepping onto the autowalk, I relaxed along with thousands of other people as the process began. While not a traditional shower, these amazing systems were designed to freshen up the busy traveler and his clothes at the same time.

Two minutes later, I emerged to see my reflection in the 360-mirror. Much better—fresh, clean, and tidy, bordering on acceptable. Not for long, I sniggered. With these lovely raging hormones, I would have to ride on a continuous loop of quick-showers to be able to stay clean.

I had the option of riding through the extended shaving and grooming station. Reflexively, I stroked my face and felt the stiffness of the stubble and the deeper resistance in my skin when I rubbed upward. It would soften in a day or two. I would keep it, as it might help in disguising me. The shaving system would need to scan the contours of my face, and a smart hacker could use that data to find me. There would be minimal protections on these systems from data siphoning.

Stepping off the autowalk, the same twenty-percent attendant greeted me—how would you guess? There could be thousands of these identical units in this transit hub alone. I was thinking about hiding in all the wrong ways; the best disguise for hiding in plain sight would be as a robot. We didn't even notice them unless we needed something. I couldn't pretend to be a twenty-percent; its center pole was only about five inches in diameter, and the uni-ball drive wheel was about a foot in diameter.

I had been worrying about the shaving systems being hacked when all these helper robots were interlinked, openly sharing data. Here at the quick-showers, a team would stay in one area and trade information with a different team stationed at the exit. It made no logistical sense to physically travel. That means these units recognized individual people and probably by face more than just by their outfits. If I was illegally searching for someone, this is where I would hack the system.

With a pleasant smile, the twenty-percent waited patiently until I returned from my mental wandering. "Any other services that I can arrange for you, sir? We have a full selection of personal and public activities designed to meet any need. How about a shave or a massage?"

"No, thank you. I'm good." I almost asked if he could fend off teams of assassins while I ate and detoxified. Food! "Oh, wait. On second thought, can you get me a large triple burger meal with everything and a mega-sized health water? I am very hungry."

In the space between us, he projected a menu of side items, and I scrolled through it quickly. I came close to ordering it all.

"I would like fries, mixed fruit, and a large brie cheese wedge—no, make that two large wedges, please," I said. These would be easy to stuff down, and they had some chance of keeping me full for a few hours.

He nodded, and a few minutes another twenty-percent robot delivered a big box of food and the large water.

"That will be six unicreds," said the delivery bot, adding with a grin, "I hope you enjoy it."

"Thanks." I fished out a ten unicred note from my pants' front pocket and handed to him. He took it and returned the change.

They both smiled and nodded as I waved goodbye. After finding an out-of-the-way section, I sat at a two-person table and dug in, never setting the burger down until it was finished. Within a few short minutes, I had devoured everything in the package. Eying the empty box, I wished that I had ordered two of them.

A few days ago, I would have gone to a posh and exorbitantly expensive restaurant where a glass of water would cost more than this meal. Maybe my voracious hunger made this feast so glorious. I suspected it was my effete gourmet snobbery that robbed me of some wonderful experiences with great, inexpensive food. I hoped to live to test this theory.

●●● ━━ ━━ ━━ ●●●

Feeling better and steadier on my legs, I rode the autowalks until I saw a transit train set to leave in a minute. That would work.

On the train, the doors closed behind me, and it began to pick up speed. A transit map appeared before me, showing a stop at a recreation district forty-two minutes away. As with all zones, there was one closer. This would be an unexpected destination, and it would put an even greater distance between me and my pursuers. Using mass transit was riskier than taking an individual transpod, but it added another dimension of randomness to my flight. Glancing about the train's cabin, I chose a seat near the middle, near a dozing older man with a long yellow beard. He had animated rec-zone badges all over his vidshirt. He likely was one of those hobbyists who traveled the megacities seeking to visit every rec-zone.

A projected screen popped up in front of me and assaulted me with one of those faux news and entertainment shows that beats its viewers with smiling, half-dressed stars, pummeling colors, fast motion, and hyperbolic emotions. With a curt wave of my hand, the screen disappeared, leaving me in relative silence. With that symphony of visual mayhem and noise going on, someone could walk up and punch me before I even noticed them, and that outcome would be a best-case scenario.

Confronted with time to kill, I found myself ogling women again. It bothered me that I couldn't blame it all on Erlin's love potion. This overdose had amplified the urges that I fought every day. People tell me that it is perfectly natural for men to look. Looking and acknowledging their beauty is fine. Objectifying them does not honor God. As a Christian, I am to hold every thought captive. Contrary to that commandment, I am good at holding improper thoughts captive and fixating on them.

Forcing my focus onto other things, I noted that there were a number of riders with large robo-pets. One woman had a real living dog. I could tell as it was not some odd color, nor did it have wings. It drooled excessively, and the drops didn't immediately disappear.

Those on the fast-moving transport were the same kind of people found everywhere in the megacity. A discreet visual sweep of the car allowed me to relax. No one was obviously out of place or showed any interest in me. For the moment, I was relatively safe. As this was a non-stop express to the recreation area, I watched as transpods delivered new riders and took some away in varying sized groups. Feigning boredom, I studied the new arrivals: teens in a group, couples, children, a few babies, and several personal movers for those needing mobility help. There was nothing out of the ordinary.

I pulled up a floating animated route map before me, and it stated that we had nineteen minutes left reach to the rec-zone stop. Considering my option to stay on to the end of the line, I was disappointed to see that the train would begin to loop back toward the station where I had come onboard.

I still felt vulnerable without my counter-surveillance gear. All that stuff needed to go, as proven by the missile strike on the armored personnel carrier. Erlin had volunteered to go with Riley to help with the ruse. Had she gone, I probably wouldn't have been drugged, and I would likely be home now.

Visions of Erlin aggressively kissing me swarmed my thoughts. No! I shook my head with vigor, trying to shake those thoughts from my mind. Stopping, I pawed at my hair, hoping to tame it back into shape.

Two rows over, the stunning woman with flowing brunette hair whom I had been leering at throughout the trip sat frozen, staring at me through her half-height fashion visor.

Sure, I was acting a bit weird, but most people wouldn't even note that. They are oblivious to their surroundings, as they are so engrossed in their visors or the pop-up screens. I'd bet she was using *Check-Me-Out!* or *How-Hot-Am-I?*—one of those popular social programs that measure the length, intensity, and the location of another person's eye contact on the user's body and displays that information on a colored 3D heat map of their figure. She likely scrolled through her top viewers and pulled me up on her display to see who was that interested. If I was running the same program, she could ignore it, send her interest, state that she was involved, or outright block me. Based on my outrageous behavior, I was shocked that she didn't throw up an opaque privacy screen between us.

I smiled, trying to reassure her that I wasn't as creepy as I was acting. Ooh...that did not work at all. At a loss how to de-escalate the situation, I did a stunted apologetic half-wave. Her eyes grew wider and darted about as if seeking someone to help. Pulling up her light blue purse, she clenched it in front of her torso like a small shield.

Four rows behind her, a new transit pod arrived, letting off a young couple. The brunette's eyes locked on mine like one of the old gunfighter realviews. The transit pod's thirty-second departure clock started. She crouched forward, coiled, waiting to see if I was going to make the first move. If I got up, I would have to walk past her, and she might think it was to talk to her or something worse, so I leaned back in my seat to indicate I was staying. She leaped to her feet and darted off in an outright dash. Just behind her, a pretty redheaded woman jumped to join her. To my irritation and self-condemnation, I checked out their backsides as they fled.

As the transit pod sped away, I could see them peeking back at me and talking. The pod's windows turned a shiny, opaque gray.

Great. I am officially in the "beyond creepy" territory. They had correctly reasoned that I am dangerous and out of control. I didn't even remember staring very much at the redhead. How many more people have I freaked out?

My heart rate increased. A series of calming waves swept over me, and my hormones subsided. Pulling back my sleeve, I half-expected to see the overstressed patch catch on fire and, in a puff of acrid smoke, turn to dust. Hesitantly, I placed a finger on the patch and found it cool to the touch. Good, there was no hint of powder. I prayed, *please, keep working.*

Employing a few deep breathing exercises, I made myself relax. Outside the window, a bright, shiny, and colorful world passed by. Happy and joyful realview people promoted products and smiled at us as we zipped past. Feeling dirty and confused, I was a startling inverse of the beauty around me, and that realization made me sadder.

Those roiling waves of patchy thinking and difficulty with recall were disheartening, and I hated it. *This all will pass...I hope.*

A lithe blonde woman in a blue dress walked past me and sat several seats away. Her haircut reminded me a bit of Erlin's. I closed my eyes so not to stare at her. Erlin. Had the EMP permanently fried her core, or had her system regenerated? She could be hunting me, like in that hokey old realview, *My Crazed Biosynth Lover*, the one where the guy's robot partner goes crazy and chases after him, crushing everything and everyone in her path. The ending left one wondering if the murderous robot had really been destroyed.

People had panicked, demanding the government install greater protections for humans in all symbioids. I thought the story and the outcry was hilarious back then. Not so much now that a super strong and super smart symbioid that didn't need to eat or sleep might be stalking me.

If I could get secure access to one of my hidden servers, I might try to connect to the pixie dot that I implanted in her neural port. That might give me her location and her state of function...unless the EMP had permanently fried her core or her motors. Then it was all a moot point.

My eyes were burning less, so I opened them. To my surprise, I found that a thirty-something blond guy with sparkling red hair stripes had come to stand in front of me. His hair was styled in one of the newest trendy cuts, and he was wearing a knock-off designer outfit. He reeked of pretension as he smiled, flashing his too-white of teeth at me. He had illuminated tooth veneers. It was another of those stupid trends that I disliked.

"May I?" he said, pointing to the empty seat behind him.

Not waiting for me to respond, he gave a spiral hand signal, and the seat turned around to face me and moved closer. With an insouciant confidence, he plopped down without looking to see if the chair had moved into place. That act told me that he wasn't a Remnant. We check first that a technology is behaving before we act; too many of us have been killed or wounded by so-called "random technology accidents."

The man leaned forward with his palms facing each other and his fingertips touching lightly, making an A-shape. He was trying to show his dominance. I thought he looked like someone sitting on a toilet. At least there was no weapon in his hands.

His hands parted, and he rotated his full right hand so that his thumb was pointing up. Ooh, the mystical knife-hand dominance move. Someone has been watching those bogus Influence Others realviews.

"Rolland Newcastle," he said.

I flinched. "Pardon?" My snide humor vanished as my eyes flicked about the cabin, scoping for others who might be on their way to join us.

"Rolland Newcastle. Anyone ever told you that you look a lot like Rolland Newcastle?" His teeth flashed again, supposedly showing confidence. I read cocky and irritating.

"I get that sometimes," I said, trying to sound disinterested.

"Cool. I believe in getting right to the point, right? I have an idea that could net you a few extra unicreds. We can all use a few more of those, you know what I am saying, am I right? Well, here's the deal, you see my wife is having her thirtieth birthday party on Saturday, and she had this thing about Rolland Newcastle. I mean, I don't get it, am I right? The guy was a major-ass clown. Not you, of course, you're different. So, what I need you to do is simple; you just show up and give her a thrill. It will be really easy for you. You'll have to dump the beard, but hey, you'll be making a few extra creds, so it's cool, right? B'sides, guy-to-guy, the scraggle doesn't work for you." He smiled like he was doing me a favor.

Offended, I brushed my hand down to smooth my poor beard. Lots of guys kept a three-day beard, and it was considered cool and stylish. In my case, it apparently added to my indigent or strung-out appearance.

"Sorry, I am not a Newcastle look-alike. I don't—"

The guy smiled wider with his teeth growing brighter, and he patted his palms downward attempting to calm me. "Right, right, right. That's the beauty of it. See, you don't have to pay to be licensed. You just show up and get all friendly with her, maybe grab her butt and go for a kiss and fifty creds are all yours— basically for doing nothing. I mean, what a deal, you get to grab the ass of a classier lady than you would ever have a chance with, no offense meant there, I am just being honest, you know what I am saying? And best yet, you also get paid to do it. That's a really sweet deal, am I right? I know what you are thinking; you should be paying me for such a deal." He laughed, slapping his knee as if we were all in on his joke.

Does he have a realview of her? Hiding out at a party would be unexpected—What? Stop it. Doing anything with this guy was detestable, and my curiosity about his wife was wrong. With effort, I stamped down that thinking and used most of my will-power not to tell him off.

Shaking my head, I replied, "No. I am sorry. Like I said, I don't do that kind of thing."

He frowned, and his sculpted eyebrows attempted to scrunch. "I can see you are a shrewd businessman. So let's just say seventy-five unicreds. Wow, right? That is really good money, don't you think? But for that, you have to give her a few gropes and tell her that she is the most beautiful lady you have ever seen and—Hey! I know, maybe you could act like you are drunk."

"No. As I said before, I am not interested. I am just a guy trying to get somewhere."

He leaned even farther forward, and his seat moved him closer so that I could see the glowing red strips glistening in his hair. He stared me in the eyes and said, "Let's you and me get real here. I am a really good judge of character. You look rough. You had a night of hard partying that didn't go so well, right? You haven't shaved in a few days, your clothes are nothing special, and you don't have any money, and you probably have already blown this month's public share. You need what I am offering."

Squinting, I snarled, "I am doing fine without your help, thanks."

He leaned back a few inches and chewed on his lip as if coming up with an idea. "What I do is deals. I am known for it. Okay, let's see if I can sweeten the deal. If you are really good at playing Newcastle at the party, maybe this could be the start of a new career for you. I have connections that can get you some more gigs. Maybe a split of thirty-five for you and sixty-five for me? After all, I would be doing all the work to get you the jobs. Not to worry, we can work out the percentage after you come to the party—I'll get you the money after the party, if you do well."

He got this look as if he had thought up something spectacular. "You know what? I just thought of this, this is good. I know how we can really make this special for my wife—You could be acting, like all too friendly and stuff, trying to cop a feel, but not her boobs, right? She just had those DNA'ed up as an early birthday gift from me to her, or should I say to me? Am I right? But they say that she has to have a few days to set or heal or something—so, right, I could come in all heated, telling you to get away from her, and then you could pretend to throw a punch, and I would block it, and then I would punch you in the face. Not too hard, but we have to sell it."

Horrified, I raised the palms of my hands toward him and growled, "Are you nuts? No. It's time that you left." Have to sell it? I would love to sell it to him in the face! As it was tough for me remain sitting upright, I was no more than a growly kitten and in no condition to put up much of a fight.

His face fell as I scooted sideways away from him and stood to leave. My knees shook with the effort. He reached out and placed a firm restraining grip on my arm. I glared at him and he reluctantly removed his hand. The city's safety systems should be asking this guy to move away from me.

"Easy, guy. Let me finish. This would be good for you. You know you need it. I'll tell you what, to make it worth your while, I would throw in an extra fifty, that's 110 UCs total, and I could even have my cousin waiting outside with one of those deluxe home med kits if by chance I hit too hard. I tell you, this would be great. It's a win-win for both of us. So what do you say, deal?" He held out his hand for us to shake on it.

Horrified, I shook my head and started walking away. "No deal. Get away from me. We're done."

Not only was he a creep, he was bad at math, or I suspected it was more that he was an outright swindler. With great effort, I briskly shuffled towards a personal transpod. It didn't matter where it went as long it was away from this guy.

He called after me, "You should be grateful for any job now that Newcastle is dead, you amateur! You don't look that much like him anyway. I was trying to help you out, you lowlife. See, that's the problem with the poor. They will always be poor because they are so lazy, and they don't want good work, even when it is handed to them."

I heard the transport safety system begin to reprimand him as I stepped into the pod. It took far too long for that to engage. What did they need to see or hear for them to act, him dragging me out of the train car? Maybe it had something to do with my invasive staring at that dark-haired woman. I don't know.

I sat down, the door closed, and the pod moved off with a whisper. Vibrating in anger, I raced through paybacks that would hurt him, including showing up at the party to reveal my true identity. That included a horrible little mental play with me taking his wife away for an innocent night or week on the town.

Wow. I am ashamed that I even thought of devastating a marriage, all for petty and pointless revenge. He was a jerk, but my idea was many times worse than what he was trying to do. I was transferring my anger at my circumstances onto him. This wasn't acceptable behavior. I apologized to the Lord and asked for forgiveness. Then I prayed for the man's wife and added, "And him too." It still was far shy of the right attitude.

●●● ▬ ▬ ▬ ●●●

After leaving the transpod, I drifted along with the milling crowds. The streets grew wider, and large realviews of smiling people and cute animated animals clamored for my attention, telling me that I was approaching Merryland. Another recreation area, I laughed. Of course that was where we were headed; there was some form of a rec area everywhere. Megacities are designed to keep the public happy and busy.

I let my frown be my guide. If I found this irritating, maybe they wouldn't look for me here.

Even before entering the park, I was already regretting this plan. Merryland was indeed merry, maybe too merry. Joyous realview critters were waving, singing, and dancing about us as we were funneled into the park. Nearby on the main street, a colorful parade erupted into the street, spewing bright, happy, dancing creatures that filled the air with catchy pop songs.

I winced at the onslaught. We were being drizzled in gooey manufactured happiness that had no lasting power or substance. How could anyone like this?

To my right, a burly guy turned abruptly and bumped into me, almost knocking me over. His thick hand grabbed my arm to keep me from falling. "Sorry. Are you okay?" he asked. I nodded, righting myself with his help. Removing his hand, he leaned close, and a big hearty smile filled his face. "Isn't this great? We come here at least once a month, and I still love it!"

"Yeah, it's great," I outright lied, eking out a smile. He gave me a thumbs-up as he rejoined his group, who were singing along with the parade.

He was not alone in his love of this place. Everywhere people were laughing and beaming.

There had to be one other person in this swirling mass of humanity who was regretting being in the park. Determined to be right, I scanned the crowds. There, headed toward the exit, an older couple was trying to coax two unhappy, crying children to follow them. The man's weary eyes landed on mine, and I nodded and smiled at him; I understood that weariness for different reasons. I was my own grumpy, hungry, tired, and over-stimulated child. I was not vindicated.

Keeping to the smaller side streets, I stayed away from the rides and sought out a quieter spot away from the major attractions and especially the water park. In my compromised state, my brain would not have been able to handle that well.

Tired and hungry again, my energy levels plummeted, and I plopped down on a comfee-bench in an area that offered multiple avenues for escape. A gentle fresh breeze whispered past me, and the warm sunlight fell on my face. It was probably manufactured, but I enjoyed it nonetheless. It was as quiet as possible with around 80,000 people milling about on vacation.

Quaint, old-time electronic signs pointed to snow skiing, water activities, surfing, hiking, biking, hypergliding, and rock climbing destinations that were within this area. Behind me was an idyllic mountain village scene with snow-capped peaks in the distance. Was this based on a real location in the past, or was it was made up? Were the mountains realview projections, or were they were using forced perspective to make something that was much smaller and closer appear to be full scale? How it was being done didn't matter; as I still obsessing about this, I decided that the mountains were utilizing both techniques. Maybe this would allow my mind to move on to something that was important, like surviving.

Trying to relax, I studied my surroundings, contemplating the least dangerous method to obtain a meal where I wouldn't create any patterns. Patterns meant predictability, and that led to capture and death. There were restaurants and little food vendors everywhere here, so technique and planning were my issues.

Food sticks! Lazarus had given me two food sticks...and I still had some snacks from the safe house too. There I sat, hungry, with food in my backpack. I pushed the backpack release, and it slid down my back and moved to the side. Turning to investigate, I reached in to pull out one of the brightly colored, hand-sized quick-meals. The label said that it was "A Scrumptious Old-Style Beef Stew Hand-Pie." That would do. Hands trembling, I fumbled with turning the blue activation knob until it turned red, indicating that it was heating the contents. The pouch changed to a spring green color, and I placed it on my lap, watching it open to fashion a simple plate. The edges of the plate turned a spring green, indicating that it was cool enough to eat. It smelled delightful as I touched the half-moon pastry shell to test its warmth. It was not too warm to pick up. Lifting it to my nose, I breathed it in before taking a bite. The crust broke, and the taste of savory beef and vegetables filled my mouth. *Oh, this is really quite good!*

A twenty-percent robot selling drinks came by, and I waved him over to purchase a bottle of enhanced sports water. I had to be running low on electrolytes, minerals, and vitamins after the last few days.

A smile was building on my face one bite at a time as I sat, enjoying eating and drinking. Sweeping over me like a cool breeze on a hot summer day, I could feel hope starting to seep in. Add a little sleep, and I might even feel almost human again. Finishing the last of the hand-pie, I fetched and activated the second quick-meal Lazarus had given me. This one was "A Delightful Grilled Turkey, Cheese, and Potato Panini."

Growing calmer, I enjoyed the meal rather than just gulping it down. I would eat again and make my way out of the park after I got a bit of rest. My mind wandered, and I found myself wondering if my second EMP had caught anyone. It had been rigged to initiate twenty minutes or so after the first blast. If I survived, I would cover the losses of the safe house's neighbors—and of

Lazarus' interventionist group. Gazing off toward the snowy slopes, I watched people skiing. There was no real way to make it up to them for what happened to Lazarus. I could send them money and twenty newer versions of Marv or something like that.

The first EMP firing had triggered a mechanical timer, and that should have pulled out the securing pin that caused the second unit's EMP shielding to fall off, and that would cause the second EMP to fire. My friend Terry Curtis and I had set this all up. We were laughing so hard at the idea of it that we almost added a third EMP to the room. We had a great deal of fun trying to outdo each other, coming up with more outrageous variations on this idea, including filling the room with foam, candy, or even pudding. We ended up adding the second, much more powerful generator. Terry (those who know him just call him Curtis) had worked the deals, and he had warned me that the second "special" EMP was so powerful that it "could ward off an invasion." Even with EMP shielding, it also would have fried the third EMP device before it detonated, rendering it useless.

Maybe the apartment was empty, and the second EMP did nothing. If Erlin was still there, she wasn't going to rise again, and I had wasted time messing with her port. If they did find the pixie dot I put in Erlin, they could use that signature to find and track the ones that I was carrying with me. That's what I would do if the dot had survived. That was enough for me. Shoving the last bite of the hand-pie in my mouth, I fetched the pixie dot applicator from my backpack and tossed it and the meal packaging into a nearby recycling drop. It was smart to assume they had the pixie dot and were using it to find me.

I glanced up to check my data-sphere screen—ugh. How many thousands of times today had I tried to check my data-sphere or tried to start some nonexistent process? It's okay. I need to relax and think. I was being hard on myself because I felt unprotected, frustrated, afraid, and alone.

The food had helped, and I was feeling pretty good as I left Merryland. A large, friendly rodent told me to "come again soon." I shrugged, unwilling to commit.

Walking along the busy avenues, I wondered how many times I had already gone over the same ideas for reaching out for help. It all had the same terrible outcome. Lazarus had likely died to save me, and that was almost more than I could bear. A bad move on my part could add thousands more to that list.

I had to get out of Heavensport. Even being hidden among 768 million people and being reported as dead, I still was too well known to be able to stay out in public and expect to remain undetected. A scraggly beard and a hormonal imbalance were not enough of a disguise to keep me hidden for long. Looking deranged and drunk was fairly normal for me in my early twenties.

A horrible thought struck me—to find me, all they would have to do is put out an offer of 400 unicreds for any verifiable Rolland Newcastle lookalike sightings. Make it one of those social sharing games, and people would go crazy with it. "We lost Rolland, can you help us find him?" or something like that. Four hundred unicreds wasn't enough money that anyone would worry about the offeror's bad intentions, but it was enough to motivate people to start looking. That deal-making fool I had met on the train would sell out me without hesitation, and so would a million others. Make the amount 1,000 unicreds—or worse, offer a deluxe robo-partner of their choice for my capture—and I was done for.

Wow. That was a negative and gross characterization of the public. Even as I tried to push that judgmental thought down, my logical side wouldn't let it go. For easy calculations, if even ten percent of the population were even a tad bit greedy, that was 76.8 million or so pairs of eyes looking for me. Even if it were five percent that would be...ah, dang. I was too tired to be able to figure out half of 76.8 in my head. What about kids? Does that take away from that number? This is stupid. A guess would be around 20 or 21 million people looking for me. The fun side of this was that there must be several million guys who looked enough like me to break them financially. If this came to be, a number of them were about to have some surprising and awful days ahead.

If they didn't find me on their own soon, it was a matter of time before they made such an offer. There had to be independent groups or individuals that had their own private face scanners that would jump at the opportunity to act as private detectives. It would be a fun and profitable adventure for them and would result in a painful death for me. Realistically, if those seeking me were pushed too hard, they would begin the full-on purge of the Remnants. This was a detestable situation.

I had to get off the streets and into another one of my safe houses right away. There I could send out information about these attacks to alert the other Remnants and maybe arrange an extraction. This safe house would have to be one of my deeper plants that I hoped that no one knew about. I gave thanks as my thinking was getting better, and I was remembering more locations.

Making a quick bathroom stop, I did a covert check of my finances to find I had a little over 7,000 unicreds in disposable credit holders and about 390 creds in loose bills. That would help me get out of Heavensport or at least let me purchase food and some different clothing to blend in better. I had to use care, as each use of these holders created a small trail. The loose bills would not be as easy to trace.

The government had tried for hundreds of years to move away from all printed bills. Somehow it stopped. I never had much of an opinion on the subject until I had to build safe houses.

Weaving my way through the city streets, my stomach rumbled and complained. I was still hungry, even after eating two food sticks a half hour ago. The war going on in my body was burning through calories at a furious pace. Once I was someplace secure and I had eaten again, I would be in a better position to make a reasonable plan.

A pastor had once told me to use the acronym HALT when making important decisions. Never make any when you were Hungry, Angry, Lonely, or Tired. I teased him saying, "What about Scared?" SHALT or HALTS. I always meant to come up with more to make SHALT NOT. I was in a full SHALT or HALTS situation. Add drugged up into that. Okay, that doesn't work at all.

Making my way through the main transit hub, I studied the dress of the people around me looking for ideas to better blend in and hide. A guy walked by with a vidshirt flashing the words "technically not available." If that weren't bad enough, the word "available" flashed brighter, drawing one's eye to it. I am sure his significant other would be so pleased with his deep level of commitment.

Everywhere I looked were endless variations on bat, angel, pixie, bird, or dragon wings, and those stupid tails and ears, all broadcasting out people's emotions. Erlin warning me against using any emotion-broadcasting gear didn't leave me heartbroken. My emotions were anti-social and troubling before she pumped me full of her lethal love cocktail. I certainly didn't need animated visual flags to confirm that I was an unstable and raging pervert.

What about robo-pets? Do they monitor us? I watched a yellow pixie zooming about the head of a woman with animated orange Medusa hair. The robo-pet landed on her shoulder, and with malice it stuck out its tongue at me. That is a programmed or learned behavior, and someone chose to keep it. No robo-pets.

Hunger was pressing in on my thinking. I was keeping my remaining backpack food for an emergency, and this was getting close. All the walk-up restaurants along this area felt too open and vulnerable. The smells emanating from them were excruciatingly delightful, and my stomach complained at my passing them.

Several times, I abruptly changed course when I was confronted with areas that were too open or where the alleyways were too constricted. The size and density of the crowds were another worry. I used these corrections as a way to inject greater randomness to my path. Contrary to my normal pattern of avoidance, I added in arbitrary lifts and even a few autowalks to change it up. If they found me now, they would attack in a full on brutal assault, not a staged malfunction.

●●● ━ ━ ━ ●●●

7

Entertaining Angels

●●● ━ ━ ━ ●●●

A heavy and unrelenting urging in my spirit sent me down a wide street to one of the artisan zones. These areas are filled with stores and restaurants run by humans. It was a thriving sub-culture for those who enjoyed managing their own business or the uniqueness of the products and services that could be found there. They still used automation or robots to conduct business, just judiciously applied. Shops here had numbers like 50/30 listed on their doors. This told shoppers that 50% of the store was run by humans, and 30% of the products were human-designed.

Given a choice, for something structural or chemical, then I will go for the precision of the automated system. For something artistic in its design, I can go either way.

The scent coming from a multi-ethnic restaurant drew my attention. Onions, garlic, and maybe chicken? Whatever it was it smelled great. The door listed the restaurant as a 60/80. The urging deep in my spirit pushed me on, and my stomach growled in complaint.

I had learned the hard way to listen and act when these deep, unexplainable pressures that tugged and pushed me. Years ago, I had this feeling and I had brushed it off as merely nerves. I woke in critical condition at a hospital, the victim of a "malfunctioning" autowalk. A few others riding with me never woke.

Other than in the artisan zones, the majority of the restaurants in the megacity were automated. It made sense. The best recipes could be copied, developed, and delivered by food systems and robotic technology. Machines could measure and modify almost everything to make sure that all the acidity levels, tartness, spice, and flavor were exactly the same each time a dish was served.

Over the years, I had experienced some of the best restaurants that were available. There is something to be said for the excitement of variation and that unique human touch that cannot be adequately explained. Though I am loath to admit it, for most daily meals, the automated food system's fare tastes better.

That pressing unease pushed me towards a narrow shop named **Starliner**. While in plain sight, the whole shop was unremarkable, tucked in among much larger, showier stores that were demanding to be noticed. The sign at the door listed it as 100/70—rare. This meant it was human-run, and the products were mostly designed by humans in small quantities.

Inside the boutique, there was a mix of clothing and electronic items. There were no realviews or automated merchandising systems here. The store was designed to sell one-off kind of goods. There were a number of lit display cylinders around the shop that held single items of clothing, a pair of shoes or some pants. Nothing I saw seemed to merit this kind of wasted floor space.

Intrigued, I stopped to read one label, which that said that it was a jacket worn by Lula DeValt in the realview *Desire by Sunset*. It had the exorbitant price of 7,250 unicreds. This place sold realview star merchandise and memorabilia to fans. Why would anyone pay that kind of money for an item of clothing that the star wore for a few hours during a realview production? I doubted that the stars had developed any kind of emotional attachment to the clothing.

Unfortunately, I know Ms. DeValt all too well. She is a vain and vapid little creature who cares only about herself. I have heard that the public thinks that she is "charming" and "adorable." I don't share that opinion of her as I have seen her throwing massive screaming fits over the stupidest things, such as the direction the wind was blowing or how her Blue Sky Island mixed drink had to be "the color of the sky in the Haulien Islands, not the Maurakala Islands!" At first, I thought she was joking. No, it was a full-blown tantrum over something that was completely meaningless and cosmetic at best. Sadly, these blowups are too frequent. It is said among those who spend time with her, "To know her is to dislike her; to work for her is to detest her." She is the classic kiss-up, kick-down kind of person.

Still uneasy in my spirit, I circled around behind a pair of tall, lit ella-glanse crystal protective product tubes and used them as cover to peer out the store's front windows. Inside the displays were two skimpy, sparkly dresses that were displayed on exaggerated female mannequin forms. Feigning interest, I stooped down and continued to peer through them to scan the street in front of the shop. I was praying that the source of my unease was just hunger.

"May I help you?" asked a voice beside me.

An attractive woman of about twenty-five, dressed in a loose-fitting gray jacket was standing next to me. Her dark hair was pulled back in a ponytail that hung past her broad shoulders. Distracted, I had not heard her approach.

"Pardon?" I said, still nervously eying the view out the front window.

"We don't sell those here."

"Right. Sorry. No pardons sold here," She wasn't leaving, so I stumbled on. "I'm just looking for food or clothing. You know, something different."

Outside the window, a flicker of motion drew my eye. The air was rippling as if the wind was boiling and thickening. Adaptive cloaking was breaking. A T-37a assault mech glided down to land by the front door.

"Oh, no," I said, my voice falling.

The saleswoman yelled out, "Lockdown!"

Metal shields slammed down to cover the front of the shop, blocking out all the external light. What kind of place was this? Turning, I saw that the young woman was already gone. She was at a dead run, headed towards the back jewelry counter twenty feet away. Rounding the edge of the display, she hesitated as our eyes met. There was indecision on her face.

Stepping forward, I mouthed the words, "Help me. Please."

Only God could help me now. Sending an assault mech of this level was complete overkill. It was equivalent to using a missile to kill a housefly.

The wall behind me groaned and bowed inward as the mech attacked the store's defenses.

"Run! Come here!" she yelled, waving and pointing behind the counter. She ducked down and disappeared.

Running furiously, my legs protested, and my chest was pounding as I heard the sounds of the wall behind me being ripped away. With a leap, I vaulted over the back counter to land with a wrenching thud inches away from the woman, who was crouching close to the counter. It was only by the grace of God that I didn't land on top of her.

To my complete surprise, the area behind the counter was empty! There was nothing there but the two of us. I expected something more than that after the shop locked itself down like some high-tech prison. Even an armored jewelry counter would barely slow that assault mech. We needed a hyper-missile or rail-cannon. I began praying.

The front of the store gave way and blew open, spewing debris and dust across the room. Powerful rays of sunlight blinded us as the powerful assault mech pounded and tore its way through the remaining wall to crash into the shop.

"Go!" hollered the woman.

"Me or it?" I yelled back.

The floor gave way beneath us, and we plummeted down to be swallowed in the enveloping darkness.

With a pop of air, the floor above us moved back into place, taking away all the remaining light. I heard smashing noises that faded to silence as we continued to fall into the darkness. The T-37a was hunting me.

An angled section rose up to meet us; it began directing our slide as we still were falling downward at a steep angle. I was elated. This was an emergency escape tube.

My happiness was short-lived. Above us I heard ripping noises and felt the pressure change followed by a muffled *ping, ping, ping* noises.

"Roller bombs," I said, assuming the worst.

Roller bombs are small, offensive tactical bouncing spheres that can be fired down tunnels, hallways, pipes, and ducts. Imagine smart, heat-seeking, bouncy flak cannon grenades that can send out multiple-shaped charges to destroy everything in a twenty-foot radius.

As we were in a big tube, we were the projectile in the barrel of a weapon that was being fired.

"Hang on!" cried out the woman, and there was a sudden change in the air pressure.

A sharp curve slammed us to the side of the tunnel. A second change in pressure blocked up my ears. I closed my eyes and said a prayer, waiting for the roller bombs to catch us and explode. There was nothing that we could do.

A tight grouping of powerful explosions reverberated through the tunnel. They were close, but not on top of us. The pressure of the nearby blast made my head and ears hurt, leaving me nauseated.

"What happened?" I shouted.

She called back, "That was a sixty-degree diverter. It reset to send the bombs down the other path."

A section of the tube had switched to direct us off at a sharp, sixty-degree angle to join a different tunnel. It had slid back in place to send the roller bombs away from us. It had saved us from a horrible and grisly death.

The detonation was so intense that I knew without us being diverted, we would have died. Our body heat was not the only trigger on the roller bombs. These were semi-autonomous smart weapons. Proximity scans showed us getting away, and an algorithm made the units explode in unison in an attempt to use the tube's materials as shrapnel. Whatever the reason, it had been too close, and my ears hurt from the pressure from the detonation. No more explosions came, and I gave thanks to the Lord for that.

In total darkness, we began to slow until we came to a stop. Before I could act to disengage my arms and legs from around the young woman, she wriggled free and scurried away.

Near me, I heard her whisper, "Go right and follow my voice. Stay low. These tunnels are only six feet tall."

I did not hesitate. Losing her in this enveloping darkness would be a nightmare. Stumbling and frantic, I moved toward where I heard her last, listening intently for any sound of her moving or breathing. My back complained at the insult of being bent over, and I stood up a bit more. I was rewarded with searing pain as I banged the top of my head on the tunnel's low ceiling. Pressing down on the throbbing ache with my hands, it was all I could do not to curse and strike at the roof, as if that childish action would somehow teach it a lesson for being too low. After taking the time to calm myself, I crouched over more and reached out to find the woman.

Not hearing her, I panicked. Did I lose her already? Darting forward and waving my hand in a zigzag pattern, I bumped my hand into her.

Taking a step back I said, "Sorry. I banged my head on the ceiling and then I thought I had lost you."

"I waited. We are not going to get far like this. Relax, I am going to take your hand and put it on my shoulder." I felt her warm, supple fingers take my right hand and guide it to rest on her left shoulder. "Follow me, and try not to step on my heels, okay?"

She moved off at a brisk pace, and I stumbled after her, worried that I would once again strike my head. She didn't seem to have that problem. Was she part bat? How was it that she so comfortable in these low tunnels? Her shoulder seemed low, indicating that she was not tall. I tried to remember her from the store. A silly thing like a rampaging assault mech crashing through the shop had stolen my attention.

After a few initial missteps, I moved farther to her left side to walk at a bit more distance. This worked well, and it allowed us to continue at a much quicker pace with minimal entanglement.

With few other stimuli, I concentrated on walking in unison with her. There was no hesitation or awkwardness to her gait, nor was there any shaking of her shoulders to indicate that she was waving her hands to avoid striking a wall. Trying to think back, I didn't remember her wearing a visor back at the shop. Did she have night lenses on? Did she get them from the jewelry counter?

These questions were bugging me, so ventured to ask, "I am sorry to bother you, miss. May I ask how are you able to move through these tunnels so easily? I am bumbling along while you are gliding through here effortlessly. Are you wearing night lenses?"

She slowed, and I felt her strong shoulder turn towards me. "It helps that I am well under six feet tall and yes, I am using a form of enhanced spectral night lenses."

"Thank you. That explains it."

Her lenses were both casting and reading a spectrum of light that was outside the human eye range, and this was making the tunnels appear as dimly-lit rooms. I was tempted to press for more exact details about her level of visual acuity. Some advanced models were so good and bright that one would even be able to read in the dark with them.

The pace increased, and after a few more minutes of loping along, I conceded the race. "Can we stop?" I dropped my hand to grasp my aching side. "I am very tired." The lack of food, crouching, and the intense internal chemical war had done me in.

With an exasperated exhale, she whispered, "Maybe you should consider exercising."

I snorted in surprise, not expecting the comment. "Sorry, I haven't eaten much in several days, and it is catching up to me.

Can we stop for a moment? This low tunnel makes it hard to run."

She acquiesced with a grunt and said, "Two minutes. No longer."

Thanking her, I slipped to bow down on my left knee, listening to the sound of us breathing. Blood was pounding a bit less in my brain, and that meant that I was alive, and after all that had happened, it was a better outcome than I could have expected. I wallowed in the thrill of being alive. It was good that she couldn't see me grinning like a fool in the dark. Wait. She could.

Crouched as I was, the instep of my left foot began to complain at being stretched and threatened to cramp. Adjusting my stance caused the neck of my outfit to funnel a puff of my own rancid scent up to my nose. It wasn't pleasant. Even with the quick-clean at the transit station, my system had been on overdrive for a few days, and I stank. I hoped that she didn't smell it. If she did, she might have been wondering if I had died a while back and hadn't the decency to quit moving. I tried not to laugh out loud at the silly thought.

In a low voice from about two feet away, she asked, "Can you go another fifty yards or so? There is a better spot for us to rest there."

"Yes." I wondered if she were strong enough to drag me there.

About a hundred yards later we came to an area where the sound, scent, and air patterns opened up, signaling we had arrived at a much larger open area. Should I tell her that it was two times farther to this spot than she had said? Not a good idea, as I still didn't know where I was or whom I was with.

We sat in the complete blackness of the tunnel, leaning up against the tube's curved wall. Lacking any light, I closed my eyes to focus on the sounds, echoes of the tunnels, and the air movement. Taking and releasing a deep breath, I opened my eyes and saw no difference in the view.

Venturing to begin a conversation, I said, "Thank you for rescuing me. I thought we were going to die in the shop and again with the roller bombs."

"We are still not out of danger yet, but you are welcome."

A bright white light pierced the darkness, hurting my eyes. The woman held a small, broad-beamed light that revealed that we were indeed in a larger space with several branches of tunnels that led off into the darkness. The walls and pipes told me that we were in the access channels that were used to supply basic city services. I noted markings near the tunnel branching. Why were these marked, instead of microdotted with location markers? Was this to help those who might get lost down here? What if you didn't have a light?

Her light waved across my face, drawing my attention. Turning, I noted that she was holding a small pistol, and it was pointed at my chest.

"What's your take on weapons?" she said her voice calm and steady.

There is something unreal about having a handgun pointed at you. Your mind doesn't want to accept it. If I lived, I was going to have to get past this.

"I have respect for them, but I don't carry one," I said, trying to sound calmer than I felt.

"We'll see about that," said a feminine voice from my right side.

Out of the darkness, a young, strong-looking blonde woman moved to stand next to me. She wore a long ponytail, and her outfit was a serviceable dark gray with navy and green accent panels. It didn't scream for attention. She had on a half-visor that I assumed was a spectral night lens.

"Hands on top of your head, please," she commanded firmly.

Complying, I raised my hands and interlocked my fingers on the top of my head and sat waiting as this new woman did a quick but thorough search of my body. A tingle raced up my spine, and I fought to lock myself down and not squirm. This was not the time to give in to my stupid body. Enough already. I wasn't that bad at fourteen—well, maybe I was, and I didn't remember it. A new wave of calm slid over me. How many more hits did these patches have left? The blonde woman picked up my backpack from the floor next to me, moved off, and lit a second light to look it over.

The dark-haired woman said, "Thanks for coming."

The blonde didn't look up as she evaluated the contents of my pack. "No problem. I got the alerts of the deployment the diverter. I did a wide-area scan. We are safe for the time being. We need to get moving to make it harder to find us."

"I agree. Did you get the feeds from the shop?" asked the dark-haired woman, keeping her light and gun tightly focused on me.

"Yes. It is bad, a total loss." The blonde briefly glanced up at the brunette with the gun. "He has lots of cash, credits, a change of clothes, toiletries, and some big tech."

Her light lingered on my face, and I adjusted my eyes to a moderate squint. She asked, "How big is the tech he's carrying?"

"Not street. More. Maybe old military. It is a few years old. High-quality for its day."

The dark-haired woman's gun moved more on target. Still and calm, she asked, "Yours?"

I nodded, still shocked that the loss of the shop wasn't a big part of this conversation. It wasn't a good idea to bring up another reason for them not to like me. I would guess that having one of the most advanced assault mechs on the planet attacking us was more of a surprise.

The dark-haired woman asked, "Why was the T-36 after you?" As my eyes were adjusting to their handheld lights, I could make out that she was wearing a visor similar to the one worn by the blonde.

I sensed a test. "Not to be rude, miss, but it was a T-37a."

From my right, the blonde woman chuckled.

"How do you know?" asked the brunette.

Despite the malevolence of a handgun being leveled at me, I felt oddly free to speak. "The T-37a has an extended cowling along the top, by the forward sensor array, to block phantom data bounce. It has better active camouflaging, and it has upgraded weapons and armor. Uncloaked it looks much cooler too."

The dark-haired woman was appraising me. "Okay, so you aren't a hack. Are you military?

"No. Not even ex-military," I said with little emotion.

As she leaned forward, the contours of her face were highlighted by the light. "Then why is it after you?"

As I tried to read her eyes, she slid back into the shadows behind her light. The blonde extinguished her beam and sat still in the darkness. I assumed she was waiting for my response to the dark-haired woman's question.

Exhaling slowly, I said, "I almost asked you if the T-37a was after you, as you certainly have sets of skills and things like guns, escape tunnels, and spectral night lenses that are not frequently needed by normal shopkeepers. But that is wasting time. It was after me."

Undaunted, she persisted, "The question is still, why?"

"Possibly they heard that I was considering returning to the music industry. As that isn't true, that leaves the possibility that they are trying to kill me. May I put my arms down? I have no weapons, and I am tired and hungry." She nodded. "I am Rolland Newcastle."

"Rolland Newcas—" Her voice drifted off. Darting up to a crouch, she focused the light on my face. I could see them both moving behind the light, trying to confirm my identity.

"I know, I am reported as dead. Despite how I look and smell, I am still somewhat alive." I fought not to add something humorous to lighten the moment. That would take too much energy.

The dark-haired woman stared at me. She said, "As I understand it, you don't go anywhere without at least a Thollo 9850 and a squad's worth of electronics."

"For about a year I have been running a Blackstorm 2360. It has much better resolution, near zero EMS signatures, and it's lighter and not as constricting."

Her face fell. "It's him," she said with no energy remaining in her voice. Her light pointed down, and there was silence.

I could make out in the dim light that the blonde was still staring at me. She said nothing, then shook her head.

The dark-haired one sat quietly for a time and then asked, "Do you swear that you are not being sought for a criminal act or taking part of any anti-government action?"

"I swear that I am not part of any anti-government action, nor am I being hunted for any criminal act."

The blonde woman inquired, "Is there anyone else who is running with you that we should be looking for, like a maybe a brother...or some friend?"

"No. Just me."

There was more silence, and it was more than I could bear. Staring at the faint shadow where the dark-haired woman had stood, for lack of a better idea and probably more due to my dreadful weariness, I said, "Do you intend to shoot me?"

Whoa. This was not my best attempt at marketing. Generally, this would have been the perfect time to be trying to persuade her that keeping me alive was the best idea, not to promote the benefits of shooting me.

Before I could correct my blunder, she said, "That would potentially save us a lot of trouble if we dropped your body off somewhere. Maybe the people who are after you would forget about us." There was a click, and a red light pulsed once, confirming that the pistol's safety had been engaged. In the faint light, it appeared that she holstered the palm-sized weapon in a small pouch at her side.

Even after my ill-advised attempts at convincing her to shoot me, I had to come clean about where we stood. Oh, this was not going to be fun.

"I am sorry that I have brought this horrible mess to you. It is important that I say it out loud, even though I am sure that you both understand the situation already. The fact that someone used a T-37a in the city shows how much this has escalated. This also means that they are desperate, and they intend to kill anyone that they even think has been in contact with me—even after I am dead. This could be the start of a coup or the final attempt at finishing the Remnant genocide. Again, I am sorry. I didn't want this to happen to any of us." I disliked bringing up the Remnant purge, as it more often caused people to want to look away from, rather than at, the real problem.

The two women looked at each other with unhappy expressions. And I could not blame them.

●●● ▬ ▬ ▬ ●●●

Narrow as the tunnels were, we lined up, with me following behind the dark-haired woman who held her light. Behind me was the blonde with her light. She was a few inches taller than her friend, so she didn't need to crouch to walk either.

Through a long, arduous maze of tunnels, we came to a U-shaped metal ladder welded to the wall, leading upwards. At the top, our leader opened a lid that revealed another tunnel. Will this never end? My back was complaining at the idea of more walking while stooped over.

She turned back and whispered, "Not much longer."

After her last measurement was half off, I was not buoyed with enthusiasm. Without any other options, however, I followed along, praying silently for God's direction and protection.

The woman came to a stop in front of me, and in the light beam, she pressed on a rounded bolt head. A long pole lowered from the ceiling, and foot pads folded down and out to create steps. The light pointed up, but I couldn't make out any opening at the top.

"Stay," whispered the dark-haired woman. "I'll check it out."

Next to me, the blonde switched off her light, and we stood silently, waiting. The brunette's light clicked off, and I heard her climbing the rungs with quick and efficient steps. Crouched in the stifling darkness, forced to wait, I could hear the woman behind me breathing softly. Above us, a strong white light poured down from the opening.

"We're clear," she called down.

As we climbed up and out, I saw that the access hole was hidden in a closet off a medium-sized workroom. The space had several stations that were covered in what I recognized as high-quality electronics. Not your normal street-quality face shields and electronics. This was hardened, specialized stuff. On the table by me there were a few Runker 2120s, a couple of Crown Eagles, and quite a number of objects that I didn't quite understand.

Looking about the room, I said, "I am impressed."

A flash of a smile from the dark-haired woman took me by surprise. The blonde gave me a slight nod, accepting the compliment. They were no longer wearing their half visors. When had they taken them off?

"Are we able to talk?" I whispered.

The blonde nodded as she sat back in a work chair and stared at me. The dark-haired woman leaned forward as she sat on the edge of a desk with her weight resting on the palms of her hands. She was still analyzing me. At some point, she had untied her ponytail, and her hair was down.

This was not about to be a fun conversation, but I had to ask, "Will those who sent the assault mech be able to find this place easily? Is it directly tied to the shop?" I was so tired that I wasn't being demonstrative. As much as I didn't want to say it, I had to ask, "Should we be grabbing supplies and gear and running? Maybe we could run to one of my safe houses?"

The dark-haired woman shook her head. "Our direct involve-ment with the store is tangential and convoluted. I would esti-mate that we have about a day and a half before they will be able to locate this place, as neither of these places are regis-tered in our names. I would suggest that we get some sleep and make some careful plans before we run early tomorrow morn-ing."

Escape tunnels, at least one weapon, high-end electronics, and hidden registrations? Who are these two women? Did I stumble upon a team of secret operatives?

The blonde pondered the question and nodded. "I think she is right. While we are tired, we risk walking into the hands of those hunting us. Sleep and planning will be our best next steps."

Slumping onto the spongy blue-gray flooring, I felt drained. My thinking was dull from lack of food and sleep. I was not up for producing a better plan. They seemed sharp, so for better or worse, I had to trust in their opinion of our safety.

"May I ask a favor?" I said, slipping off my backpack and plac-ing it next to me.

"Depends," said the dark-haired woman; her tone was cool.

"May I trouble you for some food? I was serious when I said I hadn't eaten much in the last two days."

I looked at the clock projector on the desk. It wasn't worth doing the math to figure out how many hours it had been, and it didn't matter, as I was hungry.

She stared at me as if she were trying to read my fuel gauge and agreed. "Nothing fancy."

At the hope of getting some food, I smiled. "Anything—and some water, too, please."

"Lauren," said the blond. "Don't make him beg. He has been good, right?" The blonde turned to me. "Of course we will get you some food and something to drink." Her face brightened, and she asked, "Ever have meat pies?"

"Sure. That sounds great." I was so hungry everything sounded delectable.

"Well, then I think you will enjoy these. These are handmade and really good. What about pizza?" I nodded. "What toppings do you like?"

"Jessica."

The blonde turned, looking quite irritated. "What? He needs to eat. He's not our prisoner."

"Right. I'm just warning you that we need to stay within our normal buying habits. Get the same toppings as normal. He'll have to deal or pick off what he doesn't like. We should go out separately to buy from the different shops."

I smiled. "Less obvious that you have a guest. Good plan."

The dark-haired woman named Lauren gave me a quick smile, and there was a twinkle in her eyes. It brightened up her face. She caught me staring and flicked her head to the side, hiding. My memories of her appearance at the store were weak and overshadowed by the arrival of the assault mech.

The blonde, Jessica, walked up, and I rose up partway from the floor as she handed me a tall bottle of water and a small container of cookies. I thanked her and sat down to eat. It is amazing how great the simplest foods can taste when you are ravenously hungry.

Jessica had turned to open a desk drawer, blocking my view of Lauren. This allowed me the opportunity to glance at her unnoticed. She was about five feet five inches tall with a strong yet slender athletic build. She had broad shoulders and a slender waist and a nice round backside. Her clothes were well-fitted, being neither too tight nor too loose. Lifting my eyes to avoid continuing on this thought path, I noted that there were no robo-wing attachments on her outfit. Her hair was a lovely light golden color, not the please-look-at-me glowing coloring that was common on the streets. She turned with a smile, and she had two credit holders in her hand.

"Use mine," I said trying to slide the backpack to her. It sat in the middle of the floor in between us, mocking my attempt. "There is a good sum in there."

Jessica shook her head. "We don't know if it is being tracked. Once we know it is clean, you can buy. You've got enough."

Grinning back at her, I decided that I liked her features. She was not artificially beautiful or too made up. But there was something right about her face, and I liked it. She may have been wearing minimal makeup. Seeking not to be rude, I glanced away.

Turning, I saw that Lauren was trying to read me. I smiled back at her, attempting to be friendly but also trying to be careful trying not to offend her. My attempt to smile and appear unthreatening on the transit train had failed miserably. To be careful, I looked away.

From my brief glimpses of her, Lauren was much stockier in overall build and shorter than Jessica, though her legs and arms seemed slim. It was hard to make out her figure as she was wearing looser fitting clothing.

Changing direction, I asked, "Ah, so Lauren, are you and Jessica friends or..." Lauren froze, peering at me with a surprised expression. "You two said your names a moment ago."

Jessica gave a genuine laugh and gazed at Lauren, who shrugged.

Jessica, grinning, said, "He's not dumb. We might as well face it; we are in too deep to be able to back out now."

Lauren and Jessica faced each other and mouthed something I could not make out. The interchange was brief, but some decision had been made.

Lauren steeled herself as if she were trying to overcome inertia. Still leaning forward, she straightened up and tilted her head back, revealing her attractive face and strong feminine jaw line.

"We're sisters. Jessica is almost two years older," she said with a hint of defiance in her tone.

"Cool. Nice to meet you both." It was not a brilliant statement. It would do.

Lauren scooted off the edge of the table and pulled a credit holder from her sister's hand. "I'll run to Janny's for the pies and pick up some drinks there as well."

Jessica turned to answer her sister. "I'll send in our usual and pick up more drinks at Hendro's on the way to keep it all normal looking." She turned, flicked on the benchtop screen near her, and pressed a few nodes. She noted my interest and appeared embarrassed. "It's on fast order."

I nodded with a smirk. "I have had a few of those of my own."

Standing near the door, Lauren said, "You stay here and don't touch anything."

Pointing to a comfy-looking couch, I asked, "May I?"

"Sure." She moved to a work bench and stopped. "Do you want to see the newsblasts or realviews? Or if you are so inclined, you can shave or take a shower as well." I nodded in agreement as she pointed to the bathroom door. "There is a Cleano in there for your clothes, if that would help make you feel better. You know how to use a Cleano, right?"

"Sure, thanks."

I wasn't sure if I should be offended. You put your clothes in, close the door, and in a minute or so, the light shows green and a chime sounds. You pull them out clean and wrinkle-free. Who doesn't know how to use one? Maybe she thinks I am one of those fancy rich kids who had staff who do everything for them. Well, I do, but I was raised by a family that emphasized self-sufficiency and the skills to do a wide spectrum of tasks on our own without help. My dad had no respect for those healthy people who demanded that others do everything for them. He called them "adult-sized babies" among other unflattering things. It was healthier to decide that Lauren was merely trying to be kind and helpful.

Pulling myself up with effort, I stood and started towards the couch, feeling much older than my age, and that changed my plans.

"I think I will take a shower, if that is okay. I don't want to be around me right now, and I am sure that having to look at me for long will put anyone off eating. Maybe I'll take a quick nap later on the couch if there is time."

Lauren smiled. "Be our guest." She and Jessica stopped to check the full-door screen to view the hallway before opening the thick door. "We may be a while. Don't open it for anyone. If trouble comes—"

"We'll eat at the restaurant without you." Jessica grinned.

"Sounds like a plan," I smirked as the door closed behind them.

On my way to the shower, the sudden demand to use the restroom sucker-punched me. I was shaking again and beginning to sweat. Thankfully, it was not as severe as at the transit hub. While it was not fun, I was glad it happened after they left. Riding out the internal storm, I had time to reflect.

At some point, if we stayed together, I was going to have to warn them about my hormonal overdose. Any chance that my behavior would put them at risk was unacceptable. A calming sensation swept over me, and I sighed in relief. Would these patches outlast my need? I analyzed a patch on my arm, but there was no way to tell how much was left in them.

This was a mess. Telling them now could panic them, making them run; not telling them would come back and bite me. If I sensed that I was getting out of control, or if I lost four or five patches, I would tell them. How do you broach such a subject with two women you just met without scaring them away?

Hey, here's an idea. "Thank you for saving me from the assault mech that destroyed your shop and also for taking me into your home. As we will all likely be killed in a dreadful, bloody manner, I thought that I should tell you that a symbioid tried to kill me by injecting me with a massive overdose of sexual stimulants. Because you are both beautiful women, I will tell you that I could become a raging lust monster without warning. Sweet dreams to you both." Grand, just grand.

If I weren't so tired, I would leave to keep them safe. As dangerous as I was near them, being tired and foolish out on my own would put them in greater peril. I prayed that my hopped-up, chemically induced emotions were becoming less intense and for the Lord to keep me under control.

Overall, my experience in the bathroom wasn't as brutal as before at the transit station. I could tell that the nano-docs had cleared more of the toxins from my body. While running a Cleano cycle on my clothes, I used the shower and the shaving system to clean myself up. Looking at my body, I was pleased that my translucent patches were all still in place and had not washed off.

Dressed, I came out to the main room to see that the women were still not back. Lauren had warned me that it could take a while to get the food, so I crawled onto the smooth and pliable yellow couch, and I was almost asleep before my head touched down.

●●● ⬤ ⬤ ⬤ ●●●

8

Pain in the Night

●●● ━━ ━━ ━━ ●●●

An urgent encrypted message flashed on the realview wall. A svelte, middle-aged woman sitting at a large, ornate desk pressed the button to secure the room and take the call. A tall, distinguished soldier saluted and said, "Ma'am, I am calling to inform you of some recent events."

"I just heard, Colonel Haas. Someone is running at least one T-37a assault mech in the city. One report claims that there were ordinances launched in a human-run shop. This is unacceptable and criminally breaches all the rules of engagement and public safety."

"Agreed, ma'am. As you said, we don't know how many mechs are out there and who authorized it. We don't even know the true target of this deployment. There is something big going on, and someone high up has to be part of this. It cannot be a rogue operation that authorized the use of a T-37a."

The woman took a deep breath of air and exhaled sharply, saying, "Agreed. I only know of three groups that have the power to authorize such a weapon's use. Under strict circumstances, a four-star general can authorize it if it is to prevent an imminent act of war, a coup d'état, or an invasion. It is a career ender if they are wrong. Of course, the World Congress can vote for a declaration of war or martial law for the same reasons. The EPGB can authorize it, as well, but they are under even tighter restrictions. They must prove that there is a threat to New Jerusalem's sovereignty or have proof of attempted genocide against the remaining Remnants that is not being addressed by the World Congress. I have not been made aware of any case that would warrant this action."

The Colonel nodded, looking concerned. "They can be utilized for diplomatic or Remnant extraction. I cannot imagine a reason outside of war where they would need to deploy such a powerful unit as the T-37a. In the situation in the merchants' quarter, they would have to suspect an imminent threat or the sale or use of heavy weapons to be allowed to bring in the systems they did. We have no indications this was the case, so we are acting under the assumption that there is a critical breach of our systems, and we are implementing deep, system-wide scans. We started that after the events we encountered down in an apartment in the Sterven quarter."

"I had heard that an EMP was fired in an apartment block down in the Sterven quarter..."

"Not just one, but two."

The woman's brows furrowed, and she looked unhappy. "Two? How many locations? Do we have data on this?"

"Just one location and they detonated about twenty-two minutes apart."

"One location? That doesn't make any sense."

"No. That is definitely out of the ordinary. It could be based on an old terrorist tactic of setting off one bomb and having others set to go off to harm first responders. We arrived at the site to find the burned shells of an eleven-robot tech team littering the floor of a small, one-person apartment. It is registered to a Simon Peterson. No deep record on him and no complaints. The rent is covered by the Citizen Fund as most are in that area."

"The tech team? Were they ours? That is an expensive loss for someone to have to explain."

"They come from several branches. Most are from Diplomatic Services. We are trying to keep this secret for now until we can piece together what happened. There was a T-40 Nightmare on site that was also rendered inoperable—"

"A T-40? Why in the world would anyone bring a T-40 into the city?" The woman's face was pale and pinched. "And maybe more worrisome, what in the world could have stopped something like that?"

Colonel Haas shook his head. "No one I have spoken to has any good theories why such an advanced hunter-killer assault mech would be brought into a city, other than to prevent or start an all-out war. Our top weapons scientists are checking it out, but the closest theory I have heard is that that the T-40 was just perfectly aligned with the EMP blast, and possibly one of the new composite flange housings weakened its reflective and adaptive armor. They stated that a normal EMP would not be able to take a Nightmare down. These mechs are tough and hardened weapon systems. Had the EMP blast been less powerful, it might have begun to regenerate its injured systems, but the damage was too severe."

"I guess it's good to know about this weakness now, instead of some future point if New Jerusalem were ever go to war. Was there was anything special about the second EMP to have been able to have done this?" she asked, leaning forward and looking tense.

"We don't know. The EMP melted its own core and components to slag after firing. No serial numbers survived either. Reports are that it doesn't look standard."

"I guess it is good that a T-40 didn't get sent out into the city. Even with its active camouflaging, those aren't subtle. We would have had panic and potentially a lot of death and destruction as it went after whomever or whatever they brought it into the city to get. Do we have any leads on what or whom its target was? Should we be worried about them as well?"

The Colonel said, "We don't. It is all troubling. The records on the Nightmare are missing or have been changed. We are looking, but we are seeing signs that someone is backfilling a story to meet the changing picture."

"Freeze the data streams, back them up to quantum nodes. We need to understand what is going on and who is behind this. Obviously, we cannot let this escalate more than it already has."

"That is already underway, ma'am. The backups are finished, and we are digging into this."

"Good. I'm glad that you are all on top of it—anything else?"

"Yes. At the apartment, found clothing for a woman and man with two sets of matching robo-wings. There were two similar helmets with full face visors and a different face screen visor as well. We have pulled only two recent DNA records from the room. Both were male. Based on hair and some of the oils from the clothing and sheets, a symbioid was present at some point in the last forty-eight hours in that room. The man's clothing had massive amounts of specialized designer chemicals that are used for diplomatic symbioids to...entertain male guests."

"Please relax, Colonel. I am familiar with the spectrum of services that diplomatic symbioids are designed to provide. You say massive amounts? Do we have any particulars how this happened and how much was present? Was this part of some party?"

He shook his head frowning. "There are no indications that this was a party. It is all speculative at this point as to why such a large quantity of male stimulant was released. All we have are a few theories, but nothing likely or definitive."

"Such as?"

"Well, ma'am, as I said, these are just the newest theories, and they involve two highly improbable events: a multi-trillion-to-one software glitch that caused the full payload of male-focused chemicals to be released, or this was an intentional attack."

"An intentional attack?"

"Yes, ma'am. That is the most troubling and least plausible of the scenarios, where the diplomatic symbioid's encryption was broken and its stimulants were used with the intent of bringing about a fatal event."

"Hacking a diplomatic class symbioid? Can that even be done?"

"There is always the slightest possibly, but I rather doubt it. My techs say that the symbioid's advanced encryption and software protections make this nearly impossible."

"I find that scenario deeply troubling. If there is even a chance of such a hack, then there are a great number of very important people in danger. Could these drugs been delivered by a non-diplomatic symbioid in a loading mix-up or an attempt to make it look as if there were a successful hack?"

The Colonel replied, "I asked our tech team this, and they said it would require massive amounts of reworking of the delivery systems of lower, less-encrypted classes of symbioid to even take the cartridges, all to make it appear the encryption on a diplomatic symbioid had been broken. I am at a loss as to the strategic reasons anyone would seek to do this. My team said that to give the impression of this kind of hack and to achieve a similar death, it would be easier to sedate the target and administer lethal levels of stimulants through several cheap, off-market symbioids or other such adult systems. The potential cost and time to develop a diplomatic encryption hack of this level would be substantial, and when it came into the light, the developers would fix the vulnerabilities, rendering the hack useless."

"This whole thing is beyond strange. Is there anything else to report?" asked the silver-haired woman, looking tired and worried.

"Yes, ma'am. It gets stranger, if that is possible. One of the DNA samples that the tech-bots pulled belongs to a record that has had an extensive cleaning done to it to hide the man's identity. We have a group of specialists and bots doing some record reconstruction to see what we can find out about him."

"And the other DNA record?"

"This is where it gets interesting—it belongs to Rolland D. Newcastle."

"*The* Rolland Newcastle?" the woman said, shocked.

"That's affirmative, ma'am."

"How old is the DNA? I mean he's dead, right?"

"That's the surprise here. The decay records lead us to believe that he was in that apartment two nights ago and left that next morning around 7:00. But the official report is that Rolland died at about 11:00 p.m. the prior night in his Phantom 344 pulsorjet, and that's about a half hour before the DNA tests have him arriving at the flat. We are rechecking the DNA decay records."

"This is all highly irregular. Those kinds of pulsorjets don't just fall from the sky. I would bet the exorbitant price of that 344, if I had it, that Phantom Corp will agree with that assessment. Based on Rolland's rather famous paranoia and the fact that two EMP devices were rigged to fire with a sequential delay—and in the same room—I would not be surprised if this was a safe house for Rolland Newcastle."

The Colonel nodded curtly. "I would agree with that assessment, ma'am. I will get a team searching the records and site of the pulsorjet crash looking for any discrepancies. While we are at it, I will have the team search back a few days or so for any conveniently misplaced reports of Rolland calling into channels looking for help."

"Good idea. I will see what Diplomatic Services has on him. Also, I will get my people to check if there are any feeds available from that party he was at that night, and I will have them contact those who were there. Pursue anything else you can think of. This has all the earmarks of serious trouble. Contact me if you hit any roadblocks and with any news that I need to know. I will do the same."

The soldier saluted. "Yes, ma'am."

The screen went black and disappeared. There was a raging storm in the city, and no one knew how big it was or how bad it would get. She hoped that it would not overtake and destroy them all.

●●● ▬ ▬ ▬ ●●●

Lauren, Jessica and I were sitting around the table where we had finished the meal. During dinner I had told them all I knew, from the attempt at the bathroom up to my encounter with Erlin.

During a lull in the conversation, Lauren said, "May I ask why you didn't have your security team with you? Don't you usually travel with one? That seems a bit risky."

Nodding I said, "I was being stupid. I was having a bit of a tantrum about how I had 'every right to be out on my own alone as I wasn't a prisoner.' So, I snuck out." Lauren raised an eyebrow, and Jessica just stared at me. "I figured I had it all covered with my gear, and it was time to be daring and live a little bit. You can see how well that went."

Jessica replied, "I get it. I think I would go crazy if I was forced to stay locked up in our home, unable to go out by myself for a walk."

Lauren nodded, "Me too. Even if your home is the size of a megacity."

I laughed. "I sold that one, and it wasn't quite that big, though it felt like it at times. A hundred people could be living there, and you wouldn't even know it."

Despite my earlier thinking, I knew it was time for the uncomfortable truth about Erlin's attack. They were smart and kind, and even if they didn't handle it well, it was only fair to tell them.

Bracing myself for what was to come, I said, "I don't mean to scare you, but I have to tell you something that is not so nice."

"Are you going to release another song?" asked Lauren, her eyes twinkling. Jessica sniggered and composed herself, trying to pretend it hadn't happened.

Lauren's comment was a jab at my short-lived music career when I was twenty. Back then I had been hanging around with some famous producers who assured me that we could produce a smash hit building off my notoriety. They were wrong. My album, *Songs from my Heart,* was almost universally panned as juvenile and insipid. It was my fault. Even before it was released I knew that it was horrible and that it was a mistake. I learned the important life lesson to trust your gut.

"Maybe not as bad as that; you will have to decide. I want you to know the truth. It wouldn't be fair to you otherwise." I pulled back my sleeves to show the faint patches on my arms. "They tried to kill me chemically. I have been through several days of blood-chemical cleansing and am still being treated for the overdose with these patches. There is no sensitive or polite way to explain it, but those trying to kill me somehow hacked Erlin, my diplomatic symbioid, to make her try to seduce me. When I didn't give in to that, they had her tackle me and pin me to the floor. She used her kisses to deliver massive amounts of sexual stimulants to try to take over my will. I am guessing that the plan was to make it appear as if I had gone off on a wild binge and died from a brain hemorrhage or heart attack." As they sat listening to my revelations, I felt ashamed finding it difficult to look them in the eyes. "I am sorry. For your own safety, I felt it was important for you to know and be able to decide if I should be allowed to stay here. I will completely understand if you want me to go."

Jessica said, "Rolland, I speak for both of us saying that you are welcome here and wherever we go, right, Lauren?"

Lauren nodded. "Absolutely. You needn't worry. We would never toss you out. That would be almost as bad as what they did to you, and what they did was terrible and cruel. We are so sorry that happened to you, and it wasn't your fault. You have nothing to be ashamed about." Her face was angry, and her hands were balled into fists. "I want to beat those jerks who did this to you."

Jessica said, "That is truly horrible, what they did. Are you okay?"

Nodding, I said, "For the most part, I guess. The patches are there to handle the excess that the blood cleaner couldn't re-move and for the spikes." I was embarrassed to even mention it, but it was important. "These are a gift from Lazarus, the Christian interventionist who saved me when I was about to die. He told me that my survival wasn't guaranteed, and I may still die."

Lauren's face was intense and determined. "Not if we can help it. Jessica, don't we still have Olgen's kit here? Or did we get rid of it?"

Jessica got up. "We still have it." She went back into the closet where we had climbed out earlier, pulled down a large orange case, and brought it over next to me. "We would be horrible hosts if we let you die right here, wouldn't we?" She opened the case and I saw it contained a medical kit. Pulling out two long white pads, she held them up. "Our friend Olgen had a severe stimuli problem. One evening, a few years back, he overdosed here and was in a bad way. Even though he was close to dying, he didn't want us to call for help. We had no choice, so we made the call. Olgen was like an older brother to us, so we got this kit to help him survive."

Lauren asked, "Would you feel comfortable with lifting your shirt a tad so that we can place these pads on your torso?" Her eyes were soft gray and earnest.

Complying, I pulled up my shirt. With her so close, this was another reason that I was glad that I bathed.

"Won't Olgen mind if I use his machine? What if he needs it?"

Lauren shook her head. "No. He would be the first to understand, and he would want to help you—besides, he doesn't need this anymore." She applied the first pad to my skin at the right side of my chest, and she moved around to the other side to begin to place the second one.

"Has he given the stuff up?"

Jessica looked sad and replied, "In a way. He died almost two years back from an overdose." She turned on the machine, and I could see it working.

Gah! "I am so sorry. I didn't know."

Jessica smiled and said, "How could you? Life is hard. It is all good, he came to The Lord a few weeks before he died, and now he is with Jesus."

"Amen," added Lauren solemnly. With a brief smile, she returned her focus to the kit. "This should give us a good read-out on your health and a treatment plan."

Surprised, I said, "Are you both Christians?"

Lauren said, "Yes. We are both Christians. I hope that didn't come as a complete surprise to you." She was frowning. "I would hope that anyone meeting us would not be shocked that we are Christians."

Stammering, I backpedaled and said, "No, I don't mean that. You are both so kind, and you have rescued me where there was no escape. You being Christians is really great news. Sometimes I feel so alone in the darkness with my faith. It is always a good surprise when I run into fellow believers."

Jessica laughed. "Relax, Rolland. You have been through a great deal. We can see why you would be wary of others. As it is far too evident, Lauren here likes to tease. She can be an intellectual thug."

Lauren shrugged. A beep came from the device, and she focused on reading the output. "Jessica, check this out." She looked at me in surprise. "It is obvious that you are favored by God. By all rights, you should be dead. Are you up for more cleaning? I think you should be on this machine all night. Are you good with that?"

"I would be immensely stupid not to do whatever it takes to get free of this stuff."

Lauren got a twinkle in her eye and said, "So, is that a yes or a no?"

Jessica's face pinched. "Lauren. That is enough. He is sharing his heart and the deep hurt he has suffered. Can you try and be nice?"

Lauren looked sheepish and said, "Sorry. You are just so much fun to tease."

I smiled to reassure her. "Thank you, Jessica. It is okay. I have a feeling that if she couldn't tease someone, her head might explode. The answer, Lauren, is that I cannot stand that these stimulants have taken over my thinking and have made me into who I once was, rather than who I want to be. Let's do whatever it takes to get rid of this junk."

Eyes wide, Jessica read the screen on the med kit. "I am sure it was controlling you. Those are some scary numbers, especially for someone who has already had some treatment. Did you do a lot of these kinds of drugs in your wild days or do something to build up some kind of tolerance?"

"No. I was an idiot all on my own without drugs; it was a natural gift."

Lauren chuckled. "Well, you have been kind to us and not the lascivious Rolland that the media says that you are."

Flinching, I said, "I hope I am better than what you imagined." Lauren's face fell. I raised my hands and patted the air, signaling for her to remain calm, "Wait. I mean, I hope I don't come across as the same hedonistic playboy fool I was in my twenties. I am tired, and I am in a food coma, so my words aren't coming out too well right now."

Jessica grimaced. "Not to mention you are still flying at almost twice the human max on sexual stimulants. I count us lucky that you are not acting like a raving pervert."

Lauren gave me a joking, haughty look. "I don't know if we should be thankful or offended. Should we take this as a sign that you think we are ugly?"

I stopped, trying to think of the best way to approach this. "If it helps your wounded sensibilities, you two are very far from ugly. We can thank and praise God for me not giving in to being that 'raving pervert.' Just after Erlin attacked me, the transit system contacted me privately to warn me that I was at 'substantial risk for exhibiting inappropriate behavior that may be considered extreme even for an adult zone.'"

Lauren's mouth dropped, and she said, "Excessive in an adult zone? Wow, you must have been quite a sight."

"Yeah. It was bad."

Lauren's face grew somber, and she leaned forward to ask, "If I may ask, how did you escape from Erlin? The drugs that she used are more than enough to have caused all the men and ninety-five percent of the women I know to succumb and die. Those symbioids have the same types of stimulants for women as well. Even without using the drugs to take away your will, their hack broke the harm-no-human precept; she could have easily constricted or beaten you to death. Symbioids are fifteen to twenty times stronger and many times faster than us."

I proceeded to tell them about God's still, quiet voice calling me to detonate the EMP and about my flight and about passing out as Lazarus and Marv came to rescue me. When I had recounted my time with Lazarus, I told them of how I left and how I suspected the event ended. By the end, we had covered it all rather well and they asked good and insightful questions.

I said, "Something has been troubling me about my encounter with Erlin and the encryption hack. Maybe you can help me sort it out? Why would they risk revealing their high-level diplomatic symbioid crack on someone as minor as me? It makes no sense.

Once the news gets out about a supposed glitch or a security hole, it will be fixed, and they will lose their advantage. I could see them using it on someone important like the head of the EPGB or the World Congress, but not me. Certainly, I have been an irritant in bringing The Remnant killings to the public attention, but I am hardly a big or important target."

Lauren was now spinning in thought. "Forgive my saying this, and I do not mean to minimize what they did to you in any way, but on a strictly design level, it is sickly brilliant." Her gray eyes were wide and shining. "You are right. They would want to hide their high-level symbioid encryption hack at all costs for as long as possible to be able to use it elsewhere on other high-level targets. This isn't going to sound nice, but it would be a waste of their resources to get only one use out of what was an expensive and difficult hack."

"Agreed," I replied, not offended in the least.

"They didn't count on you launching an EMP. I will bet that midway in the process, after you had lost all your ability to resist, they would have brought in a cheap love symbioid that they show-rigged with obvious additional chemical tanks and a hacked controller that was designed to override the built-in pharmaceutical delivery limitations. It would be as simple as uploading a known dosage error into the software to cause it to dump huge quantities of lesser quality chemicals, and that would hide the chemical trace indicators of a diplomatic symbioid. You'd be just another stimuli-junkie who was hiding out in a tiny apartment and who died when you miscalculated your hacked dosages trying to get an exaggerated high."

I was trying not to stare, but I was both enticed and horrified on some levels that such a sweet-looking young woman could think in such a devious fashion.

"That makes too much sense." I studied her squinting. "You weren't part of that team that hacked Erlin, were you?"

Surprised, she blinked twice in quick succession. "No, but I would love to see how they managed the hack. Had I been part of the team, I would have used a symbioid created to appear similar to one of your famous old flings to get you or inversely some nasty-looking thing to show how far you had fallen into the darkness. That would have resonated in the newsblasts more."

Turning to Jessica I said, "Please tell me that you aren't like her, are you? You are not just quiet about your deviousness, right?" Maybe it was me who needed to flee in panic from this place.

Jessica held up her hands. "No. Well, somewhat, but not completely. Maybe it is genetic or because I am around her so much. I am not innocent and never claimed that I was. She is her own creature and frankly, she kind of scares me at times." Lauren stuck out her tongue at both of us. Jessica retorted, "So mature, sis."

Lauren sneered. Staring off into the distance, she said. "Even though this didn't work on you, it wasn't a failure. They broke the symbioid's encryption and launched the attack. Because you had an EMP, that is just an anomaly, and your survival statistically would be considered an outlier. I am willing to bet that this will be used again, and it will be used sparingly on other high-value targets where an obvious assassination would have unfavorable cascading repercussions. I wonder who the first woman target will be?"

Jessica stared at her sister and said, "Well, thank you, mad Dr. Lauren for that succinct synopsis. She turned her attention back to me and said, "Thank you for telling us. I am so sorry that all this happened to you. I hope that we can survive this and somehow help catch those who did this awful thing to you."

Lauren came back from wherever she had gone mentally and said, "I am sad and angry about how they treated you." She smiled and said with kindness and sincerity, "I want to say thank you for being brave and considerate even in your pain, risking telling us something so personal to allow us to choose for ourselves. We really appreciate that. Rest assured that we will do everything we can to help you get through this."

Jessica agreed and softly asked, "Did you want to know what happened to Lazarus?"

As I was hooked up to a machine that was trying to remove a large dose of potent chemicals, I had no other place to go or much else to do. I could guess what happened, but it was important to hear the truth.

"Sure...I owe him that, he saved my life."

Jessica got up and pulled up a feed and spent a few minutes somberly going over what she found. She turned with a sad look and she said, "Should I tell you?" I nodded. "Do you want to see the newsblast or have me to read it to you?"

"Whatever is easier for you," I said not wanting to make the decision on how I would hear the news.

The realview screen at the side of the room came on and a newsblaster began, "Sad news tonight for the public and those on the edge and living in need. Long time Christian activist, Hale Stolt, better known to the community as Lazarus, is dead at seventy-eight. Police say they believe that he was brutally murdered by street criminals looking for drugs and money."

There were images of a closed floating box being led out the door of an apartment. The door was ajar, and bruisers were busy scanning the area. There were different detectives at the scene, not the two I had met at the public bathroom. That was good. We didn't need the corporal blaming this attack on the Remnants.

The newsblaster continued. "Lazarus had once been the leader of the Friends of Freedom and Cost Abatement, a group known for their outspoken opposition to repeated attempts to eliminate all public funding for social and drug programs. After his own stimuli addiction nearly took his life, Lazarus had a change of heart that brought him out onto the street on a mission to help those who were in desperate need. Civic leaders are coming forth to address this great loss and to herald the man who exemplified the spirit of compassion and mercy. Lazarus' long-time symbioid helper, known affectionately to all as Marv, was also destroyed in the senseless attack. As we get more information we will keep you updated. Funeral services for Lazarus will be held on Saturday—"

Waving the screen off, I fought crying. "I am sorry. I—"

He had died for me. I said a quiet prayer for him to the Lord.

Lauren's voice cracked. "There is no need to apologize. We understand. We are sorry for your loss. He sounded like a great man. Lord, thank You for Lazarus and what he did for Rolland. We pray that his death was painless and that he is having a wonderful time with You, Lord."

Half-croaking with emotion, I said, "Amen. I would like to have gotten to know Lazarus better."

Jessica nodded in agreement.

Lauren said, "At least he is with the Lord now. No more suffering or pain."

Jessica replied, "Amen. I only pray that this shines light into that darkness where so many are hurting and lost."

During dinner we made a basic plan to leave the apartment early in the morning and head to one of my safe houses deeper in the megacity. There we would have more time to develop some better strategies for engaging outside help. We all agreed that our time in this apartment was limited. They were expending a lot of resources in hunting me, so it would not be long before they found this location. Leaving right away would be optimal, but I was too tired, and I still needed at least a full night with the emergency overdose kit. They didn't look much more awake than me. Weariness leads to mistakes, and that was not something that we could afford and hope to live.

Even though I was enjoying the conversations and bursting to ask questions about the emergency lockdown shields, escape tunnels, and the handgun, we called it a night at 9:00. I hoped we would have more time to talk later.

Jessica walked out, and I could see a low rectangle of a compressed Softic bed was dutifully following along behind her. She pointed to a spot in the living room, and the bed stopped there and expanded. "It's not beautiful, but it is comfortable."

"It looks wonderful," I said, getting up stiffly, forcing myself to stand. As I reached for the emergency detoxifier to bring it to the bed, Lauren gently brushed my hand aside and lifted the kit to carry it alongside me.

Lauren said, "Jessica had said that you have some clothes in your bag that might be more comfortable for sleeping in. Did you want to change?"

Glancing at my clothes from the EMP locker, I said, "These will be comfortable enough to sleep in. Based on my recent luck, it may be a good idea to be ready to run at a moment's notice."

Jessica had a bemused look on her face. "Based on the level of everything that has tried and failed to kill you, your so-called recent luck has been rather spectacular. I agree that it is a good idea for us to be prepared to run. I wish we weren't so tired, or I would vote for making a run for it now. Getting some sleep is the best thing we can do to prepare for tomorrow."

Lauren nodded and said, "Good night, Rolland. Hopefully tomorrow you will feel better and back to normal."

"I am guessing that you mean hormonally. Getting chased never feels normal. Goodnight to you both. Sweet, assault mech-free dreams."

"Amen," said Lauren, adding in a grin as she and Jessica left the room to head down the hall.

Sitting at the edge of the bed, I took off my shoes. My feet were tingling in appreciation. I grunted in pain as I pulled my feet up and slid into the bed. Pulling up the modesty sheet, I felt the bed taking measurements of my frame and weight distribution to best fit my shape. A low note alerted me to turn to my side for the last measurement, and the mattress conformed again, raising the pillow to the side of my head. It felt wonderful.

What a hectic day. Glancing about the room at all the specialized electronic gear made me think about how they lit up at dinner when we briefly discussed their profession as tech builders. There was passion there. They were not just resellers of existing tech.

So, why was Lauren in that shop where we met? To my surprise and disappointment at dinner, no mention of the shop was brought up. Maybe the store was a front for them to sell some of their more exotic electronics. Were some of their clients so dangerous that they required such heavy security measures? Nothing that they said or that I could see in the apartment indicated any interest in celebrity goods. They didn't strike me as doing or selling anything illegal either. They were both intricate and interesting puzzles that I hoped that I would have time to explore. They were a certainly a gift from God on that day. I was determined to protect them so that they didn't end up dying like Lazarus. Somewhere, mid-prayers and in conversation with God, I fell into a deep sleep.

● ● ●　━　━　━　● ● ●

"We have a strong probability reading for our target. I have teams in place and ready. Will you give the go order?" began the encrypted voice.

"How strong?"

"A probability of eighty-seven percent. We believe it is the residence of the owners of that shop the T-37a raided last night. It is not clear. The word is that the apartment is a tech lab doing one-off specialized electronic stuff. Two sisters in their mid-twenties may run it. They keep a low profile, so I don't think we will have any blow-back on this."

"Good enough. Move. If asked, inform the channels that this is a standard raid of a radical terrorist lab and illegal weaponizers. Make sure that you prepare the site with the proper evidence to back this up—put in some ties to the Lord's Swords, that militant Remnant group that we have been setting up. This will be a good test run for that storyline. The public will eagerly swallow that without thinking."

"Will do. The go signal has been sent."

● ● ●　━　━　━　● ● ●

I woke with a start; something was wrong. In the faint light of the room, I saw Lauren start to bend down near me.

Her face was tense as she glided close to me to whisper, "Something's up, and it's not good. Two mass and electron spectrometers signaled me that we have a moving irregularity of too little mass and signal in the hallways."

I was still trying to wake up. "Too little?" I said, sitting up trying to rub the tenacious sleep from my eyes.

Lauren wore a knee-length, bulky, dark gray coat, and over that, it appeared that she was wearing a hyperglider harness. In her arms she was carrying another hyperglider unit, two black helmets, and some clothes. She set them down next to me on the bed.

"Countermeasures for something big and very nasty. I am going to release the pads." She pulled up my shirt and pressed the red buttons on the long pads to start their release. Irritated with the process, she started drumming on her leg. "Come on, let go already."

They were disconnecting from my blood stream and tissues, and I could feel tingling as they closed the openings. Cutting the lines might stop this process.

Lauren made sure that she had my attention and said, "This is important; they have to finish releasing. As soon as they're done, put on this jacket and then the hyperglider. I assume you know how to use one?" I nodded as I slipped on my shoes. "Move. We are out of time." She turned and darted away, fading as a shadow into the darkness.

The pads slipped off and I tossed them aside, trying to make sure I didn't trip on them in the darkened room. I rose unsteadily to my feet. After putting on the jacket, I slipped on the harness for the hyperglider, and it locked onto my body. My backpack wouldn't fit on my back with the bulky hyperglider harness in place, so I stuffed the money and what else I could into the removable cargo pockets from my backpack. Pulling them off, I adhered them to my upper thighs and felt them attach. Ignoring the aching, I ran stiff-legged towards the hallway door. Jessica stepped out of the first door on the right. She was dressed in the same fashion as we were. Motioning for me to follow her, she pulled on her helmet and disappeared into the room.

Following, I pushed the helmet's switch, and it opened like a clam shell in the back, allowing me to place it over my head. As it securely closed, the displays lit up, giving me night-sight and situational awareness enhancements.

BUFOOOM! The room shook. The massive, muffled explosion made the whole side of the apartment blow inward to freeze in a thick wall of golden frothy bubbles.

What just happened? Stepping into the hallway, I pressed the door lock button. It slid shut and it locked. Bolting into the room where I saw the girls run, I growled at my stupidity. That thin door wouldn't slow anything.

Hey! They had sprayed a layer of Foamalast on the walls and the door of the apartment. That was what that foam was.

Foamalast was a spray-on protective coating that was used to minimize damage in close-quarters demolition work. Shock waves made the material instantly foam up to dissipate the energy over a larger area. The greater the amount of energy released, the more the foam expanded. That was a big blast. I never thought of using it as a barrier to stop the breaching of walls or doors—and apparently neither had the thing outside the apartment.

Wow. And I thought *I* was paranoid.

As I got inside the room, I could see that it was a bedroom, and Lauren and Jessica were standing on the bed looking at me.

Jessica called out over my intercom, "Close the bedroom door and lock it." She could see my hesitation and said, "Just do it!" I complied.

Lauren and Jessica were still on the bed and were facing away from me towards the large window that looked out over the city. Lauren pointed a small cylindrical device at the ella-glanse window. Another muffled explosion caused the floor to tremble. There was no time left; they would be here soon.

My voice rising, I said, "You can't break ella-glanse crystal. It would require—"

"A series of sound waves at just the right frequencies, like this." She placed her hand on the pane, and it crumbled to fine, sparkling, sand-like crystals.

An explosion of wind howled into the small bedroom, causing clothing and loose items to start swirling around the room. Thankfully our helmets blocked most of the noise and the decomposed window grit that was blasting us. I understood the coat now.

Through the maelstrom and chaos, I saw Jessica attach a wheeled housing over the new opening and pull out a long line and cast it out into the night.

She called out on our intercoms, "Fly up, not down. They will expect us to go down. Jump out as far as possible to avoid being slammed by the wind into the walls."

With no hesitation, I saw Lauren, followed by Jessica, run and dive out into the dark night skies. A large, muffled explosion behind us rocked the room. Time to go! I took a running leap, bounding up on the bed, and I cast myself out as far as possible from the room. The colorful city lights lit up my view, and my gut wrenched as I plummeted downward.

Pressing the start button, I felt my hyperglider wings extend, and I powered on my unit to full thrust, heading upwards. Above me, I saw the flash of iridescent dragonfly wings in the night, and I saw the ladies arcing up to land on a hover taxi pad that was about eight floors up from where we had exited.

"Quickly, land here and get in the taxi," said Lauren's excited voice over my com. "They will not be fooled by the rope for long, and they will follow the disruption trail to where we are now."

I pulled a steep twisting arc that took me above the transportation pad. Seeing a taxi with its door open, I landed mere feet from the cab. Pleased with the effort and its coolness factor, I cut the power to my hyperglider, its sonic wings folded, and I entered the cab's open door—to find an older couple staring at me, looking scared.

"Ooh, pardon me. I didn't know this one was taken." Embarrassed, I climbed back out and saw one of the helmeted ladies waving me over to a different taxi some forty yards away. I sprinted over and climbed in the seat directly across from them.

Calling out to the taxi's autopilot, Lauren said, "Taxi, take us to the city rec center at maximum speed. Go! We are very late." The hover-taxi took to the air, picking up speed. In a calmer voice, she said to me, "So, did you make any new friends?"

"No, they were quite unfriendly and didn't want to share the taxi. Maybe it is because I told them that I was friends with you and—"

Gerrrrrrank-tauk!

A blur of blue and white passed through the cabin, bisecting it. Almost in slow motion, I saw the section with Lauren and Jessica roll back and away to fall towards the city below. The main propulsion unit in my half of the cab began flipping my half end over end. A whirring noise came closer, and I instinctively ducked. Scant inches above me, the remaining roof was cut away.

Over the com, Jessica called out, "They have released AA-30s! I repeat AA-30s have been released!"

Lauren yelled, "Rolland, are you okay?"

I didn't answer, I was a tad busy. Using all my strength, I jumped free of the spinning wreck and punched my hyperglider's on button. The cab dropped away below me, still spinning.. My hyperglider wings grabbed the air, and my thrusters kicked on, driving my stomach towards my knees, shooting me up and away.

I was under no illusions—the outcome was clear—but I wasn't ready to give up without trying. I had seconds of life left. AA-30s were military interceptors that were designed to engage and destroy fast-moving, armored targets. Their rotating vibra-blades would make short, brutal, and exceedingly nasty work of us. It was no challenge at all. Someone had pulled out all the stops to make sure that we did not survive this one.

A terrible noise came from below as chunks of the taxi struck the walls of the city, and the parts rained down on the walkways below.

Up to my left, I saw an eighteen-foot-wide whirling disk, flittering and glittering through the night's air. It was almost beautiful...in a malicious, death-bringing sort of way. I saw another one down below me that was closing in on one of the women.

With an odd clarity and calm I thought, *So, this is how I die. Jesus is Lord!*

If I am one thing, I am stubborn. Unwilling to give up, I pulled up hard and to the right. Above me, through the twirling and flashing lights of the city, I saw Lauren and Jessica's hypergliders spiraling at full thrust as they attempted to elude the second AA-30.

In the open window that Lauren had made, I saw a T-37a, and it was not even attempting to camouflage. Lovely.

An attacking AA-30 slashed in to strike at my upper body. Cutting my thrust, I pulled back as hard as possible and opened my wings wide in a canopy to pull me up and back. It was so close that I felt the leading edges of the vibra-blades cut across the harness of my hyperglider. A few inches closer and I would be dead. I tucked into a barrel roll dive and held my breath as I skirted blacking out from the g-forces.

"I'm out of ideas here," said Lauren in a panic. "OH, MY—I just lost a wingtip to that AA!"

Breathing hard, Jessica said, "I almost lost my head on that last pass too."

We didn't have many more near misses, and that thought gave me an idea. It was stupid and suicidal, and I had no other better idea.

"Pray for me! I am about to do something really stupid," I called out.

●●● ⬤⬤ ⬤⬤ ⬤⬤ ●●●

9

A Storm in the City

●●● ━━ ━━ ━━ ●●●

Before they could respond, I spiraled down to streak past the AA-30 that was closely following one of the women. Pulling upward, my vision blurred and tunneled, signaling that a blackout was imminent. I pulled a downward-looping left turn that sent me heading toward the opening with the T-37a. My monitor showed that the second AA had turned and joined the other unit to chase me. The T-37a's flak cannons moved to lock on me. Even at full thrust, I was no threat to its hardened composite armor, so it did not fire. I prayed that it was programmed to capture me if possible. We would know the truth of that in about two more seconds.

I slammed on my reverse thrusters, and my hyperglider's wings flared out in a glowing wide sweeping arc behind me. I yanked down hard on the twin emergency release handles, and the harness' straps were sucked back into the unit, throwing me forward and down. The hyperglider's maneuvering jets broke free of their mountings to go whizzing off in wild, bright loops.

Falling, I looked back and over my shoulder and caught a glimpse of the AA-30s shredding my hyperglider and passing through it only to charge straight into the T-37a. As I had hoped, both systems viewed each other as an immediate threat. I heard, more than saw, the deep ominous thrumming of the flak cannon's rapid firing. Above me, a large explosion billowed out, lighting up the night sky.

On to the next problem; I was counting on the slanted walls of the city's falling object inhibitors to catch or at least slow my plummet. This was the system that prevents objects from falling and crushing pedestrians below. Most don't know about it as it gives people unhealthy ideas about throwing themselves or other heavy objects from high up as a test.

Having said that, there I was, testing that system, hurtling downward at a sharp angle, about to slam into a nigh-unbreakable ella-glanse city wall. If I survived this strike, the resulting fall to the streets below would finish the job.

"Engage float-on, Rolland!" Lauren yelled over the intercom.

Placing my hands out before me to brace for the impact, I felt a backward thrust as if a huge hand had grabbed me in mid-air to slow me dramatically. As I struck the wall, it crumbled into dust, and I plowed through the opening.

Bright lights and loud music struck me as much as the wind vortex that howled through the space. Dancers swarmed around me as I came to a stop, dangling a foot from the floor the middle of a large, sparkling stage. A beautiful auburn-haired woman dressed in a flowing green gown was singing, unfazed by the wind or by my surprise entrance.

On a long yellow couch, amidst chaos, sat a couple huddled together in a tight ball. Their eyes were closed, and they were trying to scream despite the window grit being blown around the room. I cannot blame them. I must have looked like something out of a horror show.

As the singer belted out the crescendo, pyrotechnics erupted around us, making me flinch. The wind from outside was pushing me like a huge human-shaped balloon towards the back of the room.

"Realview stop!" I called out, and the explosions, dancers, and the singing woman disappeared. "That's better."

The wind was calming as the pressure equalized. With panicked faces, the man and woman gathered themselves up and scrambled out the front door of the apartment. They didn't appear to be hurt, just scared.

"We are here, Rolland!" I turned my head and saw Lauren, followed by Jessica, landing in the opening. "Are you hurt?" Retracting their wings, they strode into the room.

"I don't think so. Let's get out of here." My feet were floating above the floor.

Lauren said, "Disengage float on, Rolland." I dropped to the floor. She could see my confusion. "I'll explain later. The AAs and the mech destroyed each other. There is no time to celebrate. There may be more."

In the hallway, there were no signs of the couple. I assumed they had run somewhere to call the police. We took off running.

We took a few different lifts and autowalks, trying to randomize our path. This wouldn't confuse them for long. The fact that we wore helmets and coats wasn't all that odd, but the hyperglider harnesses made the women stand out. We would have to ditch them soon.

Finding an out-of-the-way hallway, we stopped to catch our breath. I reached up to release my helmet.

Lauren shook her head and said, "Keep it on. We can talk without being overheard, and it will hide us from some scans."

As we leaned with our backs up against a wall, I said, "Thank you for dissolving the ella-glanse wall. I thought for sure I was about to die hitting it or falling afterwards. I didn't expect the hovering part." I was babbling.

Lauren's helmeted head turned to face me, and she said, "There are modified anti-gravity lifter constellations in our jackets; I based them on the types used by DNA modders."

These were internally implanted or external devices used to offset and manage the great weight, volume, and movement of some of the more extreme DNA modifications. That was a clever idea.

Even through her helmet's visor, I could see Lauren was unhappy. She chastised me, "What were you thinking, Rolland? You nearly got yourself killed."

"I had to go and start an argument."

"What?"

"Not with you, with them, the AA-30s and the T-37a. We weren't going to outrun them, and they weren't going to quit. So I figured if I could get them to fight, their survival programming would kick in, and they would see each other as the biggest threat. They would try to take each other out, and that might save us. If this was a military-run attack, those units would be linked to coordinates. Then it wouldn't have worked, and we were dead. It was a long shot, maybe thirty to seventy that they were not synched, but I couldn't think of any other viable options at the time. The next iffy part of my plan was counting on the city's falling object inhibitors to catch me, or that I might be able to grab the rope dangling from your apartment. In hindsight, it was a bit crazy."

Lauren snorted angrily. "I give the odds of your whole plan working more like ten percent. That was more than a bit crazy, that thing that you did."

"I couldn't let them kill you. We were out of options, and we were not going to survive many more attacks."

Jessica asked, "How did you make the pulsorjets charge the T-37a?"

"Did they? Cool. That part was all God. I used the hyperglider's automatic survival flare function and a prayer. I had learned about them as a teen when I was playing hyperglider tag with my brothers over the ocean." I grinned, feeling slightly embarrassed. "Timothy denies daring me to this day, but I think he did. For whatever reason, I pulled the emergency releases. The jets went off in wild spirals, and I fell into the ocean from about twenty feet up. My brothers thought that was pretty funny, especially because it blackened both my eyes when I hit the water. That's when I learned not to look at the water when diving."

Lauren shook her head in disbelief. "Here you would have hit the shopping district at about seventy-seven miles per hour, making a terrible impression on those below." I was about to interrupt when she said, "Yes, assuming the city's fall inhibitors didn't catch you."

"I did have your anti-gravity float jacket too," I said.

"You didn't know that you had it," replied Lauren, her tone terse.

"Seeing that Rolland's plan worked, I guess this was a good plan," said Jessica, sounding unsure of that statement.

A couple warily walked past us. They stared at us from the corner of their eyes as they walked, hugging the opposite wall.

Over the com, I whispered, "Out on the streets, you can dress like a huge fish or wear hardly any clothes and not get noticed, but here—"

Jessica huffed, "No doubt."

Now that the couple had passed by, I turned to Lauren and said, "I have an idea—next time, letting me that I am wearing some kind of antigravity jacket and how to use it would be helpful."

Lauren snorted and gave a light chuckle. "Next time, when there is a skosh more time, I will. Right now, we need to get out of this area. I am sure that couple from the apartment has called the police, and that means our attackers know too."

"So, where do we go?" I asked as we stood up.

"We need to dump these hypergliders and helmets. They will be searching for the pairings," said Jessica. She pointed down the hallway to an air taxi terminal sign. "Let's launch them. If we get lucky, maybe they will follow them for a little while."

Lauren walked to a large maintenance access door and said, "We need to get out of view. People rigging hypergliders will certainly be noticed." A small tool appeared in her hand, and with ease, she jimmied the lock. When the door slid open I noticed that the tool she'd held was gone again.

Passing by her, I whispered on a private channel, "You are a little too good with that. What kind of misspent youth did you have?"

Through her helmet's face screen, I saw her eyes narrow. She leaned in close as someone would do to whisper, and over a private channel she said, "Wouldn't you like to know?"

Yes, I thought to myself, Yes, I would. I doubted that story would be boring.

As we stepped inside, and the large door closed behind us, the wall lights came on to illuminate the long, wide hallway. Jessica led the way with Lauren a few steps behind me.

Inside, we took off our helmets, hypergliders, and jackets. I said. "We can fas-stik the helmets to the jackets and put on the remaining two hypergliders. I am guessing with the constellations embedded in the jacket, we can make them look kind of human."

Jessica nodded. "It is easy enough to use the constellation's memory to get something that is a close proximity to us."

"We can program my jacket to float like a big balloon, and yours can drag it on a rope or something."

Jessica sniggered. "Lauren can take care of that—she knows all about really big balloons."

Lauren made a face at her sister as she pulled off her hyperglider harness and turned to set it down. When she stood, I noticed her jacket was billowed out at her chest, and I almost joked that it was a backpack, not a front-pack, when I saw that it wasn't a backpack at all. Lauren was remarkably busty. Not in the 'nearly can't use their arms' extreme DNA modder way, but Jessica's joke about her knowing all about really big balloons made sense. When we first met, I had thought that she was stocky and trying to hide a few extra pounds from view. Well, she was. Somehow, even with my overdose, I hadn't noticed. To be fair, I was tired, and she had been wearing a loose-fitting jacket.

As we began to prepare the jackets for take-off, we heard Lauren exclaim, "Oh dear."

She was shocked, and her face was pale. In her left arm, Lauren held her jacket and was holding her right hand up, studying her fingertips.

"What is it?" I said, moving to her side.

Lauren responded by holding up her jacket in front of us. From mid-waist to hip there was an eight-inch-long cut.

"Are you, okay? Are you bleeding?" Jessica moved in and knelt down next to her sister and examined the cuts in her clothing. "Thank merciful God! There is no blood or any wounds. Your clothes are toast." She pointed to a gash along Lauren's right side. "Wow. You cannot get much closer than that."

Lauren dropped her coat to the floor and looked down at her side. Unable to see, she turned sideways and placed a hand on her ample bosom and pulled it up and over as she thrust out her hip, trying to get a better look. We could see that her dark gray pants had a long thin slice cut through them at her hip and all the way up, about five inches into the fabric of her lighter gray shirt. As Lauren appeared to have a tiny waist and such a large chest, this was a miraculous cut not to have drawn any blood at all. Her arm must have been up over her head, and maybe she was arched to the side when the AA-30 hit. I couldn't figure out how this cut could have happened. Now was not the time to ask her.

Lauren looked upset. "It seems that I didn't just lose the tip of my wing to an AA-30. It also got my drag bag."

Jessica began to laugh.

"It's not funny. It cut off my drag bag with all the electronic gear in it."

"It is funny because your boobs are so big that you couldn't even see that the bag was gone," said Jessica, still laughing.

"It's not that funny. And talk to God. I certainly didn't ask for them...they get in the way."

"I am very glad that you are okay. That was too close," I added, having limited success with not staring at her surprising figure.

Lauren was distant and morose. "Thanks...I am sorry that I lost the bag."

Jessica shook her head, "Relax, sis. I still have some in my bag, and we still have you and your really, really big...brains."

Jessica gave her sister a quick hug. Lauren eked out a smile.

The three of us put together our jackets with our helmets and strapped on the two remaining hypergliders. It wasn't as convincing as I had hoped. It would have to do.

"This isn't going to fool anyone," said Lauren with a worried expression as she brushed a long lock of her dark hair from her face.

"Not if they look at it directly, but it may give us time if they just follow the signatures. It is not perfect, but it is something," said Jessica trying to sound upbeat.

"Where to?" asked Lauren.

I said, "Toward the edge of Heavensport, hugging the roofline—north or northeast might be good."

We powered the units to hover and pulled them down the hallway to the maintenance access door that led to the air-taxi port. The hypergliders' sonic wings spread, and they took to the sky, appearing much like huge dragonflies flying off into the glorious red, yellow, blue, and gray dawn. This surprising peacefulness was in stark contrast to the violent way that the day had begun.

Out in the open bay, we could hear the sound of emergency support vehicles. As this was a vehicle-only area, there were no guardrails or safety protections. Creeping out near the edge, we peered out at the disparity between the beauty of the city and the ugly commotion caused by the falling cab parts and the debris from the explosion at the apartment. None of us spoke. All the heady joy from escaping had leaked away, and we were caught by the sad aftermath caused by those seeking to kill us.

Lauren stared at the view below us. "I keep thinking about those who may have been hurt."

"Me too," I said. "I pray that no one was. I hope the fall inhibitors at least slowed the falling debris."

Jessica said, "If anyone was hurt, I pray the Lord will heal them completely."

"Amen," Lauren and I replied.

"It's time to get going," said Lauren, pointing to the large maintenance access door that we had used to access the air-taxi terminal. "It will keep us covered for a while until we have a better plan."

● ● ● ▬ ▬ ▬ ● ● ●

"Report."

The modified voice said, "The apartment was breached and—"

"I know this already, Joden."

"Sir, need I remind you to keep this conversation secure and free of any identifiers?"

"I think you can relax. No one is going to intercept this message."

"We don't know that for a fact and we don't want to risk that, sir. So, I ask that you—"

"Enough! Don't lecture me. You are the one who has failed in the simplest tasks so far. Just tell me what is going on."

There was a pause as the altered voice on the other end regained composure. "We believe that the three people in the apartment were able to escape. We are pursuing."

With an angry huff, the older man cursed. "What? Please explain to me how three people could escape a T-37—or any assault mech in such close proximity?"

"We had issues breaching the door, and that gave them enough warning to make a getaway."

He clenched his fists; his voice rose in growing anger. "Issues breaching? What kind of door could stand against a T-37?"

"That is a very good question, sir."

"I know. That is why I asked it."

"Ah, yes. Well, as I understand it, once they got in, they found that the whole wall was covered inside by some kind of expanding, foaming material. It took two hits to allow us to enter. Both attacks bounced the T-37a back, and that blowback severely damaged the T-25 and the T-10."

"Can this get worse?" asked the older man, drumming his fingers in a sharp staccato on his desk. "Okay, tell me what happened inside the apartment?"

"Our targets ran to a bedroom."

"And why was this a problem?"

"The hallway and bedroom doors had that same material on it that caused us so much trouble in the initial breach attempt. When we gained access, the T-37a's maneuvering jets were damaged, so it was unable to go airborne to give chase. There was a rope at the window that was assumed to be their method of egress. After launching AA-30s, we realized that the targets had deployed hypergliders in their getaway, and the rope was a diversion."

"Did the mechs fire on them?"

"No, sir. Missiles are not a surgical option for such small targets, nor are they in any way quiet. Even dialing the explosion of a hyper-missile back to its minimal setting, the bounce blast damage alone could still kill hundreds, if not thousands. A complete miss would take out multiple floors, and that would yield untold casualties."

"I am much less interested in collateral damage than I am in getting this taken care of. We can always claim the explosion was caused by a hydrogen leak or bombs detonated by the terrorists."

The modified voice sounded uncomfortable. "Sir, there is no way to hide that kind of damage or the trace compounds from a missile strike. The public will see this as an act of war."

The older man tone was sharp as he cut him off. "The public knows only what we tell them. They are all so happily sedated with shopping and robo-partnering that they don't care what is happening, as long as it doesn't interrupt their fun or inconvenience them in some way. Take away their realviews, and then you will have an insurrection."

"To some degree, sir, you are right. But we cannot count on—"

"Of course I am right. And I think you are the one who was wrong in how this was handled. You should have used the railcannons to eliminate them in the bedroom."

"We had hoped that the mechs' stealth and capture tools would have sufficed without the use of heavy weapons. The rail-cannons would have penetrated the closet and a half mile beyond that into the residential zone and that would have drawn the attention of those we do not wish to alert. That would have negatively affected our timeline."

Irritated, the man snorted. After some contemplation, he replied in a calmer voice, "Okay, agreed. So, what did you do?"

It may be quicker to show you. This is the brief vid feed from the T-37a of the AA-30s' attack. I have never seen anything like it."

There was a pause as the older man reviewed the event feed. There were details on the screen showing information such as velocity, arcs, and g-forces.

"So that larger one, is he Newcastle?"

"We believe so, sir."

Whirling AA-30s flowed through the air, darting, slashing, and striking at the three hypergliders. In chaotic response, the hyperglider pilots performed the most outrageous physics-defying turns, avoiding the hits.

"How long does this go on? Can we just get to what I need to know?"

"It is about right here, sir." The older man leaned forward, narrowing his eyes to watch the realview. A rectangle surrounded the larger pilot. "If I may control the feed, sir. It will help."

"Do it."

The realview zoomed in on the larger hyperglider pilot, who was being chased by an AA-30. Spinning, he took a sweeping barrel-roll turn so close to the second AA-30 that the second unit changed its course to join in the pursuit.

"He's at maximum thrust and his wings are set for speed." The older man grunted. "Now he is charging at the assault mech that is recording this event."

"Fool."

"Yes, sir. I need to slow this section down to allow you to better see what happens."

The camera zoomed in to show the pilot grasping at his harness in slow motion. With a shimmer of iridescent light, the hyperglider's wings flared out. The man was violently thrown from the harness, and the back of the unit exploded in a series of wild, brightly colored, looping spirals. Within a hand's width from the pilot's head, the two AA-30s shredded through the stalled hyperglider. The tips of AA-30s' spinning vibra-blades collided, shearing off in a bright splay of shrapnel. Collision warnings lit along the T-37a's screen and it began firing on the damaged AA-30s. The screen flared in a plume of flame and mayhem and went black.

"No! They were to get the man, not the stupid hyperglider!"

"Yes, sir," said Joden's modified voice.

After a long and uncomfortable pause, the older man said, "The pilot who fell from the hyperglider just before the explosions—I am guessing that was Newcastle. Did he fall to his death?"

"It seems highly probable, as this took place at least 800 floors up. The realview didn't show any other flight or safety gear. As there were no operational mechs or AA-30s on site, we don't know, sir."

"Joden, I am beginning to think you are bad luck."

"Sir! I will ask you again to refrain from—"

"Oh, shut up!" The older man slashed his hand forward and severed the communications. He was tired of dealing with incompetent fools. He would have to handle this before it blew up, taking them all out. Sometimes one had to remove a damaged limb to save the patient's life. It would be an inconvenience, but as in medicine, he could always re-grow that missing limb.

●●● ━ ━ ━ ●●●

10

The Pressure to Conform

●●● ━━ ━━ ━━ ●●●

We had to assume that the city's facial and identification detection system had been accessed by our pursuers, and we were vulnerable. Their ability to hack the encryption on a diplomatic class symbioid made this plausible and scary.

The previous evening at dinner, we had discussed my worries about my kit's unique electronic patterns being the tool that the enemy used to locate me. Being able to discuss tech without first having to explain the intricacies of each device was a rare and enjoyable experience. Jessica and Lauren showed a depth of knowledge that was rare even among some of the best techs. Without a doubt, beauty and brains were a great mix. They agreed that I should have been invisible to discovery. There was still no explanation for them tracking me to Lazarus other than they'd tapped into the city's security systems.

Riding down in a maintenance elevator, we accessed an electronic map and chose an open area near an internal repair hub to prepare. It would have to do. After finishing there, we planned to go down five floors and enter a mixed electronics and clothing shopping zone.

The maintenance elevator stopped and opened to reveal a large service corridor. There were no humans, and the few robotic units paid no attention to us. We found a small, out-of-the-way, locked room that Lauren was able to open in seconds. Shuffling in, we checked our supplies and began to prepare.

As I was removing my thigh bags to take a measure of what I still had, I heard Jessica cough out a short laugh.

"Guys, you know how I was teasing Lauren about her large physical charms blocking her ability to see that she had lost her drag bag?" Lauren's head spun to her sister. "It is obvious that I don't have the same problem as her, but the outcome is not that different. In all my spinning, trying not to be minced by an AA-30, I seem to have lost some of the contents of my electronics bag."

"How much is some?" asked Lauren as she moved forward toward her sister like a predator.

"All but these." She held out one facial reconstructor and a few odd items, and I wasn't sure of their purpose.

"At least we have one reconstructor," I said, trying to find the bright side.

Jessica shook her head in short, tense arcs. "Well, not so much. The NC module is gone. I checked the bag twice and all my pockets to make sure."

The NC module was the brains of the system and the part that made the whole unit work. They were rarely interchangeable and notoriously easy to lose.

"I am so sorry, guys." Jessica looked distressed and miserable.

I smiled at her and said, "Don't worry, Jessica. We survived what should not have been survivable, several times, and no one was hurt—"

"Yet," said Lauren.

I raised an eyebrow. "Maybe, Miss Positive, but in the short time I have spent with you two, I can say that there's no one else with whom I would even attempt to face this threat."

Lauren shook her head and grimaced. "Then you aren't trying hard enough. Just off the top of my head, I would go for a battalion of assault mechs and a battlecruiser to get you to a high-level security compound."

"Funny. As that is not likely to happen without a lot of people dying, the three of us are the best bet we have. Now, before you go and surrender or get too excited, Christmas is not over. I grabbed some things from my backpack and have them here in these bags." To save time, I handed one bag to each of them.

Excited, Lauren pulled out a hand full of credit holders. "Yippee. Credit holders and unicred bills."

Jessica lifted out a facial reconstructor and frowned. "A Tully Explorer 6."

"Those were good," I stated.

Lauren nodded. "Were, as in past tense. Maybe you didn't hear, but they found a major unrepairable security hole in that model that about a year ago, which practically broadcasted the user's ID. We might as well stand in the center of a shopping zone nude, yelling out our names."

With extreme effort, I fought picturing that or suggesting that they test that theory. "So, can we sell it or use it to barter for something we need?"

Lauren smirked and said, "You mean as compared to trading it for something we don't need? No, they would think we are either stupid or that we are trying to scam them. It will cause more trouble than it is worth. I say we recycle it or leave on a bench somewhere." She pulled out a thin silver neck ring. "Hey, a Yunker 50 personal assistant with a Tachy 2.1 security net. Now, this is worth something to collectors of old tech. This was quite the setup in its day. I know a guy who would pay close to three-fifty or maybe four hundred unicreds for that."

"Obviously, no one has been in that safe house in a while. Do you see anything in there that will help us now?"

Lauren laughed. "Money doesn't go out of style or get outmoded. Well, that is not true; some old credit holders have to go to a credit shop to be exchanged for new ones with the new encryption. You understand what I mean. I found some personal care items and some underwear, so you are set."

Lauren got a strange look on her face. She reached up and pulled out the neck of her blouse and looked down.

Jessica knitted her eyebrows together and said, "What's wrong? Do you have bugs? Or are you trying to test whether Rolland is over his overdose?"

"I don't think I am." I was being honest.

"Stop it, you two. I hope they are still there." Lauren stopped midsentence and gave me a warning look.

I bit my tongue, fighting against spewing multiple inappropriate comments and just watched, unable to look away. I smirked; it was abundantly obvious that they were still very much there.

She began to reach in. Seeing my interest, she turned her back to me. Moments later, she spun back to us, triumphantly holding out a palm-sized bag in her hand. Jessica was laughing, unable to keep it in. "That's enough," Lauren said, half-jokingly scolding her sister. She faced me, her face flushed and embarrassed. "I was trying to grab some last minute stuff and, well, I stuffed it where I could."

I almost said, *there is this new invention called pockets—I think they will be big*. But I didn't.

Opening the bag, she held some packets and several tubes. "Three, no, four packs of Face-Its, ear strips, and some retinal ID disrupters."

Face-Its are popular faux flesh face appliqués that many people use to change the looks of their face for masquerade parties and Halloween. These flesh-like devices adhere to the user's face and blend in automatically with their skin color and even match their pores. Simple and cheap, these were a great idea.

Still having a difficult time not laughing, Jessica snorted. "Thank God for your storage chest."

Okay, that got me to chuckle.

Lauren shook her head and said, "Funny, Jessica. And you," she said, squinting at me, "don't start."

"Yes, ma'am."

Lauren handed everything but one of the Face-It packets to her sister. Pulling open the packet, and she waived me over to stand in front of her. "Bend down and look at me."

"Cool. This is a really good idea." I complied, attempting to gaze only at her Face-It and no farther down, which is hard to do when you are about fourteen or so inches taller.

"Thanks. I got them for Halloween last year. We ended up not going to that party, so we never used them." Lauren was concentrating, working on my face, spreading the cool, putty-like mask on my cheeks, forehead, and nose. After looking into her warm gray eyes, I decided it would be more polite to look up at the ceiling. "Just so you know, I left the fairy princess costume back at the apartment."

That made me laugh. "I would have loved to see that, especially when paired with your hyperglider wings."

Lauren paused, looking me in the eye, and smirked. Returning to the process, she said, "Tilt your head down."

Following her instructions and trying to avoid staring at her eyes or anywhere else, I closed my eyes.

To my side, I heard Jessica say, "When you are done, you can do my face, and I will do yours. Not having a 360-view or a mirror, I would mess it up. While we wait, we should come up with names to use in public, in case they are audio scanning for name and subject matching. I will go with Monika."

"Monika?" I inquired, opening my eyes.

Instinctively, I recoiled as Jessica slowly reached her index finger towards my face to tap my nose and cheeks. "It is close to setting. That looks pretty good. He doesn't look too much like that guy from the newsblasts."

"Good," I muttered. "That guy is hard to look at for long."

Lauren smiled and nodded in agreement. "Simply ghastly, and the chicks he is hanging out with are not much to look at either. Done. Jessica, you are next." Jessica came over and Lauren began working on her.

Laughing softly, I said, "I dunno. I think they were pretty darn cute." I chose cute over beautiful as not to go too far. She had a look on her face that I couldn't quite decipher. It was better to let this drop. "For my name, I will go by Sanders."

"That is not a name that is correlated with you in any database, is it?" queried Jessica, trying to stay still.

"No, it is from an extremely old Earth kids' book. There is this bear that lives in the woods under that name. It is so obscure, I am sure no one will know it."

Lauren smirked. "Okay, Winnie. Sanders it is."

I tried to hide my surprise. She knew about Winnie-the-Pooh and the name of Sanders over his door. One would be stupid to underestimate either of these young ladies. "How about you, Lauren?"

"Who?" she said, feigning confusion. "My name's not Lauren, I'm Leahnen." I think I flinched.

"You certainly are," snipped Jessica, who was pointing to Lauren's chest. Lauren shot her a dirty look. "Don't blame me if you get teased, you chose it."

I fought not laughing at the exchange. It was time to put in a few of my own digs. "So, why stop there? Why not go for the whole name or just Fanalone?" Leahnen Fanalone was the name of one of my old girlfriends who was famous for her more-than-substantial physical attributes that made her torso resemble a figure-8 with a head.

Lauren laughed. "I couldn't resist the opportunity to tease you. Call me Chipper."

Jessica huffed and said, "Dang. I should have gone for that."

"Chipper? Why Chipper?"

Lauren stopped working on Jessica to see if I was kidding. "You know, from the realview *Millennium Seekers*?"

I shook my head. "Sorry, it doesn't register."

"It came out about ten years ago. There was a super cool tech in it who was named Chipper. She was smart and beautiful, and she solved things that no one else could. Still, no?" Lauren looked disappointed.

"That was about the time when I was at the peak of my stupidity. I didn't watch a lot of realviews back then."

"But you dated a lot of the starlets. How about Mellina Beywood-Right?" asked Jessica.

I was embarrassed to admit it. "Yes, I dated her a few times."

"She was the actor who played Chipper. Was she nice?"

I was thankful for the Face-It as it may have been masking my blushing. "We didn't do much talking. I—think so. Sorry. That was a bad-mannered time of my life and one that I never want to go back to."

We moved past this topic, and over the next few minutes we worked together to add a Face-It to Lauren. We were as good as we could be under the circumstances.

My Face-It had already begun to feel as it were part of my face, though it was a tad heavier. Soon, we would forget about it all together.

To prepare for electronic surveillance, Lauren gave me a vial of contact lenses that would change my retinal patterns to confuse any ID scans. It wouldn't likely match any record, and it wouldn't pull up mine either. Placing the cup over my eye, I felt the cool vapor and heard the faint beep signaling the successful transfer of the liquid lenses. After about eight hours they would naturally dissipate. I handed it over to Jessica, who followed the same steps.

Lauren reached up and pressed a small, flesh-colored strip across my forehead. "These will cause electronic facial scanning systems to report back incorrect facial spatial data."

"Cool tech. I have never heard of them before."

Jessica replied, "That's because we came up with them."

"We haven't tested them yet. We also have ear gloves...we need a better name for them." Lauren placed a thin translucent material over my ears, and I felt them adhere. "Ear shapes are as unique as fingerprints. These sheaths should help mask our identities. Ear sheaths or ear sleeves."

Then, to my own embarrassment, I found myself trying to compare Lauren's and Jessica's ears. They were nice and small, and they looked different from each other. Ears had different overall sizes, and some had attached or unattached ear lobes. I had never paid attention to the different shapes and structures. That was as foolish as never noticing that people could be different heights or that they might have different colored eyes.

Lauren warned me, "I don't have a way to hide the pattern of your teeth and lips, so don't smile too much. If they deploy a subcutaneous spectral vein scan, we are toast. Those are unique, and I don't have a good fix to hide that."

Great.

"What about walking gait analytics? Everyone's walk is unique," said Jessica.

Lauren frowned. "I was trying not to go there. Can't you see that he is freaked enough already?" Was I showing that? Wonderful. "Maybe we can pick up some shoe nudgers, like they use to keep distracted pedestrians in line. If we can find a cheap personal system and a visor to hack it, we should be able to send differing rhythms. Realistically, though, we could get to a safe house faster than I could hope to rig it. We will have to try to walk differently and hope that it is enough."

Spying a workbench nearby, I went over and searched the area. Returning, I held out several odd and flat little pieces of smooth plastic.

"Put one of these in different spots in each of your shoes." Lauren stared at me confused. "It is an old actor's trick. They irritate the foot enough that subconsciously, you walk a little bit differently. Swing your hips a bit more or tighten your knees and arms as you walk. Throw in something you have seen in someone else's walk."

I mimicked a guy I had met years ago at a conference. He had a peculiar walk where he held his hands tightly to his sides as if heavy weights were pulling his hands and shoulders down toward his knees. Despite this visual weight, when he walked, he rolled up to his tiptoes, like someone trying to peer over the heads of a milling crowd. I don't remember his name, but I remember his walk.

Lauren slid into a sly grin, and she said, "Well, what do you know. Sanders may be worth keeping around after all." She patted the air with the palm of her right hand. "You may want to tone that down a tad, or it will bring you notice."

Jessica gave a quick laugh and said, "With that kind of walk, we will have to fight the girls off."

"No doubt," I replied, nodding with a serious expression before letting a grin slip.

As we split up the credit holders and cash, we planned what to do if we got separated or were attacked. We mentioned a well-known tower in the megacity and a couple of random times. It gave us the hope of meeting up if we got separated. We even suggested several visual flags we would wear or poses we would use if we got caught to warn each other to avoid meeting. No one wanted to go there, but we understood that if that happened, we would be on our own.

Out on the shopping street, we moved at the pace of those around us, pretending to be out for an early morning of casual shopping. A projected clock said it was 4:45 a.m. Okay, a very early morning of shopping. All around us were other people out doing the same thing.

We were headed towards a safe house that I had stashed in a shopping quadrant, about a thirty-minute walk away. I checked a transit map, and it confirmed what I feared, that we were skirting the edges of the New Paradise adult zone.

It was a zone that I knew too well. My brother Paul had a huge apartment there that we frequented during his wild days. He and his wife kept it after they returned to the Christian walk. I don't know why; I wouldn't have. Maybe she kept it after his death as a reminder of how far they had come. I had no interest in visiting that apartment because it had the potential to suck me back into a way of thinking that would not honor God or Jessica and Lauren.

Even on the outskirts, we were too close for my comfort. The realviews and the dress of the people here were wilder than normal, and I fought the urge to stare as zone-pleaser outfits were being stripped off, and the display of flesh became more abundant. Getting out of this area was a high priority for me. The pull of the addiction kept trying to drag me back to drown in the sickness.

The constant press of advertising grew more adult as we approached, and I was getting a crick in my neck breaking off so many contacts. I no longer had Riley to block them. Lauren and Jessica had stressed looks, and I guessed it was not just due to the worries about being hunted. These realviews used parallax point projections of sound and visuals that served individualized ads directly to each of us, based on our perceived interests. As we were heading towards an adult zone, they assumed that our interests were more adult in nature.

I was about to suggest to Jessica and Lauren that we should give a wider berth to the New Paradise adult zone when the screens around us sounded tones, indicating there was an important public message. We stopped and looked up anxiously.

A smiley woman with a flowing mane of blonde hair filled the realview screens. "Newsblast. The New Jerusalem and Heavensport Security Forces have issued an alert for three people suspected of planning terrorist activities." Unflattering images of Rolland, Lauren, and Jessica appeared. "The leader, Gary Lee Yudizio, a failed celebrity Rolland Newcastle look-alike, and his separatist girlfriends, twenty-five-year-old Lauren Jocelyn DeHavalynd and twenty-seven-year-old Jessica Simone DeHavalynd, two sisters, are being sought by the authorities. They are considered armed and dangerous."

The outside view of the destroyed shop popped up. "Here's what we know. Security forces launched a daring daytime raid to capture the suspects, who were allegedly holding out in a small shop thought to be a front for the Lord's Swords, a radical Remnant supremacy group." Images of us and a flaming sword logo covered the store's damaged front. "Confronted, the fugitives used hidden tunnels and roller bombs to elude capture." The screen view changed. Through projected crime scene shields, one could see hints of a blackened hallway and some twisted mechanical structures. "At about 3:40 this morning, based on information from concerned citizens detailing illicit activities, the counter-terrorism task force raided what is believed to be their hideout in a densely populated public housing area of Heavensport. During this raid, two assault mechs were destroyed when the fugitives detonated explosives outside their apartment. Then, without regard for the welfare and safety of the public, the terrorists used a stolen military assault mech, flak-cannons, AA-30s, and modified hypergliders to evade capture." The three unflattering images of us filled the screen again. "If you see these people, do not try to apprehend. Please contact the New Jerusalem and Heavensport Security Forces immediately. Again, do not try to apprehend. They are considered armed and dangerous. A reward of 50,000 unicreds is being offered for information leading to their apprehension."

Lauren turned to us, her eyes wide and scared. "Oh, dear. This is bad. I think we better get off the streets fast. Those dangerous people could be near us."

This made me glad that we had hidden our conversations as we had. Now that this was considered a terrorist event, the city's systems would have been listening for our names and event keywords well before the newsblast. Now, millions of people would be talking about this. Not that this would slow the system to any great extent, but it would require more analysis and lead-checking. I prayed that they did not have Jessica's and Lauren's voice patterns. As I am somewhat famous, mine was everywhere, but they couldn't apply it to the search, as it would raise flags that I was alive.

Using one of the projected city maps, we had a brief and cryptic discussion and decided to flee to one of my safe houses several hours away in the Cormonoy business sector. While it was riskier to get there, it had a deeper cover. My friend Terry Curtis, whom most call Curtis, had set this one up too. He had concealed its ownership under several layers of shell corporations and dummy accounts years ago during my inquest into the deaths of the Remnants. It was designed to hide important informants or even myself there if things went bad. I never visited it, as my comings and goings were being monitored, and that would have put it in danger of discovery. Curtis said it had more comforts than the first place. How many more, I could not recall, and it didn't matter as long as we could safely hole up there for a while.

The sun was still an hour from rising over the megacity as we boarded the transit tube up to one of the transportation layers. There we took an automated air-taxi to the Cormonoy business quadrant that was near the safe house. Then we would walk a distance to help hide our destination.

In the taxi, Lauren and Jessica sat on the seat across from me. I asked, "Do you want to have a full view of the city, or should we use only the side windows? We could always opaque them if that is better."

Jessica's eyes looked drowsy as she said, "I will likely sleep, but I am up for the full view if that is good for you both." None of us had slept much before the attack at the apartment. I could see that we were all feeling tired. We were running on adrenaline with a healthy dose of fear.

Lauren nodded. "I love the city at night...well, early morning. I vote for a full view."

"Taxi, full view, one-way visibility, please."

The outer shell of the taxi faded away, and we could see in every direction. It was as if we were flying through the stunning vista of the megacity without a craft. Asking for the one-way privacy option meant that we could see out, and no one could see into the taxi.

Gliding silently over the bright caverns of Heavensport, all around us the realview signage and lights from the city glistened and sparkled. The taxi rose, moving to join a faster sky-way. Below us, we could see the large swaths of the city that were lit up like a bright sunny day. These areas are called day zones. They are designed to allow people to enjoy outside daytime activities regardless of the time and to maximize the balance of public use and their internal clocks.

"That looks like fun," said Lauren, pointing at a huge water park in the distance.

We were so high up people looked like tiny, multi-colored lines. In the air before her, Lauren drew a large rectangle over a section by the wave pool. With her index finger she stroked down, and the view zoomed in closer, allowing us to see the faces of the people walking about and swimming. Many were dressed to impress rather than to swim.

"You'd never go," said Jessica.

Lauren scanned the image and sadly shrugged. "You are probably right."

"Why is that?" I said. "Can you swim?"

"I can swim fine." Lauren looked embarrassed, and after a moment, she replied, "It's because of my chest, okay?" She pointed to her prominent bust. "I get enough stares, rude comments, and inappropriate sexual offers without wearing a swimsuit out in public—and that really irritates me. I shouldn't have to hide my figure, but if I don't, I am treated like a brainless robo-partner rental in an adult zone."

Jessica giggled. "Nice visual with that one, sis. It would almost be funny if it weren't true. Let's just say, a sizable number of people have found out the hard way that it is not polite, never mind acceptable, for them to try to touch her. Chipper here has a future as a mixed martial artist."

"I have no doubt about that. I am sure that many people regret underestimating either of you. Chipper, I am sorry that this kind of stupidity still happens in this day and age. Sadly, I understand it far too well, as I am often treated like an exhibit in a traveling petting zoo. For some reason, some people think they have the right to inappropriately touch or spew insults at us, just because we are out in public."

Lauren paused with a raised eyebrow as she considered my statement. "You get it." There was an odd little smile on her lips as she turned to look out the window.

Keeping our conversations clean of any personal identifiers was tiring. The exchange drifted off and we took to being quiet and resting. Lauren was looking out over the city as Jessica was sleeping peacefully, snuggled against her shoulder.

Even though I knew it was incorrect, I was beginning to accept their new looks as being them. Would that happen if had I known them for several weeks before we used the Face-Its? It was odd, even though a few of my friends and I often used facial reconstructors. Why was this so different?

Looking down at the city, I noted that my vision seemed sharper. Maybe it was because I wasn't wearing a data sphere that was filtering everything and filling my head with pointless information. My mind seemed much calmer, and I was coming to enjoy it. Occasionally, I still looked to screen locations, seeking data or wanting to run some service.

I had been filling my head with so much stuff that I was blocking out life. Worse, I was telling God that I didn't trust Him to help me and that I had to take over. Emotions flooded me, and I fought to rein them in. I repented of this self-reliance, and I asked God to forgive me. Self-reliance is something the world says we need more of to thrive; in actuality, it's the direct opposite of what we really need, which is complete reliance on God. He handles everything perfectly when we completely surrender and submit to Him. I am so weary of trying to manage everything and failing catastrophically at it. For some reason, I still resist giving up any control.

Wiping my eyes with the sides of my finger, I noted that Lauren was studying my face. Flashing what I hoped was a reassuring smile, I wondered if she could tell that something was up.

Cautiously she smiled and asked, "Are you okay?"

"Yeah. I'm good. Just thinking about things."

She nodded and politely turned to look out the window at the city flowing by us. Jessica was still asleep. Strong, quiet, and self-assured when she was awake, in her sleep, Jessica's Face-It-modified face was still sweet and innocent.

I knew so little about them, and they had only the media portrayal of me to go on. Based on that, I wouldn't want to meet me either. I could understand Lauren teasing me about my past, so I cut her some slack.

Long ago, the newsblasts had chosen the image of me that they would use to represent my life in the media. They were unwilling to believe that I had been transformed into a new person. You can't blame the newsblasters; it is easy money to bet on catastrophic relapses by those surrounded by the deceitful glamour of fame.

I had created much of my own pain, and I self-medicated in all the wrong ways for years. Now that I was professing to live the Christian life, the media watched closely for any cracks in my public face.

Little of it mattered. I hoped we were headed to where we could hide for a while to rest and eat while this storm blew over. Eat. I was very hungry again. At the safe house, we would have time to eat and to work out a plan to safely get help. With so many narrow escapes, I wondered how long we could expect to evade capture and death. As I had dragged Lauren and Jessica into this, I was determined to do all that I could to protect them.

The ride was peaceful. A stupid plan burst forth, one where we would ride the cab to the farthest edge of the city, and there we would find some out-of-the-way traveler's stay. What? I had been watching too many realviews. All we needed to add to this tired old fantasy is some grizzled old man with a banged-up old hover truck who would cover us in the back with a tarp and drive us away to safety. It was stupid. The longer we stayed out in the open, the greater the probability that we would be caught or even shot down. They had downed a government APV with a missile, cut a taxi into slivers with an AA-30, and destroyed a business and an apartment with assault mechs with no repercussions. Taking out another air-taxi was nothing.

About four minutes later, we landed at a location that was about a half mile of walking and about 105 levels from the safe house. I hoped it would be enough to confuse our path.

After we climbed out, three people climbed into the cab after us, and I watched the cab glide off into the darkness. I was pretty sure they were safe. How would you even go about warning them without sounding like a lunatic or alerting the police? Hearing no explosions, I turned to catch up to Lauren and Jessica, who had already traveled several yards ahead of me.

As I jogged briskly to join them, Jessica's face was tight and her brows were knit. She said, "What's up?"

"I was thinking about the people who got into the cab and what happened to the vehicle I was to ride off in a few days ago—I was praying for their safe passage."

There was a look on their faces that didn't translate well though the Face-Its. Hiding our conversations from the city's heuristic audio interceptors made everything so much harder.

Lauren shook her head and whispered to us, "If they can break the protections on a you-know-what," she meant a diplomatic class symbioid, "a hover-taxi would be easy. Its new records would show that the people were dropped off in the city, but no one would ever see them again. And far away, a remote section of the grasslands would become a tad bit greener."

I blinked and said, "I am really thankful that you are good and not on the other team."

Lauren merely nodded and said, "She tells me that all the time."

"I am sure she does," I replied warily.

Jessica nodded. "It's even scarier that she looks so sweet and innocent, and something like that comes out of her. And you can't argue against its sick logic."

Lauren looked nonplussed. "What can I say, it's a gift."

Lauren and Jessica both smiled at me. Everything was going to be all right. Without another word, we began walking to the safe house, and I enjoyed the walk.

In this zone, the buildings were glossier and the main floors taller, and they sought to outdo each other in their grand, sweeping designs. Dramatic architectural entrances led to massive vid-glass walls and noisy fountains of every shape, size, and height. Were these hissing and crashing water features thought to be calming?

Confronted with these elements, I tended to wonder more about the programming of the audio dampeners, micro-cleaners, and robotic groundskeepers and how they managed to clean the rocks and plants. Maybe this was all a realview projection, an ecology program that mimicked an outdoor environment.

Having been in hundreds of such sectors in megacities over the years, it was difficult to remember any of them, as they tended to blend together the more they tried to stand out. Maybe it is due to standardized robotic architectural programming or the construction constraints of building in megacities. The odd part about it is that I enjoy architecture.

We strolled along the business avenues, and I noted that it wasn't as odd to have one guy walking with two girls as I had feared. Everywhere there were variations in the number and sexes of the groups that filled the streets.

I heard or read that the majority of the workforce worked from home; all this activity appeared to contradict that. It was an anecdotal reaction and not at all scientific, as it is almost impossible to think in terms of three-quarters of a billion people in a single city. Even seeing one million people standing in one place, I don't think I could comprehend that it would be a mere 1/768th of the total number of people in Heavensport.

The people here wore fewer robo-wings, and their color palettes were muted, with less animated logos. This didn't mean that they didn't dress to be noticed.

After about fifteen minutes, we arrived at the location where my safe house was hidden. We found the freight elevators, and after walking a distance, we found the one marked 379fd.

We got in and I said, "Heaven is a great place if you have tickets." The elevator doors closed, and we moved up to the 453rd floor, where it stopped. "I have special tickets." In response, the elevator moved sideways for a few seconds and stopped again. I said, "I have been called."

The elevator moved up once more and stopped, and the doors opened to a hallway with indirect lighting. We stepped out, and I walked to the end of the corridor in front of a large, sturdy door and stated, "And sanctified." To the left, several yards down from the door, a section of the side wall opened to reveal a lit entryway.

"Where does that door go?" asked Jessica.

"That? That's a honey pot—a door that looks legit, but if someone messes with it, we get a silent warning, and they waste time only to find just an empty space behind it." I pointed to the section that had opened for us. "We're here."

I led the way to the opening. The warm light revealed a hallway trimmed in deep reddish-brown polished wood walls with brushed metal accents and ella-glanse crystal. A natural stone floor led to a bright and welcoming room farther in.

A voice from inside said, "Welcome. I am glad that you are here."

11

Respite

●●● ⬛ ⬛ ⬛ ●●●

Both Lauren and Jessica took a step to the side of the door when they heard the sound of the voice from within the room. Their eyes were wide and worried.

"We're good. It's the house's butler," I said.

A six-armed, uni-ball-based robot rolled up to meet us at the door. He was a Model-30CB, which is a more advanced Model-20. He smiled and welcomed us in. Jessica and Lauren peered in, still unsure.

"Yes, that is correct, sir. Allow me to introduce myself; I am Hugo, the house's butler and chef. I will be assisting you during your stay. For your safety, please come inside." Gracefully, he turned and glided into the hallway, beckoning to us to follow him. "If you would prefer to give me a different name, you are most welcome to do so." He glanced behind us and asked, "Is this the full party, or should I be expecting someone else?"

I shook my head. "No. This is all of us."

When we were all in the hallway, the door behind us slid closed with a whisper, and we could hear it seal. The worried look on Lauren's face was almost comical.

With a calm voice, I said, "Relax. We are as protected here as we can be." For now.

Hugo said, "I have set the security to its maximum level of 5.6. Will this suffice?"

"That's great," I said. That was indeed a decent level, and that helped me relax.

He smiled and said, "Now if you would care to follow me."

Pivoting about on his uni-ball, he rolled with the faintest sound down the hallway's stone flooring. Gliding to the side, he let us pass.

Hugo motioned with one of his six human-like hands over the extent of the apartment and said, "While you are here, this is your home. Please let me know if there is anything I can do to make your stay more enjoyable."

The open floor plan was of a good size, suitable for comfortably hosting a nice party for about thirty people. Straight ahead and leading off to the left was an open and inviting living room. To the right of the entrance hallway were the kitchen and the dining area. The galley-style kitchen had a long work island that butted up to a black stone-topped table in the dining room. Around the table were five comfortable-looking chairs, one of which faced the cooking area.

The living room's furniture was offset nearer to the dining space to deliver the maximum realview stage possible. Two sleek white couches made up the long sides of a cozy conversation rectangle. The ends were capped with one yellow and one orange rounded lounge chairs. The back walls were showing the glistening morning sky over the city. As we were hidden deep within Heavensport, this was the realview system at work.

Hugo rolled to a curved entryway that was opposite the kitchen and dining room. "If you are looking for the bedrooms or to use the restrooms, they are down here."

Following behind him, we were led down the short hallway to stop in a cylindrical foyer that held five concave translucent doorways that matched the shape of the space. The doors glowed a soft green, indicating the rooms' availability.

Hugo pointed to the two doors on both sides of the hall and said, "We have four bedrooms here, and at the end is the guest bathroom."

Lauren walked straight ahead and opened the centrally located door to reveal a shining bathroom. "There is a shower, toilet, and Cleano in there. We may want to create a basic schedule for bathing."

Jessica had walked into the first door on the right and then returned to the hallway. "Well, Rolland is all set. This must be his personal room. The bathroom is almost bigger than both of our old bedrooms back home combined, and you should see the tub. It is huge."

Hugo smiled and said, "Not to worry, miss. Each of the four bedrooms is the same size, and each has its own master bath, robo-tailor, and more. I can set the realview walls and ceiling to a décor of your liking, or you can do that yourself. Just let me know your preferences or how I can help you settle in."

Lauren's face grew bright as she looked in the last bedroom on the right. "Wow, realview walls and ceiling in a bedroom? This is like staying at some fancy hotel. I'll take this one."

Jessica, still standing before the first bedroom on the right, said, "This will do nicely." She walked in and I heard, "This is so cool!" as the door closed behind her.

For no particular reason, I chose the first bedroom on the left. As I was about to walk into my room, I heard Lauren. "Rolland, to release the Face-It, just press firmly on each of your cheeks for about five seconds, and it will come off."

I stopped and turned to peek my head out into the hall and said, "Got it. Thanks."

Bringing my other hand up, I touched my face, surprised that I had forgotten I was still in disguise. The fleshy appliance felt normal to me, but now that I was thinking about it, it felt restrictive, and my skin needed to breathe. The contacts needed to go as well. Stepping into my room, I closed the door behind me.

After taking a short 360-shower, I used the air puff dry cycle. Fresh and clean, I stepped out and used the robo-stylist for my hair and to neaten up the lines of my beard. Looking less like a dirty face, the scruff would stay for now in case we had to run. I checked out my wrists and down my body, and I was shocked that the booster patches were still in place. I would have expected them to have given out a long time ago. Maybe they weren't needed anymore.

Before I showered, I had placed my clothes in the Cleano unit, so they were ready and waiting for me. Lifting them out, I placed them up to my nose and took a big sniff. There was none of my scent on them, and they smelled fresh. Why I sniffed them, I don't know. Maybe a part of me didn't trust that they wouldn't stink. Later, I would fire up the robo-tailor to give me a few more clothing choices. A quick, ten-second bite-down on the full-mouth cleaner topped everything off, making me feel ready enough to give a newsblast conference.

Stopping at the door, the humor drained from me. Even after checking to see if the medication patches were still there, I had been more fixated on cleaning up my exterior than on finding out where I stood medically.

I called out for the house robo-doctor. A few seconds later the door opened, and a robot came into the room. This unit had a humanoid head set on an extensible neck; its three arms were mounted high on a slender white rectangular body with rounded edges. This was set above a low and wide base. For complex surgeries, it could remotely control or add on modules for a total of eight long and thin arms, giving the appearance of a robotic octopus.

After giving it a brief summary of the situation, I asked the robo-doctor to run a full set of medical diagnostics on me. It asked a few questions as it worked. It applied two four-inch square pads to my stomach and to the middle of my back and lowered my shirt.

The robo-doctor finished the tests and retracted its arms. Its face pursed as if thinking, and it said, "You are a most interesting case, Mr. Newcastle. Under normal circumstances, I would love to submit your data to the medical community for further evaluation and study. Maybe your situation will change, and that will become possible. The nano-docs have been most helpful in giving me data on your overall health, hormonal levels, and the extent of the damage. You are a very lucky man to still be with us. I will continue to monitor your health during your stay with us. I have given you some additional boosters and attached some tissue cleaning pads to your torso to help."

"So I am good to go?"

"Most assuredly," said the robo-doctor. Happy and relieved, I went out to meet with Lauren and Jessica.

Out in the foyer by the kitchen, I was a bit surprised that I was the first one out of the bedrooms. Hugo stood near the dining room table waiting for any commands. Not having a better idea, I walked over to appraise the living room. It was nice and appeared quite cozy.

What should we do? My stomach growled out its suggestion. Food. What better way to celebrate our arrival than with a good meal? Walking to the kitchen table, I was confronted by a delicate etiquette puzzle concerning the best seating plan. There were five seats total, with two sets of seats across from each other on the right and left sides of the table and one seat that faced the kitchen. A bad decision here could lead Jessica and Lauren to an incorrect conclusion about their value to me.

If I sat at the single seat at the head of the table, they might think I was asserting authority. If they sat at opposite sides of the table, I would have to keep looking left and right constantly like someone watching a tennis match. Even if they sat on the same side, my neck would hurt from being twisted to that side. Placing my hand on the back of a chair I noted that it swiveled. Constantly swiveling back and forth would look stupid. *Hey, maybe I could get Hugo to add a squeak to the swivel to make it even more obvious and irritating.*

If I chose to sit on the left side, facing the entryway hallway, that would leave their backs to the exit, and that could give them the impression that I thought they were expendable. Ultimately, if someone breached the front door, a few seconds' head start or a dinner table in between us would not matter in the least. Taking a deep breath, I exhaled slowly and sat on the right side of the table with my back to the entry hallway. Laughing, I shook my head. *Watch, they will decide to eat in their rooms.*

Jessica came out and sat down across the table from me in the chair closest to the kitchen. She had removed her Face-It to become the woman I remembered from the night that we met. I preferred it.

Jessica glanced at Hugo and nodded. Her eyes narrowed as she scrutinized my face and posture. "You know, your back is to the exit."

I grinned. "I know. I was trying to be polite. I figured if they break in, a mere table between us wouldn't make much of a difference."

She smiled and nodded in agreement. "True. Thanks for the thought anyway." She turned to look around the room. "This is place is impressive. And this is just a safe house for you? This is much bigger and much nicer than any place we have ever lived."

"I wish I didn't even need to have safe houses. Saying that, I am glad it's here."

"Me too."

Lauren came out, free of her disguise; she was all aflutter. "You were not kidding about the size of that tub. I am definitely taking a bath today." Sitting down in the chair next to her sister, she looked at me and froze. "Did you know that your back is to the hallway leading to the exit door?"

Jessica bobbed her head in suppressed laughter. "He knows. He is being all gentlemanly about it."

Lauren nodded sagely. "Thank you. If it makes you feel any better, if they can break down that door, a mere dining room table will not be enough to save us."

"Were you listening in?" I asked, not putting it past her.

"No. Why?"

Bemused, Jessica said, "When I pointed it out to him, Rolland basically said what you said."

Lauren replied, "That's either good or a bit weird."

My stomach growled loudly enough to change the subject.

Jessica laughed and said, "I agree with Rolland. I'm famished."

Lauren agreed. "Me too."

I said, "So, do you want breakfast or lunch...or even dinner, here at the table, or do you want to eat it in your own tub?"

There was a struggle on their faces.

"Eat here, bathe later...and I am leaning toward lunch," said Lauren.

"I agree, lunch. Then I may go for a nap and then a bath. You're Mr. Gourmet. Why don't you suggest something?" said Jessica.

"Sounds like a plan," I said. This was a good opportunity to get better acquainted and to thank them.

Pulling up the menu, we could see that the kitchen was nicely stocked. It was able to provide an exceptional dining experience using food components kept in a specialized cryo-storage system that was similar to the cryo-sleep used by space explorers. This system that Curtis had put in kept ingredients fresh almost indefinitely, and they still tasted great. What would happen when the supplies were used up? Knowing Curtis, he had that worked out as well.

Poor Hugo...our six-armed butler and robo-chef was going to get a workout. This was going to be fun. With glee, I scrolled deeper into the menu, pulling up exotic meals. Realviews of luscious, colorful dishes were projected in 3D in front of us, each with their accompanying aroma, making our stomachs growl in hunger.

Lauren and Jessica grew more uncertain with each new suggestion. There had to be something amazing here that would get them excited, so I continued to pull up more selections. When I looked up, I realized what I'd thought was going to be fun had become painful.

I said, "I was wondering. What is your favorite comfort food? I mean, what do you typically choose after a hectic day of running from AA-30s and a T-37a?"

"Typically, when that stuff happens to us?" replied Lauren, her eyes twinkling.

"Sure, your normal day. So, if you could have almost anything you wanted, in around ten minutes or less, what would it be?"

Lauren's face lit up with a big open smile, and without much of a pause, she said, "In ten minutes or less? I'll tell you what I want; I want a robo-chef in my next home. Okay, I want an avocado and thick sliced turkey on a toasted bagel, with a hint of pesto mayonnaise. Iced tea—and brownies for dessert."

"Okay. That was pretty direct. I think that Hugo can manage that. Jessica?" Hugo had already begun working, pulling out pans and bowls and preparing the cooking surface, and he was rapidly printing out parts of the meal.

He smiled and said, "You got it." Without stopping his cooking, one of his arms delivered a glass of iced tea to Lauren.

Jessica slipped into deep thought. "What do I want? Hmm, that is difficult. What sounds good changes all the time. Let's see...got it, channa, no, wait, chicken tikka masala, basmati rice, chapati, a mango lassi, and pakora with green and brown chutney and the traditional rice pudding, kheer, for dessert."

Lauren's eyes lit up. "Make that two mango lassis."

"Hugo, make that a pitcher of the lassis and make enough of each order for all of us to share, please."

"Yes, sir. It will be my pleasure."

Jessica said, "Rolland, what are you going to order for yourself?"

"Do tell. It will help peel back the layers to reveal who the real Rolland Newcastle is." Lauren lifted the glass of iced tea to her mouth and took a sip. "Oh, that is good."

"I am glad that you like it. Well, I was hoping that your suggestions would give me an idea of what I want to eat."

Lauren scowled. "Oh, no. You are not getting off that easy, 'fess up."

As I was thinking about it, an image popped into my head. "A combination, spicy steak and bean burrito smothered in that queso blanco cheese, a side of Spanish rice, salsa, and chips."

"Fiesta time," said Jessica, laughing.

Lauren stared at me with a sly smile and shook her head. "Of all the foods you might have picked, and you choose that."

"What is wrong with that?" I said, trying to decide if I should be offended.

"There is nothing wrong with that. I like it as well. It's just that I had imagined you would have chosen some strange, exotic food that I had never even heard of before."

Jessica said, "That costs one hundred thousand unicreds per serving."

"Oh, I already looked for it. We are all out," I said.

Lauren rolled her eyes, and Jessica's eyes sparkled. It was great that we were all relaxing and continuing to connect as friends. There was life here, and it was good. A tiny bit of hope was seeping in.

"What about dessert for you, Rolland?" asked Lauren.

Taking a slug of my mango lassi, I set it aside, trying to slow my pace. "A small wheel of brie drizzled with caramel, shaved almonds, and dried cranberries."

"That sounds decadent. I was beginning to believe we had a fake Newcastle with us."

"Yeah," I murmured, off in thought. "Hey, we could eat it with a nice Chateau DeSorignal 32."

Jessica looked intrigued and asked, "Is that good? I'll bet it is pretty expensive."

"I doubt it. I just made it up." Jessica threw her napkin at me, and we all laughed. It felt good.

Standing up I waved for them to join me. "Oh, before I forget and our meals are ready, let me show you some of the defensive features of the safe house. Each of us needs to understand what is available."

● ● ●　━　━　━　● ● ●

"Ma'am, we have found hints of records that led us to believe that Rolland Newcastle did call in an NC-22 the night his Phantom 344 pulsorjet went down."

The svelte woman nodded. "I assume you dug deeper, Colonel?"

"That is correct, ma'am. It took some doing, but we gather that the call came in from a public bathroom in the Dreseldek Market Center. It points to an assassination attempt by a human on Rolland, and he personally thwarted it."

She sat up in her chair. "That sounds far better than the party story that was sold to the newsblasts. The validity of the vid feeds and recollections of the people who were attending that party are murky at best. I doubt that Rolland was even there. What do we know of the assassination attempt?"

The colonel shook his head and said, "The would-be assassin was not injured, just tranquilized. I interviewed the two human detective responders who had been called to the restroom. If I may be frank, the younger one, Corporal Lewis DeGris, was one of those angry fools that equate all the planet's problems with the Remnants. I think he believed that I would agree with him." Measuring his statement, he said, "They look past all the good that the Remnants have done."

The woman nodded, leaning back in her chair. "It because of their kindness that we are still living on New Jerusalem. They had every legal right to remove us all and to keep all the wealth for themselves, but they didn't. How many people do you know who would have done that?"

"Not many, ma'am. After all these attacks, even they might re-think that kindness. I just don't get these anti-Remnant groups."

"People need to identify a physical, delineated group as their enemy. We see this to some degree even with sports teams. If we allow ourselves to assign inhuman characteristics to these groups, we are able to justify committing horrific acts against them that we would never consider doing to someone from our own peer group."

He nodded. "These anti-Remnants haven't done the research, or if they have, they have decided that it is all faked."

"I agree. So, you mentioned that there were two detectives. Was the other detective more helpful?"

"Yes, ma'am. The senior detective, Karl Skjold, was helpful. He was genuinely surprised that the record of that night's arrest had been erased. He told me a Diplomatic Services symbioid named Erlin and her tactical team took over Rolland's care. Diplomatic Services said that those records were 'lost' in a rare database corruption."

"Lost? These coincidences are quite amazing, don't you think?"

"Yes, ma'am. There is no record of where Erlin is now. She may have been decommissioned. It is unclear."

"Did the detectives see Rolland and Erlin leave?"

"I interviewed them separately, and both of them had a similar story. When the detectives were leaving the premises with the prisoner, they saw the T-10 tactical team move a diplomatic or embassy defensive cube with Rolland and Erlin into the waiting APV and then leave the area at a clip."

She frowned. "Do we have a rough timing on this?"

"Yes, a few minutes before the time when the Phantom 344 pulsorjet was said to have crashed. My hunch is that it was the APV that went down. I have Diplomatic Services checking for the location of Erlin, the APV, and the tactical team. Phantom has been repeatedly denied access to the crash scene as an investigation is underway. As crashes are incredibly rare, it's standard operating procedure to ask the manufacturer's technical teams to attend crash sites for their input."

"Colonel, get our teams out to the crash site right now. Have them take a Phantom rep and one of their top teams to join you. We need to be there in person before there is nothing left at the site to see. If you get push-back, I will get you the backing of the World Congress, and if that is not enough, I will get the Earth Planetary Governing Board to bring its forces to bear. I hope I am wrong, but I think we are up against something much bigger here than just an assassination attempt on a single Remnant."

"I agree. If they are hunting down Rolland with assault mechs without it causing a stir, they may be working towards a full Remnant genocide. We can't allow another disaster like the Fall of Heaven."

"That would be far more catastrophic than what we may want to believe. There is a planetary ownership clause that states that if ninety-five percent of the Remnants are eradicated, the EPGB could rule it the genocide of the legal owners, and they could rescind the New Jerusalem charter and take away its sovereignty. The citizens could be forcibly evicted to other planets, and the EPGB would have the options to put the planet back into the New Earth Lottery, keep it, or maybe even sell it to the highest bidder. There would be many influential bidders vying for this planet. So you can see that this is a very serious situation."

"Is it time to brief the World Congress?"

The silver-haired woman frowned and said, "I hate to say it, but no. There is still so much that we don't know, and we cannot risk this information getting out quite yet. We only have actions, and we don't know who is behind this. Rushing it now may merely serve to alert them, causing them to disappear or making them go all out and begin a full-on purge. Until we know more, we cannot trust anyone, and we can't stop this or catch them. If the EPGB gets involved now, they could get in the way or try to assert their control. What about the assassin? Can we interview him or her?"

"As there was no report of an assassination attempt, and the weapons he was carrying disappeared, there were no charges for them to hold him on. Our mystery man was quietly released, and he has vanished. This is a high-level action by someone with power."

"I find this more and more disturbing. Now tell me, Colonel, what do you know about the terrorists in the Browlbek merchant quarter?"

●●● ▬ ▬ ▬ ●●●

During the meal, I took a chance and said, "May I ask why you had that Foamalast painted on the walls back at your apartment? That has really been bugging me. You don't have to tell me if you don't want to."

Jessica sniggered and looked at her sister with a bemused expression. "You want to take that?"

Giving a smile and raising her eyebrows, Lauren said, "Believe me, using it wasn't our idea. It's all because of this stupid guy that we know. He is one of those wheeler-dealers who are always looking for the next big score. He got this 'great deal' on a big tub of the Foamalast, and he was sure he could sell it quickly and make a huge profit. Of course, he was surprised that he couldn't find anyone who wanted to buy it. Simple research would have told him that ninety-four percent of all destruction is now being done with nanobots and construction robots, and it is illegal for private citizens to possess or sell Foamalast without a Class-A construction permit. So, Red decides that it is in his best interest to hide it in Jessica's closet."

"Great, huh?" replied Jessica, as she scooped some chicken tikka masala and rice with her naan bread.

Brushing off some pakora crumbs from my shirt, I asked, "How did he get in? I mean your place wasn't exactly an open door. I saw at least four levels of security, and I am sure I missed a few."

Jessica looked proud. "Those came after we found his unwanted gift. Despite some of our clients having rougher edges, they have always respected us and our property. Even though we were not doing anything wrong or out of line with our Christian beliefs, we realized that we were being naïve and that we shouldn't always count on good behavior from others."

Lauren said, "So, to top it off, after we find this illegal substance in the closet, we find that Renegade Red had stolen two of our custom headsets and a Thollo 7220, and he had traded those to get it. I was furious. We demanded our gear back—or the fair street value for it—and that he get the box of the Foamalast out of our apartment. No big surprise—the trader Red worked with couldn't be found, and Red decided that he didn't want the Foamalast back. Then he demanded that we pay him for his 'loss of use' of the product, even though he stored it at our place without our permission."

"Really? Red sounds like a real prince."

"Oh, he gets a high grade from us—on the Psychopathy Scale," said Jessica, laughing.

Lauren nodded her head vigorously. "He had the gall to threaten to turn us in if we didn't pay him the street rate for the Foamalast. I told him there was no 'street rate' as no one wanted to buy it, and he could have it back when he reimbursed me for the gear that he stole from us. Of course, he just wanted the money. I told him that this would be robbing us twice—once for the gear that he stole and again if we were dumb enough to pay him for a product that we never wanted."

"Wow," I said, amazed at the stupidity of this fellow.

Jessica said, "Tell him the best part."

"The best part? Oh, you mean why we used it and didn't just turn him and the Foamalast over to the police? Well, one night the jerk vid-called us. At first, he tried sugar, and when that failed, then came the threats. He kept going over the same song about how I had to pay him for the stuff as if repeating it often enough would convince me. When I didn't agree, he threatened to blow us up if we didn't cover his losses. This guy acts impulsively on his emotions, and he is a magnet for people looking to sell some very dangerous and illegal things. So, we took his threats seriously. We got thinking, what stops explosions?"

"Couldn't the police have stepped in to stop him?" We Remnants take all threats as being serious.

"That could have taken years in the system, and he warned us that he had friends who would immediately carry out his plans if he was arrested or detained."

"I can see your quandary," I said.

Jessica squirmed in her seat, bubbling with excitement. "According to the law, you are not allowed to have this material in a form that can be applied or sold, but there was nothing in the rules about having it on a surface that technically belongs to the city. We wanted to make sure that the jerk couldn't get it back, as we would be considered accessories if he sold it." Jessica's eyes were alive with mirth. "We had so much of it to dispose of that we painted all the outside walls, ceilings, and floors rather thickly with it. It was overkill, to be sure. We found it quite funny at the time. To be fair, there was a bit of drinking involved with the decision and application."

"That is pretty funny. I think that I can already guess the answer, but how did Red take it?"

Jessica said, "Better than I expected, but he didn't have much of a choice. We had asked for a day to discuss it, and we took that time to compile a very nice realview of his vid conversations with Lauren and me about his Foamalast deal."

Lauren was enjoying this. "We included a detailed list of our missing property and the actual footage of him pilfering our property. We had him talking about his trading our items for the compound, his demands for payment, and his raving threats to blow us up. We added the uncut feed of the product being applied robotically with no identifiers to us. It was all clear-cut. We put it on a few kill-switch global pods in case we met with an accident and made sure he knew it too."

"It almost sounds like a deranged sit-com. Didn't he understand that his vid-calls with you were being saved?" I asked.

Lauren ran her fingers through her dark hair and said, "Aren't most vid-calls auto-saved? Ours were marked on the screen throughout the vid stating that they were. I guess that statement is so common that he didn't think about it. Whatever the reason, he was angry with us, saying that we had betrayed him. Somehow to him, his theft, threats, and extortion weren't a betrayal."

Jessica shook her head and said, "We found out later from another friend that Red has had numerous experiences with the legal system. We didn't know it then, but when he stole our gear, he was out on parole. I made it clear that he would be going away for an extremely long time if he persisted in contacting us or even attempted to carry out his malformed ideas. He must have decided that a trip back to prison wasn't worth it and moved on."

"Has he tried to contact you since then?" I said.

Lauren nodded. "Once. He vid-called from jail asking for us to vouch for his whereabouts and asked for money so he could post bail. I told him that I had no idea where he had been or what he had been doing for the last eight months, and under no circumstances would I post his bail. He asked me to lie for him 'as a friend.'"

"That is astonishing."

Lauren agreed. "I try never to lie, and there is absolutely no way that I would ever lie for him. I still don't think he got that every vid-call from prison was definitely being recorded and that it would be used against him in court. Yet, for some unknown reason, he still believes that he is ten times smarter than everyone else, when he is actually dumber than most. Some mutual friends told us that he is still in jail and will be there for quite some time, as they have taken a strong liking to him. Most likely that's because of his charming personality and willingness to see the law as sets of malleable suggestions. I never pressed to find out what he did to end up in jail for so long. Sometimes you have to turn away from that kind of thing."

I finished chewing my bite of my burrito and agreed. "He certainly was not one of the nicer or brighter people around. So, I have another question about the Foamalast—wouldn't it lose efficacy over time when it wasn't used?"

Lauren finished a sip of her iced tea and held it in her hand, making it wiggle in the glass. "It needs a substantial energy release or pulses of specific UV spectrum light for it to disengage and begin to dissipate. We painted the walls to block it happening by any chance exposure. We figured that when they came to renovate that section of the town, that one apartment will be a bit more difficult. They could send in nano destruction bots to molecularly break the bonds or remove the paint for the pulses to work." She glanced about and with a puckish grin. "Overall, I still think the whole thing is rather funny. I never thought that we would have to use it. Now that the event has occurred, at least those areas will begin to degrade."

"It's funny how God caused all these odd occurrences to work out, isn't?" I laughed, lighter in my spirit.

Lauren and Jessica were also laughing. Cool.

●●● ◖◗ ◖◗ ◖◗ ●●●

12

The Impetus to Change

●●● ▬ ▬ ▬ ●●●

We had finished eating, and we kicked back, enjoying each other's company, lingering hours past what we had originally planned. Our baths would wait.

I studied Lauren and Jessica in the warm light of the table lamp, and there was something right about their looks. It wasn't that they had perfect features or overly enhanced bodies as did so many of the women I had met. I was trying not to be obvious about it, but I did note that they had wonderful figures.

"May I ask a somewhat personal question of you both?" I said.

Lauren and Jessica were relaxed, and they had opened up during the meal, so I was optimistic.

"Sure," said Jessica.

"Am I right that you two haven't had any cosmetic modifications done?"

Lauren's face grew cross, and she spat out, "Are we are so odd-looking that this is your assumption? Or are you saying that we are in need of some bigger upgrades, modifications, or maybe reductions?"

"Goodness, no. Not at all. The exact opposite, in fact. I am trying to say that I love that you *haven't* had any work done. It is incredibly refreshing to find anyone who is willing to be the person that God intended them to be and not give into society's ever-shifting, twisted idea of manufactured beauty. I have lived in the warped world of faux celebrity for far too long. We lose all sight of reality. Everyone is trying to outdo each other without the ability or willingness to see that they have gone too far. When people have to have anti-gravity lifters installed in a controllable constellation throughout their bodies just to be able to stand and bear the weight of their overly inflated DNA enhancements, that is just too much."

Lauren's gaze was intense. "Sorry if saying this destroys your fantasies, Rolland, but nearly every great body out there is shaped and controlled by either internal or clothing-based adaptive anti-gravity lifter constellations. In fact, those amplified anti-gravity lifter constellations in our jackets allowed you to float. So, don't be too harsh in your judgment; this tech has some value."

"I can attest that it worked amazingly well and it saved me. I am not implying that the tech is bad or that it has no good application, but having to use it to be able to live, breathe, or move after extreme and purely cosmetic body modifications might be a sign that there is a deeper problem. I am not trying to paint everyone who uses this tech as being foolish, as I have a number of close friends who have to use this technology, and other than their physiques, they are quite normal and well-adjusted. I know quite a bit about it, as constellations and alterations are daily shop talk for my friends in the DNA world." I sighed and continued, "My point is that after so many modifications, people look fake."

Jessica looked uncomfortable and tried to lighten the conversation. "So, have you had anything done?"

I leaned back in my chair, seeking to look less aggressive. "Me? No. I guess deep inside I always fought against it, and it is not because I think I am perfect in any way. As you can see, I am not the pinnacle of male perfection. My nose is too long, and I am not a wall of walking muscles; I don't take DNA enhancers; I have no neural ports or implanted electronics, and I don't have any tattoos, nor have I had medical enhancements for vanity's sake. It's not because I couldn't. It just never seemed right for me to do it."

Lauren's eyebrows rose, and she looked at me with her arms crossed. "And yet you keep showing up almost every year on the newsblasters' 'Hot One Hundred' lists and in the top five for a few of those years."

Rolling my eyes, I replied, "Those are pointless popularity polls that are skewed toward money, fame, and power. I am completely aware that if I hadn't been born into wealth and power, and I was some guy living off the monthly public share, I would go through life unnoticed." Lauren was unconvinced. I said, "Did you see that last year Leyland Melcurate, the Viceroy of the EPGB on New Jerusalem, made that list? Would you call him sexy or handsome?"

Jessica shook her head. "No, I wouldn't. And it is not his age either. He is okay-looking, and he dresses nicely and carries himself fairly well, but I would never put him on the list. There is something about him that creeps me out. I can see him having people locked up against their will in his basement."

Lauren's face pinched like she smelled something rotting. "Ew. Thanks, Jessica. That's an image that has been seared into my brain." Her face softened and she said, "Oh, I have one! What about Bredforth Ablefrock, the Director of the World Cup Sailing League? He had to have bought his way onto the list. He is an ancient old codger who looks every one of his one hundred and twelve years of age."

Jessica shrugged. "I don't know. He has a twinkle in his eye that I like."

"Just say the word, and I can set you up on a date with him. He recently divorced his eighth wife when he found out that she willfully and maliciously turned thirty. You still may have a couple of years with him if you play it right."

"Funny, Rolland—but when you get a chance, get on that, okay?"

Even though I'd brought it up in jest, this hit a nerve. "I was only kidding about setting you up with him. I care far too much about you to put you even near that creep. He is a lecherous, demanding, and cantankerous old coot who hunts beautiful and naïve young girls to charm them into becoming one of his trophy wives or mistresses."

"So, you guys are best buds?" asked Lauren, feigning innocence.

She was kidding. I still harrumphed in disgust. "On his best day, he is a cheat and a scoundrel."

Jessica shook her head. "I wasn't serious about getting to meet him, Rolland. But be assured these women know what they are getting into. I doubt he had to drug them to get them to marry him."

"I wouldn't put it past him."

Jessica smiled as if she were explaining something complex to a young child. "I cannot imagine that they are all grossly naïve about the payments they are exchanging and the expected time frame. He gets the prestige of having a very attractive younger wife, and they put in five to ten years and get wealth, comfort, and fame. I am sure that a few of his ex-wives saw marrying him like taking a horrible job that pays extremely well. After those years, they will have some social standing, and they'll be well off for the rest of their lives."

"Probably not all that well off. He is a cheap SOB. I don't think he has paid for his own lunch in a hundred years, so I am sure he guards his money and property with some harsh one-sided marriage contracts." Lifting an eyebrow, I said, "You don't strike me as one who would even consider dating, let alone marrying, to obtain that kind of lifestyle."

Jessica laughed, leaning back in her chair. "Me? No. You are quite right about that. I want real love with the right man. I am just making a case that even if Bredforth is a horrible creep, it is not as one-sided as you are portraying it to be."

"I openly accept that I am too sensitive to this, but I have seen it too many times. The women or men who marry for fame and fortune usually end up paying a far higher and more painful price than they ever could imagine. Male and female predators like Bredforth are under no illusion as to why these people are interested in them, even if their victim claims it is true love. They resent and abuse these people, seeing them as pretty, opportunistic prostitutes or disposable robo-partners. I just hate seeing it."

"Then you don't believe that a person can fall in love with someone much older? Love and respect are not tied to how many years we have spent on this planet," said Jessica.

"I do believe that people fall in love for almost any reason. In the general, medium-income population, I would highly doubt you would find such dramatic age gaps as you do with the rich and famous. With a huge difference in your ages, what would you have in common other than you both breathe air? One says, 'I am 326 years old; I saw the survivors being brought planet-side after the Fall of Heaven.' And the other says in response, 'I just got out of high school and went to the prom. My dress was awesome. Wanna see the realview?' and he says, 'The real-whatsy-hoozit?'"

Lauren laughed. "Whatsy-hoozit?"

"You like that? You can use that to impress your clients. That is more than a bit of an exaggeration. Case in point, I remember, I was about twenty-five when I met a nice young woman at some event; she had to have been about nineteen—"

Jessica smirked and said, "Nice? You mean built, right?"

I scowled at her. "I don't recall her figure or even what she looked like in particular. That's not the point. I don't even remember what we were talking about—"

Jessica laughed, "You don't remember what we were just talking about? Are you feigning old age memory loss?"

I rolled my eyes and shook my head.

Lauren raised an eyebrow. "You sound like a politician on the witness stand, where you cannot recall any of the particulars."

"Should I stop or do you want me to continue?"

Lauren giggled, "Sure, please continue."

I looked at Jessica for confirmation, and she nodded, saying, "You're right; he is fun to tease. Please, go on."

"Great. Now, I have two of you teasing me. I'll make it short. So this woman, out of the blue, asked me how old I was. When I told her I was twenty-five, she said, 'Wow. You are practically dead.' And she was serious. This shocked me as I still felt like a kid. Actually, I still feel about twenty-four."

Lauren's brow furrowed. "Funny, you look about the age of Bredforth."

"Funny. The point is, most young people tend to think of anyone a few years older as ancient. It is not as big an issue when we get much older."

After taking a sip of water, I continued. "I'd like to circle back to the topic—the effects of living in isolation. I didn't realize just how insulated and removed I have been from the real world until I met you two. What are the odds of me meeting either of you in our normal lives? Pretty much zilch, and my life would be much emptier for it."

Lauren raised her index finger as if she'd had a brilliant thought. "What about when we are the only two standing in line to meet you at the signing event for the release of your next album?"

"Neither of you would be there, as I think you have taste. This will sound conceited, but even if I were foolish enough to put out another album, there would be long lines to meet me, and we both know it wouldn't be about my music unless they were there to tell me to stop before someone gets hurt. There is no end to the people who have created some convoluted fantasy world with me, where I whisk them away to some fairytale castle. Some of them are so aggressive that it is scary." Setting down my drink, I said, "I cannot thank God enough for putting us together. Well, maybe not running for our lives, but He has pulled us through this, and that has given us time to connect and get to know each other."

Lauren said, "Seeing that we are sharing, I should come clean—I did have some work done." She waved her hand over her whole body, "Up until two years ago I was a guy."

Shocked, I cleared my throat. "Really? Wow, I would have never guessed. That is remarkable." There was *nothing* about her that even came close to whispering she had once been a man.

Jessica and Lauren burst out laughing. In between her laughing jags, Lauren said, "Tell me that you didn't really fall for that. You can relax, I was joking. For the record, neither Jessica nor I have had any work done, and I wasn't a man. This is how God made us, nothing more or less. Wow, I had no idea that you are so gullible."

Once Jessica regained her composure, she said, "Should I tell him that once I was a twenty-percent robot?"

Lauren nodded vigorously. "You can see how tiny her waist is—I built her from a kit. I did a decent job on her, don't you think?"

Sighing, I submitted to their humor. "An absolutely marvelous job, for sure—I am being gullible because I trust you both, and I want to embrace who you are as you tell it to me—that, and I am tired to the point of being stupid."

"You are well past that point, and you are wading neck-deep into stupid," said Lauren.

Jessica was enjoying this. "That's enough. You forgot that we did use tooth directors when our adult teeth were coming in, as most kids do."

Lauren nodded in agreement.

"Well, without a doubt God did amazing work with you two, inside and out."

Lauren smiled. "Thanks. No one gets to pick how they will look, right? Well, other than the DNA modders or the implanters. So, seeing we are sharing personal information, if you don't mind telling us, have you ever been married?"

There had been rumors several years back that I got married in secret to a woman I met at a restaurant.

"No, I have never been married, and for the sake of time, I'll answer your next questions. No; no; yes, once when I was twenty-two; then no; no; and 7,934,852.

"Pardon?" Lauren started chuckling. "A few more details would be helpful."

"Oh, you want details? I do not have any children, and I haven't been seeing anyone. That woman who claimed that we got secretly married was lying to become famous. I have never met her nor been to that restaurant in years."

Lauren leaned forward, intent in her focus. "What was it that you did when you were twenty-two and what is that 7,900,000 number? Is that the number of your old girlfriends?"

"The number twenty-two I made up to see if I could get a rise out of you. That's one point for me, and the seven million figure is the number times that the press has claimed I am dating, engaged, suing, or at war with someone I have never met or may have met in passing at some function."

Lauren's eyes twinkled. "So how many of those almost eight million did you actually date?"

"Only about half. A guy's got to sleep at least a few hours a night—seriously, I have never been engaged, and I avoid those people I do not like. I am not particularly litigious, despite what the press claims. I don't sue over nonsense such as broken cookies at a restaurant or get angry when I have to wait for some frou-frou drink at a bar." I was referring to a famous incident where I supposedly became unhinged waiting for a fancy drink at a posh restaurant.

Lauren said, "Really? The newsblasters made it sound as if you were the one who went berserk."

I nodded with a harsh laugh. "Notice that they don't offer to play the realview of the event? There are plenty of feeds, and I have seen them. This is because it was Lionettia Navililan who completely lost it. I brought it up as I still hear whispers about my supposed behavior."

Jessica's face fell. "I have heard that Lionettia Navililan is as nice as she is beautiful."

"And at one time she was...fame twists people. Who knows? Maybe she just hid her behavior better early on. I don't know."

Lauren asked, "Were you guys out on a date?"

"No. We hadn't dated in over a year, and I ran into her there by chance. She asked me to join her for a drink at the bar. I don't remember the drink taking all that long to arrive, neither of us was drunk, and I never saw the infamous cookie, so I don't know what caused her blow-up. I was thrust into the middle of it and I was trying to calm the situation. Let's just say that it did not go well. Since then, her marketing team has tried to covertly push her inappropriate actions onto me as people don't want to believe that she would have done that. Me, well, I am an easy target to hit."

Jessica leaned forward slightly and brushed a strand of her blonde hair from her eyes. "So, you never found the right one?"

I shook my head. "As you know I dated quite a bit, but I never found the right person. They are or they are not. I believe that it is God that picks your perfect mate. This didn't stop me from trying to find something other than God to fill that God-sized hole. Only He can fill that. I can tell you from painful experience everything else leaves you dry, empty, and unfulfilled. And that leads to addiction as one tries to fill the horrible emptiness."

Lauren perked up and said, "That leads me to my next question. So what's it like to be a trillionaire playboy?"

"You should have remained a guy and you would be a third of the way there." I enjoyed getting a dig back in.

Jessica laughed. "I think you may end up regretting that joke, sis." Lauren took the jibe and waited for me to respond.

"So, what's it like? I haven't known anything else, so it is hard to explain. As freeing as it sounds—and to some degree it is—it is also majorly tiring always having to be on guard, not trusting the motives of those around you. Even those with great wealth and fame are always measuring themselves against you. Every time I go out, I have to have teams sweep the area where I want to go. Aside from the risk of assassins or accidents, there are always women and a few men who try to sneak in to meet me, thinking that when we meet we will fall in love. They can get quite nasty when they think others are trying to keep them from me and the rich and famous lifestyle they feel is rightfully theirs."

Jessica blanched and said, "You don't think that Lauren and I are doing that, do you?"

I barked out a harsh laugh in surprise. "Dear sweet Lord, no. If you remember, I dropped in on you two, and it was me who dragged you into this mess. I welcome you into my life, I mean, into my normal life, not whatever this is. Actually, I need you both, or I don't think I will survive—my point is that there is a big difference in knowledge about someone and really knowing someone. There are some who know all about the little details of my life, like where I went to school, the names of my pets, my favorite color, and that sort of thing, but they have never met me, and they don't really know me. Seriously, you two probably know me better than most people do or ever will."

With a sad face, Lauren inquired, "Don't you have any close friends?"

"I have a few, like Curtis, the guy who set this place up, and there is my family. I have met a lot of people but not too many who are that close. You can't just go out and have a conversation with normal people—once they realize who you are, they always seem to be angling, or they get awestruck and have a hard time just talking to you. I am just a guy."

"That was made clear by your failed attempt to compliment us," said Jessica with a sneaky grin.

"That was marginally better than some guys we have run into," Lauren agreed. "So, your attempt to fill the God-sized hole was wine, women, and an album of horribly lame songs."

"Keep it up, and I will find out if we have it in the media library and make you listen to it."

"Oh, please do. My favorite from **Songs from My Heart** is 'I Love Your Really Big Boobs.'" Lauren was smirking gleefully.

In my head, I ran over a few exceptionally inappropriate responses. "Yeah, that is a classic love song. I could sing it to you right now, but I wouldn't have the chorus. That would be a shame, as it added so much depth to it. Maybe I will update it and add it to my next release and dedicate it to you." That slipped out.

"Oh, thank you. I would be so flattered," replied Lauren, pausing between each word, her face and tone comically void of expression.

Jessica huffed at her sister. Turning to me, she said, "Who you were is not who you are now." Then, to Lauren, "Even though it is fun to tease him, we have to be careful not to keep shaming him about his music career and his old lifestyle."

Sheepish, Lauren dipped her head, her gray eyes searching mine. "Sorry, Rolland. It is not fair to push that back in your face. You have asked God for forgiveness for all that, and He took it away, right?"

"Yes, but the old lifestyle and those behaviors keep trying to come back in."

"Of course they do, but you don't have to let them. The shame that you feel is not from God. He forgave you and healed you, and He has forgotten that past. You don't have to keep living in it or bringing it back up. That lie is from the devil, who wants you to live in perpetual self-loathing, shame, and bondage. You need to stop punishing yourself for it. Just avoid it when it comes up and move on. 'Resist the devil and he will flee from you.' If you hear that same old song of accusation, say something like, 'I know who you are and I don't accept that.' Add in, 'Why don't you say it along with me, Jesus is Lord!'"

A short laugh burst forth, and I felt better. "You are right, thanks."

She was right. I was beating myself up for the past and continually bringing it up to feel badly about myself. That wasn't of God.

Tired of drinking water, I asked Hugo for another mango lassi. Both of the ladies agreed with me, and soon he returned with three tall glasses of creamy delight.

Taking a sip, I murmured, "This would be perfect for a warm summer's evening. All we need now is a veranda at night, overlooking a nice tropical beach and a warm gentle breeze—wait, that gives me an idea. Let's see what we can do. Realview: Sail Island, 10 p.m., no clouds, south veranda view of the beach, small sidelights on low, summer, 74 degrees Fahrenheit, gentle breeze." The living room responded, and the room faded away and a glorious view of the island filled our senses. A delightful fresh breeze wafted over us as the environmental ventilation system modified the air to meet the requirements of the location.

In the gentle lights of the veranda, I watched them staring silently up at the realview sky. Jessica's eyes widened as she peered up at the stars. "This is just awesome. This is some realview setup you have here. You can even see both of the moons, and those stars are amazing. With this setup, you would never have to leave home."

"Oh, I don't know about that. It's pretty good, but it can't even touch the real thing," I replied in a low voice.

Lauren continued to gaze upward, her face serene and sad. "We wouldn't know. We have never left Heavensport. We have only seen the realviews and visited the cityscapes. You can't even see the moon and stars outside when you are in the city because of the light pollution. In fact, I wouldn't even swear that I have ever even seen a real sunrise or sunset."

It was too easy to forget that others didn't have my level of freedom. It was embarrassing that I did not even recognize the extreme blessings that I had been given. "If we are able to get out of this alive, maybe you will let me take you both to the beach and on a fun tour of New Jerusalem?"

In the faint light, I could see tears welling up in their eyes.

"That would be great," said Lauren.

"Absolutely," said Jessica softly. She had a lock of her long blonde hair and she was playing with the end as she studied the sky above us. "We would love that."

"It's a bit late in the game to ask, but is either of you married?"

Jessica harrumphed and released her hair, letting her hands fall to rest in her lap. "Nope. We are both free as this breeze. A couple of relationships in the past, but none that were right."

"You can say that again. A few major duds as well," said Lauren.

"Not good, huh?" I asked.

A frown grew on Jessica's face. "About three years ago Lauren was engaged. The guy ran off with a woman he met in one of the adult zones."

My heart sank for her. "I am so sorry. That sucks."

Lauren smiled weakly and said, "No biggie. It's far better to find out before you get married than after—I was young and stupid, and I thought I could change him and help him grow up." Lauren got up from the table. "Nice as this has been, there is a bath and a bed with my name on it. I'll see you later."

We waved and I watched Lauren leave. Jessica continued looking at the sky.

After hearing a bedroom door close, I said, "Do you think she is okay?"

Jessica smiled at me and nodded. "Lauren is tough—but it hurt her when Marcolo left."

"He's not the ex-friend with the Foamalast, is he?"

Jessica shook her head. "No. Marcolo is a different idiot. Lauren found out about Marcolo and that woman when she walked in on them in, shall we say, a romantic embrace on her bed in our old apartment. Same old story. He begged her to forgive him and said that he would stop, but of course, he didn't. A few months after their breakup, we heard that he married her. She was one of those DNA inflators who was trying to look like Leahnen Fanalone."

"Oh," I said. "I am sorry."

Jessica was weighing her next statement as she studied my face. "Supposedly he told Lauren after he was caught that she 'needed to get some major DNA work done because she didn't fulfill his needs.'"

My heart dropped, and I felt horrible. "I really stepped in it with my stupid questions, didn't I? I may be the exact opposite of what she needs to be around right now." Unable to look Jessica in the eyes, I fumbled with my empty glass, seeking some other focus.

"Relax, Rolland. You didn't send Leahnen to seduce Marcolo. All you did was date a woman many years ago whom Marcolo's girlfriend, now wife, tried to emulate. You cannot get much more removed than that. I thank the Lord that Lauren didn't marry him. I never thought he was nice to her, and I told her that, but she didn't listen. As you may have noticed, she can be stubborn. He had other issues too. Sometimes he was just a little too friendly with me when Lauren was not around. He also loved to make helpful comments about how great I would look if I got 'a lot more meat added up on top and on bottom.'" Jessica's expression was sour.

"He sounds like a first-class fool. Don't listen to that junk. It sounds like he needed a lot more brains added up top, but instead he got meat. You are perfect as you are."

Jessica gave me a grateful smile. "Thanks. You are right about him. He hated the fact that Lauren and I were so much smarter than him. As for me, the right guy will come along, and he will appreciate how I look and, more importantly, love who I am."

"Without a doubt. He would be a fool not to love everything about you, and if he doesn't, then move on, because he doesn't deserve you."

"Thanks. You are most kind." She paused and said, "Oh, and so you don't have to ask Lauren why we had a third hyperglider in the apartment, yours was to have been a gift from us to Marcolo. He kept telling us it was his dream to learn to fly a hyperglider and for us to go on a sky tour to some exotic beach location. As part of the surprise, Lauren and I had taken lessons so we could start planning the trip. Thankfully we got pretty good with them, or the AA-30s would have gotten us."

"I am so glad that you both made it through with no injuries."

A chagrined smile drifted across her face. "A few bruised egos after losing the gear, but we will mend."

"Did Marcolo ever learn to fly?"

"No. We even gave him lessons as a gift. He never found time to take them. He was a big talker and ultimately just lazy. Any day of the week he could have traveled fifteen or so minutes to a local rec zone and learned."

I set my empty glass down, and Hugo came over and picked it up. "So why did you buy them instead of renting them?"

"That story is a bit more involved. After the whole Foamalast fiasco, we started hearing street buzz that a few of our ex-clients had been talking about the kinds of equipment we carried and making comments about our figures. This was not comforting, so we had been discussing plans for surviving a violent home invasion."

"Those comments would certainly make me uncomfortable."

"It was definitely creepy. We had to up our security even if we ultimately got out of the business. As we had only the closet access hatch and the front door, we were faced with the real potential of being trapped in our bedrooms with no way to escape. In typical Lauren fashion, she said, 'This is easy. If we are invaded, we will sprout wings and fly off to safety.' At the time we thought that was really funny.

"About a week later, a regular client of ours came to us and asked if we would be interested in trading some of our custom helmets and visors for three high-performance hypergliders. When we did the math, it worked out that after our equipment discounts, we would own the better units for a bit over the cost of renting some slower units just two more times. We liked hypergliding, so we went for it."

"That is a no-brainer—and hypergliding is far more fun when you are not being chased by AA-30s."

"Or assault mechs."

"Or assault mechs. Definitely."

Jessica's eyes glistened in the light. "We didn't buy them as part of our emergency plan; that just sort of happened. I have to say, it's totally amazing how it all worked together. Even Lauren's surprise experiment where she mistakenly turned ella-glanse crystal into powder came in handy."

"Surprise, huh? I will have to tease her about that—I agree this was wild how it all fit together. By the way, I want to thank you both for letting me use the hyperglider. I will gladly replace them when this is all done." A passing breeze made me look up at the twinkling stars. Even though they were not real, they were beautiful. With a soft voice, I said, "I pray that I am here to help in healing and not just adding to the pain."

"I don't think that you are adding to her pain. As cool as she is, Lauren is in need of some deep healing. I think it is coming. God tends to put people and circumstances in our paths to bring up areas that have to be healed. Sometimes you have to open wounds to get the infection out before you can fully heal. We all get hurt in this life, both physically and emotionally."

"Agreed. Sometimes the physical healing is easier than the emotional healing...though I did spend several painful weeks in the hospital when they replaced my tibia and fibula with a pair of carbon nanotubes in my left leg."

"Ow. I bet that hurt. If you don't mind telling, what happened?"

"I was on an autowalk that became a high-speed people launcher. This so-called 'malfunction' managed to kill two people and mess up about seventy of us." I lifted my left leg up and pointed along the shinbone. "You won't be able to see the scar anymore, but they had to abrade the wound to get the infection, shattered bone, and other junk out. Even with meds to help, it was horrible. Thankfully, they were able to save my life and my leg."

"Why didn't they just re-grow the bone in place?"

"That is my fault. After they got me stable in the intensive care unit, they worked on my leg and the other wounds. As I said, the pain was miserable even with the drugs. They told me that they could put in this fancy carbon nanotube and graphene tibia and fibula, and they would be hundreds of times stronger and lighter than my bone. What sealed the deal was that it wouldn't take as long, and they said it would not be as painful. I was already going through enough mental stuff as it was, so I signed up for it."

Jessica's eyes were sad. "I am so sorry. That must have been so horrible—wait a moment. Have you ever run a scan on your leg to see if they added any kind of homing device to it?"

"Repeatedly. Nothing. It has shielding, so it doesn't act as an antenna or a capacitor. It is pretty non-reactive."

Jessica scooted forward in her chair. "What about a biometric scan? Is there a different density, or does it show up in security detectors?"

I could see where she was going. "It would show up in a density scan showing the change in the mass of my leg—"

Jessica sat straight up and finished my statement. "As compared to your right leg. Someone could legally run flood scanners over whole sections of a city street and pull out anomalies in bio-symmetries. They would get a bunch of anomalies, but after locating you once and getting a measurement of the variance caused by your left leg, they would just do a search for your specific data structure."

"So I have been a huge, walking ID beacon. I haven't been blocking density scanners to any great level, and I didn't have any electronics running at your shop, so I will bet that my leg is how they found me and sent the T-37a. Wow."

Jessica's face was bright and excited. "Yeah, wow is right! We are shielded here, correct?"

Scooting to the edge of my seat, I asked, "Hugo, how well are we shielded?"

Hugo rolled up and said, "Completely. About two floors and eight rooms in every direction from this apartment are filled with equipment rooms that are needed for this sector's functioning. This apartment has active phase blankets running, and it reads on the city's plans as if it doesn't exist."

"Thanks, Hugo." I turned back to Jessica and said, "That is part of Curtis' genius. Even the normal maintenance bots don't register this cube of floors. My own repair bots do the work like it is their own planet."

"Does this apartment have a robo-doctor?"

It was clear what she was getting at. "It does. We knew that those running here may have been the target of some pretty severe attacks, so it is a good one. In fact, I had it check me over in my room to see where my numbers were."

Jessica was leaning forward with her elbows on her thighs and her curled hand's knuckles to her lips as she thought. "I hope that you are right that it is a good one. I think we will need to do some operating, if you are up to it."

I slouched in my chair, deflated. "This sounds absolutely terrible, and I am not up for it, but I will. It has to be done. When do you think we should do it?"

"Now," she said, without a pause.

My eyes darted to hers and I scowled. "Now?"

"Yes. We aren't the ones operating on you, so us being a bit tired is not an issue. Your update from earlier will help save time. Also, will give you more hours of healing and less time for worrying and waiting."

There was a peace in my spirit. "Let's do it." Jessica got up and walked toward the bedrooms. "Where are you going?" I called after her.

Over her shoulder, she replied, "To get Princess Bubbles from her bath. We need her expertise on this."

About fifteen long minutes later, Lauren came out to join me. Her hair was pulled back, and she was wearing a different outfit than earlier. It was nice-looking and flattered her impressively curvy figure. There was no jacket to hide her physique now.

She noted my scan and said, "Oh, this? There is a robo-tailor here, and I thought it would be fun to play with it and see what it can do. I hope you don't mind. This place is great."

"I am glad the place is getting used." Struggling to look only at her face and not her figure, I said, "I am sure that Jessica has you up to speed with what we are going to do."

"Yes. Jessica is in working with the surgeon. The nanobots should be about ready for insertion." She sat down next to me and smiled to reassure me. "We will do the operation in your bedroom. The cleaning bots have already sterilized the room, and the ultraviolet final cleansing is almost finished. We cannot be in the room during the surgery, as we need to keep it sterile, but we will watch by realview from the living room." Lauren placed her hand on my arm and gazed steadily into my eyes. "Please understand that I will check the system before you go in for prep. I mean, I will really go over the system. Jessica is taking this seriously too. It will go well. We have been praying for you and will do so throughout the surgery."

She couldn't have said anything better to me. I was in their capable hands, and their prayers meant a lot to me. I felt both calm and emotional. Weird.

Jessica came out. "It is all set."

I smiled at them. "Thank you both. May God bless you and keep you. I also pray that you can forgive me for getting you into this and for offending you." That was all I could manage without crying, and I was determined not to go there.

Lauren gave me a big hug and a kiss on the cheek. "Forgiven. Don't give it another thought. Please forgive me for being so snappy and teasing you mercilessly."

"I forgive you too. That was never in doubt." Blinking, I tried to stop the tears that were forming.

Jessica gave me a kiss on my other cheek and a hug. "Forgiven, without a doubt. Now go and get ready."

In my room, I closed the door and said a prayer as I stripped and walked over to the bed and climbed into it, pulling up the modesty sheet. Did they just see me strip via realview? They said they would be watching. Before I could think more about that, the robo-doctor administered a painless air puff injection that was beginning to take effect. The bed was shaping itself to me, and I felt more than I saw the robo-doctor begin to prep me for surgery. My vision began to degrade and darken as I slipped below the veil of consciousness.

●●● ▬ ▬ ▬ ●●●

13

Growing New Support

●●● ⬤ ⬤ ⬤ ●●●

"Report."

Joden's encrypted voice said, "We have retrieved the hypergliders, their helmets, and some jackets at the northeastern border of Heavensport."

"This is good. I assume that means that we are close to capturing or eliminating our targets?"

"Ah—I would say no. Not in that area there, sir. We believe that the occupants had removed the units and relaunched the hypergliders. We couldn't risk detection by accessing the low-orbit monitoring satellites for surveillance or tapping into the city's surveillance systems. We have noted deep scans showing that some of our activities are being noticed, and they are looking for breaches in the system. This required us to observe the hypergliders' flight paths from high-altitude commercial monitoring platforms. From those, we could not implement the scans that we would have liked."

"Even with the reduced viewing capability, wasn't it obvious that nobody was in the hypergliders?"

"No. We were using their unique electronic helmet and hyperglider pairing to follow them, not visuals."

"And this fooled you?"

"Our team was deceived, for a while, yes. It wasn't until a few hours into the flights when the units began crashing that we realized they were not being piloted."

"How so?"

"When the first one crashed, the other one just tried to go on. Apparently, the two were dragging one of the outfits, and that didn't have a hyperglider, but it had a helmet that had been paired earlier to the hyperglider that was destroyed. The rope got tangled with a rooftop cyclone energy collector, and that pulled them all down. That is when we sent a seeker drone to the location and found out about the ruse."

"Did we have eyes on them when they dumped their hypergliders in the first place?"

"No, sir. This escalated too quickly, and if you remember, we thought it would have stayed as a cleaning mission within the sector."

"Yet you had two AAs at the ready?"

"We always seek to be prepared."

"But not enough to have at least a seeker drone or a floating monitoring platform in place?"

"We didn't want to draw outside attention to the mission. We were also trying to limit anything that would have alerted our target," said the encrypted voice.

"Okay. Is there any other bad news you are trying to avoid telling me?"

"Not actually trying to avoid telling you...our operator had informed us that he believed he had viable intel on a safe house of one of Mr. N's deceased brothers. It's located in the New Paradise adult district. After the hyperglider ruse, we took the risk to run a quick set of large-area biometric abnormality scans. A strong return led us to believe that our target was headed to that sector. The operator made his way to the location, and there he gained access to the house using a facial reconstructor tuned to Mr. N.

"Once inside, the operator was met by four friendly and help-ful symbioid robo-partners. Later, as he lay in wait for the tar-gets, the operator was attacked when his facial reconstructor mistakenly became disengaged. During the struggle, he was able to decommission all four symbioids, but he suffered some minor injuries that required him to retreat."

"This man is useless. I am done coddling him. I want him permanently removed now. I will not tolerate him any longer."

"I am in agreement, sir. We sent a team to clean him as he was recovering. He managed to extract himself and in the pro-cess eliminate the cleaning team."

"What's the damage?"

"Two T-10s from Diplomatic Services. We have culled their records and have listed them as decommissioned and indicated that they were used for training exercises. They were taken to a weapons range and have been destroyed there."

"What do we know of the operator's location and his ability to harm our program?"

"It's not good, sir. He knows more than we would hope."

"And why is that?"

"Well, sir...the operator is my brother-in-law, Miken."

"You fool! You don't bring family or friends into this kind of thing. That is the first rule of this kind of work. They know too much, and it makes it harder to make the proper decisions when they are involved."

"Yes, sir."

After an extended pause, the older man said, "Well, I am not displeased that you made the attempt to clean this issue without being told. It shows the right attitude to handle the problem. Keep trying to locate him and clean the problem. I am counting on you to do this. Do you understand?"

"I do, and I will, sir."

The screen showed that the encrypted connection ended. The older man pressed a second encrypted connection.

"Yes, sir," replied a man with a strong voice.

"You know that problem that we spoke of?"

"Yes, sir."

"I need us to be ready to remove that leg including the foot, if the leg doesn't take care of that infection. I want the connections severed and the area tidied up so you cannot see where we stepped. Is this clear?"

Yes, sir."

"Monitor Mr. J's progress and move as needed if his program is in danger of discovery or failure. Is this understood?"

"Yes, sir. We will get on it now. Is that all?"

"No. Say hello to your mother for me, would you? Please tell her to come over for supper sometime soon."

"Yes, Uncle. I will."

●●● ▬ ▬ ▬ ●●●

I woke to a throbbing discomfort that was running up and down my left leg. My thoughts were incoherent, and I couldn't quite place the reason for it. Had I been drinking? I smacked my lips and ran my tongue over my teeth, but there was no telltale taste of being on a bender. Struggling to sit up, I was unable to move my leg.

A human faced robo-doc glided into my view. It was smiling and calm. It looked familiar. "Please lie still, Mr. Newcastle. You are still under sedation after your leg surgery. I have alerted the DeHavalynds, and they will be here shortly."

The head of the bed lifted me up to an inclined position. My face felt funny, so I rubbed it haphazardly as I noticed that under my sheet, there was a long shape encasing my left leg. A twinge of pain shot up my leg as I tried to move my torso to a more comfortable position.

I heard a knock at my door, and Lauren and Jessica entered to stand by my bed. The robo-doc moved back to give them room.

"Are you feeling better?" asked Lauren, as she and Jessica came and stood by my side.

I nodded. As my throat was sore, I reached for a drink next to my bed, and Jessica handed it to me.

She smiled and said, "You are doing remarkably well for someone who had his old tibia and fibula removed. The nanobots are busy internally building new ones out of your stem cells. Soon you will not even know that you ever had a problem with your leg."

My voice was rough. "Good. How long have I been out?"

"You have been in and out of sedation for about twenty-one hours," said Lauren.

"How long will I have this thing on my leg?" I said, pointing at the long shape.

Jessica smiled and said, "You still have about a day before the length of the bones are completed and then another day until it has all the blood flow it needs and your tendons are properly connected. That is very fast." She looked toward the robo-doc and said, "Feel free to jump in doctor, if I miss anything." He looked content to listen. "It appears that they have made great strides in nanotechnology and stem cell incubation since your first surgery. You should be up and moving in about three days. You will be a bit weak, but the robo-doc has that covered as well. He has the bed running a whole-body muscle stimulation program and massages to help you heal."

Lauren said, "You are on fluids and bone replacement exciters. You won't need to eat for about another day. The doc says that you may drink some water to help with your throat's dryness. In the meantime, we suggest lots of rest to heal and to pass the time. We will be out in the kitchen, picking out more foods to try. So call us if you need anything."

The next two days dragged on. Each day I was stronger, but I was still unable to move as much as I hoped. To fill the hours, I watched some old realviews that were in the media library. To the girls' surprise and joy, we found **Millennium Seekers**, the realview that got Jessica and Lauren so interested in technology as teenagers. Armed with brownies and milk, we sat together in my room for my grand premier showing. Lauren and Jessica sat in their orange and yellow chairs and I in my bed.

Because they loved it, I wanted to love it. Not far into the story, I would have settled for liking it. It was contrived, overacted, wooden, and unrealistic, making it an unintentional comedy. Flaws aside, I could see how some young people would find Chipper's character exciting. I was pleased to find that seeing

Mellina elicited no emotional response or flood of inappropriate memories. She was just a person I once knew in passing. Should I be worried about this?

Partway in, Jessica said, "Time has not been kind to this show."

Lauren agreed. "It's pretty bad...and I used to love it. I always thought Chipper was so mature and beautiful, she looks like she is barely twenty and still a kid."

"You are both much prettier and smarter than her." I hoped I hadn't overstepped. I could always blame the drugs. "Time and experience influence how we see things. Back then, **Millennium Seekers** resonated with something in your teen selves. I would say don't be too hard on it, as it helped you find your passions and made you who you are. Also, you have the added stress of wanting me to like it. There is no better way to kill your enjoyment than that...I almost brought up a painful story about me playing my album for my family."

Jessica nodded and with a smirk said, "I think I understand why it took Mellina two years to find work after this...and it wasn't because of typecasting."

Lauren chuckled and said, "Can you believe she used a Hawkleve to break the encryption on the bomb? The writers certainly were not techs."

"I loved the extra lights they added to make it more futuristic," added Jessica.

We ended up laughing at the realview and having a good time. Sometimes our cherished childhood memories are best left alone.

Speaking of best left alone, I had the unpleasant experience of hearing my songs from **Songs from my Heart** being played too loudly from the living room. I was sure Curtis made certain that it was in the media library. One of the many problems with that album was that most of the songs originated not from my heart but from a location about eighteen inches lower. It was embarrassing to hear how shallow and stupid I was.

My favorite bad review was, "Rolland Newcastle's music is an infantile, sugary overload. It forces the listeners to 'take candy from a baby.'" Hearing the album now, I had to agree with that review. I had been an immature baby, forcing people to listen to bad, overproduced, candied music.

Lauren popped in with a joyous smile on her face, asking if I wanted to get up and dance. Even if I could have stood up, I had my fingers in my ears and was pretending not to hear her.

"I can send the realview to your room for your viewing pleasure," she said with a helpful smile.

"Watching a younger version of me belting out a lame song from **Songs from my Heart** would bring no one any pleasure, other than you. May I remind you that New Jerusalem has some strict rules against torture."

"And the courts still haven't brought you to justice for it either."

"Touché. Hugo? Please destroy the media files for **Songs from my Heart.**"

Lauren was unfazed. "I have backups."

"Of course you do. Hugo, scratch that. Rescind all brownie rights for Lauren or Jessica if they continue to play, or in any way cause the playing of, and in any form or parody, any of the music or video from **Songs from my Heart.**"

Lauren's face froze, and she studied my face. "Realview, stop playback." Blessed silence. She leaned in close, her face stern, and said, "Just know that this will go against you in your court case for torture." She winked.

Nodding, I said, "Duly noted."

Later that afternoon, she and Jessica sat at the foot of my bed, innocently savoring brownies. I didn't say anything about it, as I tried to pretend I didn't find it funny. They are adorable stinkers.

It was difficult to wait, unaware of what was going on in the outside world. To play it safe, we decided it was best to avoid pulling in any outside data streams. This left us time to talk and to prototype ideas with the 3D replicators.

The bed, the robo-doctor, and Hugo took care of my hygiene needs. They cleaned and even shaved me. My hair was washed in an interesting massaging head sphere that had micro cleaner brushes that delivered moisture and soap at the base of the scalp and massaged it. Sections of hair were washed and wiped outward, taking the soap away. It felt nice, and it dried and styled my hair as well. The bed pampered me, giving good massages. Despite this, I was becoming anxious, and I wanted to get up soon and get moving.

Lauren had offered to reprogram the hair machine and barber "for something different." There was too much levity in her request, so I declined her kind offer. We had to get her out of there before her sense of humor was released on us all. Jessica was showing similar signs of ornery merriment. She was just quieter and potentially more devious. That scared me.

By the third day, I was able to get up and put weight on my new lower leg. It was a bit sore, but I felt much better. My plan was to surprise the ladies and come out to the common areas to join them for a meal. After getting cleaned up, I came out to find Lauren and Jessica covered in sweat in the middle of a grueling realview exercise class. As they were wearing form-fitting exercise clothing, I excused myself and headed back to my room to give them some privacy.

From behind me, Lauren huffed out, "Sorry, Rolland. We thought we had time to squeeze in a workout before seeing you today."

"No problem," I said over my shoulder, fighting the urge to turn around and stare.

"We'll be done here in about five minutes and showered and out in thirty. We have to...keep fit to be able to run," said Jessica, out of breath.

"And fight," added Lauren.

"Have fun. See you in about an hour," I said.

I didn't need to exercise as I was getting muscle stimulation and strength-building programs as part of my recuperation. Without them, I would be about as useful as I was with Lazarus when trouble came.

About an hour later, I came out and found that the ladies had been busy. The realview setting was that of a bright desert. I walked down a brick road to a rustic, brick-walled cabana that overlooked an endless yellow-white desert under a sparkling blue sky. In the cool shade afforded by a large white canopy, Lauren and Jessica lounged in flowing white dresses on the yellow and orange chairs from our living room. They waved to me, as if that were needed to get my attention. Coming around the front wall to join them, I saw they were sitting across from one of the white couches, sipping drinks, looking stunning and peaceful.

Eying them carefully, I moved to sit on the couch. "If you pull out a coat of many colors and call me Joseph, I am running."

Lauren laughed, her eyes flashing. "I hadn't thought of that. Can you give me about ten minutes with the robo-tailor? Relax, Rolland. We figured that you have been cramped up in your room for a few days, a wide-open view would probably be appreciated."

Jessica smiled demurely, setting down a curved, clear glass of tea and said, "What better way to serve Turkish but in an outdoor cantina in the desert." She waved her hand over the startling vista before us. "Of course, you can have anything that you want to eat. We found this realview location, and we thought it was quite beautiful."

A gecko wandered past us in no hurry. Hearing a noise, I turned to see Hugo dressed in some fanciful ancient desert garb. It was fun, even if his six arms and uni-ball base broke the illusion.

We ate shish kabobs, roasted vegetables, rice, flatbread, and hummus as we drank hot tea and soaked in the feel of the desert. The women had kept the heat of the air down to moderate levels, making it a fine experience rather than a painful way to test our tolerance to heat stroke and dehydration.

This was another bit of proof that Jessica and Lauren were enjoying our stay. Good for them. They deserved some fun after our last few days. I studied them as they ate and spoke. Lauren seemed the most changed, lighter in her mood. It seemed cruel to pull them out of this enchanted world. Without saying it, though, we all knew that this had to end. Those who were hunting us had not given up, and I would bet that they were even more desperate. How much longer did we have before they found us or started some bigger action? All I knew was that I needed to heal faster.

14

Forgiveness, Trust and Healing

●●● ▬ ▬ ▬ ●●●

We had finished the evening meal and were lounging in the living room to allow me to extend my leg on the couch. Jessica and Lauren were relaxing in the orange and yellow chairs, which had been placed next to each other to save me from having to keep turning my head to speak with them. Ottomans supported their legs. The two young women appeared to be happy and comfortable.

The room was lit for evening, and a realview of the Maurohaa mountain range filled our view. As this was one of the highest and coldest locations on the planet, I appreciated that they had chosen a view from a nice cozy lodge.

The realview room was an inviting mix of natural stone and wood surrounded by floor-to-ceiling glass exterior walls. An old-fashioned stone fireplace was inconsistently yet delightfully radiating heat from the crackling fire. A wall of cool air brushed past my right shoulder, contrasting with the fire that warmed my front and face. Shivering, I found the extremes exciting as I leaned in closer to the fire. This is what life must have been like three or four hundred years ago, when there were unintentional warm and cold sections in a room. As the faint scent of burning wood wafted by, I savored a hot mug of cocoa that was nicely warming my hands. Outside, palm-sized snowflakes were gently falling. It was beautiful and serene. The snow should have consisted of tiny flakes due to the cold, dry, and brutal wind. None of that mattered; I was enjoying the show.

The ladies were relaxed. Hearing them laugh helped alleviate some of my guilt about my disruptive entrance.

"Lauren, may I ask a question?" I said.

Jessica feigned surprise. "Oh-oh. This is how it started three nights ago." She let slip a mischievous grin.

Taking a pause, I measured my question. "What I am referring to is how much your spirit has lightened in the last few days. I mean, the night of my surgery, I had stepped in it."

Jessica leaned forward in her orange chair, waiting for a response from her sister. Her ottoman slid back under her chair, letting her feet drop to the floor.

Lauren mused, trying to put together the words. "Well, you know how it is with God. The truths are simple, but the path is often complex. I am trying to think how to explain it. First, it is not about you. Sure, what you said angered me—no, please stop before you start apologizing again. But you meant it as a compliment. Sometimes God has to dredge up the deep, hidden, and hurtful memories and point out our unforgiveness before He can begin to heal us." Lauren stopped in thought. "I think I will have some more hot chocolate. Do you guys want anything?"

"I'm good," I said.

Jessica shook her head, and the robo-chef began preparing Lauren's cocoa. A minute or so later, Hugo brought over her drink order.

"Thanks, Hugo." He nodded and left to return to the kitchen. Lauren's face was serious as she took a sip and leaned back, trying to avoid spilling her hot drink. "Your well-intentioned statements brought up my buried feelings about Marcolo, which I thought I had dealt with a few years ago. All that junk had fes-tered and was rotting me on the inside. While I was soaking in the tub, God revealed to me my unforgiveness and resentment, and I saw that I had to let go of them so He could heal me. Unforgiveness doesn't hurt the other person in the slightest, but it makes you a slave to that resentment and anger, and that will continue to destroy you until you repent of it and hand it to God."

Lauren removed her left hand from her cup and pointed to my leg. "Your surgery required your leg to be opened, and all that stuff that we didn't want to be in there had to be removed. It was painful, I am sure. And I am also sure that you didn't want to do it, but it had to be done."

"Or it would continue to lead them to us, and that would get us all killed," I said, agreeing.

Lauren said, "Right. I too was rotting and dying, living in bondage to that memory. The thought of Marcolo, off having fun with his starlet-wannabe, with no repercussions for what he had done to me, was eating me alive. Jessica told me that she re-peated to you his comments about my looks and my needing some major work done."

I tightened up, clenching my fists, fighting an outburst. "That was stupid and terrible, and he was just plain wrong. You are beautiful and perfect as God made you."

"Well, thanks. I agree that what Marcolo said was unneces-sary, especially after he had already ripped out my heart. Then, when I heard that they were married, that hurt, because I thought she had gotten what I was supposed to have."

She could see that I was ramping up and headed it off by raising her hand to calm me. "Yes, I know, you can relax. I am good now. At that time, I thought he was the man I wanted, so I developed all kinds of horrible scenarios where I would win him back and then dump him for revenge."

Jessica interrupted with a sharp release of air. "That only works in silly romantic comedies. The problem there is that you end up marrying your best friend or an alien or something stupid like that. In real life, it never works out."

Lauren smirked at Jessica. "No. You are right, it doesn't. And seeing that you have been my best friend, Jess, marrying you would bring up another set of other issues."

Jessica just grinned, nodding emphatically.

"Besides, that was just a passing childish thought," said Lauren.

"The marriage thing?" asked Jessica. "Good thing too. You aren't my type at all."

Lauren frowned and shook her head. "You are such a doofus."

Scowling, I said, "All joking aside, this Marcolo guy sounds like a complete fool. Based on what I have heard, I wouldn't trust him if he told me that the room lights were on."

Lauren chuckled. "It is funny how we can hold on to someone else's twisted opinion of us when we wouldn't trust their judgment on anything else. Yet I did, and I wallowed in it as a reason to continue to live in my bitterness and anger."

Lauren brushed a strand of dark hair from her face. "This is not about him. It is about how I responded to what I perceived as a gross injustice directed against me. I am thrilled that I didn't marry him. That would have been a huge and painful mistake. I have repented of my anger and unforgiveness, and I have given all that to the Lord, for He is the judge and He passes sentence and repays evil.

"He revealed to me that in my anger and bitterness, I had been applying the same judgment to all men that I felt for Marcolo. It was sucking all the joy and happiness from me. But when I acknowledged it and repented, choosing to give that junk up, the Lord healed me. I mean, *bam!* I was free of that weight. I know that sounds as if it comes from some bad realview. I would find it hard to believe if someone told me that happened to them, but it really happened to me. Honestly. There was a wild effervescence that swept through me from head to toe."

Jessica said, "That could have been your tub's massaging jets." Lauren frowned at her sister, and Jessica laughed. "Relax, Lauren, it is quite evident that something has changed. It's not that 'turn that frown upside down' kind of psychobabble that people spew. You are just lighter, don't you think, Rolland?"

"It's obvious that I do, or I wouldn't have risked asking about it. I can see that something amazing has happened to you. I understand it, as I have been there as well."

"Oh? Do tell," said Lauren, scooting forward in her chair, eagerly waiting.

She reached to set down her mug, and a small table slipped out from the side of her yellow chair to meet her drink. Measuring the contents, it signaled Hugo, who came over to pick up the empty mug.

Hugo said, "Lauren, did you wish to have another beverage—more hot chocolate, tea, coffee? I can project other options for you to choose from."

"I am thinking about it. I'll let you know, Hugo."

"Do I get my first post-op beer?" My mouth and throat were dry even after drinking the cocoa.

Jessica called out, "What do you think, doc?"

The robo-doctor glided into the room and shook his head. "Not until tomorrow." It was a bit creepy that the robo-doctor was always listening. At least he was not coming to sit and join our conversations. Could he even sit?

Jessica said, "You heard the doc. How about another mango lassi? I have been enjoying those."

Lauren smacked her lips happily. "Make it a round of them—and some nice chewy chocolate chip cookies." We heard Hugo moving into action.

"I wonder how they will taste with the mango lassi?" I said, unsure of the blending.

Lauren sat back and said, "No better way to find out, right? So what happened?"

"Obviously you know all about the accident with the autowalk when I was seventeen." I pointed to my left leg that was extended on the couch. "I was angry at God for letting it kill and hurt all those innocent people, and most of all, I was even angrier with God that He let it happen to me. It was then that I made a vow that if God couldn't or wouldn't protect me, I would do it myself. Despite being told my whole life that God loved me, I didn't think God really cared for me. He seemed distant and disinterested in me at best. I grew up being told that I was His vessel, but I felt I was a vessel that God was using as his toilet."

Jessica shook her head in utter disbelief. "Really? I know you said it was lonely and that you couldn't trust anyone, but you have had everything you could ever want—loads of money, power, fame, and lots of beautiful women. That is exactly what most people would see as a dream life. How could you see that as being, to use a kinder phrase, dumped on by God?"

Hugo glided over to hand each of us a cold, frothy glass. Thanking him, I took a sip and continued, "Oh, that is good.

Thanks, Hugo." He smiled and nodded as he went back to the kitchen. "Yeah, it all looks so glamorous on the newsblasts and in the realviews. All the big parties filled with all the perfect, fake, smiley people. That would make them PerFake, wouldn't it? I just came up with that." I laughed.

Lauren shrugged, unimpressed. "Yeah—so, wasn't it ever fun, or are you trying to tell us that secretly you were like someone eating sour pickles the whole time?"

"No. Of course not. There were many times that it was great fun. Most of us love to get positive attention because it feeds your ego. Without God, though, it is all completely empty. You sit there surrounded by everything or everybody that should make you happy, and you think, 'Is this all there is?' Have you ever eaten so many sweets that no matter how great they tasted, your body is sickened by the thought of eating more and demands real food?"

"Sure." Lauren nodded and paused for effect. "You do realize that there are several simple treatments for blocking the addictive nature of sugar."

A few hundred years ago, sugar was the legally addictive substance that was used to drive up sales. Studies found that it was eight times more addictive than some of the worst street drugs. Hiding under the guise of several public rights groups, the pro-sugar industries sued to block the use of sugar addiction blockers, claiming those therapies took away consumer's ability to self-regulate and choose for themselves, which was funny, as that is what most addictions do.

There was the inevitable battle of fake science, covertly funded "consumer groups," fear-spreading media campaigns, lawsuits, and releases of new addictive sugar variants that "by sheer chance" were not affected by the treatments. Science was so warped by this mess that people started "going with their gut," which led to a mess.

The government could no longer overlook the long-term public health crisis and costs caused by sugar addiction. After many protracted years of court wrangling, the World Courts finally got sugar listed as a Schedule One addictive substance. This required industries that added sugar to their products to offer brain resets and sugar addiction restrictors to the public free of charge.

The outcome: Sugar added "for flavor" started disappearing. People still enjoyed sugar in smaller portions. The health of the public got better, and medical costs dropped. Producers became sneakier, which led to every product being routinely tested, and fines and sanctions became more aggressive to dissuade such actions. The sneaky and convoluted ways that industries have tried to beat these regulations could be a story in itself.

"I am sure Rolland knows about sugar addiction therapies." Jessica squinted, staring at her sister. "I wonder if there is a brain blocker to stop incessant teasing. Please go on, Rolland." Lauren twirled her finger, indicating that I should continue.

"When my family started dying, the newsblasters hunted me without mercy. They asked insightful questions like, 'Are you upset that your family has died?' hoping that I would explode in some rating-grabbing way. For the most part, I pulled back and hid, becoming even more untrusting of everyone, especially God."

Blinking to clear my eyes, I said, "My problem was that I was a Christian who did not have the proper foundation to deal with the inevitable storms that come to everyone, regardless of their position or wealth. There is deep and searing pain in life, and no one gets a pass from it."

Eyes questioning, Lauren said, "Was this when you went through your wild phase?"

"It certainly helped start it. First came my parents' deaths, and for the record, I still don't accept that as an accident. Then my brother Paul and my sister Mary died. That really destroyed me. I was very close to Paul. He was there for me after our parents died and then to help me navigate all the problems and stresses that instant celebrity brings."

Paul was a little over four years older than me, and he had been the first big celebrity in our family. The media had followed some of my older brothers and sisters with interest, but when he showed up, the media and public went wild for him. He was suave, handsome, and deeply kind. There was something special and electric that effortlessly radiated from him.

Jessica's face was pinched and distraught. "I had a major crush on Paul." She swallowed hard and looked off into the distant realview mountains. In a voice just loud enough for us to hear, she said, "Even though I never met him, it still hurts to think about him being gone."

The sadness on her face was one I understood far too well. "For me, too, Jessica. My heart is still raw from both of their deaths. He was even more gracious and cool in person. I think he would have really liked you. And you too, Lauren. I wish we all had the chance to see him again," I said, fighting back the tears.

Jessica gave a wounded smile and nodded, trying not to cry. I meant every word of it.

"You would have liked Mary as well. She was quite a character, and she was very funny. We had our ups and downs, but she was easygoing if you were living as she expected you to."

"Which you were not?" inquired Lauren.

"No, I wasn't. My brother Timothy said some of our head-butting may have been because she felt that she was set to be the next big celebrity in our family, and then I showed up at that party, acting the wild fool. It is hard to say."

Lauren's face was deep in thought. "Mary was beautiful. I always wondered why the newsblasters didn't chase after her."

"It's because she was always doing what was right and proper. She was the perfect dinner guest—elegant, engaging, and witty, with perfect posture and poise. Those are great qualities to be sure, but they don't make for exciting newsblasts. They love mayhem and salacious stories. At sixteen, I showed up at my first big gala and got caught kissing a twenty-year-old, engaged supermodel."

"You left out her two supermodel friends too," helped Lauren.

"Ah, yes." It was a big story back then, and it was what vaulted me into faux fame. "It really wasn't quite as wild as they made it out to be. Should I stop about this, or should I tell you about how God healed me?"

"I want to hear both. First, finish this story about how you believe that the media misunderstood your mega-hot babe make-out fest," said Lauren.

Jessica nodded in agreement.

"I didn't know anyone at the party, so Paul introduced me to them. He had this ease about him that allowed him to bring people of different backgrounds together and to get them to talk. As hard as it may be to believe, I was shy and especially around attractive girls. These weren't girls either. They were grown women who had been in the fashion industry for a few years. We couldn't have been in much more different places in our lives. For some reason, maybe to shock the kid, they were talking about kissing, and they asked me who had given me my favorite kiss, and I said that I had no reference as I had never been kissed. They said something like it was important for me to have a sampling as a future reference point. That is when I got my first kisses and also, more importantly, when I found out that even the distant corners of these events are realviewed because that is where people go to have secret moments."

"Wow, that is amazing. That is exactly how it happened with me," said Lauren, with her eyes open in surprise.

"Really?

"No. Not even close. Billions of us have seen that realview too many times to count. Frankly, it was impossible to miss it for years after it happened, even if you tried. It looked like a group of pretty stick insects were taking turns trying to eat the same teenager, lips first."

Ouch. "I hadn't gotten my full height yet."

"That is not my point." Lauren radiated frustration; with considerable effort, she softened. "Look, I am sorry. In my anger I made it sound as if I were blaming you for what happened. I am not. I am mad at those women. You were the only innocent party in that whole mess. Paul should have guarded you better, but he walked you over, and he handed you over to hungry carnivores."

I studied her face, unsure of how to react. "I am not sure I understand. Paul did his best, and I cannot claim that I didn't want to do it. It was kind of a dream situation for a sixteen-year-old boy."

"And that should have stayed a dream until you got to be older. Your first kiss should have been something private and extraordinary, just between you and someone special in your life, maybe a bit fumbly and awkward in how it happened, not something that was turned into a twisted stage spectacle by those seeking fame."

My face felt warm, indicating that I might have been blushing.

"No, Rolland. Relax, you did nothing wrong. Let me explain, because I sense that you may still be holding some guilt about your part in this. Your table was not hidden away as you seem to remember, and the whole 'spontaneous' and 'innocent' kiss competition was an intentional shock and awe campaign that was carefully designed to get them noticed by the newsblasters. They planned to use that notoriety to launch their careers into the top tier of modeling. Sadly, their ploy worked."

I was about to defend the ladies when Lauren held up her hand, signaling for me to stop. "Please let me finish. I can see that you are going to go all noble, and that isn't going to help you heal. You were a perfect candidate because of your age, your family's fame, money, and influence, and especially because of the similarities that you had to your dashing older brother. They solidly cast your future media image right there, and they didn't care how that would affect you as it suited their twisted needs right then. Modeling is an adult and ruthless industry for humans, and they are always fighting for notice against ageless biosynths, which can be made to fit any order or style.

"Remember Bliiondii and the shock and uproar when she turned out to be a biosynth? Before her, they said that biosynths lacked that deeper glint of humanity in their eyes and that special something in their movements. These women decided that they had to do something wild and risqué to get noticed, and that was you. And what they did to you was child abuse. Imagine if it had been three male models of their same ages and an innocent sixteen-year-old girl at that event...I imagine there would have been quite a different outcry."

Jessica said, "Maybe not. Our society loves beautiful people. Had the girls or guys been average-looking, it would have been soundly condemned. You may be being a tad hard on them. Science supports that the brain is still developing into our early twenties and those with deficient or socially distorted upbringings may have a more difficult time making decisions that fit into what could be seen as the social norm. I cannot speak to their upbringing or teen years, but it would not be hard to believe that these women may have fit into one or more of those categories."

Nodding in agreement, I said, "I give them some grace on this. Those of us who live in the light of fame are indoctrinated from early on into believing that the same rules do not apply to us. We get away with bad behavior because of who we are—well, rather, how important we are told that we are."

Lauren frowned and said, "Maybe, but you didn't stay that way. I haven't heard much good about them to believe that they are not still behaving as they did. And before that incident, they were not famous or in demand for their modeling; in fact, they were getting old by modeling standards, so they had no good excuse."

I sighed deeply. "I can see your point. In hindsight, it doesn't seem as impromptu as I remembered it to be. Whatever their plan, I will choose to forgive them, as they likely got a payback for their show that was far more painful and destructive than they would ever have expected. As I said, fame is cool at first, and in mere days it can downright suck. Once you are out of the spotlight and you want to stay in it, there is a horrible withdrawal, especially if your income is based on being famous. How many times do you see people who were once big stars attempting to do something spectacular to get noticed again? That usually comes off as sad and desperate, which is pretty much the case. The fact that I am different and not living as a self-centered jerk is all because of God. Believe me, I fought hard against Him, trying to stay stupid."

Lauren smiled. "I am so glad that this Rolland is here and not the old Rolland. He wasn't all bad, but you have grown up into a nice man."

"Thank you. That really means a lot to me."

Lauren crossed her arms as if to finalize her point. "Good. That is why I am stressing this. It is important to understand the nature of it and not see it as your failing or your fault. I am sorry that it happened to you, especially with all the pain that was going on in your life at the time."

Ruminating on it, I said, "I have had mixed emotions about that night since it happened. That whole event was a turning point for me and my family and not necessarily a good one. After it happened, I was too immature to know not to feed the wild and insatiable newsblast machine."

Irritated, Lauren unfolded her arms and sat bolt upright in her chair. "That is exactly why your family should have stepped in and wrung the necks of those involved and got you some help for you to heal. Instead, it looked like they encouraged you to dive in."

"I had just lost my parents. I am not sure anyone could have reached me in my pain. Paul, Timothy, and Mary tried, but after eighteen, I was considered an adult, and I had unfettered access to much of my inheritance, so I was able to do as I wished. All my brothers and sisters were dealing with their own issues and pain. Again, I thank you for what you have said. I will have to pray more on this and for God's healing."

"I am so sorry, too, Rolland. I cannot imagine the horrible push and pull of your early life. I am not sure that I would have done any better." Jessica briefly chewed on her lower lip. "There is something that has bothered me for years. You don't have to tell me, and we can drop it if it is too painful, but did Paul and Mary really die hunting goliaths in a two-seater pulsorjet?"

My face grew pinched. "No, they didn't die that way. Sorry, Jessica. I am not mad at you for asking this. Their explanation was a complete load of junk, and we couldn't prove it. They claimed that they were out hunting goliaths in the Great Naritu Plains in a tiny, two-seat Raptor. The biggest problem that I have with this story—and it was not common knowledge—but Paul was deathly afraid of flying. He did it rarely and only if he could not avoid it. He always went as a passenger, lightly sedated, and where he couldn't look out the windows.

"Mary, well, how do I explain this? It would be a gross understatement to say that she was morally opposed to any kind of hunting for sport. Besides all that, no one in their right mind would ever think of hunting even a single goliath by themselves, especially not in a ground-hugging Raptor. I don't care how big the cannons you could put on one of those ships might have been…goliaths are so fast, huge, and mean that it boggles the mind. Paul and Mary were sharp, and they didn't have a death wish. There are many much nicer ways to die than that."

Jessica nodded. "The explanation we heard never seemed right to me. I appreciate your willingness to talk about it. I know it is very painful."

After taking another sip of the mango lassi, I said, "It is nice to have someone you trust to share things with. It helps in the healing. As I said, I am alone a great deal, and that is not good. It is like hiding in a cave to protect yourself from the pain in life. At first, it seems like a good idea, but the air gets stale, and you are unable to feel anything outside the cave, and that separates you from everyone that matters. You begin to fixate on your problems, sadness, and disappointments. When you cry out, the call keeps echoing back. It becomes magnified until it's all you hear. We are to live a Christian walk, and that requires getting out and facing the world. You cannot walk when you are hunkered down, hiding in a tight cave."

Jessica and Lauren replied, "Amen."

"So, I guess now is a good time to tell you about how I came back to the Lord. It is complex. Essentially, after all this stuff had happened, I put the ultimate blame on God. I felt that if He controls the universe, and if He really loved me as they say He does, then He should never allow bad things to happen to me or those whom I love. Angry, hurt, and feeling betrayed, I turned my back on God. If He didn't care for me, then I wouldn't live for Him, only for myself.

"Nearly dying made me realize that I hadn't yet lived. So with youthful aplomb and indiscretion, I ventured out to explore all that I could. I know now that I was merely masking my raging loss and gaping emptiness with lots of wild parties, beautiful women, flashy pulsorjets, and bigger, fancier stuff. I am sure you have seen the realviews. I am thankful to God that I never got into drugs, but I drank enough to be stupid and dull the pain. My addictions took over as I tried to fill my God-sized hole with everything but what can fill it, which is God. I still resented Him and was bitter."

Lifting my leg and easing it to the floor, I wiggled my toes. The smell of the cookies baking in the fast oven was filling the room, and even though I had just eaten, the smell was heavenly. "I watched my family dying off in freak accidents that could not just happen to any family that was not under God's curse. People told me that it was all a bunch of sad coincidences and that I was being paranoid for no reason. Tired of this accusation, I ran the numbers, and there was statistically absolutely no chance of it being a bunch of weird coincidences."

"Is that when you went to the EPGB for help?" asked Jessica, setting her glass down on the arm tray that slid out to meet it.

The smell of the cookies was permeating the apartment, making it hard to concentrate. Hugo pulled out the tray and put it into the rapid cooler.

Hugo said, "Do you want the cookies to be hot, warm, or room temperature?"

"Warm," called out Jessica.

"Warm for me too," said Lauren.

"For me as well," I said.

The rapid cooler gave a pleasant little ding, indicating that the cookies were down to the proper level for eating. Hugo brought them over with a smile, and we thanked him.

Taking a bite of a cookie and sipping some of the mango lassi, I savored the combination.

"They are not bad together. Not quite as good as milk, but it will do. To get back to your question, Jessica."

"My question?" responded Jessica who was covering her mouth with her hand after having taken a full bite of her cookie. She stopped and analyzed the oozing morsel approvingly. "Oh, those are good."

"You asked if that was when I went to the EPGB for help. Actually, I went to the World Congress after I couldn't get anyone else to listen to me and to start an inquest. When they patted me on the back and did nothing, that is when I went to the Earth Planetary Governing Board. I am sure you know the rest of that." They nodded. "It did help put some safeguards in place for Remnants but apparently not enough." Motioning to the room, I said, "I still didn't trust my fellow man." I took another sip. "It wasn't long after that that I came back to the Lord."

"What happened?" asked Lauren, scooting forward in her chair, holding her glass on her knees.

"It wasn't a crash and burn, though that was coming. I was about twenty-six years old, and I was visiting my sister Martha's house. Neither of us was living for the Lord, so it was a good place for me to hang out, because there was no pressure as I got from my brothers who were back in the walk. I don't even remember the cause, but I was angry about everything and nothing. In my desperation and frustration, I angrily cried out, 'I don't trust you, God. And I don't know if I can continue to follow you.'

"It hit me. I hadn't been following him at all for over eight years, so that wasn't much of a threat. It might sound silly, but that took me by surprise, and it shook me. I was acting like a spoiled child, expecting God to be my servant and to work on my timelines and in a way that I expected Him to act."

Jessica stated, "He is the God of the wild country. He cannot be tamed, controlled, or quantified. He is outside of time, and He is God."

"Amen. He is that. Even with my realization concerning my bad behavior, I still didn't stop with my temper tantrum. I told Martha that I was angry with God for taking Paul and Mary and our parents. I said that because if God was good as He claimed to be, then He could have done something to prevent it from happening, and He didn't. And that, I reasoned, told me that He was ultimately complicit in all the world's evil by allowing it to happen. I said that God was therefore either grossly incompetent or evil himself."

"Whoa!" said Lauren in surprise.

Jessica froze, her eyes glued on me.

"Yeah, that's really bad. But that was what was in my heart. It was not like God didn't know what I felt or that He *was* shocked by it. He was the one bringing it to the surface. It was ugly, and it made me sick to say it, but I was having it out with God, and I hated Him—here's where it may sound weird, but God gave me a vision. It was not a dream or some hallucination. I had my eyes open, and I was seeing it as if it were superimposed over my normal sight. Calmness came over me, and I spoke out what I was seeing to Martha. I knelt down beside her where she sat, and I began crying as I spoke. I was overcome with the sheer power and beauty of the vision."

Revisiting this event, my eyes were welling up. "In the vision, I was standing on the Mountain of God. I don't know how I knew this, but I did. The light and air were so pure and clean that I have never felt or seen anything similar in all my travels, ever. I could make out that there was a steep drop-off before me, though I never worried about falling down it. I saw the white rock and delicate moss on the ground in precise, ultra-sharp detail. The colors, light, and air were far more vivid and real than our daily life. It was as if we are living in a faint, washed-out shadow of that real world.

"I became a young boy, and I looked up and saw Jesus stand-ing next to me. I just knew it was Him. I can't really describe Him...he had a beard and longish dark hair. But it was his eyes and the expression on His face that were so beautiful. He placed a gentle hand on my shoulder, claiming me as His own. He had the most incredible look of love, acceptance, affirmation, and kindness that instantly healed so much that was broken in me. There are no words to explain it.

"He removed the spirit of cynicism and the spirit of perver-sion of authority from me, where I saw all authority as evil and twisted. Then He revealed before me a fresh, clean, and new stone foundation laid down in the rocky mountain soil that I knew was my new foundation in Him. Then I was a man again. A silver tree appeared behind me, not made of silver, just silver in color. I leaned back against it, and a table was set before me as in Psalm 23 where it is written, 'You prepare a table before me in the presence of my enemies.' I didn't see the food on it, but that didn't matter.

"God did what biblically is called 'removing the scales from my eyes,' revealing that I believed the accuser, who had been blaming God for all his evil, and I had willingly believed him. It was the devil or his demons who were punching me from behind, and when I turned to see who had struck me, they would say something like, 'Wow. Did you see what God did? He just socked you. He is being such an enormous jerk to you.' This fit in with what I believed was happening, so I foolishly took the devil's word on it. There is a massive and bloody war going on, and while we know that God wins this war, it is foolish to expect that we will not come under fire or be hurt in it."

I was emotional, and tears were welling in my eyes as I continued, "After it was done, I had a deeper calmness, a peace, and quiet that I had never experienced before. All the noise that normally flooded my head was gone. There were no more of the constant barrages of flashing images, sounds, or thoughts. It was like I had never seen the world before. I truly saw everything with new eyes. I mean, I knew that something was a chair or a light, but it was as if I was seeing it for the first time. I had to ask God to show me how I was to see the world and how I was to live in it. Martha was sitting there, softly sobbing. Her face was radiant. Somehow my explaining it out loud moved her, or maybe God allowed her to see it too."

Jessica said, "Wow. That is amazing. This fits in with what God showed me a while back. It's not what was said, but who said it. The devil is the father of lies, so we do not need to listen to him and—it's more than that—we should never agree with those lies about who we are and whom we follow."

Lauren's face was filled with joy. "I tend to forget that God's words do not tear us down or destroy us. So if we hear accusations about ourselves or cutting, biting words, it is not of God, but the other guy—so, how long did this new feeling last?"

I sighed and shrugged. "Maybe two or three days with that same intensity. I have not been the same after that vision. When I woke the next day, I was still seeing the world in a totally new and fresh way. I took a pulsorjet out of the city, to be out on the grasslands around Heavensport, just to think and revel in the quietness of my mind and spirit. To my joy, the light and air had a similar feel to that I saw on the Mountain of God, and there was a pure and steady wind. It was the closest I had ever experienced God before or since. God did that for me so I wouldn't think it was just a dream or a story that I made up in my head. I still remember sitting on this large boulder that poked up above the tall, waving grass, enjoying the stillness of my mind and the unique experience of being new and spiritually clean and fresh.

"When I was walking back to the pulsorjet to head back to the city, I had a second vision of me walking, with all this black particulate matter blowing off me like granular dirt that could not stick to me anymore. I believe I was being shown all the years of lies and false beliefs that were being blown off me. While I am not looking at the world in the same way as I did those two days, the experience has changed me, and I have never been the same since. I still have to fight going back to my old worldview of years ago. That night I gave up all the worldly junk and came back to following the Lord. What is so cool is that Martha came back to the Lord that same evening as well.

"I have come to learn that you have to be at peace with whatever comes, saying, 'Even so.' Even when I have to put up with some suffering or loss, my God has that covered, and He will help me through it. He doesn't usually pull us out of trouble but through it. We tend to learn something and grow if there is a substantial struggle involved, or—and I wish it weren't so—with pain."

Jessica asked, "Have you been successful in keeping this 'even so' thinking in the midst of our current struggle?"

"Not as well as I should be. I am trying to get back to it. It is not easy, as we are almost wired to worry and fret, which adds nothing good to solving the problem. As sorry as I am to have pulled you both into this mess, having you two with me has helped me feel less isolated and alone. You give me hope, as the Lord put us together."

Lauren grinned. "I am glad. This certainly isn't how I imagined this week was going to go. All joking aside, I find when I allow myself to be inconvenienced and my schedule to be disrupted, that is when I have the most amazing adventures and where I am changed by God." Lauren gazed at me with her eyes wide. "May I ask, in the hover-taxi on the way here, I thought I saw something going on in your eyes."

Pausing, I nodded. "Yes, you did. That vow that I made, saying that I had to protect myself if the Lord wouldn't, has hindered my relationship with Him. I didn't trust Him, and you cannot have a relationship without trust—wait. I have to break that vow. In the Name of Jesus Christ, I break the vow of having to protect myself and the vow of self-protection now and forever more. I take back any rights that may have been assigned to the enemy, and they have no power over me any longer. I command this in Jesus' mighty name. Lord, please forgive my not trusting You. It is wrong. I turn my life back over to you completely, and I ask for your help in regaining my trust in You. Lord, I ask for a fresh in-filling of the Holy Spirit to heal and guide me and to seal off those entryways that the enemy has into me. This I ask in Jesus' mighty name. Amen."

"Amen," said Lauren and Jessica.

"It was in the taxi where I realized that I have filled my head with constant electronic noise because I didn't trust that God would speak to me or come to my rescue. I have claimed that I was too busy to sit still for a while without doing something else. Or I would do it lying in bed before I went to sleep. It kind of turns into, "God, I need to know you more—snore. Not a great relationship-builder, is it?"

I paused to swallow. "What it comes down to is that I just couldn't face that rejection if I were to be quiet and still, and the Lord didn't come to be with me. Fear has made me take control again. It is so frustrating that when you think you have gotten past something, it sometimes sneaks back in."

Jessica and Lauren were wiping their eyes. They understood.

Lauren said, "Take it to the extremes. What is the worst that would happen if you put yourself all out and God didn't show? Would you die or shrivel up?"

All kinds of horrible scenarios flashed before me. None were shattering beyond what I could bear. "No. It would suck and hurt terribly, but I would survive."

"Right. The enemy always tells us that whatever our fear is, even the act of looking at it is beyond what we could imagine or withstand. This effectively gives us two outcomes: if you were to die, then you are with the Lord, and there will be no suffering any longer, only eternity living in perfection with a kind, perfect, and loving God, so that is hardly a threat. The other outcome is surviving with that fear or pain. Dig deep into that and figure out the worst-case scenario. What is the ultimate pain that it could give? Even living a hundred years with it, as compared on the scale of eternity is almost a two-dimensional tiny little point. Yes, whatever your worst fear is, it would suck very badly. You would survive it, and after a point, you would remember that God is always with you whether you feel His presence or not. The enemy loves to keep you emotional and in bondage to fear; he is the one who lies and tells you that God doesn't care for you or will not come to your rescue. That jerk also doesn't want you to remember all the times that God has come to your rescue to help and heal you."

Jessica nodded and said, "God has come for you and protected you through all of this. He could have done nothing, and you would have died somewhere along the walking street in the market. You would have been just another sad, random attack by a drugged-up thug who was seeking your money and possessions. But He warned you, and you survived. He reminded you about the EMP and got you to use it before you would have died. Then Lazarus caught you as you were dying.

"He made you come into the store when probably anywhere else in Heavensport you would have died at the hands of a T-37a. It goes on and on, doesn't it, where God has come to protect you? Can you imagine the odds, out of nearly a billion people, that you would run into people with three hypergliders and a way to break through ella-glanse crystal?"

"Or an apartment thickly coated in Foamalast," I said, laughing.

Lauren lifted an eyebrow and added. "Also, you met two really amazing, smart, and beautiful women."

"Absolutely, to the 10th power, minimum," I said. Lauren stifled a laugh.

Jessica interrupted our banter. "Whatever you want to say, God has done a lot of healing here, and He has turned what was meant for bad into something good. I for one am glad to know you, Rolland."

"I agree, wholeheartedly," said Lauren.

"I feel the same about you both," I said, leaning back on the sofa with arms up and my fingers interlocked behind my head. "No matter what the other team says."

Lauren frowned. "The biggest marketing success ever was when the devil convinced mankind that he never existed. He convinced many of us that he and his demons were just scary fairy tales made up by primitive people to explain thunder or concepts that they didn't understand."

"So true," said Jessica.

Lauren leaned forward with her hands folded in her lap and said, "How can anyone expect to defend against an enemy if you refuse to believe that they even exist? That would make you look for other things to hold responsible for your problems, and you would try to treat the symptoms not what contributes to the cause. These jerks act as amplifiers on our natural urges and that cranks up the level of the problem. Whenever you hear 'It is just the way I am,' it is a lie to hide what is going on, to make it so that you don't seek to change the behavior. It is written that the angels were beyond number, and a third of them turned evil and became demons. A third of a number that is beyond numbering—that is huge."

I agreed. "And they are an eternal, powerful, and never ceasing enemy, who has no mercy whatsoever. Their primary purpose is to destroy us. They are horrible. Thankfully God is on our side, and He will provide and restore us—hey, that reminds me, there is something that has been bothering me."

Lauren giggled. "I am not sure that I want to know what that is." Jessica coughed out a short laugh.

I shook my head. "No, well, maybe. It's about the shop where we met. I wanted to tell you that I fully intend to pay for the damages to it, if we make it out alive."

Lauren stated, "When."

"Wow, she must have plans for that money," said Jessica, shooting a sharp look at her sister.

Lauren's head snapped to stare at Jessica. She sported a shocked expression. "No. I mean *when* we survive, not when will Rolland pay us. I am determined that we stay alive. The store was not important, Rolland. The day that we met, Jessica and I were thinking about closing the shop."

"I am not sure I understand."

Jessica said, "We had recently inherited it from our aunt. I am sure that you have wondered why we had an escape tunnel and enhanced security shutters."

I said, "That question has been nagging at me since we used them."

Jessica said, "She put those in due to the dangerous nature of her business."

Leaning forward, in a low voice I asked, "Was she an arms dealer?"

Lauren laughed and said, "Are you worried that someone is going to break in and arrest us? It wasn't illegal. She sold realview star memorabilia."

"The stuff I saw in the store? Realview keepsakes and that kind of pop stuff? That is dangerous?"

Jessica's expression was serious. "That low-end stuff that you saw in the store was just a front for the more exotic, one-of-a-kind items that she had for sale. She was famous in the industry for having access to some of the world's top stars' personal goods and finding those willing to pay the price to obtain them."

"Like what, a vehicle or a musical instrument?"

"Sometimes. Often the highest priced items were those personal items worn by the star—and how should I say it politely?—especially those that were not washed," said Jessica.

My face fell. "Really? Unwashed underwear and stuff like that?"

Lauren said, "And dresses, necklaces, socks, shoes, and swim-suits. Especially if there are realviews and DNA testing to back it up. Even their robo-partners are big in the market."

"Why would anyone want a used—?" I stopped. Oh, for the symbioid's memory and tactile playback of the event. "To relive the star's and robo partner's..."

Lauren raised her eyebrows, bemused by my difficulty in explaining the obvious. "Experiences. Yes. With the right gear, they can play it back from a first-person viewpoint, even with neural networking experience syncing, that kind of stuff."

"That is just gross."

I knew many of the biggest stars, and I didn't understand their appeal and especially not when it came to anyone wanting to buy their dirty private clothing. They stink just as badly as everyone else, even if they didn't want to believe it.

"I am glad that I never sold any of my old stuff."

"That is not what we heard, right, Jess?"

I almost choked.

Jessica nodded in agreement. "Not you in person, but it is the standard operating procedure to have someone from a star's team make the arrangements and deliver the goods. The stars get extra unicreds, and the buyer gets what they are seeking."

"I would never have authorized that. I certainly wouldn't do it for the money. I want to know who is selling my stuff and why. Whatever the reason behind it, I intend to stop it immediately." It never occurred to me that anyone would ever fixate on me in that way. It was somewhat flattering with a heavy dose of creepy at the same time. "So, do you remember any of my stuff that was sold and who brought it in? I guess it is even stranger to me that anyone would be stupid or crazy enough to want to buy it."

Lauren's eyes twinkled: "This is a very sick world that we live in, and people are clearly not making good decisions about who they should fixate on. Obviously, we do not have access to the store's records, though I think I remember my aunt saying that over the years she got some clothing, undergarments, and a ring."

"Years?" This was a surprise. "Wait, you said there was a ring? Was the band made of fiery ulananabite and with a large, square, bright blue and white colnathon stone in the middle?"

Lauren said. "I think so. Our aunt showed us a ring like that. Why?"

Taking a deep breath of air, I released it slowly. "Do you remember if it was a stylish woman, about six feet eleven inches tall, with bright red hair who brought it in?"

Lauren nodded. "Probably. We weren't there, but our aunt talked about her calling her 'The Red Tower.' She was the only person who met with her and knew her real name."

Jessica said, "Our aunt told us about her adventures when we went to dinner with her or when she came over. She was into this world, and she could talk to us about it, as we would never tell anyone. Some of the stories were rather funny."

"That description of the 'Red Tower' more than narrows it down for me. I will have to talk to my security team about my soon-to-be ex-stylist. She said that ring was lost or stolen. It is just a thing, but I don't appreciate that there was a side business selling my personal goods, especially the dirty ones. I would like to find out who bought my clothes so I can get them the psychological help they need."

It was weird to think that anyone would ever be interested in buying my undergarments. This was an uncomfortable revelation.

"So, selling this kind of stuff can be that dangerous? I mean enough to have it set up like a fortress? And just for the record, I am grateful for that."

"It is most decidedly dangerous. People take their favorite stars very seriously. That is why the shop had all that security and we carried that pistol." Jessica's face became drawn and sad. "Maybe you heard a few months back about the death of Lorlee Thornton?"

"Yes."

"She was a close family friend whom we called our aunt when we were growing up. The shop where you first met Lauren was Lorlee's shop."

"I am so sorry. That was a truly tragic event."

The sad story of Lorlee Thornton had caused quite a stir. While I had never used her services—well, up to that day, I didn't think I had—it was not uncommon that famous people wanted to dispose of their more personal property to make a few extra unicreds. In their aunt's case, an irate fan had brutally murdered Ms. Thornton in her shop when she told the young man that she was not interested in buying any of the pop star Ochin Harashaw's clothing. He persisted in his sales attempts, asking for enormous sums of cash for the goods. The leaked surveillance realview showed an irritated Ms. Thornton telling him that Ochin was 'a poorly manufactured and soon-to-be-forgotten third-tier starlet,' and she only purchased and sold major stars' items. Those were her last words. It was terrible and senseless. The murderer saw his act as justified, as he was defending the honor of Ms. Harashaw. Later, they found that he had stolen the clothing from the starlet. Some honoring.

The day I showed up was the first day that Lauren and Jessica had reopened the store after their aunt's death as a way to honor *her* memory. Neither of them had any interest in keeping the business going. That explained Lauren's less-than-exuberant face when we met. Their test lasted less than a day before the shop was destroyed. God apparently wanted them out of the business.

Jessica said, "As she was an aunt-by-choice, that is one reason we thought it would take longer for them to find our connection to the store."

Lauren nodded. "That and the convoluted ownership trail that she hid through various corporations and trusts. She carefully cultivated the perception that she lived like a spy. Her clients liked this extra privacy, though she mostly did it to protect her own privacy and to hide where she lived. There were lots of unsavory competitors and collectors looking to make a score off of her."

Lorlee "the spy" had saved us, and I was thankful for her paranoia.

We spoke for about a half an hour longer as we finished the cookies and drinks. I called it a night, as I was still fatigued and drained.

●●● ━ ━ ━ ●●●

15

Dealing with Darkness

●●● ▬ ▬ ▬ ●●●

The screen popped up signaling an important call, and the silver-haired woman answered it. Colonel Haas greeted her, saluting sharply, "Ma'am, I think we have had a break."

"Yes, Colonel?"

"The crash site was not where a Phantom went down. It had some parts from a Phantom pulsorjet, but the rep said that the surrounding area had no Phantom signature chips."

"I am not familiar with these chips. Please explain."

"Yes, ma'am. They aren't well known. These are microscopic ID chips that are built into some high-end ships and Phantom's products. They are used to measure impact forces and damage in just this type of catastrophic event. A crash of this magnitude would have scattered millions of these IDs over a large area, and investigators would have used those patterns and other information from the chips to help them understand the crash site.

"The government crash team at the site claimed that everything else was destroyed in the explosion or had been already taken away for processing. The rep definitively stated that without the pulsorjet impacting a sun or a black hole, there was theoretically no chance that all the crash IDs could be destroyed. He also stated that the parts he studied at the site were not from a Phantom 344 pulsorjet. They were from two or three much older and less expensive models 22 and 25. Furthermore, he said that fragments of the wreckage showed signs of age corrosion and inconsistent damage patterns for the orientation and location where the pieces lay."

The colonel eked out a sly smile. "According to the Phantom rep, they have no record of Rolland currently owning, leasing, or subleasing a Phantom 344 pulsorjet, or any of their vehicles for that matter. He hasn't owned a Phantom craft in about six years."

"So, this is a completely manufactured crash site," said the woman.

"No, ma'am. Something big did blow up in the sky and then crashed there. It was likely the armored personnel vehicle that Rolland had called in. The site has been thoroughly scoured to remove all contradictory data. I believe all the signs point to this pulsorjet debris being overlaid and staged by the crash team."

The woman scowled. "This confirms to me even further that someone or some group that is high up is directly involved in this. There is too much action around Heavensport that pops up and disappears below the surface to be just a coincidence. I think our elusive Rolland Newcastle is still very much alive and causing his enemies some real pain. I hope that if his God is real, He saves him or lets us come to his rescue. This has to stop this before it gets even worse."

"Yes, ma'am. He will need all the help he can get to survive this—and so do we."

● ● ● ▬ ▬ ▬ ● ● ●

I woke the next morning feeling good. I had full use of my leg without any pain. The incision was healing well, and I was sure that in a few months' time, it would be difficult to even tell that I had any kind of surgery performed on that leg. After bathing, I put on some new clothes that the women had made for me a few days back. It was the first outfit I had been able to put on that wasn't designed for medical recuperation.

Walking out to the dining room, I saw that Lauren and Jessica were just starting a pancake and bacon feast at the kitchen table. They were dressed in nice new clothes. It had become fashion week here at the safe house, and the robo-tailors were getting a workout.

Jessica waved me over to join them. "My, look who's up and looking healthy. There's plenty to eat. Help yourself. How do you like the outfit?"

Sitting down across from them, I tried not to be inappropriate and fixate. "You both look very beautiful."

Lauren giggled. "She was asking about your outfit, not ours. But thanks anyway."

"Oh, right. Yes, mine is very nice as well. Hugo, I would like what they are having. It looks wonderful."

"Right away, sir."

A minute later he placed a plate and a glass of orange juice before me. With a prayer of thanks, I savored the sight and inhaled the delightful aroma.

"How are you feeling?" asked Lauren.

"Really good. I could run if I had to." Placing a bite of pancake into my mouth, I chewed slowly, enjoying the sweet taste and the spongy texture. Next, I sipped some of the orange juice. "After we finish our meal, I was thinking we might try to covertly contact my friend Curtis to get a feel for what we are up against."

Lauren halted, posed with a chunk of pancake on her fork. "Is that wise? Wouldn't that potentially reveal where we are?"

"Yes. But we are sitting here insulated and blind. We may be safer to stay hidden, or we may be giving them the time they need to get more teams in place before springing their trap. If they find us here, it won't be a good outcome. In my security training, I learned that those who stay in one place when under attack tend to die. Movement is life."

Lauren frowned and set her fork down. "It's hard to think of giving all this up. But I think you are right."

"Do you trust Curtis?" asked Jessica.

"Completely and with our lives. He is one of just three people whom I can think of right now that I will entrust my life to."

Lauren said, "Who are the other two?"

"Isn't it obvious?" With my palm up, I waved my hand over both of them. "It's you two, of course."

Lauren's face hinted at a blush, and Jessica smiled, saying, "Thanks. Up until we met you, it was just Lauren for me."

Lauren nodded and said, "Same here—so, if you trust Curtis, I will trust him as well."

"Agreed. How do you intend to contact him?" asked Jessica before she took a small bite of her toast.

"Curtis and I have a secret electronic connection that works outside the normal channels. It is pretty slick. We set it up a while back as a way to get in touch if things went bad and we needed to disappear."

Jessica finished chewing and swallowed. "How long have you known him?"

"Since I was twenty. He is about my age, and I heard about him from another Remnant after Curtis helped him solve some problem that other techs said could not be done."

"What was that?" asked Lauren who was fiddling with her fork, pushing a piece of pancake about the plate, driving it to sop up some of the lines of syrup.

"I knew that would pique your curiosity. He was the guy who figured out the Mantiel verifiability, veritability, and variation function. MV-cubed."

"He did? I thought it was some big, secret military think tank that came up with that," said Jessica. "I use that all the time in my equipment builds."

"You and every other good tech do," I said, raising my orange juice glass in a toast, and they joined me.

After finishing her sip, Lauren said, "So, Curtis' last name is Mantiel?"

Rolling my eyes, I grinned, shaking my head. "No. In typical Curtis form, he didn't want the spotlight, so he made up the name. His real name is Terry Curtis, but most people call him Curtis. He got rich enough off the MV-cubed patent and a few others, so he doesn't have to keep working, but he loves this stuff so much he can't stop." Jessica and Lauren understood this.

"It's funny who becomes a long-time close friend. Curtis is not one of those people I would have pegged as someone destined to become such a close friend. Does that make any sense? Others come and go, and he and I just get closer. He is loyal to a fault and smart as they come. I don't know what he gets from me. He usually tells me that he is only taking on my projects because they are interesting. When I demand a bill, he only charges me for his material costs. He certainly doesn't want any fame or notoriety."

Lauren sat back in her chair and smiled happily. "It sounds like you are honest and straightforward with each other, and you are just as loyal back. I can hear that you care about him, and that goes a long way."

"I hope that you two get to meet him in person someday." I shoveled in a few more bites of pancake and took a long and deep drink of orange juice. Pushing my chair back from the table, I stood. "No time like the present to get this started."

I moved to face a wall along the back of the living room; with my index finger, I wrote the letters Z and A in the air. A section of the realview changed to an image of the Degalian deep sea trench filled with thousands of odd-looking fish. Pointing to the center of a school of yellow fish that made up a circle, I then drew a square around a group of blue fish that mimicked an infinity symbol. The screen went gray. I looked at Lauren and Jessica, ready to explain. They didn't seem worried at all. About thirty seconds later, I heard a low pinging noise.

The screen fluttered, and a data feed loaded a specialized security program. In a low-quality realview live feed, my friend Curtis appeared on the screen. He looked the same as always, tall and slender in build, with tousled dark hair. His face sported an infectious, friendly smile.

"Rolland. It is great to see you, bud. I knew they couldn't kill you. Hey, oh—I am sorry. I didn't know you had guests with you—oh, and they are *really* beautiful too. Is that why you have been hiding? And to think that all this time I had been feeling sorry for you."

"Easy, Curtis, I missed you too." We were both grinning. "Allow me—this is Lauren and her sister, Jessica DeHavalynd. They are both extremely smart, cool, and they have exceptional tech skills."

"My, that is high praise from this guy. Beautiful, cool, and with great tech skills; that is a great combination. It's a pleasure to meet you both," said Curtis, his smile growing even bigger.

"Flirt later, chum. I am guessing that we don't have much time on this line."

"That is for sure. The world is churning, and there is no public mention of the growing storm. I looked at your feeds from the NC-22 at the bathroom. That guy was a pro operative, and it was embarrassing how easily you handled him. Too bad they let him go."

"He got away? I am disappointed that he walked, but I am not shocked."

Curtis nodded. "I also saw that the safe house in the Sterven quarters was activated and that you fired off both EMPs. By the way, I still think that is hilarious—you disappeared after that. When I got word that there was something big like a T-25 or some say a T-32 in—"

"It was a T-37a," said Jessica.

"Really? They were running a 37a in the city? That's not good. That means we have even bigger troubles than I first thought." Curtis scowled, hunching his shoulders.

Lauren said, "Allow me to save time here, the T-37a was chasing Rolland and me. We fled and made our way back through some tunnels to our apartment. They ended up tracking us there and launched an attack early in the morning. The three of us bugged out using hypergliders. Two AA-30s and the T-37a almost got us but we managed to escape again and make it here."

Curtis said, "Two AA-30s and a T-37a? And you made it out alive. Wow."

I grinned. "As I said, they have some great skills."

Curtis was intrigued. "You have me almost ready to break protocol and come and visit you to hear about it. Hey, wait a minute. I know you two; you are the insurgent women from the newsblasts with the Rolland look-alike. By the way, the images they used did not do you justice at all. Clearly, they were trying to cover their use of weapons of war in the city and still be able to go after you. There is some majorly scary stuff going on here." Curtis was lost in thought as he stared at me. "So a quick question, by chance, did you put a data sprite in Erlin?"

"Yeah. She tried to kill me, and I put one in at the safe house. It's a long story."

Curtis' face lit up. "Oh, that is too funny—I don't mean the where she tried to kill you part—because of that sprite we have a deep connection in a silent tech house that I have never even heard of before. I almost severed it thinking it was a reverse hack. I will have to explore what I can find there—also, we have had some heavy, deep probes being thrown at your file pods, and they are hunting all of your safe houses in Heavensport. I would count them all as compromised or soon to be compromised. The best plan would be to go low out of the city and not watch the commercials. Understand?"

"Can you pull the passes for us?" I asked.

Terry Curtis shook his head. "I would love to, but I am being watched." Curtis addressed the ladies. "Few people know about Rolland's and my friendship, yet they are trying to stake me out. That tells me that they are desperate and throwing a big net. Yesterday I did a test by sending out a private booking interest to an exclusive desert villa that is known for its remote location and security. I attached feelers on it, and it lit up. It was stalked by at least eight different trackers. Whoever is behind this is just a few steps from going to war. My hand on it will send up red flags. Can you get it done without me?"

I looked at Lauren and Jessica and replied, "We should be able to figure out how to make it happen." If they couldn't, I doubt others could.

Lauren said, "I see from the data feeds you are using DarkScatter 2.3 for this call. Dump it after we are done. Would you look for build 1.9.167 and send us a copy over this feed?" We could see Curtis begin working. "When you build it in a replicator, do it at Mod 3.2, and did you ever see the realview *Millennium Seekers?*"

"Sure. Who hasn't? There, you should have the program."

Lauren said, "Got it, thanks. Now, modify the casting module by Chipper's regret before starting it, if you know what I mean."

"Chipper's regret, I don't...oh, she had..." Curtis' eyes grew wide, and he nodded. "Interesting. How do you know about DarkScatter?"

Jessica smiled demurely. "Lauren and I wrote DarkScatter. We can discuss that topic at another time. We will do the same build, and we can talk later as needed."

Curtis was impressed. "Agreed. I highly recommend quietly sneaking out as soon as possible. I would suggest that Brainos would make a fine meal."

I said, "Thanks for the meal suggestion; that sounds good to me. Maybe if all goes as planned, we can cook some of it up tomorrow for a late dinner. Oh, before I forget to mention it, did you hear about the attack on a street interventionist named Lazarus?"

"Sure. It is lighting up the newsblasts."

"He was sheltering me and died to give me time to run. If you can, dig up what you are able. It wasn't a random attack for drugs. They came after me, and he died to keep me alive. The truth needs to come out."

Curtis nodded, his face somber. "I'll see what I can find. Talk to you soon, and be careful."

The screen went back to the original realview projection of the underwater reef. I could smell the air as one would at a beach.

Lauren interrupted my errant thoughts. With narrowed eyes, she asked, "Brainos? The kid food? I hope that was code, or you and Curtis have terrible taste in food."

We moved to sit in the living room. Plopping down on the couch, I said, "Curtis is telling us to stay away from commercial passenger travel systems and to use the food transports out of the city and head to the farms in Kongesgaard. There we will plan our next steps."

Jessica said, "Isn't that trip through the Great Plains where the goliaths roam, where Paul and Mary died?"

"Yes. That's another reason those hunting for us would not expect us to be there. Any path we take will have some level of danger. Out there, huge defender robots keep the automated transport trails free from trouble."

Concerned, Lauren leaned forward, her eyes scrutinizing my face. "Even with that, are you emotionally okay with going there?"

"Yes. Goliath attacks are extremely rare, and we will be hidden among the thousands of transports that make it safely there every day. I would say that we are at greater risk by staying here much longer," I said, trying to sound stoic.

"How did you get that destination from Brainos?" inquired Lauren.

"We arbitrarily gave code names and travel modes to various things. They had to be completely unrelated so correlation databases and spectrum quantum computers couldn't guess the meaning. It took us a little bit of time to do the memorizing." I paused and shrugged. "Full disclosure: we didn't come up with that many escape plans, so it wasn't that hard. A question for you, why have Curtis build an old version of your kit? Oh, and what did you mean by Chipper's regret?"

Lauren gave a sad head shake as if she felt sorry for me. "That was two questions. We put the newest version out in the wild with a lower number designator in case we need to get it when we cannot access our own systems, like now. Everyone else will pull down the highest number version, thinking it is the newest one. If they do stumble on it, they have to create it with the right mod setting, or it runs as it were an older version of the kit. We added a silly twist from that old realview to add another security layer. Chipper's regret is that Mellina Beywood-Right couldn't find a role for two years after playing that character, and she said that she wished that she had never played her. Adding two to the casting module will allow the two units to sync their scatters."

"Interesting. Then, unlike Chipper, I have no regrets that she so greatly influenced you both. So, if I understand it correctly, DarkScatter uses all the available spectrums and disruptions caused by the environment, even down to the leaves and people and refractions on buildings to break a signal into worthless bits of micro scatter until they hit the exact inverse variance of another unit. Then it uses the same techniques to gather and unscatter it, and that allows it to develop sync. Is that right?"

Jessica and Lauren smiled. Lauren raised that sneaky eyebrow of hers and said, "So you know about our program?"

"I was the one who found it and set up our private link. As I said, it is slick. That should have told me that you guys made it."

Jessica beamed, and Lauren appeared to blush slightly again. "I didn't know about the version or the casting and the mod settings. I just wanted you to know that I am not just a pretty face here."

Lauren laughed merrily and said, "Oh, you needn't worry about that."

Jessica got up and looked back as she walked to the replicator. "Don't worry, you are beautiful to us." Lauren nodded.

That was a great compliment, and I offered my thanks. I wiggled my toes, and my leg felt good. "That's enough about my haunting beauty. Having us use the food transport cars to get out of the city is a good plan. No one would choose to ride one when there are so many other easier and faster transports available."

"I'm in. I always wanted to see a live goliath in person," said Lauren.

"At a distance," I said.

In the hall between the dining room and living room, Jessica finished setting codes on the replicator. She turned back to us and said, "I agree. At a great distance. I'm in as well."

I looked over at Hugo. "Hugo, have you kept current on the procedures for getting transit passes?"

Hugo nodded. "Yes, sir. Once every two weeks I get updates brought in. I am sorry to say that sales of public tickets have been suspended. There has been a rash of theft and contraband being shipped via the transit systems. Only employees of the transit authority and their families or those who work for one of the four largest farms in Kongesgaard have permission to travel."

"Could we buy or create false IDs?" I asked.

Hugo said, "My sources say that they have new specialized encryption that has to be tied into their systems. It is a hack that would be difficult and dangerous to attempt from here."

Jessica's face fell. "Lauren isn't going to like this...but we need to contact Sandrah to help us get into the transit cars."

"No way," spat Lauren.

"Put your grievances aside for a moment. Sandrah is our best chance of getting to where the cars are and out of the city without being noticed. She has connections where she can get the proper permits and clearances—and she owes us."

"Is she trustworthy?" I asked as Lauren continued to glower at her sister.

"No," said Lauren without hesitation.

"Yes, she is. She isn't completely scrupulous, but she understands and can work the transit world better than anyone else I know."

"Jessica, I think you are too trusting with her, and you want to believe that she has a better character than she actually has. I don't care if she was a marginal friend in school. That was too many years ago, and she has spent those years living too deep in the dark. She is probably the reason they had to lock down the system. You know her; she is always scheming, looking for what might be the next big score."

Jessica came back to sit in her chair. "That's why we offer to square her with us, and we throw in a few hundred unicreds. We show her Christian love, and maybe it can help move her back to the light. God can work on her in ways we cannot understand. I am sure she has hated being in our debt. I never thought I would ever have to call in that marker, so adding some money makes it a win for her, and we get safely out of Heavensport without notice. Lauren, I know you don't like her. She has never turned on me—"

"Yet," spat Lauren. Jessica crossed her arms over her chest and huffed, frustrated with her sister's interjection. Lauren's face was tense and focused as she said, "All she needs is a good, or even a mediocre reason, such as making a few extra unicreds, and she will sell anyone out. Her only regret is selling too low when she could have squeezed more unicreds from a deal. I doubt she even remembers that we helped her."

Jessica exhaled through her nose and reluctantly released her crossed arms. "Okay, I hear you, and I accept your concerns to some degree. Can you think of anyone who knows this stuff better than her and whom we can contact?"

Lauren was sullen as she shook her head and conceded, "No. I can't."

Her expression softened as Jessica pleaded, "Think it through—can you think of any reasonable scenario where Sandrah would ever come into contact with the powerful people that are behind this attack on Rolland and the Remnants? I will almost guarantee that they are not the low-end contraband runners and petty criminals from the free housing districts that Sandrah runs with. They are probably high up in the government or in business or something like that. I will freely admit that she is damaged goods, but I think we can trust her enough on this one, and frankly, we don't have a lot of options or time to waste."

I raised my hand cautiously and said, "I have a few contacts who could get this done."

Lauren shook her head. "They are closely watching your contacts. I am sure they are flagging your voice's parameters, looking for you to surface. The only risk we might want to take would be to call in the EPGB or someone high up like that."

Ruminating on this idea, I said, "Hey, there is this behind-the-scenes kind of guy named Joden at the EPGB. He seems competent, and he is well-placed. I have met him only in passing, so there is not a direct tie between us. He could be a good person to reach, and maybe he could get some help from higher up." The more I spoke, the less right it felt. "No. I don't feel at ease about this. It could be the timing or plain old fear that is stopping me. It makes sense that those hunting us will expect us to run to them. It sucks not knowing what to do and to sit here floundering."

"How much do we have in unicreds?" asked Jessica.

"Hugo, bring the bank," I said.

We watched our robot butler shoot off into the kitchen. When he returned, I pointed to Jessica, and he handed a pouch to her. She spent some time checking it over.

Her face grew white. "We have 60,000 unicreds in unmarked credit holders and loose bills, not counting the money you brought originally."

I frowned. "Is that all, Hugo?"

Lauren's jaw dropped, and she sat up abruptly. "Is that *all?* Sixty—no nearly sixty-eight thousand unicreds, and you ask if that is all? That is more than most people make in a year."

Hugo waited patiently for the drama to play out. "Yes," I replied, "it is a lot of money for normal living. If you are running for your life and need to bribe people or buy things with no questions asked or records kept, that will go very fast."

Lauren visibly relaxed and softly said, "Sorry, Rolland. I am new to this."

"It's okay. It is a strange new world we are in. So, Hugo, do we have other tools and financials to help us?"

Hugo nodded. "Miss Jessica missed the two bearer bonds worth 6,000 unicreds each."

Jessica reached into the pouch and pulled out and held up two matte gray cards. She winced in embarrassment. "I didn't know what those were. We don't deal with such things."

"No problem. This is a good start. More importantly, we can add some brownies, food, and drinks for the trip."

"That would be my pleasure," said Hugo.

We discussed a few other possibilities and decided that Sandrah was our best bet for getting out of Heavensport undetected.

Jessica prepared an audio-only DarkScatter to Sandrah and sent it out.

After ten long minutes of waiting, we heard a voice. "Yeah."

"S-rah. It's me, J. You clear?"

"Clear. You?" asked a woman with a husky voice.

"440. I wouldn't do that to you. I need some help," said Jessica.

"You aren't part of that trouble at your old place, are you? I don't want any part of that."

"Yes and no. We did not bring or set off any of that junk, nor are we doing anything wrong. It was all them. We are running, and we need a pro to smooth a pass, if you get me."

"I would say no to a go. It's too thick for me, branch. I don't want any part of that," said the voice.

"We don't either. I would not be contacting you if we were not desperate. We need to pull in that special favor."

"I shouldn't have answered your scatter," the voice protested. "Why do you have to go and do that to me?"

Jessica's face grew pinched. "S-rah, did you think that the favor would be something like picking up a pizza for us or robo-dog sitting? When I helped you, the storm was all around you, and you got shelter. Can you spare us some help in our storm?"

"Tell me what's involved, and I will tell you if it is too messy."

Jessica relaxed and calmly said, "Three passengers: you know the two females, and the one is male approximately six foot three inches tall and with a medium athletic build. We need proper sheets, train trans passes, and outfits with headgear to Kongesgaard for tomorrow before twelve noon."

"Sheesh. You are crazy, girl. That is too fast to pull it unless we load some creds to pull a boost."

"How much?"

There was a pause and the voice said, "Three thousand for the stuff, and one thousand extra for me to do what I have to do. That means you and me, we are clear, no debt and no more callouts to me for free help."

Jessica looked at us for our agreement to the terms, and we nodded. "Stiff, but done. Unicreds at delivery. We need you on this, S. I know this is a lot. I wouldn't have asked if we didn't need your special kind of help. I will throw in one thousand extra, all non-traceable, if you don't tell anyone anything about this, who it is for, or where we are going. You good with that?"

"Done. I can get it by 11:00 a.m. Will you meet your own part then?"

"Good to go. Where and when?"

"Meet me in the service entrance for Hymindahl's Restaurant, Laffland Street, North 233, level J-459, 11:30 a.m. Go to the back and use the access code of 498857 to get into the back. No one will bother you if you do that quickly? Got it?"

"Got it."

"Find the delivery access door near the back oven and use it to get to the hallway. The lock will be disabled. I will meet you there. Let me make this clear—it is just you three. No weapons, no electronics running, or any disguises where I don't know it is you. If I get even a whiff of trouble, or you come in another way, I will not show, and I will consider my debt paid and that you still owe me for the full amount. You 440 on this?"

440, S-rah. Please come alone too. This has to be still and quiet, or a lot of innocents could get hurt. The other side isn't playing nice at all."

"440," said the voice and disconnected.

I stared at Jessica in awe. I have sat in on high-level negotiations that were not so delicately and skillfully played. "That was interesting. Remind me not to negotiate against you—ever. So do you think we are good?"

Jessica didn't answer. She stared at me and her sister and then said, "Eighty-eight to twelve in our favor with a margin of error of about fifteen."

"You're an optimist," said Lauren, "but we don't have much of a choice here."

"Does she normally talk like that?" I said.

Jessica gave a half-hearted shrug. "No. That is her business slang to get it done faster, and she likes it as it is dramatic. Sandrah is a wary one, and that is why I trust her to help."

Lauren didn't respond.

●●● ▬ ▬ ▬ ●●●

We had worked together until fairly late in the night to give us all the best shielding possible from electronic surveillance. I was impressed with the skill of Lauren and Jessica. Each had a unique way of approaching problems that I felt complemented the other's skills.

We created a projected variation of a facial reconstructor that mimicked the ear and forehead strips in a simple neckband. While it was not perfect under close scrutiny, the illusion was decent, subtly changing our looks, making a nose seem larger, widening the separation between our eyes, or casting a different shade on our hair. They would do.

Originally we had debated using wigs and homemade versions of Face-Its. As simple and useful as they were, we scrapped this idea due to the difficulty in quickly applying or removing the face applications. Lauren was quite adamant that because Sandrah felt forced into working with us, she would use any excuse to pull out of our agreement, leaving us out in public with no ride and still owing her money. If Sandrah thought she wasn't going to get paid, that made our situation even more dangerous.

Even with the projected facial reconstructors, we didn't relish the idea of being out in public. Jessica and Lauren had been debating simple additional methods for disguising us.

Being tired and a bit silly, I said, "The best disguise would be going out dressed as robots. No one notices them, and they are everywhere."

Hugo spoke up. "If I may interject; why don't you?" Before I could say something snide or witty, he said, "Not so much as one, but *in* one." Hugo pointed to the wall near the living room. It opened, and a four-foot tall rectangle that was about twelve feet long and three feet wide glided into the room and parked in front of us. "This is an MT-3424J. They are one of the most common materials transports in the city. This one has some features that you will not find in other units, such as fresh air circulators." The lid and sides opened to reveal a spacious interior. Seats inflated in a line, leaving storage space below each chair. "And comfortable seats," Hugo continued. I would be coming as your driver and eyes until I get you to your next point of departure." A 360-view from Hugo's eyes was shown on the interior walls of the transport.

Jessica looked worried. "What will happen to you then? Will you come back here?"

Hugo appeared surprised. "No. Once we leave here, the safe house will automatically lock down, wiping all records and DNA evidence. After I get you safely underway, I am to deliver the house's system core to one of Mr. Curtis' upload points around the city to enact a transfer and then to do a full wipe of the house data and recordings. Then I will be taken in as part of the next safe house. Maybe someday I can serve you all again."

I smirked, sighing with a huff. "I am hoping that this is my last need of a safe house."

Lauren looked at Hugo with a big, reassuring smile. "We will make sure that you get a good place to work." She glanced at me and said with a serious face and pointed tone, "Right, Rolland?"

"Sure. No problem. If this keeps up, I may have to join the crazies in the Robot Freedom Movement. They have been fighting for years to have all robots legally declared fully human citizens and set free. *Free the blenders!* Seriously, that is one of their battle cries."

In the morning after eating a good breakfast, we packed our backpacks with food, clothing and the new equipment that we fabricated. We decided that retinal ID disrupters would not be too much for Sandrah to tolerate. We would remove the neck-ring facial projectors before we met her.

The thought of leaving the apartment was both sad and ex-hilarating. There was no boisterous idle talk. After a last check to make sure we hadn't forgotten anything, we headed toward the MT-3424J materials transporter that was stationed in the area near the foyer.

Hugo was there waiting for us. He smiled and said, "I have the coordinates for today's journey from your conversation with Ms. Sandrah. Shall I use that?"

Lauren nodded and said, "Can you take us to a delivery area near the restaurant? She only wants us to come in the front door."

"I think so. We will have to see what shows up on the transit maps once we get closer to it. Scanning the area now might alert watchers to our current location and our destination." Hugo bowed, tilting his upper frame forward at a hidden joint located at approximate waist height on his center pole. "It has been my pleasure serving you all. I wish you all a safe journey."

Lauren strode up to him and gave him a big hug and a kiss on the cheek. I was about to say something when Jessica did the same thing. Hugo looked at me expectantly, and I gave him a quick hug, too, forgoing the kiss.

Yes, I knew that he was a machine, but there was something right in hugging his rigid plastic frame. It was a physical demonstration of our thankfulness for finding sanctuary and healing in a time of fear and uncertainty. Our restorative stay had changed the dynamics of our flight. While we were still running, this time we had more thought and say in how and where we were going. And that made a great difference.

Stowing our backpacks below our seats, I took the back seat, Lauren the middle seat, and her sister up in front of her. Hugo lowered his center pole to allow him to look at us at eye-height. He made sure we were seated before handing us each an ear comm that would allow us to talk quietly between the four of us. The screens of the transport began showing us the 360-view through Hugo's eyes. To our right, we could see ourselves seated in a box that looked like an odd amusement park ride.

Hugo said, "Obviously, I will not need to move my mouth to communicate privately with you. Your cabin is soundproofed, and there is a phase blanket in place to block external scans. Most of our trip will be in the back transportation and delivery halls. Does this meet your approval?" Each of us agreed verbally as a way to test our comm levels. "Off we go. You have an important appointment to keep."

The transport's walls and roof closed in around us to lock. It didn't feel claustrophobic. The vid walls and air circulation made it feel as if we were sitting in the middle of a room. When Hugo raised his center support to his normal height it was as if our seats had risen up and glided forward to take a position at the front of the materials transport.

Lauren let out a gasp, and Jessica giggled.

"What's wrong?" Anxious, I said it a bit louder than I had intended.

Lauren tittered and said, "So, this is what it is like to be tall."

Over the comm, Hugo said, "I am only 5'8" tall. I can extend my center pole to show you how Rolland sees the world."

"That is not necessary..." I said.

"Please do it, Hugo. Just for a moment," pleaded Jessica.

I was overruled, and the view moved up. Lauren gasped again, and Jessica snorted out a chuckle.

"I would get altitude sickness up here," said Jessica with surprising mirth in her voice.

"Sick? Heck, you could die from a fall from this height," teased Lauren.

"Funny. If the ladies are done playing, we need to get going, and Hugo, you need to get back to your normal height so you don't draw any attention."

"Yes, sir. Off we go." The view lowered, the wall in front of us opened, and we moved out, building up speed. Hugo's vision switched to a low-light spectrum mode intensifier to better show the trip through the darkened private corridors that led away from the safe house. As we looked back, the apartment went dark, and the wall closed behind us. We rode into an elevator at the end of the corridor, and the doors closed. There was a change of motion as we moved in several directions and floors, seemingly at random.

The elevator stopped, and the doors opened to a long hallway, and Hugo silently moved us forward at a generous clip. The darkness was broken in a flash of bright white light when the wall at the end the passageway slid to the side to reveal a busy hallway packed with fast-moving transports. We weren't slowing at all. We were picking up speed, and I clenched my seat, bracing for the coming impact. Side protection pads inflated next to us, and over the comms, I heard Lauren and Jessica gasp as we flew toward the robotic transport stream. Our transport turned sideways, and we held on tighter as we slid lengthwise. With a sharp acceleration that forcibly pushed us back in our chairs, we careened in to merge with the traffic. There was no terrible crash; not even a bump.

Relieved, I had to force myself to unclench my muscles and release my breath. I said a private prayer of thanks that we had survived, and I had not wet myself or done much worse.

Hugo said, "I apologize for that on-ramping. There are few human comforts or concerns in these transport lanes. I submitted that I am transporting delicate desserts and they allowed me a slower than normal merge."

Lauren said, "That's 'a slower than normal merge'? Whoa." I agreed with her.

With a childlike light in her voice, Jessica replied, "'Delicate desserts'? Aw, Hugo, that was sweet."

We came to sections of the transport lanes where we saw some people walking. Through Hugo's eyes, we all noted that they looked past us as if Hugo and the other robots didn't exist. I got to thinking about this. Social rules are complex. We only acknowledge those on the sidewalks that we almost bump into or with whom we have some required interaction. So maybe I have over-thought this robot blindness.

After ten minutes, Hugo said, "We are almost at our destination. For your safety, I will project a realview dome of me stopping the transport, and this will help shield your exit. You will have just a few moments to exit the transport, leave the transit hub, and to make your way out onto the street. There will be no time for saying goodbye."

Why was I having difficulties saying goodbye to a robot? One of the girls, maybe both, cleared their throats; they were fighting similar emotions.

"Good plan," said Jessica, her voice cracking.

"Sure. Good plan," snuffed Lauren in agreement.

I nodded and kept quiet. There was nothing more I that could say that would help ease our thoughts. Nor did I want to encourage their membership in the Robot Freedom Movement.

●●● ⬭⬭⬭ ●●●

16

The Labyrinth

● ● ●   ━ ━ ━   ● ● ●

Hugo laid an animated three-dimensional map of our travel over his projected 360-view. Red no-entry bars covered a large swath of buildings above and below the restaurant where we were to meet Sandrah.

"As you can see, we are unable to gain access nearby," said Hugo. Orange bars lined the whole block and across the street. "And there are no safe or available drop-off points nearby." A green circle appeared on the floor plans of the buildings that were across the street and down a few blocks. "I can get you here." A yellow line moved across the map, showing the path to the restaurant. "It is as safe as reasonably possible; the hub is currently free of humans, and there is minimal pedestrian traffic when you exit through the access door."

"That will work great. Guys, make sure your facial projectors are on," Lauren reminded us.

As Hugo was bringing the transport to a fast stop, he said, "You will have to move at a moderately fast pace to make it there with a few minutes to spare." The projections ended, and the transport opened. We did not hesitate. Climbing out into the dimly lighted hub, we grabbed our backpacks and put them on. "Once you are at the restaurant, drop your comms in a recycler. A safe journey to you all. Go."

With a quick hidden wave, we headed to the access door and slipped out into the busy street. The shock of the bright sunlight, swirling colors, noise, realviews, and people struck us, causing us to shield our eyes. It was overwhelming.

Lauren grunted her disproval, and Jessica hissed, "It's like being thrown into a colorful tornado."

Gaining our composure, we followed the path set by Hugo, moving at a good clip, winding our way through the meandering foot traffic. The streets were becoming increasingly garish and noisy. Realviews pushed products and shopping experiences with a vigor that was bordering on abusive.

Clenching my teeth, I kept breaking off contact from the realviews. More came to replace those, reminding me of an unfortunate camping experience I'd once had with a swarm of voracious mosquitoes and biting flies.

With point-projected realviews, advertisers sent each person their own personalized video and audio stream, like thousands of precise little spotlights. Everyone got their own stream based on what the system thought would best sell to them.

They must have mixed me up with someone else, which meant our projectors were working better than expected. While this was good news, and the ads were not adult in nature, it still sucked, as my personalized ads were filled with clowns. I loathe clowns.

Arriving at Laffland Street, we found it to be full of over-the-top specialty boutiques offering flashy street-show outfits and wild costumes. Jessica pointed to a small building crammed between two large and boisterous shops. Hymindahl's Restaurant.

The restaurant was small, dull, and out of date, in a word, unobtrusive. It had the feel of a timid little old man who found himself uncomfortably wedged in a crowded transport that was full of DNA modders, fancy-dressed street braggarts, and dealmakers like my buddy from the train. Walking to the restaurant, my eyes fought to slide off to either side to look at those more visually stimulating shops. This was a perfect place to stay unnoticed.

A sign by the front door welcomed us to seat ourselves. Not surprisingly, the restaurant was nearly empty with most of the diners sitting along the edges by the high-mounted realviews that showed sporting events from around New Jerusalem. I felt eyes on us as we made our way to the kitchen access door. This reminded me of one of those cliché gangster restaurants from the realviews.

Lauren punched in the code, and we slipped inside, closing the door behind us. This was not some nefarious gangster hangout. It was more like a fairy glen where the locals were surprised that anyone happened upon their secret entrance. When we accessed the kitchen, they probably worried that we were health inspectors or investors looking to turn their place into a ubiquitous Cheezy Burger franchise.

Inside the kitchen, we dropped our comms into a recycler as we made our way past the mechanized workforce. As there were few patrons, most of the robots and robo-chefs were inactive. It looked more like a museum exhibit than a working kitchen.

Jessica, who was in the lead, said, "We are about eight minutes early."

The delivery access door didn't budge. It was locked. Sandrah was wrong. Before I could comment, sleight-of-hand magician Lauren hacked the simple lock and opened the door to reveal a hallway leading to the back service area. In the secluded corridor, we turned off our electronics and put them away to avoid any chance of frightening Sandrah off.

Rounding a corner, we were surprised to see a slender woman leaning against the wall dressed in a form-fitting orange and yellow one-piece work outfit. Her yellow safety helmet, coupled with a short semi-opaque visor, was focused downward, giving us a profile view. She was not what I had expected. From her gravelly voice, I had imagined that she would be on the husky side and not stick-thin. Maybe she used a voice changer to disguise her transmission.

Reeking of feigned insouciance, the woman turned her helmet towards us and then rocked her shoulders to push off the wall. She stood upright, facing us as we approached. Lauren stopped a few yards back, and I took her cue and did the same. Jessica walked up to the slightly taller woman, and they hugged stiffly. Even though we could not see her upper face through her visor, I got the impression that she was eyeing us coldly.

"Lauren." Her voice was chilly, distant and gruff, sounding the same as we had heard back at the apartment. Was this her real voice?

Lauren acknowledged her with a nod. "Sandrah."

The woman struck a dramatic pose as she surveyed the area behind us, checking for any threats. Satisfied, she turned her attention to me, and she began circling around as if judging a farm animal at a fair. At least she didn't touch me or check my teeth. Standing still and looking forward, I glanced only at her face shield, trying to be polite. Her helmet and visor hid the upper half of her face. Soft, shiny blonde hair cascaded down past her shoulders. She had the potential to be rather striking without the headgear.

"You need a new line of work," she rasped.

"I know—Rolland is dead."

"No. It's because you don't look a thing like him."

Attempting to be charming to ease the tension, I said, "I'll take that as a compliment."

"Don't. He was much better looking than you."

Wow. And it is a pleasure to meet you, too, thanks.

"But loads of money makes even plain, dumpy-looking guys like you much hotter." Her helmeted head turned back to Jessica. "Speaking of money, this guy's about to become 5,000 unicreds uglier. You got it, J?" Jessica produced a pair of credit holders and Sandrah took them and ran a check on them. "They're clear." She pointed to two large gray bags that sat by a service door. "There. Get the gear on and leave the bags by the wall. Do it fast; it is too open to stay here long."

After removing our backpacks, we pulled the plain orange and yellow work uniforms over our clothes. Mine began adjusting to better fit me. Looking over, I noted that neither Jessica's nor Lauren's uniforms had done so. After Sandrah's sweet greetings, I doubted that this was unintentional.

Sandrah ordered, "Don't put on your helmets or visors yet. I have to take your ID realviews."

Obedient, we stood as Sandrah walked up and pointed a small device at each of our faces and swung it in an arc around the fronts and sides of our heads. She took Jessica's photo without a comment.

To Lauren, she said, "You should have brushed your hair." I didn't notice anything wrong with her hair at all. Lauren said nothing. There was the faintest hint of a flinch. I was proud of her.

Sandrah stepped up to me and in her gruff voice said, "Say, 'Duh.'" I merely smiled softly as she took my photo.

Sandrah said, "Put on your safety helmets and visors. Make it snappy."

Once on, the screens gave us detailed maps covering the service tunnel's layouts for hundreds of floors and levels near us. The view glided in tighter to focus on our current location, giving us pertinent information for the area where we stood.

A small device mounted on Sandrah's arm pushed out the three ID tags. She handed our credentials to Jessica, who in turn gave them to us. I glanced at Sandrah's ID on her helmet, and it read, Ms. Glamorlee A. Fantastica, Supervisor, Investigative Services. Glamorlee?

Our displays showed that our IDs were now paired with our gear. My ID said I was Mr. Dummel Dummelstine. Great. Jessica was listed as Ms. Mary Lorcat and Lauren as Ms. Messa McBlobb. Creativity and kindness were not her strong suits.

I looked for a location on my suit to place the ID when Sandrah snipped, "Put the IDs in an internal pocket in your clothes. If you lose them, you will be locked out, and security will be alerted." We quietly complied. The proximity of the ID made my fake information appear on my chest badge.

A row of lights flared to life alongside us, pacing just ahead of Sandrah as she strutted towards an access door that opened before her. I am not proud of it, and it was wrong, but I snuck a quick peek at her derrière, hoping to find it as unattractive as her personality. It was a bit flat and square, but it was better than she deserved.

Sandrah led us down to a walkway avoiding the elevators. Our visor displays showed us that we were being led to the closest transportation hub for the network of automated carts that fed the businesses and homes of Heavensport. A city with three-quarters of a billion inhabitants needed a staggering amount of food and services every day. We were getting a glimpse of this massive undertaking.

We moved deeper within the inner workings of the city. Sandrah kept quiet and we followed suit as we continued, taking a lift down to a lower level and out across more suspended walkways.

Sandrah stopped outside a large, heavy airlock door and said, "If we meet anyone from this point on, let me do the talking." Her helmet turned towards me, and she snapped, "And don't mess with anything."

Passing through the door, our visors told us that this huge open area was a destination point, listed as 2,938,372 of the autotrack system. This area accepted and coordinated the standard, apartment-sized, sixty-foot-long by thirty-foot-wide by ten-foot-tall automated food carts. Focusing on a cart, our visors pulled up layers of information listing the types of products, bio-health scans, weight, financials, and other facts about each bin and section in the huge carts.

We watched the process of unloading. Nothing came to a stop—it was a fluid dance in which the tracks moved carts to where whole sides of the carts were lifted up to connect with a long conveyor belt, and the empty carts moved on. As the interior bins moved along, more pieces were removed. It reminded me of how the trunk of a tree keeps dividing into smaller branches and up finally to the leaves.

Fully immersed in watching the logistical dance, I didn't realize that the group had moved on. I heard Sandrah's harsh voice over my helmet's com say, "Hey, bad Dumbcastle Not-look-alike, keep up. Last warning."

I didn't say a word as I ran to catch up.

I heard Sandrah say, "J, I don't know what you see in that fool."

Jessica said, "S-rah, he is a good guy and my friend. Please be kind to him on my account, okay?"

This was no mistake; Sandrah intentionally sent that private chat to me. She was hoping to draw Jessica into saying something unkind. With care, Jessica had stood up for me, choosing not to bend to her pressure.

I understood Lauren's reluctance to work with Sandrah. No matter how beautiful she might turn out to be, her personality was a negative twenty detractor on a scale of one to ten. I suppressed a grin.

Stop. If she thinks that I am laughing for any reason, we will be in serious trouble.

Sandrah was a vindictive bully. And this was a dream situation for a bully; she had power over three people who were temporarily unable to defend themselves, and she loved it, especially as there was some bad blood with Lauren.

She had her money. Angering her for any reason would result in our passes and helmets being shut down. She would disappear into the labyrinth, leaving us in the dark to be arrested by the security systems, and that would alert those who were hunting us. The saving grace was that we know her real name and one of her aliases. Smugglers are about self-preservation and staying hidden. Being on the police's scanners would make her life much harder. Hopefully, that thought was enough to make her fulfill her part of the deal.

I was being judgmental, and I was willfully unrepentant. I *hate* bullies—even more than clowns. Clown bullies? That's a whole other level of bad. *Stop it now.*

We rode a fast-track personnel carrier to the main depot. Lauren and I sat in the back seat while Jessica and Sandrah sat up front.

Despite the amazing views around us, none of us spoke. Jessica and Lauren were smart; they knew that all of our private conversations were routed to Sandrah. We were at her mercy, and I doubted that she had any.

Without the night vision and data overlay from our visors, we would have had no idea of the complexity and enormity of the autotrack systems that honeycombed the megacity. The endless miles of interwoven tracks were humongous capillaries, and the continual lines of cart trains were the lifeblood that kept the massive megacity of Heavensport alive.

As we were in a better-lit area, we watched as multiple levels of train tubes crossed over, under, and next to us. They moved produce and goods to and from the millions of restaurants, grocery stores, and homes. As unbelievably large and busy as this section was, we knew that it was one of the thousands of delivery ports that ran in mazes in and about the megacity's base.

On flights around the city, I had often seen the ports and the long train lines that fed the system. Until now I had not focused on their actual size and complexity. It was as humbling as seeing the night sky when you are away from the influence of a city's lights. I was feeling small and insignificant, and that was making me feel secure. We were a few tiny dots of life on a journey.

The fast-track personnel carrier exited through a short tunnel and came into one of the biggest bays that we had seen yet. Here the carts were being delivered to be added to the skeletal frames of thousands of massive train cars.

The train cars' design was simple; without the carts in place, it was an empty rectangle made up of a floating base with two end-caps that held up a long, train-like passenger cabin that sat like a backbone across the top. The bottom section housed the motors and lifters, and the caps held the elevators and the vacuum air disrupters that made high-speed ground travel possible.

Each of the train cars was 640 feet long by 120 feet wide and 120 feet tall, and they carried 400 carts per car. Each side of the center cargo bay held ten decks, with each side holding twenty carts per deck that were lined side-by-side with their noses pointing in towards the center. There are millions of these train cars in the megacity.

Not a motion nor an inch was wasted in this intricate ballet of machines and components as the lead carts slid in to park side by side and were pulled together to create a long and wide blocks. Large robotic lift arms glided in from the sides to lift up and slide the line into the open sides of the large transit cars. This motion was so fluid that it had the feel of a wave of liquid blocks being poured into place. Finished, the train car swung out and moved off at a frightening speed to join the lines leaving the city. A new car moved in to replace the one that had left.

In a mass evacuation situation, the transit system would automatically convert carts into cabins. Passengers would be loaded in the transit hubs throughout the city.

Our visors told us that we had arrived where the cars leaving for Kongesgaard were being loaded. We came to a gentle stop, got out, and pulled on our backpacks.

Sandrah walked us over to a car and said, "This is yours. Randomly chosen, no markings or identifiers that would make you stand out. Your passes are keyed to your destination, and they will automatically activate the cabin's comfort features. You had better get going. It will wait only fourteen more minutes before leaving you stranded."

I know it is completely immature, but I really wanted her to remove her safety helmet and visor so that I could see her face. It was going to bug me. What did she look like? Was she so beautiful that people tolerated her horrible attitude? How would I even ask her to take off her helmet to show me her face?

To my surprise, Sandrah reached up and removed her helmet. With a dramatic flip of her head, she swung her full, shiny, golden blonde hair like she was in some hair commercial. It fell back into place across her shoulders, and she posed, staring at me for the full effect.

I stood there dumbfounded. She was positively and absolutely average in every way. Okay, she did have great hair. Her makeup was well done, and some of her features were nice, but altogether she was *completely underwhelming*. In fact, her demeanor made her hideously ugly. Yes, I am being unkind. I cannot believe that all her horrible attitude was caused by us putting her in a bad spot.

She saw me staring at her, and a haughty smile slithered to rest on her face. I couldn't look away as I was determined to solve the mystery of how she could hold such an inflated opinion of herself. Her eyes didn't flash, her lips didn't demand a long slow kiss, nor did they promise whispers of unbelievable delight.

The chorus and orchestra had built to a stunning emotional crescendo, and the prima donna, bathed in the stage light, had lifted her chin to belt out a song—but she couldn't hold a note.

Sandrah stood before me, her eyes defiant, arms akimbo with her chest and chin thrust forward. Smiling cruelly, she said, "Sorry there, Not-Castle, you and I will never happen. Not even a taste. I am completely out of your league. You would have to have the unicreds of the real Rolland Newcastle for me to even look at you."

Holding back my retorts, I said nothing. My greatest desire was for her to leave and never to see her again. An ill-timed laugh or comment could still destroy everything and accomplish nothing.

Sandrah turned and walked to Jessica. My eyes were drawn to the slightest motion; Lauren was clenching her fists, fighting the urge to beat this woman senseless. *Hold tight,* I prayed, *she will leave soon.* Lauren looked at me and I saw her begin to calm.

I heard her gruff voice say, "We 440, J?"

Jessica nodded. "440. Be good."

"Whatever."

Sandrah sashayed over to mount the fast-track personnel carrier. Sitting bolt upright in the front seat, her eyes landed on Lauren and on to me with no real emotion. She pulled on her helmet and stared straight ahead. The carrier glided away from us to disappear into the distance. She couldn't go away fast enough for me.

Jessica softly said, "We have to get moving, or the car will leave without us."

We didn't argue. As we headed toward the car a countdown timer appeared on our visors warning us that our transit car was scheduled to leave in six minutes. This was less time than what Sandrah had told us, which was no surprise. She wanted us to panic.

Inside, we rode the elevator up the eleven floors to the top passenger cabin. It was much wider than a city transit train cab-in, and it had hundreds of g-seats set in rows under the arched ella-glanse canopy.

With urgency, I directed them to right-side windows seats not far from the front. There was a question on their faces as they complied without comment. This was their first trip out of the city; they needed to be by a window for the wonderful surprise that was coming. Stowing our backpacks in the compartments below our g-seats, we climbed in and were auto-strapped in place.

A realview projection of an earnest young man appeared. "Thank you for joining us today. Please relax and enjoy your journey to Kongesgaard."

The car rose and moved forward with no sound or vibration. The silent repulsors and the vacuum air disrupters were doing a marvelous job. The underground world around us moved past the windows faster and faster as we began picking up impressive speed. As in a race, other cars were sliding up to pace us. They moved forward or slowed to merge together to become a single, almost endless line of cars leaving Heavensport.

Gaining speed, we left the darkness of the underground to be thrust into the glorious light of the day. The ella-glanse canopy afforded us a spectacular, unimpeded view of the spacious grasslands and the bright blue sky that surrounded Heavensport. I heard Lauren and Jessica gasp over our headsets. They had their heads cocked to the right side, watching the extraordinary sight. Long, glistening lines of white train cars were coming and going in different directions. The pressure from acceleration faded, and our visors told us that we had reached our cruising speed of 620 miles per hour.

The realview man appeared and said, "Feel free to move about the cabin. We will arrive at our destination the city of Kongesgaard in three hours and twenty minutes."

The miles flew by as we watched the terrain changing. Their translucent face shields could not hide the excitement in their eyes.

Jessica whispered, "It is more beautiful than I could have imagined."

Lauren said, "God is great. 'The heavens declare the glory of God, and the sky proclaims the work of His hands.'"

A few minutes passed, and Lauren got up and signaled for us to take off our helmets, visors, and uniforms. Complying, we took them all and placed them in a storage compartment that was farthest from us in the long cabin. Returning to our seats, we huddled together next to the side windows.

In a quiet voice, Lauren said, "We need to talk quietly about any plans. I don't trust that—girl. Seriously, how long do you think she has practiced leaning up against walls trying to look all mysterious and cool? She is worse than the bully she was back in school."

Jessica looked unhappy. "Easy, Lauren. I admit it. She was horrible and dramatic. I am sorry, Rolland. Maybe this was a mistake."

I whispered, "Don't worry, I have heard worse. How do I say this nicely? I kept thinking she must be really beautiful under her helmet and visor."

Lauren turned pale, and she looked horrified. "You didn't fall for her, did you? You realize that she took off her helmet to show you her 'famous' face? I am shocked that she didn't find some reason that she had to remove her top—or to just strip down bare, to give us the full show."

"Are you kidding? Fall for her? Not a chance. I would rather kiss an angry goliath or Bredforth Ablefrock than her," I spat.

For some reason, Jessica appeared confused. "Sandrah says that she hasn't met a man who doesn't want her."

"Sure—to leave and never come back," I said a little louder than I should have.

Lauren studied me carefully. "I caught you looking at her."

"That is because I was trying to find something, anything about her that would allow her to be able to hold herself in such high regard. When she removed her helmet, I was shocked that she was so average and unexciting."

"Wow. I wish Sandrah could hear that," said Lauren in a low voice that had a healthy dose of exuberance.

"She would just think I was bitter because she told me that I couldn't have her. I cannot imagine that she hasn't heard a negative statement or two about her looks and personality. She is either overcompensating for some serious self-esteem issues, or she believes herself to be a once-in-a-lifetime beauty, which to me, she is definitely not. She shoveled all that attitude on us because she is intimidated by the two of you."

"By us? How so?" asked Jessica.

I stared at her, unsure why this wasn't blatantly obvious. "As you both know, I have dated quite a lot, and many of those women have been considered to be great beauties by the world's standards. In my misspent youth, I acted as a judge in several worldwide beauty contests. I am only bringing this up to help with establishing my credentials on superficial, worldly, purely physical, and meaningless things. I am quite the expert on being shallow and self-absorbed."

Lauren snorted. With a sly grin, she said, "We bow to your excessive youthful indiscretion and experience."

I dipped my head low in a mock bow, which is difficult to do when crouched down. Thankfully I didn't fall over. "In my professional opinion, setting aside my ruffled feathers, I would say that in a straight beauty competition, with no personality penalties or bonuses, that you are both far superior to her in every category. Insecure people use intimidation and bluster to try and hide that they feel grossly inferior."

"Do you really think so?" inquired Lauren, half whispering, her eyes wide.

"I am telling you the truth. You saw the outfits that Sandrah gave you. They were baggy, and they didn't conform at all to your figures, where mine did. That wasn't done to help you hide. It was visual sabotage by someone who knew that she couldn't win in any kind of comparison. She wasn't bright enough to figure out how to make you cover yourself in mud, or she would have done it. I can say that with some confidence when you look at the horrible names that she made up for our IDs. Her digs have no merit."

"So, nothing about her was all that great?" asked Jessica, who still sounded hesitant in her delivery.

I didn't want to concede it. Rocking my head side to side, I said, "Well, to be fair, she did have great hair, and her butt was okay, but that alone can't sell the musical. She is slender, but not shaped."

Lauren eyed me up. "You looked at her butt?"

"As I said, I was trying to figure out why she was sporting such a huge ego. By the way she was swinging it, she thinks it is far better than it is. It was kind of flat and square, but overall not too bad."

Lauren said, "I thought so too."

I gave her a sly grin. "So you looked too?"

Lauren shrugged. "Girls check out girls. It's a competition thing. We are just subtler than guys are."

"Agreed—oh, I want to thank you both for standing up for me," I said softly.

Jessica said, "I don't understand. We didn't do anything."

"Sandrah intentionally sent your private channel for me to hear you when she asked you what you saw in me. You could have sided with her to keep her happy, but you asked her to be kind because I was a good guy and your friend. Thank you for that; that means a lot to me. And also, thanks for getting this set up and putting up with Sandrah for us."

Jessica smiled and said, "No problem. I meant every word. I just hope that dealing with Sandrah has actually helped us and in some way helped her."

Lauren shrugged. "We made the decision together with the best information that we had at hand. Whatever happens, we will have to live with the outcome. Why did you thank me for standing up for you? I didn't do anything."

"Precisely. I could see that it was taking every bit of your will-power not to jump on her and beat her when she was talking to me."

Lauren appeared taken back. "You noticed that? I was trying my best to remain calm."

"It helped me to not respond. Had I ripped into her, that would have certainly caused us harm, especially if I'd told her who I am. The childish part of me would have loved to see it, but she strikes me as the type that pays back thirty-fold for even the slightest perceived affront. Oh, for the record either of you could take her in a fight with ease." I frowned, frustrated with myself, and said, "I am sorry for attacking her so. It is not how I should respond, regardless of how she acted toward us. We are, for the moment safe and on our way. I am sorry, Lord. Change my heart."

Jessica said a prayer for Sandrah, and we agreed saying, "Amen."

●●● ▬▬ ▬▬ ▬▬ ●●●

The ride was smooth and fluid as the transit cars floated almost two yards above the ground on anti-gravity lifters. I pulled up the train's specs, which said that these lifters did no damage to the soil, plants, or wildlife beneath the trains, and if needed, the cars could rise up to 115 feet off the ground to avoid obstacles in their path. So cool.

We relaxed, enjoying the beautiful landscape as we headed to Kongesgaard. In the distance, we could occasionally spot a gleaming white train line that we assumed was headed back to Heavensport. We passed by streams, valleys, mountains and vast open areas filled with large grazing animals, but not a single goliath was to be seen.

We ate some of the Insta-Heat food and brownies that we had brought with us. If things continued to go right, we would be in Kongesgaard about an hour before nightfall. There we would find shelter at one of the local inns that catered to those on vacation or those who had come there to work.

●●● ▬▬ ▬▬ ▬▬ ●●●

17

A Goliath Nightmare

●●● ▬▬ ▬▬ ▬▬ ●●●

The coded message line blinked. "Yes?" answered the man with a hint of apprehension in his voice.

A husky female voice at the other end of the encrypted line said, "You don't know me, but I have something very special that you will really want."

"I have a wife, and I am not interested in those kinds of services, thank you—"

"It's not those kinds of services. I have information that you want."

"Yes, we all have information. It's that kind of age. We are all interconnected. Good day—"

"Joden, wait."

The fact that the call had come on his private encrypted line made him pause. "Okay. I will give you a moment. First, how did you get this line's connection information?" asked Joden with a firm tone in his voice.

"As you can see, I have access to information that others don't. Like, I know that some very important people are hunting for a particular Rolland Newcastle look-alike and his two lady friends. They seem to want him pretty bad."

336 - THE FALL OF HEAVEN

"Yes, I saw that on the newsblasts, just as nearly a billion others did. Is this all you have?"

The voice sounded irritated. "No, of course not. I have information about where they are right now. The chatter out in the most private of channels is that this information is so important to you that you might pay, say, 250,000 unicreds to get it."

"Two hundred and fifty thousand? You have got to be kidding. I don't have access to that kind of money."

"My sources also say that you would have access to liquid accounts again and likely much more if you got this information while it still was fresh. It could put things straight again and maybe with a sizable promotion attached to it?"

Joden paused. "How do you know that I am the right person and that I am not just trying to kill this guy?"

"And his two female partners. What you do with them is not my issue. I am 440 on this."

"440?"

"Free and good. So, do you want to deal?"

"A question first—why did you contact me and not one of the others who may be interested in this information?"

"Those who want it more will pay more. Also, it never hurts to have good relations with someone in your position when they move up in the world. A girl has to be thinking of her future. I am sure that you understand."

"Perfectly. Let's say I am interested and that we make the deal. How do we get the information and deliver the money to you? As I said, I don't have immediate access to the electronic transfers as I once did. I can get you half now in an untraceable credit holder, and once I know that the information is correct, I will get you the remaining half, plus another fifty thousand to make it an even 300,000 unicreds, but that will require a strict promise that no one else gets this information, and our little deal is kept as a secret between us, and us alone, or the deal is off. Are we in agreement on this?"

"Oh, Mr. Falkaal, I like your thinking. Consider the deal struck and signed on those terms. This leads me to believe that we will have many mutually beneficial encounters in the future. If I may be blunt with you, we don't have time to play around on this, as there is a small window for action when I can definitely tell you their location. I have this knowledge firsthand, as I set it all up, so I know it is good. Normally, I wouldn't do this, but I trust you, so I am prepared to forgo the games and safeguards that I would normally use for securing the delivery of the funds and information. I am sure you will act honorably in this deal. Do I have your word on it?"

"Yes, of course. You are correct, this must be taken care of in the next few hours, or none of us will get our money, promotions, or what we rightfully deserve."

"Good. So, we are 440 on this, right?"

"We are."

There was a pause and the woman said, "I am Sandrah Orgel, your wife's friend. I'm the one who gets her all those special items that are nearly impossible to get elsewhere."

"Ah...Sondra..."

"Sandrah Orgel. You met me a few months back at the party that your wife threw for her Uncle's reelection launch at the Stratus Ambassador Hotel. She needed Loma oysters and Prat shellfish that were not available anywhere else at the time due to some strict government harvesting bans. I am sure she told you that I got them for her and at a great price. Your wife introduced me to you by the champagne fountain. I have long, golden hair and, not to sound too prideful, but people don't forget me when they see me."

"Right, Sandrah. Now I remember. I am so sorry that I didn't place you right away. I would say it is the stress of this whole project and the looming deadline. So, it was my wife who gave you the way to contact me?"

"Of course. I called her telling her some of the story, looking for the right person to contact about it. She immediately saw the value in what I was proposing. I think this is more than luck. As I have such a good working relationship with Vernina, I figured that we could expand the business circle, and we could come to an understanding that would allow you and me to work out a good deal as well."

"Most assuredly, Sandrah. I will deal with you fairly in this."

"I know you will. And who knows what this all could lead to?"

Joden smiled. "This is great. Can I get your particulars, so I can have your payment delivered directly to you right away? I need to get the full details on where I can meet up with these three people as soon as possible. Again, I appreciate that you understand that we don't have much time."

"Of course. As we speak, I am transferring the location information of the three you are seeking and my address, to which you should send payment."

"I see it. Thank you. Hmm, this is most interesting and very helpful, indeed."

"A wise woman has to understand whom she can trust."

"Agreed. You are obviously very wise. Oh, I know that I don't need to say it again, but this deal has to remain completely quiet. No one can know about it. To use your line, are we 440 on this?"

"Of course. Good business is all about keeping confidentiality and dealing fairly. Saying that, I am open to meeting with those whom you trust to explore additional opportunities. I am passionate about business."

"That is good news. It's funny that you should say that—when you meet with my proxy today, I will have an extra activity for you to perform that I am sure that you will be most passionate about. I would meet you myself to finalize the deal with you, but I am sure you understand that I have this new business to attend to, thanks to your help. You will not be forgotten."

"This all sounds delightful," she said.

● ● ●   ▬▬   ▬▬   ▬▬   ● ● ●

"Uncle?" asked an encrypted voice.

"Yes, Drayonev?" said the older man.

"We have a problem. The cleaning that you assigned us was spooked and has fled. We believe he is no longer hunting the operator. I have teams searching for him now."

"How do we know that Joden has done this?"

"We received an encrypted message earlier today from him saying that he knows that you had put a cleaning order on him after the problem with his brother-in-law, Miken. He is asking for more time to remedy his situation, as he has some leads that may solve all of our problems."

"I gave him time, and he did nothing. Why should I give him more?"

"He claims that he has compiled a kill-switch package that will be released to a wide and dangerous audience for us if we try to harm him or his family in any way."

"Do you have faith that he can do this?"

"I think he is desperate enough. He included a few clips from your conversations where somehow he had bypassed the encryption, and based upon what I heard, they would be damning if they were released. The fact that he contacted me directly shows a level of knowledge of our structure that is worrisome."

The older man cursed. "Had he done what I asked the first time or even the second time, we would not be having this discussion. Do you think we can convince him that we have no intentions of cleaning him? Can we pull him back into line, or is this situation beyond repair?"

"He states that the cleaning demand for his brother-in-law has put him at odds with his wife. I don't see a good way out of this unless we can find him and extract the kill-switch media override codes. As paranoid as he is, I think we have a worst-case scenario here with the media release," said Drayonev.

"Are we scanning for his recent activities to help find the packages? He is just a government worker, so he cannot have access to the tools and money that would help him to escape our notice for long. He's not like Newcastle."

"No, Uncle, you are correct. He is not like Newcastle. But we would be foolish to underestimate him. He does have electronic countermeasure training and has spent a number of years in your employ. I believe that he is capable and has a moderately strong level of cunning."

"I will agree with that on some level. Are we able to track him by any of his equipment or that biometrics thing that we did with Newcastle?"

"We have feelers out for any activity in any of his family's financial accounts. I have—can you wait a second, Uncle? I am getting something that may be of importance."

The screen showed that the secured line was on hold. After a minute, the voice came back on. "Good news, we have tagged a private pulsorjet rental on a long-dormant account of Joden's wife. The destination that was given is likely bogus. We can get a signature from the pulsorjet and monitor it from global sources. I think Joden is on the move. His wife is staying with her family and keeping a prominent public position on her Uncle's reelection campaign. She is too exposed for us to take her as a hostage to be able to exert leverage."

"Hostage? I don't think that we want to go that far. We are not barbarians."

"Barbarians? Uncle, may I be frank with you? We are not negotiating a peace settlement. We are talking about killing Newcastle and his group, Joden, and his brother-in-law, Miken. If this fails, and they can link us to the deployment of the assault mechs, the AA-30s, or the hypermissile, they will lock us up for the rest of our lives. We are well past the point where we can feign innocence or plausibly deny any culpability."

"Those are good points. That is why I hired you. Do what you must. We have come too far to stop now, and all this bother may cause us to have to speed up the overall timeline of the project."

"Agreed. I will be in the air to engage as soon as we get a location for Joden or Miken."

"That is good. Please keep me updated as soon as you are able."

"Will do, Uncle."

●●● ⬛ ⬛ ⬛ ●●●

"Yant?"

"Yes," replied a quiet voice on the encrypted line.

"Joden here."

"I heard that you were running."

"Just for now. I have something that may change the song altogether. I need a favor. I have a loose nut that needs to be removed before it causes a much bigger problem."

Yant asked, "Not the whole mess with you-know-who?"

"No. I have Miken on that one, and I am going with him to make sure that gets done right. I need you to take care of someone else. I think you will enjoy this one."

"Flying lessons?"

Joden said, "You might, but I was thinking of something more along the lines of what the symbioid almost did to Mr. N. I am assuming you can break other non-diplomatic class symbioids' encryptions, right? It should be even easier to do, as you will have direct physical access to the symbioid."

"Yes, that will help speed up the process. Either way, I can break the encryption as before. I do want to state in my defense that in the first test case, it wasn't my fault that the task wasn't completed. My process worked flawlessly. There was an EMP that was deployed in the apartment. Did you hear about that?"

"Yeah, I did. There is no EMP in this apartment, and now you will get field data on its efficacy on a twenty-something woman."

"That sounds good. That data will help."

"Once I get back in good with you-know-who, we can get your proper payment settled. I hope that works for you. It shouldn't take long for me to be welcomed back in," said Joden.

"I would hope so. He cannot function without you. I'm sure that even as dense as he is, he will understand that. You should consider letting me take care of him too. I have worked for that arrogant windbag for fifteen years, and I still don't think he knows my name. He called me Grant yesterday. He is dangerously stupid, and that puts us all at risk when he starts thinking that he is the thought leader on anything."

"He is more like the thought loser than the leader. I would love to give you the go ahead, but for the public phase, we will need to have a face for the project. Think future assassination target, and that may help. There is always hope that he will stab himself to death trying to eat with a fork. For the time being, we have to pretend to suffer this fool gladly."

There was a pause and Yant said, "Okay, agreed. So, tell me more about our first female test subject."

"She is a perfect candidate. She is young, greedy, self-absorbed, and shallow."

"You just listed at least a third of the population of Heavensport."

Joden laughed. "True, but this one is a direct threat to us and an extortionist. She is demanding that we deliver 300,000 unicreds to her today, just to keep quiet about what she knows of our plans and who is involved."

"300K? Seriously? I am not going to let some dumb, greedy girl derail all of our hard work. She is going to get paid back in full today. It's fast, but I can manage it. Do you have more on her? It will help in creating a plausible backstory."

"Sure. She is a petty smuggler with too much ambition and too little wisdom or intelligence. For some reason, she also seems to think that she is some great beauty. I don't remember that much about her other than she was kind of plain, but she did have beautiful blonde hair. I would suggest picking a symbioid that is handsome or beautiful to go and meet her at her door. You're the artist in this. Oh, get this, she told me that she is 'passionate about business.' We will test that theory, huh?"

Yant laughed. "That is too funny. This project sounds like great fun, and I am confident it will work. I may try loading the symbioid's hand and a fake credit holder with doses of highly concentrated stimulants to start the process. After that initial dosing, we will be able to lead her to do whatever we want."

"Good. If you can manage it, we don't want her death to appear as a symbioid stimulant software malfunction like we planned with Newcastle. That whole event was too rushed, and it ended up biting us. We don't want to risk any further chance of exposing your brilliant hack. Any ideas how to hide it?"

Yant sounded excited. "I did some research a few months back for such a future project. How about if I dress the scene as if she is one of those do-it-yourself chemical stimulant experimenters? I can fill in her apartment records with materials and data to show her progression in experimentation and her escalating addiction to pleasure."

"That sounds good. After the initial contact and control using the symbioid, we can put the rest of the show in place. Maybe you can you rig one of those inexpensive, barely human-looking pleasure models to make it look like she rewired it to remove the safety functions? The more wild- and wicked-looking, the better. People will write her off as just another sick person."

"Consider it done. I will probably get one of the dark-market Armageddon Love Twenties or one of the Love Storm models.

They are popular with that crowd, as they are easy to modify, and they have already killed a few people who have taken the modifications too far. I'll record a realview of the event for our data review, and if necessary, we can shore up public opinion by dumping a tightly edited version onto the newsblasts. I can make it look like one of those secretly obtained self-recordings of an event that went tragically wrong. That should throw off any deeper inquest. It will go wild crossing the globe. So, who is the lucky lady?"

"Her name is Sandrah Orgel. I will send you the particulars that I have on her."

● ● ● ◗ ◗ ◗ ● ● ●

We passed through the mountains and on through the foot-hills. The view changed continually. Rolling, grassy hills were spattered with dark gray rock outcroppings that starkly forced their way out of the tough soil. We had seen many interesting creatures along the way, some quite large and majestic, but we had not seen a single goliath.

"Still no goliaths," said Jessica with a sad tone.

"No problem." Lauren said, "Realview goliath information." With a flick of her wrist, she chose the recommended selection.

A slender and attractive woman with auburn hair filled the space before us. She smiled and said, "I am glad that you have decided to learn about the elusive, imposing, and sometimes downright scary goliaths. During the next few minutes, I will try to give a brief overview of these magnificent and misunderstood creatures. My name is Dr. Sophia Bulton, and I am the Director of Goliath Studies at the R. D. Newcastle Foundation, a special organization whose mission is to better understand and protect the environment and the creatures that inhabit this wonderful planet of New Jerusalem."

"Pause, realview." The realview stopped and Lauren turned to me and asked, "Is this R. D. Newcastle your organization?"

"I told them that this information didn't have to be on any of the realviews that they were making. It makes it sound as if I am doing this for publicity. I didn't even want my name on the foundation, as I got others to help me pay for it, but I was over-ruled."

Jessica was surprised. "You are giving them money so that they can study goliaths?" I nodded. "Even after they killed your brother and sister?"

"If goliaths did it, it wasn't personal. They didn't come and knock at the door of their house and kill them when they an-swered the door. I don't know how or why they died. As I said, the whole premise stank. They attributed their deaths to being attacked by goliaths."

Jessica's eyes were wild and angry. "If you even had the slightest belief that they did, regardless of what provoked them, why would you give money to learn about these things?"

"They are amazing creatures. Yes, they are cranky, quick to anger, and almost impossible to stop once they decide to ram-page, but did you know that some of New Jerusalem's most im-portant crops can be fertilized only by goliath dung?"

"I would have, if you had let us watch this realview," said Lau-ren.

"My dear miss, I believe that you were the one who stopped the playback, so let me finish. We understand little about many of the important creatures and environments on New Jerusalem, and not understanding them leads us to dumb, snap decisions that may imperil us all. Everything is interconnected, even if we don't immediately see the connection. Man is the interloper on this planet, and because we have the technology to save or destroy species, we should give a little consideration and seek a bit more information before we decide to annihilate a species or a habitat."

Exhaling, I continued, "Before you think I am being all noble here, I started the goliath study for all the wrong reasons. I loved Mary and Paul very much, and I was hurting and angry. I wanted to develop plans on how to kill off the goliath without causing them to go crazy, wiping out whole cities or any of our crops. Did you know if you kill or wound one, it can create a chain reaction among their pack that causes them to go absolutely insane with anger? We still have no idea how to calm them once they get going. They are forces of nature, like enormous, beetle-shaped tornadoes or hurricanes.

Undaunted by my explanation Jessica said, "So, did you try to kill some as a test?"

Trying to read her, I said, "No. I spent over two months with one of the teams that were studying them. I learned that they can dig through bedrock easier and faster than our best machines. They appear to be intelligent, and we know that they care for each other. They have six to eight chain-brains randomly placed through their bodies. Even after taking massive damage, they can function on a single brain. This and their extremely tough exoskeletons make them hard to kill. And no one has had any success in domesticating them.

"As much as I wanted to hate them, after spending time studying them at a distance, I learned to respect these incredible wild creatures. It comes down to this: I can't prove that they killed my brother and sister as the report says. I do know that they were not hunting them, and Paul wasn't piloting the Raptor. It is either a bogus report, or the goliaths were provoked to kill them."

With a wry smile, Lauren said, "I am not sure that we have to watch this realview now."

Jessica appeared satisfied with this. "Fair enough, but I have a few questions about them yet. We can watch the realview, or you can tell us, how big and how old do they get? How fast are they, and could we outrun them if we had to?"

"We saw a few large males that were about 180 feet long, 95 feet wide, and 75 feet at the head. We still don't know how old they can get. It is estimated that they may live to be about 120 years, maybe much more. Sophia and her team clocked one at about 64 miles per hour, so no, you cannot outrun them on foot without an exoskeleton war suit. I say stick to a pulsorjet, and go high to get away from one."

Lauren arched an eyebrow and said, "Sophia?"

"Yes, Dr. Bulton. I funded the mission so it wasn't as if I were an employee. When you spend long hours camouflaged in a pulsorjet, everyone is on a first-name basis."

"So, how well did you get to know her?" Lauren asked, her gaze and voice tight. I got the drift.

"Pretty well, but I was closer to her husband Dr. Trey, who was with us. He is a great guy, and he has a deep love for the goliaths that you cannot help but catch. Their two teenaged kids, Samantha and Sorren, helped in logging our realviews and data. Someday soon they are going to be great scientists as well. You would like them all."

With a sheepish smile, Lauren said, "Cool. That answers my questions."

Jessica nodded. "For me as well."

●●● ▬ ▬ ▬ ●●●

We were about forty miles from the city of Kongesgaard when the train system told us to take to our g-seats immediately. Auto-strapping in, we felt a pull on the train, and the cars began to decelerate rapidly and change their course. We lifted to rise over a row of tall trees that grew on a long, wide stone ridge to our right side. Topping it, we slid into a deep, wide valley that was ringed by high hills about two miles away.

Lauren called out, "Look!"

To the left of the train, a powerful, 115-foot-tall, bipedal Defender robot, using its silent lifters, had moved to pace us a half a car up from ours. Its plasma cannons were moving as if following some unseen target. As big as the train was, this impressive white, green, and blue mech held our attention. It looked tough and mean.

I watched it moving nearer. "I would hate to mess with that thing."

Jessica pointed to the other side of the cabin, "There's another one."

A second Defender had moved in on the other side of the train a few cars back. Something bad was up.

Secured by the safety harness, I strained forward, trying to sit up more to get a better look, "This is not good."

As I said that, a loud, clacking thump struck the right side of our window, making us jump in our seats. The ella-glanse window held, but we could see that some greasy, green-brown substance was covering it and blocking a portion of our view.

Lauren popped up a floating screen in front of her and was busy pulling up an image of the smear and studying it. She sent the feed to our chairs for us. "What do you suppose that is?"

"I have no idea. Maybe it was a bird or some huge bug that hit it. Whatever it was, it really stinks," said Jessica, wrinkling her nose as the putrid smell began entering the cabin. "I'll try to get the cabin to clean it off."

The tree-lined rock ridge to our left was steadily rising up to become taller than the train car. As we slowed more, the Defender slid back alongside our cabin. Its cannons were moving even more aggressively.

Jessica was scared. "I don't like this—"

The Defender began firing large volleys of shimmering blue and red plasma blobs up towards the wooded area. Lines of trees were being shredded along the ridge following our train and gaining on us. We still couldn't see what was doing it. I was about ninety-eight percent sure what it was. The plasma bursts were lighting up the darkening sky, and we heard a deep, angry whistling growl that was much too close to us.

"That is a goliath call," I said.

With a lurch, all the cars around us broke formation, scattering like a school of fish trying to avoid becoming dinner.

Trees were disintegrating closer to us. A blur of rage and fury vaulted over the ridge to land on top of the Defender. It was a massive, dark reddish-brown, beetle-looking creature with a single enormous front pincer. The goliath was about 160 feet long, a good eighty feet wide, and sixty feet tall at the head. Using its giant front pincer and two of its long, spiny, jagged legs, it grasped the Defender, enveloping it. With a sickening crunch, it reduced the huge robot into a pile of jagged metal.

"Dear God, protect us," cried Lauren.

More plasma deterrent blasts were fired above and to the left of us. In a blaze of green and yellow pulsorjet flames, the remaining Defender rocketed over us to engage the goliath. The battle was intense as the Defender sought to keep the goliath away from the train and to stay out of grappling distance of the rampaging creature. The plasma blasts were designed to redirect, not to hurt or anger the creature. At this moment, they had little effect.

Lauren's eyes were wild and scared. "They are like angry pulsorjets."

Our car began dodging as a second goliath launched over the rock hills, destroying large sections of the trees like a missile strike. The Defender backed up, firing all its cannons in a wide burst pattern. The sky lit up in blue and red pulses that knocked the goliaths backward. The shockwaves pummeled our car, making it lean to the right side. The car's survival systems were hard at work, trying to help us evacuate the area.

Jessica face was flushed and strained as she gripped the side of her g-seat. "Why aren't we racing away from the area? This car can easily go 400 miles per hour. We could leave these goliaths in the dust."

Lauren didn't look any better as she held on for dear life. "If we hit one at that speed, even with a glancing blow, we would die." Her voice rose in panic.

I said, "They have us surrounded, so we cannot break free and hit higher speeds."

The first goliath broke to the right and moved around to the back of the Defender, sending up wide torrents of churned soil. The second goliath launched itself up to land on the Defender. Despite taking direct plasma weapon blasts, it slammed the massive robot down to embed it deep in the tall grass and dirt. The large, wicked pincer chomped down on the Defender's head, popping it cleanly from its torso.

"Brace for impact!" yelled Jessica.

With an explosive crash, the first goliath broadsided our car, driving it sideways into the ground. Even with the car's leveling systems on high alert, we almost rolled upside down.

Our g-seats held us tightly in place, trapping us, as the car attempted to right itself to a seventy-degree angle. We heard the unmistakable sounds of the cockpit's walls being punctured. We watched in horror as several long goliath leg spikes tore into the sides of the cabin, piercing the hull.

With a crescendo of power, the emergency escape engines jettisoned our wounded cabin up and away from the rest of the demolished train car. The embedded spiny leg claws were tearing down the walls, cutting jagged swaths as the powerful lift continued. With a deep, whistling howl of anger, the goliath fell off, and the long cabin jerked skyward like a tensioned spring had been released.

Wind and pulsorjet engine noise roared in the long open gashes in the wall of our cabin. The rank organic smell from the goliath permeated the air, nauseating me. Through the slashed airframe walls, we could see the sun setting and the distant outline of a city as we rose higher into the sky. With a loud metal ripping sound, the starboard pulsorjet broke free, taking an eight-foot-wide section with it.

"Hold on!" I cried.

"To what?" yelled Lauren.

Good question, and I had no answer. "Jesus is Lord!" I shouted in fear as the craft shuddered and groaned under the pressure.

The cabin began to shake and rattle as it began to slow in its upward trajectory. The remaining jets were firing, shaking and flexing the damaged cabin where it began breaking apart. Shards blew outward as the more of the engines tore off and flew away. With no forward thrust, the air pressure brought us to a stop. Momentarily weightless, we felt gravity grab hold, and we began to fall. Emergency chutes deployed, and we slowed until we heard the tethers being ripped free one by one. The long, thin cabin started spiraling as we dropped.

A rush of air pressure surrounded me as an ella-glanse canopy enclosed my g-seat. With a pop, the cabin's ceiling blew out and away. With a silent rush of acceleration, my seat shot upward, out of the doomed module. I started to black out as I blasted away into the fading light.

Far in the darkness, indistinct voices were yelling. Groggily, I came to at the sound of pulsorjets pushing my escape pod and saw that I was close to landing. To my sides, I noted that there were two more pods in the process of landing by me. My attention was drawn to a huge cloud of dust that had risen up around a mangled wreck about 1,000 yards off towards the setting sun. It was coming back to me. That was what was left of our train car's cabin.

Lauren's voice broke the deafening silence. "Rolland! Jessica! Are you both okay?"

I heard Jessica reply, "I am."

Attempting to reclaim myself, I grunted out, "I am, barely. How about you?"

"I am good, but I am not sure how much longer that will be. Look off to the northeast."

Jessica moaned, "Goliath."

Over the hills and valleys, we saw four enormous red-brown goliaths swarming over the hills and grass, moving toward us at a terrifying clip. They didn't bother swerving around trees or terrain, but plowed over and crushed everything as they passed on their six long, spiked, and armored legs. They were charging the cabin's crash site.

Still descending, we watched in horror as two of the goliaths seemed to notice us and changed course to intercept us.

Jessica cried out, "How do you get these pods to change course? Take us to the city! Don't land us by them!"

A man's voice over our pod's intercom said, "Goliaths are attacking. Please remain calm. We will direct your escape pods to one of our goliath-proof bunkers. For your safety, after landing, please be prepared to exit your pod as quickly as possible and follow directions."

Goliath-proof? There was no such thing. I had watched them tunneling. You have to hope that they get bored and give up. This, however, was not the time to share this information.

Our descent began to slow, and the goliaths seemed to speed up. Below us, three cylinders of dirt and grass lifted up and slid to the side, revealing three smooth white tunnels. It seemed implausible that we would make it to these openings in time. We were like three plump sausages being slowly handed to hungry dogs.

"This is not good!" called out Lauren.

From behind us, a pounding sound wave shook the air as a blue and red plasma blast sent the lead goliath reeling on its back legs. A Defender flew in from the left side and planted itself between us and the charging goliath. Dirt clods and plasma bursts rained down as the clash intensified. In the distance, I could see more Defenders flying in to our rescue.

There was a sharp clack as something hard smacked into my canopy window. My heart leaped, and I jerked back as much as possible while being restrained by the g-seat. There was that same greasy smudge and awful stink as we had seen on the window of the car.

"My canopy just got hit by another pheromone bullet! That was what hit our car that started this whole mess. Someone is targeting us to die by goliath." I finally realized what was going on. They had found us.

In the distance, I saw the other two goliaths at the cabin's crash site, turning to converge on our location. We watched their rage magnify. The blocking Defender was shattered and tossed aside as they powered over the terrain to try and catch us.

"Pull up! PULL UP!" I yelled at our escape pods. "You are going to kill us!"

Like bullets being shot into the barrels of weapons, we blasted downward. Spiky goliath claws slashed at us. I watched as a claw filled my view, and cold darkness slapped my vision.

It took a moment to realize that it had missed, and I was shooting down my tunnel.

"Are you okay?" I asked, afraid of the answer.

"That was too close!" called out Lauren.

Jessica's voice was quavering. "One of their claws scraped my canopy and scratched it. What kind of claws do these things have to be able to scar ella-glanse?"

Light struck our eyes as we dropped into a large open hallway, and with an upward arc, we continued to fly along near the ceiling. I could see one of the women's escape pods in front of mine.

"Why didn't they just fly us to the city?" asked Lauren.

"The goliaths might have followed us, and that could endanger thousands of people," I said. "This is standard operating procedure out here."

From above and behind us, we heard a terrible grinding and crunching noise. Still strapped in, I turned in fear to catch a glimpse of the roof of the corridor being torn away. The goliaths had not given up. They were digging through stone and reinforced graphene as if it were crumb cake, and they were gaining on us.

●●● ▭▭▭ ●●●

18

The Wheat and the Tares

●●● ━━ ━━ ━━ ●●●

"Did the goliaths get them? I can't see." Joden was focusing on a small screen that was linked to an external array of amplified tactical sensors and lenses.

Inside the electro-camouflage nest, the two men lay on their stomachs facing toward the goliath's rampage. They were wearing bulky electro-ghillie suits, which, even though they were inactive, still made them difficult to see.

Miken frowned as he focused through the scope of his TechCat 60 long-range sniper system and replied, "I can't tell; a goliath is blocking my view. Can you send up a micro drone?"

"We left that satchel back in the pulsorjet. This will be over by the time I go and get them. I still think we should have just shot them all."

"You mean *you* left them. I have the gear that I was supposed to bring. And for the last time, we didn't shoot them because there is no way to make it look like an accident. Let me make it simple—fatal goliath attack, rare but no deep inquest. Three people with their upper bodies blown away and burned by long-distance sniper shots, and there would be an intense inquest and prolonged chase with no statutes of limitation. Hmm. Let me think about this. No, shut up." Miken watched as a second Defender swooped in to block the goliath that was digging ferociously at the tunnel entrances. "My biggest reason, death from rail-bolt is too quick." Miken sent off another pheromone bullet near the same spot. "I want Newcastle to suffer."

Three more goliaths charged the spot and turned the two Defenders into nasty, jagged scraps. They joined in to begin tearing up the ground, throwing streams of boulders, soil, and bunker materials behind them. Where they dug was becoming a wide, deep, and angry ravine.

Two Defenders that were hovering above the fray sent a barrage of non-lethal plasma bombs to deter the goliaths. The blasts slowed them, but they remained unwilling to give up their attack.

Joden grumbled and said, "I don't get it. Why don't the Defenders just use deadly force?"

Miken's eyes never left his scope. "Because even wounding one of them enrages all the goliaths to the point they destroy everything around them until they die, which can be a long stinking time. It's like a chain reaction in a nuclear blast. With the city nearby, they don't want to risk that."

"Why don't they just figure out a way to kill them all off, like with poison, and not have to deal with these stupid things?"

Exasperated, Miken snorted and turned to look at Joden. "Question: did you skip school, or did you do a lot of drugs?"

"I went to the best private schools, where we were not concerned with the lifestyles of farm animals."

"Goliaths are not farm animals! No one has had any success domesticating them. For your information, private school boy, their droppings are the best fertilizer on the planet and the only thing that feeds some of the most important crops we have. We would all be in serious dung without their dung. In fact, their droppings are the best-smelling part of them, and just a couple thousand pounds of it is worth more than your whole stinking education. I mean that figuratively and literally. Now, can I get back to my job, or do you have other stupid questions?"

Abruptly, the Defenders ceased firing and began flying away from the area, moving to take up defensive positions leading to the distant city's walls. Somewhere an actuarial program had counted the three humans as lost and set the defense of the city as the highest priority.

Joden was scanning his monitor with a grin on his face. "The Defenders just left. That should speed things up." His joy was short-lived. "Oh...I think we have a problem. We have three faint inbound signals moving in fast and masked. By the signal spread and shape, the system says that they are—Wraiths. They are scanning for advanced electro-camouflage and life signals. They are looking for us."

"Or Newcastle. Send me their positions. Do you think your old boss is on one?" asked Miken, who was methodically scanning the skies with his weapon's scope.

Joden's face grew pinched and angry. "What makes you think he would come out?"

Miken rolled to his side and with a smooth practiced hand began changing out the TechCat 60's receiver and ammo cartridge. "Because Wraiths are command craft. They are one of the few frontline attack ships that can carry people, important people, those who have the authority to make instant decisions."

"What are you going to do?" asked Joden, his voice rising in alarm as he watched Miken charging the weapon.

Linking his scope to the two outlying railgun barrage sniper turrets that he had set up earlier, Miken slid back into his prone firing position. "If we wait, we will die. I think it is time to send them some friendly little greetings."

●●● ▬ ▬ ▬ ●●●

Moving in a stalking stealth formation towards the City of Kongesgaard, three attack Wraiths were high up, surveying the live data coming from satellite feeds. They could see that the southwestern ridge near the city was under siege by four aggressive and angry goliaths. The two remaining Defenders backed away and move toward the city.

"Sir, we have picked up a faint bio-scan signal from the hills. It could be Joden and Miken or Newcastle and his team. It could even be civilians taking cover; I doubt it is local animal life. What are your orders, sir?"

Drayonev sneered and said, "We all have to die sometime, don't we, sergeant? Commence firing on that position."

Ironically, as he said that, a barrage of super-hypersonic railgun bolts struck the craft in its main pulsorjet motor coupling, severing the rotor from the shaft. The ultrasonic rotor blew through the housing and ripped through the Wraith's cockpit and weapons bay, causing it to disintegrate in a fiery blossom high up in the atmosphere.

The second Wraith fared only slightly better. It had been hit with a second salvo of railgun bolts, inflicting extensive damage on the craft, but it was able to maintain its altitude. The two remaining Wraiths began evasive action and fired on the hillside, causing it to erupt in a continuous and thunderous volley of roiling flames.

●●● ▬ ▬ ▬ ●●●

Our escape pods began to open as we glided down to land on a fast-moving autowalk. With the sight of the roof being torn free above us, we leapt free and started running on the down-ward-sloping autowalk. Pounding down the hallway, my eyes were losing focus, and I was having tunnel vision as I went into survival mode.

The hallway narrowed, and I glanced back to see the three pods moving off to some unseen location. I hoped the goliaths would chase them and not us. If any of the pheromone scent was on us, I knew they wouldn't stop until we were dead or that scent was gone. I wasn't feeling too optimistic.

In front of me, I saw Jessica stagger and fall head-first off the autowalk. I darted forward, snaring her upper arm, roughly pull-ing her back to safety. She turned, her face radiating fear, hands up ready to fight. Seeing it was me, she allowed me to guide her to stand on the fast-moving walkway.

About thirty feet in back of us, the ceiling ruptured loudly, spewing long, churning goliath legs. The fading light of the sky was coming from behind the goliaths, making them even more frightening. The hallway lights where the creatures dug kept blinking out as they were ground up by their fast-moving claws. We ran with all our might.

In the distance, we heard the sound of powerful rolling ex-plosions. The ground shook, threatening to make us fall. The go-liaths seemed unfazed as they continued their sustained digging and tearing.

"There! A decontamination shower!" yelled Lauren, pointing to a sign down the hall on the left.

We ran to it. Jumping off the autowalk, we skidded into the room. The crashing and grinding grew closer behind us. Each of us dove to pull on the red emergency handles hanging from the ceiling around the room. With a loud rush of cool air, the room disappeared in a billowing white cloud of gas.

It obscured our vision and covered us top to bottom in a liquid that had an odd chemical scent. The awful grinding, crunching, and rending noises of the shelter being torn asunder grew closer.

I could hear Lauren and Jessica moving and coughing.

"Come to me," I called out to them. Blinded, they bumped into me, and we pulled each other close. We scuttled back to the farthest corner of the room, away from the approaching goliaths.

●●● ▬▬ ▬▬ ▬▬ ●●●

Joden and Miken bounded over the terrain as the Wraiths' first barrage pounded the distant areas where their sniper turrets had fired. The ground shook and trembled so much that they fought to keep from falling. Torrents of charred dirt rained as a towering orange wall of wrath grew upward, and the noise of the sustained blasts pummeled them. High above them and miles in the distance, a separate large fire blossom was rumbling and growing as it began falling from the sky. Miken's first shot had brought down one of the targets, but that left two Wraiths that were still hunting them.

Their active military electro-active camouflage suits were the only thing that had saved them. The faint visual smear that was Miken's electro-ghillie suit turned and raised the huge TechCat 60 long-range sniper system to his shoulder again, and he scanned the sky, looking for an opportunity.

Over the encrypted comm Miken snarled, "Get in the pulsorjet. Don't start it or we are dead! Wait, I will be there in a few seconds."

Joden didn't need to be told twice to flee. He didn't have any weapons or skill that could make any difference in this fight. He bounded down the rocky and grass-covered hillside to reach the electronically shielded Stratos M380 pulsorjet. He ran to the other side of the craft, and the side swung open, presenting a g-seat for him like an orange tongue. He threw himself into the g-seat, and he felt the racing harness close about his bulky electro-ghillie suit. In a swift, fluid motion, the seat pivoted, pulling him into the streamlined racing cockpit, and the ship closed.

Anxious, his adrenaline flowing, Joden sat peering out the opposite side's window, keeping a twitchy palm by the race launch button. He chewed on his lower lip, waiting. The pressure was unbearable! For a moment he considered pounding down on that red button on the center console and taking his chances. No. That would get them all killed. If somehow he survived, he would spend the rest of his life expecting Miken to show up and bring him to a horrendously gory and painful end. Sweat was dripping down his brow, and he nearly started the ship's environmental systems to cool off. That might alert the Wraiths. Dragging the back of his hand against his brow, he wiped away the sweat before it dripped into his eyes. He swallowed hard as his throat was tight.

Looking up the slight incline leading away from the pulsorjet, he watched as a ghostly faint blur slid over the rough ground, moving towards him, looking like a gust of wind. Even with the encrypted signal from Miken's camouflage suit linked to his visor, he was still difficult to see. The shape stopped, and the telltale sound of the big weapon being fired was heard. Two more times it hammered in rapid succession. An explosion rocked the air several miles away. Miken had hit another of the Wraiths.

The passenger side of the ship opened. Joden was about to say something when he was struck in his right shoulder and neck by the huge sniper rifle as it was tossed sideways into the pulsorjet.

"Hey! That hurt! Watch what you are doing!" cried Joden.

The small racing pulsorjet lurched to the side as the blurry shape of Miken slid into the cabin. "GO! GO! GO!"

Seething at being hit, Joden smashed down on the race launch button. The pulsorjet leapt to life, taking to the air, snapping them painfully back in their g-seats. In their monitors, they saw the hillside where they had just been as it turned to flaming dust. The ship took a sweeping right and hugged the hillsides as it continued to gain speed.

"Send the package!" yelled his brother-in-law.

"Did you get the other two?" asked Joden, who was having difficulty with the heavy g-forces.

"Send the package, now. I dropped another one and put two bolts into the other, but we don't have much time. We need to get out of here NOW! I need to get to another vantage point as far out of this area as possible for me to try again."

There was no turning back if he sent it. Deep down inside, he knew that he had no other choice. With a heavy voice, he said, "Launch package Revenge. Initiate."

A smiley face appeared on his face screen. He turned to his brother-in-law and gave him a thumbs-up. That was dumb—with his suit on, Miken wouldn't be able to see that.

"We're done," called out Joden.

"Good. Let's end this!"

With those apt words, the cockpit disintegrated into a bright and angry orange inferno of fire and malice.

● ● ●   ▬ ▬ ▬   ● ● ●

19

Retaliation

●●● ▬ ▬ ▬ ●●●

The remaining Wraith had sustained such catastrophic damage that it was having trouble keeping aloft. Explosions in several of the weapons bays had come close to ending its journey. Even with that, it had managed to launch a full retaliatory missile strike with its remaining payload. The high rolling hillside where the shots had come from was now a long, deep, ragged, and smoking valley. The scatter of sophisticated metal alloys was proof that an aircraft had been obliterated. Anyone or anything unlucky enough to have been within a mile and a half range of the center of the strikes had been eliminated.

The wounded Wraith's warning systems were lit up. It needed to land, or it ran the risk of falling from the air. The sole human on the Wraith, a tech sergeant, took inventory of the functional armaments. Four T-20s, two T-10s and the whole drop line of twenty Malcat-92s and fifteen AA-30s were all showing damage beyond use. Only two T-40 Nightmares were still able to come online. He powered them up and set them on a search-and-destroy mission with the focus on the area where the goliaths were rampaging. Eliminate the goliaths first, then any humans found in that zone. He was going to fulfill the mission.

The huge beetle creatures were not a real threat to the T-40s. He would order them to use close contact melee tactics rather than hovering out of reach and blowing the stupid bugs to slime. The mechs would look so awesomely cool, coming in close, spewing death and destruction, and maybe they would rip through one of those huge bugs with their claws while shooting another with their rail-cannons. They would play this encounter back for years, as it was going to be so awesome. He fired off some battle recorders to find the best angles.

Tremendous elation made him quiver as he pressed the T-40s launch key. It was almost too much to believe. Holding his breath in anticipation, he watched the situational awareness screen and his armament reticule as the two assault mechs shot out of the side of the Wraith. As designed, they deployed their glide fins and electronic countermeasures to soar away cloaked so not to draw enemy fire to his hidden attack craft. Once free of potential backtrack tracing, the Nightmares' attack thrust engines kicked in, and they streaked in a blaze of avenging fire toward the target.

What a day it had been. No one that he knew had never fired more than a single missile, and that was only during training. He had just launched a full Wraith salvo and two Nightmares. *Beat that, Robert. Two Nightmares!* Nightmare, that is the proper name for these T-40s. He spat out a laugh. Anyone down there was in for a horrible night before they permanently slept.

An imminent failure warning came over the system. The Wraith was dying, and it had to be set down immediately. He keyed in the landing site to be near enough to watch the battle even if he had to evacuate the ship. The T-40s would end this fight so fast that he would not be in any danger, even being so close. The Nightmares would have his battle suit's signature, so they would protect him at all costs. After the engagement was over, he would call in an evac-rescue ship for his pick-up. This would be so cool. Strolling in with two T-40s at his side. This would make him famous among the other tech sergeants. Maybe he would even get a battlefield commission.

He had to think of what to say when they came to pick him up as he stood valiantly amidst all the carnage, acting as if it were nothing. They would be recording it. "Hi honey, I am home." No, that didn't work. Or "Oh, nothing much, just another day. How was yours?" "Spare a lift?" "Just doing my duty, sir." The right phrase would make him famous beyond the military. He would come off as totally cool, and he would get lots of hot babes wanting to date him. Maybe he would get a realview adventure star contract.

This called for some music. He pulled up his playlist and punched the Death Marchers' *Lament for the Dying*.

"Oh, the chicken goes, buck, buck, buck, squawk and the—"

"Stoli! Keep your freakin' hands off my stuff! It's not funny, you jerk," yelled the tech sergeant, killing the audio. This was his moment and that jerk Stoli had messed with his tracks. This was supposed to be all-powerful and cool; that dumb kid's song was certainly not cool. He frowned. Maybe he could get them to edit this out of the ship's recording.

He found another of his favorite Death Marchers' songs. Yes! Cranking up the pounding drum and throbbing guitar riff throughout the wounded ship, he watched the screens with obvious joy and anticipation, waiting for the awesome show that was about to begin.

The rain falls with no mercy, drenching friends and foes alike,

Death from the sky, pouring down missiles, like kisses of endless spite,

Death from the sky!

Death from the sky-aye-aye-aye!

●●● ━ ━ ━ ●●●

The sound of the walls being torn away filled our ears and minds with terror as we huddled together against the back wall of the decontamination shower. We had nothing that would harm a goliath, especially not an enraged one. I held on tight to Lauren and Jessica as we sat helplessly, surrounded by the dense fog of the chemicals. The noise of the goliaths stopped. The silence was just as horrible.

We could hear long, spiked goliath legs scraping the floors and walls, feeling about for us. We held our breaths, and I kissed Lauren and Jessica on the tops of their heads; our lives would be over in a moment.

I don't know who started it, but we were whispering "Jesus is Lord" over and over. Our speaking would draw the goliath to us, but the small size of the room made the outcome inevitable. Crumpled together, we waited for the inevitable sting of death. We were about to meet our Savior.

Explosions thundered above us, sending earthquake shock waves along the corridor and the walls. The hallway outside the decontamination room lit up as if we had collided with the sun. Not two feet from where we were, we saw a six-foot-long, spiked goliath claw highlighted in the intense light, moving forward to snare us. It jerked back as the massive goliath retreated out of the room and scurried down the corridor.

Lauren and Jessica were gripping me so hard it hurt, but I would not have pushed them away for anything. I held them tighter in the sweltering heat of the room.

●●● ▭ ▭ ▭ ●●●

When the T-40s were about two miles out and closing fast, they began firing their cannons and hyper-missiles on the goliaths. Erupting in fire, chunks of the creatures sprayed across the ground. The rear goliath reared to lift its body and claws high to protect the others. The T-40s swept in low from the right and left as that goliath fell to the soil, writhing and dying as a concave shell.

The remaining three goliaths bellowed with deep, resounding rage and released their fury on the landing assault mechs. The T-40s met them head-on in a blaze of weapons fire that eviscerated the next goliath.

The third goliath vaulted over the first and pounced on the nearest T-40. Wrapping its barbed front legs around the assault mech, its massive front pincer clamped down on the midsection. The T-40's shoulder-mounted rail-cannons continued to pound the two goliaths mercilessly as its battle frame began to buckle and separate. With a snap, its upper body, with its cannons still firing, spun free, flipping end over end, barely missing the other T-40.

Hypersonic projectiles sprayed upward, striking the Wraith, which was sixty feet from landing. The craft erupted in a thunderous, concussive explosion that finished off the wounded assault mech and launched the second T-40 directly into the maw of the remaining goliath.

The battle was intense and brief. The damaged T-40 rose from the burned wreckage, stench, and gore. The goliath rampage had ended.

● ● ●　▬　▬　▬　● ● ●

The sound of blasts and a sustained barrage of continuous cannon fire were shaking the walls around us. A line of two-inch-thick holes appeared in the ceiling above us and continued on through the floor next to us.

"Rail cannons," cried Lauren.

We scrambled, moving as fast as we could to the corner of the decontamination shower trying to offer as small a target area as possible. A series of rolling blasts shook us out of our daze.

"Run!" I yelled.

We scrambled to our feet and dashed into the corridor. More explosions shook the air around us as we turned left, away from the war above us. The roof had fallen in, blocking most of the hallway, but we squeezed through a tight gap and crawled on skinned knees and sore palms to move further down the hall. The lights ahead had somehow managed to stay on throughout the furious battle.

Suddenly it went still. There were no more blasts, shots, or sounds. Our ears rang in the stifling quiet. We looked at each other, not daring to hope that it was over.

Then there came grinding noises from behind us. A large and powerful mechanical claw was tearing away huge chunks of re-inforced bunker walls with ease. A section of the blockage fell away to reveal a battle-scarred T-40 Nightmare. We began to run.

In a panic, I yelled at the top of my lungs, "In the Name of Jesus, I command you to stop!"

To our surprise, all the hall and room lights went out. We stopped in a few short feet, as we were unable to see. This would not stop the assault mech.

We turned to see, framed in the fading light from above, that this aptly named Nightmare had stopped, frozen in place, and had slumped forward. Why? I stared wild-eyed, expecting it to finish what it had come to do, but it just stood there, motionless in the gap. Thick dust drifted in lazy circles around this awful monstrosity. Hollow silence greeted us. My head throbbed, and my eyes burned. Still, it didn't move.

Lauren and Jessica were weeping, and I gathered them to me and said, "It's okay, It's okay. We are going to make it. We need to get out of here." I didn't want to say it, but the T-40 could be in the process of regenerating its systems.

We were all shaking, and the emotions flooding us were overwhelming. Our eyes were becoming accustomed to the faint light that came around the motionless assault mech.

Creeping out into the destruction of the hallway I asked, "Should we attempt to go past the T-40 or head down the hallway and try to find a way out?"

"Away. That thing didn't come to save us from the goliath, but to kill us," said Jessica. "We don't know what else is up there."

Lauren said, "We have a problem. There is no light, and we will be in total darkness in a few yards."

"Lights on," I called out. Nothing happened. "Emergency power!" Still nothing. "This won't work. We have to head back the way we came."

No one said anything more as we turned about and moved stealthily in the direction that every part of us desperately wanted to avoid.

There was a noise coming from down the hall. Prepared to run, we heard, "Rolland! Newcastle, Jessica, Lauren! Are you there?"

My heart leaped with joy. "Curtis! Curtis! Down here!"

Peeking past the frozen T-40 was the helmeted face of my dear friend Terry Curtis, wearing a black armored gigasuit. He was pointing a large blocky weapon in our general direction, and then he lowered the barrel, pointing it to the floor. After this harrowing day, I had a moment of mistrust.

Through the visor of his helmet, I could see Curtis smiling broadly. "Come on. Let's get out of here before something else shows up." With a fast perusal, he asked, "Does any of you need a robo-doc?"

Each of us gave ourselves a quick check, and we shook our heads. We were sore and bruised, but no blood or major damage was evident.

"We're good," I said.

"I am so glad to hear that all three of you are all right." As he led the way past the T-40 that was still blocking the hallway, he said over his shoulder, "Did you see those goliaths up there? They are huge, and they really stink."

"Far too much and far too close, thank you," replied Jessica.

When we were past the imposing assault mech, Terry stopped and gently placed the tip of the large weapon against the crumpled chest of the T-40 and pulled the trigger, but there was no sound. He moved the barrel to the unit's sleek black and gray helmet head and repeated the process. There was still no noise. After the olfactory abuse of the day, it was hard to say, but I thought I smelled something that brought back memories of my misadventure with Erlin.

With another quick smile, he nodded his helmet toward the weapon and said, "It's a focused EMP rifle that I designed. T-40s can regenerate from some of the most severe attacks. If you would move back a bit, I have another gift for it to make sure that it doesn't survive. I think you are going to enjoy it."

Once we were back about fifteen feet, he turned and took careful aim at the matte gray mech's main processor panel on its chest.

Terry glanced over at us and said, "I don't know how loud this will be. It is my first field test."

Lauren and Jessica covered their ears, and I stared, waiting. There was a startling bang, and the midsection of the mech jerked back, revealing a large, thumb-sized hole that ran through its thick armored chest.

Curtis laughed and exclaimed, "Wow, that has a kick." He stepped forward to examine both sides of the hole created by railgun projectile. The hole in the back of the T-40 was about twice the size of his fist; the hypersonic bolt had burned and punched through and continued on through the reinforced wall behind it. Smoke was billowing out, and a faint glow was evident from the intense heat.

"That is so cool. I wanted to test this, but that is not something that one should do in a city." He analyzed the gaping hole. "Even without its active armor functioning, I would say that this was a successful experiment. Did you see that? It turned the T-40's battle controller and its AI core into a molten railgun bolt and punched it about two hundred feet, probably more into that wall. What little is left in there is all burned, fused, and shredded, so we don't have to worry about it regenerating." He lifted the rifle up and nodded to it and said, "This is a railgun too. As I was designing it, I saw that there was room for both systems, and I could adapt them to use the same power source...which by my readout is nearly depleted. There is about one more railgun shot or a small EMP blast left. I call that energy well spent. We really don't want this mech waking up and chasing us."

"That is a major understatement," I said, wondering when Curtis had become so chatty.

Outside, Curtis led us up through a deep and wide angry war wound of a crevasse. As we walked past the putrid carcasses of the goliaths, I saw the wreckage of at least one airframe of what might have been a Wraith, two halves of a T-40, and what could be the parts of a number of Defenders. It was hard to tell what all was there. War had ravaged the land. The stench was unbelievable, and I don't dare try to describe it.

We followed, stumbling along behind Curtis, who held his large weapon at the ready. Just past the burned area containing the most devastation, Curtis stopped and pointed to a line of large burned and cracked boulders. As he moved his hand, there was the faintest blurring near the center. His ship had cloaked itself as a large battle-damaged rock outcrop to avoid detection.

Through his helmet's shiny face screen we could see that Curtis was smiling, trying to reassure us. "Head to that darker section there. That is the door to my ship."

Lauren's face was concerned, and I understood it. Even the appearance of going back underground was unappealing.

I said, "I can go first if that will help."

She stepped aside to stand next to Jessica. Curtis stood behind us, standing guard with his weapon, scanning the sky and terrain with his tactical visor.

Stepping through the dark section, I was surprised when to see a sixty-year-old Stargazer camping pulsorjet, not the sleek ship I was expecting. This is the kind of ship that your grandparents would have used for camping back in their day. A plaque by the door said, *"Stargazer 22 - How real adventurers roam."* Despite its age and subtle signs of wear, it was clean and it looked comfortable. A shower and a simple bed would be awesome.

Lauren and Jessica stepped in and stopped glancing about the boxy, outdated cabin that had a retro-cool feel to it. We were alone. Curtis came in and gingerly stepped around the ladies. The outer door closed behind him. Opening a wall cabinet by the door, he clipped in his large black weapon as the ship took to the air with ease and speed.

"Please take your seats. We may need to hit some heavy speeds to evade any threats."

I was thinking that we could run from the area faster than the top speed of this old beast. I was tired, though, so I just kept quiet.

We climbed into the non-standard g-seats, and they locked us in place. With a smooth rush of power, the ship began to reach an amazing speed, far more than should have been possible from such a large and notoriously slow craft. Curtis is full of these kinds of surprises.

After we reached cruising speed, Curtis unhooked his g-seat harness and took off his helmet. Turning to us he asked again, "Are you all right?"

We nodded, still in shock from the day and the surprising launch speed of the old Stargazer.

"Good. Do you want any food or drinks?"

I shook my head, revolted by the idea. "No thanks. I have too much of that smell of goliath and war in my lungs and mouth to bear the thought of eating anything right now."

Both Lauren and Jessica agreed.

Jessica returned to her intense study of the older-style cabin. Bemused, she said, "This isn't a standard camper pulsorjet, is it?"

Curtis' affable grin filled his face and he said, "No. But I am curious, what makes you say that?"

"Well, first off, I am not an expert on pulsorjets, but I would imagine that we just raced past speeds that would have made a normal camper of this age shred and explode in the atmosphere." Jessica pointed to an ancient wall unit. "That is an old Netcome realview, but it has had a few modifications to the outer bezel to hide the new realview projectors. Doing that to keep it looking stock is cool, but I sense that there is more to it than that. Overall throughout the cabin, there is wear on odd areas that wouldn't be worn. That usually points to goods faked to look old."

Impressed, Terry said, "What if that wasn't a Netcome, but a Lumidail knock-off?"

Lauren replied, "Then the input would be on the upper right, which was irritating as it got in the way of the face-mounted controls when you plugged in with a fifty-six adapter."

He laughed. "Caught red-handed. Rolland, you weren't kidding. They are sharp, even when confronted with ancient tech. It would be dangerous and foolish for anyone to underestimate them."

Jessica shrugged, "You just happened to have the bad luck to have some of the gear that Dad had when we were kids...until we made him recycle them."

Curtis shook his head, trying to hide his smile. He turned back to Jessica and said, "This old boat once belonged to my grandparents, and they took us camping in it when I was a kid. They were going to sell it for scrap when I bought it from them. I did some modifications...which led to other modifications." He grinned and waved his hand over the ship and said, "It has more in common where it counts with a Makay Railjet."

That was not surprising coming from Curtis. It was impressive in the same way as hearing some old mass transit bus could smoke some of the fastest pulsorjets on the planet. In a way, the vehicle was similar to Curtis, gliding along under the scans, unnoticed but full of surprises.

Jessica gave a wry smile, slowly nodding. "Wow. That is fast. I'd like to learn more about it later. I don't mean to be rude, but at this point, I am most interested in seeing if this rig has a shower and maybe some new clothes that we could put on. I can't stand being encased in this putrid smell much longer."

Aghast, Curtis darted to his feet. "I am so sorry. Where are my manners? Please feel free to do whatever you need. You have been through so much. There is a bathroom in the back," Curtis pointed to the hallway, "and the Stargeezer—" Embarrassed, he said, "That's what I call her. She can sleep six comfortably. I had my system make some guess at your sizes from our brief realview contact but ended up getting a few other sizes to play it safe. There is a robo-tailor there, as well, to help make anything that I might have missed or that needs adjusting. There is food in the galley if you get hungry later. Sorry for my blathering. It has been an exciting day."

"That it has. Don't worry, my friend. We understand." I motioned to Lauren and Jessica and said, "Why don't you two go and shower first? I'll hang out with Curtis."

They didn't argue and disappeared into the back of the ship.

Curtis smiled at me. "You okay?"

"Yeah. Just tired. I will probably feel more like talking after my shower."

He tried to hide his disappointment. He was giving me my space, but I could tell he was bursting with questions and information to share.

Climbing out of my shock, a small part of me was beginning to feel some semblance of normal again. From my past training, I knew shock comes and goes in disproportional waves. One moment you are talkative, and the next you shut down. The lasting results from the day's adventure could last months or years even with treatment. A hot shower would help in removing the stench of the goliath experience from me.

As I wasn't showing interest in talking, Curtis had turned his attention to working on something on his terminal. He was preparing everything for our arrival, wherever it was that we were going. Maybe I should have been showing more interest, but I didn't have it in me. All I wanted to do was get clean and, if time permitted, to sleep for a week straight. There was no need to check on Curtis' planning. He was thorough, smart, and paranoid... or maybe wise.

I took a deep breath and let it out. Relaxing, I gazed out the window at the dark night skies. I could have set the windows to counter the internal lighting to view the stars better. My vision was still soft and unfocused, so it didn't matter. The dark windows matched my mood, and that suited me.

I had a lot to be thankful for, even if I was weary and had experienced far too much in the last few hours. Too much, that kind of summed it up—everything had changed so fast. How long had I been on the run? What day was it? Did it matter?

It had all begun with what was supposed to be a nice stroll in the cool night air. Who was I kidding? That wasn't true and I knew it back then. That walk was a weak excuse to take a naughty and dangerous excursion, foolishly sneaking off, leaving my security team back at home. I had no inkling that it would all blossom into this...mess.

What would have happened that night if I had taken my security team with me? The assassin from the bathroom was brazen, but he probably would have waited for a more opportune moment to strike and still be able to disappear. The attack would have been far bigger and more brutal, like throwing several flak cannon grenades at me out on the street. The number of people killed and wounded would have been horrifying. That would have created a much different storyline.

Had he not attacked that night, I would have probably returned to living out a sad little sedated life, full of watching pointless realviews. This was all a hideous mixed bag of noise and conflicting emotion. I wouldn't have been alone with Erlin to be drugged, and I wouldn't have had a reason to meet Lazarus. Then he would be alive helping others. Not being on the run, I would not have gone into that shop to meet Lauren and Jessica.

Even if I had found out about my stylist stealing and selling my stuff, it would have been a security and legal team that contacted them and other memorabilia shops to build a case against "The Red Tower," not me. As Lauren and Jessica and I didn't run in the same circles, it was improbable that we would ever have met. What a terrible loss that would have been. Even after a few short days, I couldn't imagine my life without them.

My head began filling with worry. What if I was more pain than I was worth, and they were sick of the constant trouble that stalked me? When we got free of this mess, they were going to run from me. My heart sank, and despair tried to wrap its arms around me and pull me under.

A gentle light came to my thinking, and under my breath I said, "Even if that is so, my Father has already taken care of that."

"Pardon?" replied Curtis, who turned to face me.

"Nothing, I'm just talking out loud to myself."

Curtis smiled at me, taking this as the opportunity to speak. "Cool. It has been a tough day. I am really glad that you guys made it out intact." His face fell. "Seeing all that was going on when I arrived had me fearing the worst."

"Thank you, Terry. I can never thank you enough for everything."

"No problem, Rolland. You would do the same for me. Can I get you anything?"

Shaking my head, I said, "Just a shower, then we will see. My head is still ringing from the noise. It was—terrible. Absolutely terrible."

Seeking something else to think about, I quickly examined the extent of my injuries. I was bruised and scratched, but there were no obvious wounds. "Maybe later I'll check with a robo-doc. I don't think I am hurt, just beaten up pretty good."

He nodded. "I'll bet. You are all lucky to have your lives and limbs after this adventure."

"No doubt."

There was more than luck involved here. God had been at work.

Lauren and Jessica came out of the back, refreshed and dressed in some nice clothing. I couldn't speak to their scent, as I still stunk of decontamination gas, dead goliaths, burned metal, explosives, and blasted dirt.

Smiling, I waited until they sat down to make my way to the rear of the pulsorjet. There, I found the shower, and after closing the door to the room, I stripped off my clammy and stinky clothes and dropped them in the recycler.

Once I was inside the poly-walled shower, the 360-degree water atomizers began covering me. The nasty smells of goliath and warfare were deep in my chest. Hunching over, I exhaled as much as possible, trying to expel the stench from my lungs. It stubbornly lingered, but after a time, it reluctantly it began to fade, and an invitingly clean scent filled the air. The water ended, and I was blown dry from all angles. Outside, I found clothes in the pop-up closet and put them on. I knew Curtis had my biometrics, so I was not worried about the fit.

What? I laughed to myself. After all that we had gone through, I didn't care how some clothing fit. I was just happy that we were alive. I gave thanks to God for His rescue and His great love. Whatever would come, He would help me through it. A glimmer of hope was rising in me.

● ● ● ● ▬ ● ● ● ▬ ● ▬ ● ●

With the pulsorjet's flight systems on high-alert and electronically shielded, we had time to sit and relax and try to regroup. Feeling better, we told Curtis of our side of the adventure, and he told us what he had found out.

The electronic sprite dot that I had installed in Erlin had been helpful. It revealed that there was a large, sophisticated group behind the attack. Curtis had been busy, compiling all we knew about them, including the realviews and data feeds. He had loaded all this into several kill-switch packages that he had set to self-deploy if hacked or if something bad had happened to any of us.

With his normal buoyant enthusiasm, Curtis said, "Somehow they found one of my data pods, and despite the clear warnings, they used brute force and ignorance to pry it open." He laughed, nervously running his fingers through his dark hair, seeking to calm it. "They didn't even try to isolate it. Launch codes went out, firing all the other kill-switch packages around the planet. They couldn't have made a dumber move if they wanted this information to stay private."

"How far did the release go?" asked Lauren.

"It is probably easier to list who didn't get it. The media, military, World Congress, the Earth Planetary Governing Board, Remnants, and the Planetary Stewards all got detailed information covering all that we knew about the plot. Global communications slowed by nearly ten percent after the launch, with everyone discussing the information."

He was being too optimistic about how much anyone cared, but I appreciated this and took it as a sign of his deep friendship.

Jessica sat up in her chair and said, "So, I have some nagging questions. First, how did you find us? It is not as if we were at the train station or we had our location IDs up."

"When I flew in, I was heavily cloaked. My plan was to call you on your DarkScatter, but when I saw hundreds of train cars scattering, I knew something big was up. As we needed this documented, I immediately launched a net of stealth realview drones to covertly record everything over twelve square miles. When I saw a goliath tackle a train car and then the top cabin launching into the air with one of those ugly beasts hanging off of it, I pretty much knew where you were. I am embarrassed to say that I didn't come prepared to fight off goliaths...or Wraiths."

Terry looked upset as he swallowed hard. "I didn't know that the Wraiths were there until someone else started the war with them. Had I even popped up on their screens, I would have become just one more smoldering wreck next to all the other burned-out stuff that was littering the area.

"It was wild. Wraiths were exploding in the air. Missiles were turning hills into valleys. Everywhere there were explosions. Did you want me to play any of this back? I have some amazing footage of the event." His excitement faded as he watched our faces. "No? Yeah, sorry, it is all too soon. The sheer amount firepower and level of weapons being used made it obvious that you were the focus of their assault. I didn't know how they could get goliaths to attack, but that wasn't a chance happening."

I interjected, "They used pheromone bullets to cover us in the stench of an aggressive male or of one of them being hurt. It doesn't matter what the message was; the outcome was the same—bad."

Terry nodded, "That sounds about right. Whatever the reason, both sides seemed to want you and each other dead."

Lauren said, "Somehow we are a threat to them. I take it that the kill-switch release happened before the Wraiths' attack?"

Terry nodded. "About four hours earlier."

Lauren pursed her lips and said, "I am surprised that we are still being hunted with such ferocity after that went public. Killing us will not change the outcome other than to maybe speed up their plans. It could be something primal like seeking revenge for causing some internal rivalry or schism to boil over. Had the T-40s been coming to help us, then I would have said that they were the good guys trying to stop the attack. That was not the case, as the one in the hallway acquired target lock before it died."

Terry paused thinking. "That makes sense. Did you want me to continue, or is this too much right now?"

Jessica said, "Go on. I am curious." We nodded our agreement.

Terry smiled at her. "Before leaving my home, I had taken two of those special EMPs like the one that Rolland used on Erlin, and I made one into the railgun rifle that you saw earlier. The other one was huge, far too big to carry, even wearing a gigasuit. I shielded and amplified that one to crazy levels and mounted as a turret on the nose of the Stargeezer. I hid it as an old 4D terrain camera mapping system. Even with the amplification, I wasn't sure it would take out a T-40 or a Wraith without a ton of luck."

He paused and smiled apologetically. "An EMP would not help against a goliath. Back when Rolland was being Mr. Goliath Conservationist, he had told me that goliaths have five or so chain brains, so unless I had more than a few lucky shots, my railgun would be a rampage-inducing irritant. My plan was to crash-land the Stargeezer on top of them. Before I could act, though, they all wiped each other out, leaving that one T-40.

"Then it went inside the trench that the goliaths had made." Terry shrugged and zigzagged his finger in the air. "So I just fired continuously about 3,500 feet around that position. I figured with a rampaging T-40 on the loose, blanketing the area with heavy EMP blasts was the best chance you had. I touched down and came running with the EMP rifle in case I missed."

"I thought that Rolland had called down the wrath of God on the T-40, and that is why it stopped," Lauren said, giving a smirk and appearing more at ease.

"I think it was God who made that happen; look at the odds that any of us could have made it out of this alive," I said defiantly.

Curtis paused and said, "This does seem unreal, doesn't it? Maybe there is something to your God stuff after all, Rolland."

"Oh, there is, Curtis. There definitely is," replied Jessica.

* * * * * * * * * * *

To my great pleasure, a few hours later we arrived at my secluded beach home on Sail Island in the Great Azura Ocean. This was one of my favorite places. Curtis was correct when he had said that we needed a vacation.

The inevitable barrage of legal inquests would start, and we would be called to be witnesses. That meant that our schedules would be full for at least a year, if not much more. I still wasn't sure how seriously that they would take what had happened to us. I hoped for the best, which is asking a lot from any government or agency.

It was about 10:00 p.m. when I sent my security code. The terrace and house lights came on as if to greet us. Lauren and Jessica leaned closer to the windows, trying to make out our location.

We landed, and a walkway extended to the side of the Stargeezer. The door opened, and we were welcomed by the warm breeze coming off the ocean.

I said, "Walk ahead to the large white oval section in front of us." The ellipse began to glow gently to guide them. I could see them trying to walk and look up at the stars splayed above us. "Don't worry. Once you are out and stopped, I will turn out the lights to let you look at the stars."

Curtis, Lauren, and Jessica dutifully took their places on the landing pad. I knew from experience what would happen if I didn't. There would have been a pileup in the dark as each one would step out and just stop, unable to move forward, as if pinned in place by the dazzling display of the stars above us.

Joining them, I said, "Lights out."

All the manmade lights went out in unison, and the heaven's majesty filled our eyes, and there was a collective gasp. There is no way to prepare someone for their first encounter with the infinite. Breathtaking is an overused word. It will weakly suffice.

There is a point where superlatives fail, and you are just quiet in the sight of such beauty. I had seen this view thousands of times, and I was still moved by it. There were more stars than I remembered. The scent and sounds of the ocean wafted over us.

We waited for a few minutes, just letting the view seep into our bones. My eyes adjusted, and I watched my friends' faces, and they were even more moved than they had been back at the safe house.

"Rolland, this place is amazing. How could you even consider not living here all the time?" asked Lauren.

"It is amazing indeed, and I have spent quite a bit of time here. You haven't even seen it in the daylight or the house or the white sand beaches yet." Lauren and Jessica were thrilled.

"I am going to turn the lights back on so we can head to the house. I am sure you are all tired. Lights on," I said, and the lights slowly rose to light our way.

Lauren was looking out at the lush greenery and flowers that surrounded us. "I hope we don't bother the neighbors coming here so late."

"Not likely," I said.

Jessica and Lauren appeared confused.

Curtis grinned and said, "The nearest neighbor is about sixty-four miles away. Mr. Moneybags owns this whole island."

I don't know why I felt embarrassed by this. Lauren and Jessica stared at me in surprise.

"I bought it after my parents died. I had wanted to avoid people for a lifetime…or two."

Though sad, the three of them pulled out smiles. I pointed forward and watched as Lauren and Jessica went on, only to stop a few yards ahead to look at some of the night-blooming flowers that lined the path.

I took this opportunity to confer with Curtis. "Do you think we are safe here?" I asked, keeping my voice low. It was a little late at this point to begin the conversation, but I hadn't felt up to it earlier.

Curtis merely shrugged and said, "If they really want to take you out, a single Murkadan Mark II would remove all traces of this island. Would you be happier holed up in a safe house in a megacity where that strike could mean millions dead, or would you rather spend time here in paradise?"

Curtis let that sink in and gave me a sly smile. "Besides, I have already set up the best scans and defenses that I can. If they do fire a missile, I have played with the global geo-mapping systems, and it will land a good ten miles southeast of here. If they use aircraft to attack, I also set up some stabilized geo-projectors to add a copy of this island to those coordinates. We have an electronic and geo-projection covering this island and its surrounding waters that will make it look like the open sea to any flyovers, satellites, or any other kind of prying eyes. I am sure that Jessica and Lauren will help harden this place even more. I have an alert set up to warn us if anything tries to probe or counter the system. You can relax."

"Wow. When did you do all this?" I inquired.

Curtis cleared his throat. "Well, I did it when you first disappeared. I figured if it was an all-out attack, you would need a place to hide. If you hadn't survived, well, I would need a place to get away. I hope I didn't overstep my bounds."

"You are my great friend, and you always welcome at any of my homes. I am thrilled that you came here. Were they after you that much? I am sorry, that didn't come out so well. I am tired and not thinking all that clearly right now."

He half-nodded. "Relax, I understand your point. Some, but I...ah...well, I did it more because I could not bring myself to believe that you might not make it. Rolland, I would really hate anything bad to ever happen to you. That would hurt me deeply. You are my best friend. I was thinking I would need a place to recover, if you...didn't make it."

"I feel the same about you, Terry."

He was fighting back his emotions. He looked up at the stars and blinked. "And I needed some place to plot my revenge."

"That would have gone very badly for them."

Surprised and pleased, Terry smiled at me. "I take that as a big compliment coming from you."

"Please do. I mean it that way."

"Oh, so you know, I already told Jessica and Lauren about the security I set up. It kind of came up when you were getting cleaned up. They are pretty sharp."

I nodded. "You can't put much past them, for sure." That was one less thing to worry about.

We stopped talking and took in the night air. The soft breeze and the gentle sound of the waves lapping at the shore were leeching the aches from my body and the noise from my head. Calmness began to take root. I watched Lauren and Jessica walking, filled with wonder at the beautiful island setting. On the surface, they were holding up remarkably well, considering what we had gone through. Having been through some of this junk before, I knew the odd swings one's emotions could take.

Curtis coughed, cleared his throat, and said, "Oh, yeah. If you must, you can add your 'touches' to the island's defenses as well. I am sure we can fix whatever you break."

"You are most kind," I said, giving him a big smile.

We watched the women kneeling down and looking at some of the glorious arrays of night flowers that lined the bright white walkway. If they thought they were beautiful now under the overhead walkway lights, wait until they got to see the other flowers open in the daylight.

He leaned closer to me and studying my face, he asked, "I keep asking because I don't know what else to ask, but are you really okay?"

"We are alive, and we will heal." I contemplated Lauren and Jessica. "They are great young ladies. They are the best thing to come out of this whole mess by far. I wouldn't be here if it were not for the three of you."

"I am glad you are all safe. You had me worried there for a while." He took on a sheepish grin and said, "I know that this is not the best time to ask, but as we will be hiding here for a little while, do you know if Jessica is seeing anyone? You know, if you are not, like, interested. If you are, I can back off."

Gazing at them, I knew that I loved them both, but I was drawn to Lauren in a way I had never experienced before. There was something about her spark and the light in her eyes that drew me to her.

"I love Jessica—"

Curtis stammered, "Enough said. I—"

"Let me finish, you oaf. I love Jessica, and she is awesome and beautiful in so many ways beyond words, but I am falling for Lauren." I studied Lauren who was involved in a quiet conversation with her sister. She was so marvelous that it went beyond my understanding. I prayed that she still wanted to be around me.

Curtis was staring at me. I turned to him, and he began to grin—a little at first, and then it became a huge, bright smile. "I can see that. Wow, I think she could be your match, Rolland." He studied her and said, "No. I am wrong. She is far too good for you."

I ventured a laugh and said, "Obviously. Oh, and a warning, you better be good to Jessica."

"Yeah, I get it—or you're gonna come after me."

"Oh, no. I have no part to play in that. She may be kind and beautiful, but that is only a small part of who she is. Jessica is one tough and very smart lady who can take on and take down all comers by herself. A fool would underestimate her, and they would do it at their own peril. I would say inversely that if the right person treated her as the amazing person that she is, I cannot imagine life could get much better than that."

Curtis was watching Jessica as she crouched over, sniffing a flower in the dual moons' light. He didn't turn to look at me when he asked, "She's a Christian like you, right?"

"Yes. Lauren too."

"I have some questions about that. They are pretty tough."

"I am sure they are. We would be glad to answer them the best we can—or you may want to talk to Jessica privately." Raising my eyebrows slightly, I said, "That would be a good way to get to know her better."

An odd smile crept on his face. "That sounds good."

We walked up to Lauren and Jessica, who stood from studying the flowers. I said, "So, shall we head to the house?" I noticed that the women were still glancing up at the night sky. "Or did you want to take a few minutes to see the night sky from the beach, or should we save that for tomorrow night?"

"Even though I am tired, I don't think I can wait...unless you all want to," replied Lauren, her eyes wide and hopeful.

Jessica nodded, her blonde hair flowing across her shoulders. "I have always wanted to see a beach at night. How about you, Terry?"

Terry smiled, offering his arm to Jessica, and without hesitation she took it. He said, "Please lead on, Rolland."

Lauren followed Jessica's lead and snuck her hand under my arm, and we walked to the lift to the beach. The sounds of the waves were growing louder, and peace was driving the weariness from my bones. Seeing the house would wait; tonight we had a date with the moonlight on the beach. I hoped that it would have the same healing effect on my friends as it always had on me. Already, I felt much better, and I had hope.

● ● ● ● ▬ ● ● ● ▬ ● ▬ ● ●

20

The Casting of the Morning Star

●●● ▬▬ ▬▬ ▬▬ ●●●

"Ma'am, we have another mass data dump concerning New-castle," said the colonel.

"Should I assume this is different from Rolland's first kill-switch?" asked the silver-haired woman.

"Yes, ma'am. This is another one, apparently from Joden Falkaal, the Special Assistant to the Viceroy General of the Earth Planetary Governing Board."

She paused and her eyebrows knit together. "Leyland Melcurate's Joden?"

"The same. He sent a global package that gives their side's version of events."

She leaned back in her chair and rolled her eyes. "Oh. I am guessing it's one of those 'we're not guilty, we were framed' dumps?"

Colonel Haas shook his head with a slight grin. "No ma'am, this is the opposite of that. The data categorically states that they are solely guilty of a lengthy, well-orchestrated campaign of genocide against the Remnant. Joden sent what we believe is definitive proof to back that claim."

Normally placid, the silver-haired woman's face showed surprise. "What?"

"That was my reaction too, ma'am. This data lays out the structure of their organization, including who knew what, did what, and when they did it. All the dirty underpinnings of how their orchestrated genocide plan was being applied to the Remnants. It puts all of this on the shoulders of Leyland Melcurate and a few others. This is so damning and detailed that I would bet this release was from a kill-switch package. I would be amazed if Joden is still alive."

The silver-haired woman nodded in agreement. "My guess is that Melcurate must have turned on him and backed him into a corner. Knowing Leyland, that is not hard to believe."

"We are still going over all the details to confirm, but so far it is all one hundred percent accurate and verifiable. As I said, this was a long-standing campaign designed to eradicate the Remnants. It was bigger than anyone would have guessed, and there was a great number of important people actively involved with it. They just bit off more than they were able to chew with Rolland Newcastle."

"Speaking of Rolland, do we have any word on him, if he is alive or dead?"

"We don't, but we fear the worst. Outside the city of Kongesgaard we have troubling reports that a goliath attack has escalated to a small war. We don't have a full analysis, but at this point, we believe that four goliaths attacked a line of transit cars heading to the city. They destroyed an emergency outpost and at least five Defenders. It gets worse—we have all the global signatures indicating three Wraiths and most of their payloads were deployed."

The woman sat bolt upright, her face flushed. "Wraiths? Is the city still there? Do we have any idea of the number of casualties? Are the aircraft still active?"

"No, ma'am, they are not still active in the area. I will get to that. The city is unharmed. No casualties reported as of yet, though based on our satellite feeds and reports from the city, a large hilly area outside the city is now a large, smoldering valley. To be frank, ma'am, I will be shocked if we do not have numerous casualties. Wraiths don't fire unless there is a target, and by the size of the area, there must have been many targets."

"Launching Wraiths outside of open war is the act of a madman or someone who is beyond desperate. This would certainly fit Leyland's predicament. He wouldn't risk sending Wraiths unless he thought he would eradicate Rolland or stop Joden from releasing this most recent data dump. Are we tracking the Wraiths? We cannot have them in play."

"Not to worry, ma'am. We believe that all three Wraiths have been destroyed in this action, but not before at least one launched several assault mechs. The goliaths are dead, and we have a huge mess to clean up."

"Please keep on this, Colonel. All this has to stop now. Round up anyone involved with it. And please detain Viceroy Melcurate for 'his own safety' until we can get more of the details. We have enough to get an arrest warrant. He will claim diplomatic immunity and walk. We can hold him for his safety for a day before we level charges on him. The EPGB will complain bitterly, but we will have more time to look at this data and confront them with what we find. Maybe that will be enough to stop the EPGB from quietly shipping Leyland off-planet to avoid embarrassment and the legal entanglements."

"Ma'am, this kill-switch went almost as global as the first Newcastle media dump. The EPGB and the media all have this data. They cannot claim ignorance or attempt to hide it." The colonel let a grin slip. "There are quite a few people at the EPGB who are no fans of the viceroy. How bad this will be for the EPGB is not yet clear."

With a harsh laugh, the woman said, "The leader and the public face of the EPGB on New Jerusalem, whose primary task is to protect the Remnants and their rights, is found to be leading the cabal that is actively causing their extermination. That is about as bad as it can get."

"Agreed, ma'am. The EPGB cannot afford the harm that this could do to their reputation on all the other planets, especially with those planets that are looking for a reason to get out of their planetary contracts. I believe they are going to make the viceroy a stark and ominous warning to others for many years to come."

The woman smiled slyly. "Well, let's help where we can. Please bring the viceroy in to talk."

"Yes, Madam President. It will be my pleasure." The colonel saluted, and the screen went black.

Gloria Mescula, President of the World Congress, leaned back in her chair with a smug and satisfied smile. Leyland and his minions' devious plans had come undone, pulling them all down with a resounding crash. It couldn't have happened to a more pompous, arrogant and selfish—

● ● ●　━　━　━　● ● ●

A small long-haul spaceship lifted off, headed out to deep space. On board, disgraced ex-Viceroy General of the Earth Planetary Governing Board for New Jerusalem, Leyland Melcurate, was licking his wounds from the unfortunate unraveling of his plans. The beautifully detailed strategy that he had put into place was now in smoldering ruins.

With the global release of Joden's kill-switch, Leyland had not waited for his inevitable arrest. He had fled using a backup emergency plan he and Joden had put in place. Had he been detained, his rank and diplomatic privileges would have secured his release pending the court case against him, but the monitoring and controls put in place would have made his flight much more difficult.

It would be an entirely different matter with the EPGB; they would have immediately arrested him. They were embarrassed and would act out of self-preservation to try and keep their lucrative global contract and their position of power on New Jerusalem. He was sure that the EPGB, which needed to save face, was already putting the team together to start their inquest for his permanent removal and punishment. It would be filled with those with a personal grudge against him and those vying for his vacated position. It would be brutal and unforgiving, that is, if he were so foolish as to allow himself to be captured, and if there was one thing that he was not, it was foolish.

He was on his own. He began to feel sorry for himself again. Even his assistant Joden, whom he had trusted in all his private matters, had abandoned him over a few minor misunderstandings and had viciously turned against him in a traitorous and cowardly act. As a great leader, he had planned meticulously for that worst-case scenario; that planning would now serve as the key to his return to power. Just as this spaceship had lain hidden and waiting, so would he for a few years until his triumphant return.

Leyland lay back in his g-seat as the ship continued to build speed. There were no signs of alarm or pursuit. He was safe. The shielding was doing its job.

He smiled. *Idiots*, he thought. They were all bumblers and fools.

A light blinked on his console indicating everything was ready to enact his next plan, moving his liquid assets off the planet. His remaining family and his two ex-wives would have to sell off property and goods to pay their bills. That was their problem now as he had supported them all far too long. The remaining assets at their disposal would be sufficient for them if they managed the funds carefully, but he knew they wouldn't.

As most were citizens of New Jerusalem, they still had their base planetary share to live off. That would be a shock for them. He had seen their bills in court as they asked for increases in their support to be able to sustain their extravagant lifestyles. They often spent far more than the monthly base share on a pair of shoes or a single fancy meal.

He found it funny that they were bound to become some of the common people that they complained about, those who lived off the system and got money for doing absolutely nothing. They were never any different; they were just fancier leeches with better clothing and more expensive tastes. His family and his exes had lived lavishly at his expense for years and did nothing other than complain that it was not enough. They deserved to suffer. He was sorry that he wouldn't be able to see their faces when they learned that they were flat broke.

Leyland had a few more details to attend to before he could disappear for a while. His best and final act of revenge—he was about to drain all of the EPGB's New Jerusalem Planetary GDP income for the last two and a half years and move it off-planet into his secret accounts. In the span of a few minutes, he would become one of the richest people that ever lived. A wealth that was greater than that of many established planets was going to be all his. This would fund his plans for a long time.

For a few years, he would live in luxury on Zandandos, an extremely money-friendly, no-questions-asked, EPGB-free planet. As remote as the planet was, he knew that he couldn't hide there for long. The EPGB would not rest until it got its money back and put him in jail. Generous payouts and the nicest remote military villa wouldn't protect him for long. Only as a global ruler would he have the legal protections, a worldwide military, and the orbital space control that he needed. It would also afford him billions of expendable hostages.

He would return to New Jerusalem as its ruler. He had lost it only due to the incompetence of a few people. No, not lost. This was just a short delay in his gaining ownership. By all rights, it should be his. He knew the planet well; he knew its key players, its strengths, and its weaknesses. All this knowledge would lead to his inevitable victory.

If he failed to mount a successful coup d'état, he knew that his future years would be spent running from planet to planet or living in a prison on New Jerusalem. Neither of those scenarios was acceptable.

Planetary takeovers take planning, resources, and the extensive use of force. He would return as their new emperor or whatever he chose to call himself. They would submit or die. He didn't care which, but he was leaning towards die. The planet didn't need billions of do-nothing loafers sucking off it. If they didn't like it, he would be most satisfied to bring their destruction. That would be fair retribution for the years of planning that they had destroyed. Had they left his original plan alone, it would have meant less pain for them in the long run. There would have been just a few million or so cleansed during the initial revolt as compared to the extensive toll that was coming.

With the wealth he was about to claim, he wasn't worried about achieving his plans. He would be able to afford the best automated siege and protection forces possible. Weapons brokers were easy to find when you had several quintillions of unicreds to spend. A few million T-40s and Skyraiders, combined with tens of thousands of heavy battle cruisers and a few planet-breaker bombs, and the Earth Planetary Governing Board would run away.

Their contract offered planets only limited military and legal support for their yearly percentage of Planet Production Shares. He knew from his training and experience that the EPGB would take only a few embarrassing, high-profile losses, and then they would write New Jerusalem off and try to suppress the bad press. After about two years of vitriolic rhetoric, they would send ambassadors who would offer peaceful relations and seek to become trading partners once again. They would reason that some part of New Jerusalem's profits would be better than none. Greed smooths all transitions and transactions.

All Leyland had to do now was start the process, and the automatic systems would take over, draining accounts and hiding assets, and he would be whisked away in princely comfort and safety. The EPGB would have immediately suspended his account access, but they would not have counted on the secret backdoors that Joden had installed for him.

He would arrive in Zandandos after about one year and four months of cryosleep. To him, it would feel as if he had slept for a night. His agents on the planet would be already engaged and would have every detail of his stay prepared. All he needed to do after arriving was to finalize the purchase and delivery of his invasion forces and set the date to begin his conquest of New Jerusalem. He estimated it would be a total of about three and three-quarters years before the war began, and if all went to schedule, six months more before he became their king. A little under three of those years would be spent in cryosleep during interplanetary travel. That left about a year and a half of work until he became King Leyland Melcurate. No, Grand Global Emperor Leyland Melcurate of New Jerusalem sounded better. He could even rename the planet to something like Melcure or Melcurator.

A green light flashed on the projected monitor. It was time. With elation, he started the access procedure. A white smiley face appeared floating midair before him, and Leyland gave a grunt of disgust. Joden had always been too childish. This wasn't quite the auspicious start he had expected. The smiley face morphed into the traditional pirate's white skull and crossbones on a black flag. *Better,* he thought, *that's the spirit.*

Joden's smiling face appeared. "Greetings Viceroy General Melcurate. Do not worry—this is a recording."

Duh, thought Leyland. *You are dead.*

"By now you are a good distance away from New Jerusalem and on your way to safety. I am guessing that everything has gone wrong, and I am not with you. That means if you are seeing this, I am dead or soon to be dead. That is a shame; I like me." He wore a small frown.

Leyland rolled his eyes. "Just do the transfer and let me sleep."

"I know that you are ready to be on your way, so let's get this started. The ship's course has been set and is now locked. There will be some pressure as the ship is moving to new coordinates. This will change soon, and I hope that you are comfortable."

"Just shut up, Joden, and get on with it," snapped Leyland.

"It will be just a little longer before your long sleep. I have sent for another ship to join you, and it should rendezvous with your ship in about seven minutes." Joden's features darkened and he said, "That is about how long you will be panicking when you realize that it is coming to ram you. I took a page out of the *Assignation* playbook. You remember that freighter that rammed The Remnant colony ship, *Heaven*? I have to say I found that quite hilarious when I thought of it."

Alarmed Leyland cursed and sat up. He began examining the armrests of his g-seat, looking for the spaceship's controls. Frustrated he demanded, "Joden! I order you to release control of this ship to me this instant."

The recording of Joden went on. "Ah, yes. I would love to see it, the Grand Viceroy Leyland Melcurate, who has worn his technological illiteracy as a badge of honor, is now trying to figure out how to get the ship to work. I assure you that this spaceship is far more complex than the simple realview controls that for whatever reason were beyond your grasp. And how sad, you cannot even call me for help. What a shame, huh? Hey, what was that noise? Right, it was all the escape pods jettisoning. Don't worry, they'll all come back to join the *Assignation II* to ram you."

Joden was pleased with himself. "I hope you like the name I gave it. Though I have to say that you way overpaid for such an old container ship, and that all but drained your retirement account. Then there was a sizable penalty for taking out an early withdrawal for non-retirement purposes." Joden stopped and then barked out a harsh laugh. "Wait, I guess that is wrong. The ship that is about to ram you is for your immediate retirement and your penalty. That is too funny. I hadn't thought of that aspect until now."

He regained his composure. "I'll bet you never even wondered at the name of this spaceship that you are in. I won't keep you guessing, it's *Heaven*. You always said that those that don't pay attention to the details die from them. That was so ironic and incredibly irritating because you never did." Joden made a mocking face and said, "Oh right, that's why 'you have people.' But you don't have any people anymore, do you? Those whom you did have, you left back on New Jerusalem to take your punishment while you fled to a life of comfort and ease.

"I know that you never even questioned how any of this would work. That is tech stuff, and you can't be bothered to try to understand it. Actually, I don't think you are smart enough to understand it. I cannot tell you how many times that you told me 'I don't need all the details. Just tell me what it will do for me.' Well, one last time for old time's sake, okay? Big ship ram your little ship and go boom. Or was that still too detailed for you to understand? Don't worry, Viceroy, you will have a very easy-to-understand demonstration of the process very soon.

"The only things you were ever good at were bullying and scheming. You only got to be viceroy because of your family's connections and their massive payoffs to get you into power, even though you were clearly not fit to lead. It is shameful what people did to New Jerusalem for money and power. A goliath could have done a better job as a viceroy than you did. You were oblivious to how many times we had to clean up your messes. So many of those times I dreamed of telling you off and punching you squarely in your arrogant face. I suppose this ship will do nicely as a proxy." The screen changed to show a long dark rectangular ship rising on an intercepting course with Leyland's spaceship.

Leyland's eyes were bulging as he pounded his hands down on the g-seat arms in a rage.

"Joden, I command you to stop this charade and turn the ship over to me now!"

To his surprise, a set of manual steering controls came out from the arms. Leyland seized upon them and to his frustration they did nothing.

"Oh, darn. Those didn't work, did they? I thought that I would give you some hope. Kind of like you gave me over the years, just to snatch it away. Wow. I sound so bitter, don't I? To be fair, I did record this while on the run from your nephew's 'cleaning crew.' You liked to use that term, thinking it was so clever. Do you really think that if others were to listen in, they wouldn't get it? It's not clever at all. In fact, it's old and extremely lame. It is something out of a really bad old realview program. People only suffered your presence because of your position and power. Not so secretly, they thought you were an idiot."

Joden exhaled and his shoulders slumped. With a soft voice he said, "It's funny, but I continued working with you because I had put in too many painful years to quit. I kept holding out hope that my talent would be noted and that I would move up at the EPGB. When that didn't happen, I kept making moral concessions that ultimately got me in so deep in the planned takeover of New Jerusalem that I couldn't back out. As you could barely function without my constant help, I figured that I would get a prominent post in your new government. That was a foolish thought, as it would require you to actually think about something other than yourself for even a nanosecond."

Leyland was half listening as he had left his g-seat and was trying to get other consoles about the ship to respond. He had given up trying to be subtle and he was pounding his balled fists on the surfaces, trying to make them work. As that hurt, he tried to kick the front panels with no effect. In desperation, Leyland scurried to the ship's emergency evacuation station.

Joden smiled broadly. "Oh, in case you are wondering, I put tiny holes in the ship's emergency jumpsuits. Depressurization in deep space would be a painful way to die. So, please feel free to go ahead, if you haven't done so already. I wonder if you are throwing a tantrum, demanding that I return the ship to its originally planned course, or are you begging my realview recording for help? Are you offering it money, forgiveness, or some high position in your new government?"

A faint voice came from off camera, and Joden briefly turned away. "What? Yeah, right, I will be right there. I am finishing up something important." Turning back to the camera Joden said, "That was my brother-in-law, Miken. We are off to set our ambush for Rolland. I think it is probably too late to put things right, but I told you that I would try—" Joden reflexively cringed.

Without missing a beat, the viceroy yelled, "Saying that you will 'try' is building in failure!"

Regaining his composure, Joden sneered. "Oh, yes, I said it, 'try.' Deal with it. I'll bet that you are throwing a fit as you always did whenever I said that I would try to do something. 'Saying you will try is building in failure.' No. That means I acknowledge that nothing in life is ever one hundred percent certain and that I see that there is always a chance that things will not go as planned, and yet I will do everything possible to achieve the outcome that we desired. To set the record straight, we are still trying to get Newcastle only because I promised Miken that I would help him seek revenge. If it works out as we hope, then you'll never see this. Part of me hopes that you do, and somehow I will get to view the feed."

Tiredness moved over Joden's frame, and he sat as if he had deflated. He managed a heavy sigh. "So, Viceroy, do you think that there is life after death? I have been thinking about it a lot lately while dodging your assassins. I have begun to empathize with Rolland Newcastle recently. Here's a good question, one that I wish I could hear your answer to: Why couldn't you just leave him alone? He never bothered you. I never could understand your fixation with him in particular."

A despondent Leyland Melcurate glanced about the ship and walked back to climb into his g-seat. The image of Joden paused thoughtfully. "I always thought I had more time to decide if there was anything to Christianity and life after death. It's funny, isn't it? We avoid looking at death, pretending that it isn't coming. We figure that we will all get 150 or more years to figure that out. None of us knows how long we have."

Chortling, Joden said, "Well, actually, you do—and it should be right on schedule. Enjoy the ride. I hear that the upper atmosphere is lovely this time of year. And just for fun, I have been broadcasting this back to New Jerusalem, where you will return in a fiery ball of twisted metal. Smile nicely for the realview and bye-bye now. Hope that you rot in—"

Far above New Jerusalem, a bright comet streaked across the sky and disintegrated in the atmosphere. Ex-Viceroy General of the Earth Planetary Governing Board for New Jerusalem Leyland Melcurate had returned to New Jerusalem only to immediately check out again.

●●● ⬭ ⬭ ⬭ ●●●

21

Joy Comes in the Morning

On our second day on the island, I slipped on my robe and stepped onto the veranda outside my bedroom. Greeting the sun, I took in a deep breath of the ocean breeze. Even though I had been here so many times, I was still amazed by the stunning vista of the sparkling eastern bay. White sand surrounded by dark rock and lush greenery lay before me. A tall rock spire protected the bay's entrance from storms. The water was sparkling blue and calm. It was a bright and beautiful day.

Lauren's, Jessica's, and Terry's rooms had equally spectacular views. If they didn't care for them, they could always reorient their apartment's floor to view a different section of the beach, mountain, coves, and island. They had 360 degrees of beauty to choose from. If that was not enough, they could move to one of the underwater apartments or one of the lower beach houses for a different view.

The only reason I was up so early was that Lauren and I had planned a day of swimming and relaxing on the beach.

Inside, my robo-butler had laid out a nice outfit for me near my bed. With drowsy slowness, I dressed for the day.

We hadn't slept in as I had hoped that we would. Lauren and Jessica got us up early on the first day to watch the spectacular sunrise on the beach. That first night viewing the stars on the beach had hooked them. Seeing two sunrises and a sunset had them handing out marching orders for where and when we would all meet to view the next solar event.

Terry and I made no attempt to rein them in, as it was fun seeing them so excited, and this gentle purpose was helping us heal. We still had moments of quiet despondency and worry, but it was amazing how much being there was helping us deal with the events of our adventure. We would have many more days or even years of healing ahead of us.

That morning's sunrise was a wondrous display of blue and slate grays leading to red, yellow, and orange. It was a huge, beautiful sign that said that I'd better give up any hope of sleeping in, at least for a while. Who could blame Lauren, Jessica, and Curtis? It was addictive to watch sunrises and sunsets on the water. As we were on an island, we had front row-seats for both events. I had some success in talking them into letting us at least nap in the afternoons. After the sunrise that morning, we did come back for a few extra hours of snoozing. My sleep pattern was a wreck, but it was worth it.

Yesterday, I attempted to quietly bring up Curtis' interest in Jessica to Lauren, but she stopped me and said that it was mutual and that we should make sure to give Terry and Jessica some space. I was good with that. It was great to see both of them happy.

I took the elevator down to the main entertaining floor, and in the large living room I found Jessica and Curtis sitting on the long, low white couch watching the realview that took up much of the center of the room. Jessica was a lovely splash of color as she had on a cute white and citrus-colored outfit that was perfect for beachcombing. Terry was dressed in tan shorts and a simple lime green and yellow top.

"There is an absolutely beautiful day starting out there. You two aren't going to spend it sitting on the couch watching newsblasts, are you?" I had been avoiding the outside world, and now it was back front and center.

"Pause realview. We were sitting down to eat, and we thought we would see what is brewing in the world, but you are not going to believe this," said Terry.

Jessica's face was flushed and her eyes alive. "I was just about to call you and Lauren."

Hearing a noise to my side, I saw that Lauren had come down from her room, and she had moved to stand next to me. She was dressed in a flowing, light sky blue sun-robe that wonderfully yet modestly showed off her abundant curves. She was beautiful. I tried not to stare at her.

"Morning. What's all this noise so early?" she said, rubbing her left eye. So she had gone back to sleep after seeing the sunrise. Good for her.

Jessica snorted and patted the seat next to her. "It's 8:30 a.m.. It is not exactly early, but never mind that. Come sit down and watch this."

"It's not *Millennium Seekers* again, is it?" I said.

Terry shook his head. "No. This is important."

It had better be. Lauren and I had plans.

Jessica pointed to the realview. "Realview start, audio on low." A newsblaster with flowing orange hair was talking, and images of politicians and leaders were being shown next to her. "While we have been relaxing, it appears the world has been churning. The newsblasts are all aflutter. It seems that the Viceroy General of the Earth Planetary Governing Board for New Jerusalem, Leyland Melcurate, was the driving force behind your problems and the leader for the Remnant purge. He is no longer with us."

Lauren and I sat down on the couch next to each other, and I said, "Really? Leyland Melcurate of the EPGB? Did he escape, or did he commit suicide?"

"Kind of an unintentional suicide. He turned on his Special Assistant Joden Falkaal, and Joden rigged his spaceship to reenact the Fall of Heaven," said Curtis. He was not hiding his enjoyment at the outcome.

"The Fall of Heaven? The whole ramming and burning up kind of thing?" asked Lauren.

Curtis nodded enthusiastically. "Including launching escape pods. There is a whole realview of it that Joden had programmed to be broadcasted. Joden was one angry guy, but it is kind of funny in a sick sort of way. So, did you know Leyland well?"

"I met him a couple of times. I got the impression that he was a pompous jerk, but we never exchanged even a harsh word that I can remember. I have no idea why he would hate me so. Joden was always polite and professional with me."

Lauren was focused, deep in thought. "I don't think it was so much that he hated you personally, but you were the one who brought the issue of Remnant deaths out into the open and got more Remnant protections put into place. If you were killed without any repercussions, they could be freer to go after others until it was too late or too obvious. Even if it blew up as it did, and Leyland Melcurate's involvement stayed hidden, the Earth Planetary Governing Board would declare it an ongoing act of genocide against the Remnants. They would immediately implement emergency governance powers that would give them full, planet-wide military control. And Melcurate, as the Viceroy General, would be made the ipso facto ruler of New Jerusalem with a weak EPGB overview.

"When he had complete control of the military, I bet he would have quickly moved to dissolve the World Congress, and he would have suspended all the citizens' rights due to terrorist activities and external threats to the safety and sovereignty of New Jerusalem. The EPGB on New Jerusalem would cease to exist, as they and anyone who opposed Leyland's power grab would be purged as enemies of the state. The EPGB would be too slow to react militarily, as their nearest forces would be a minimum of one or two years away.

"By that point, Leyland would rule the planet. He would build a massive military force with all the funds that were once being used to pay the EPGB and to feed, clothe, and house the public. The rest of the story would have been the standard Emperor for Life, Beloved Father of the Country, while the masses starved and waved tiny flags in front of realviews of Leyland."

"Wow. That makes horrible sense," I said. "I am not sure whether I should be impressed or worried that you are able to figure out the details of this scheme so rapidly. More to the point, I cannot express how glad I am that you show no signs of turning evil." That was a ghastly thought. I looked to Curtis and Jessica. "Leyland and his gang's machinations would be nothing next to what she could release if she were so inclined."

Lauren shrugged mischievously, but she didn't respond. Terry wore an expression that I understood.

I said, "It's okay. I should have warned you about our dear Lauren's ability. It is a bit shocking."

Terry said, "She looks so sweet and innocent, then..."

Jessica spoke, drawing our attention, "I would say to Leyland, 'How you have fallen from heaven, O morning star, son of the dawn! You have been cast down to the earth, you who once laid low the nations!'"

"Amen," said Lauren.

Curtis appeared confused, and I said, "She is comparing Leyland's fall to that of the Devil being cast down from heaven in Isaiah 16 or 17."

"Isaiah 14:12," said Jessica. I am terrible at remembering verses, let alone verse numbers.

"You guys memorize lines from the Bible?" asked Curtis.

"Some people do. It is comparable to having a wide range of tech knowledge—it comes in handy for figuring out what to do in different circumstances," I responded. Curtis was taking it in and thinking about it.

As we ate a lovely breakfast, we watched the other side's version of our story unfolding. I said, "Joden Falkaal was the guy whom I mentioned back at the safe house that I thought about contacting. I almost handed us over to the people trying to kill us. It just didn't feel right at the time."

Jessica laughed. "I am glad of that. I guess it was good that we ended up going with Sandrah, after all."

Ironically, the newsblasts reported on the attack at Kongesgaard and how we were ambushed and presumed dead. It filled in a few details that we didn't know, and it was hard to watch as the realview showed the devastation of the area outside Kongesgaard.

Curtis casually remarked, "I will have to send them my feeds from when I arrived at the city looking for you and saw this all unfolding. Mine are far more impressive and scary."

The next biggest news revelation was that Jessica's old friend Sandrah Orgel had been the one who had sold us out to be assassinated by Joden and his brother-in-law Miken. From accompanying realview overlays, I recognized Miken as the assassin who had tried to attack me in the bathroom.

The media loved that Sandrah's payment for betraying her friends had been death via a massive passion drug infusion by a robo-partner symbioid. The conspirators had tried to hide the use of a symbioid by bringing in a nasty, dark-market adult device to finish the process. The newsblasts repeatedly and joyfully went over this subject in more detail than necessary.

There was footage of the arrest of an EPGB tech guy named Erlzile Yant who was charged with breaking the symbioid's encryption and Sandrah's murder. Throughout the program, they showed too many images and realviews of Sandrah in swimsuits and revealing outfits. Maybe in their search of her media, that was all she had. She was self-absorbed enough for me to believe that. I still saw nothing that great about her face or figure. The newsblasts never called her a beauty, though a femme fatale a few times, and shortly that was deliberately changed to femme fatality.

Lauren was uncharacteristically quiet about Sandrah, and she seemed sad. "Her greed cost her, her life."

Jessica wasn't happy at all. "I should have listened to you, Lauren. I was expecting better of her. I pray that she was saved before she died." Lauren and I agreed. "Well, I guess one good thing that came out of all this; now we know how they found us on the transit cars. That was bothering me."

I frowned. "Me too. I had been thinking it was due to our transit car registering a non-standard weight permutation and because our cabin's human comfort systems had been engaged. I guess Sandrah telling them what car number we were in, its destination and time of arrival, and how to access its location beacon was an easier solution."

"I love it when you get all science-y on us, Rolland." Lauren grinned, nudging me with her elbow. "See, I told you that they were going to use the symbioid to kill that way again, and now we know who was the first female test subject. It is sad, as they put their own deaths in motion by their actions."

Curtis was looking at the somewhat racy images of Sandrah splayed across the screen. "Well, I guess the best you could say about Sandrah was that she had nice hair."

Jessica raised an eyebrow. "Do you think she was beautiful, Terry?" There was a challenge in her voice that I hope Curtis heard.

Curtis didn't bat an eye and replied, "Beautiful? No. At most, I would say that she was barely average. I guess she did have an okay backside, but it was not great. It's a bit flat and square for my tastes."

Lauren and Jessica stared at him with surprised looks on their faces.

Curtis was quite confused. "What? Was I being too blunt? I am sorry. There was just no spark to her. She didn't even rate as compared to you two."

Both of the ladies looked at me accusingly, and I held up my hands in front of me, deflecting. "I swear, I didn't lead or tamper with the witness." I glanced over at Terry and said, "I said almost the exact same thing about her. Sandrah believed herself to be a once-in-a-lifetime great beauty, completely irresistible to men."

Curtis made a face like someone smelling something awful. "I don't see it at all. I would have had no problems resisting her."

It was my turn to act smug. "See, I told you."

This made Jessica and Lauren laugh.

To my displeasure, the newsblasts did reveal that I was the first victim of the implementation of the "symbioid passion death plan". At least they mentioned that I was also the only one who had resisted and survived the assassination attempt. I was just waiting until this would change to something like I had survived because I had built up so much resistance due to my unsavory past.

The group found it fairly funny, as it later mutated into Erlinmination and Erlinuthanasia. I did hear a few mentions of someone dying this way as being Sandrahed and San-dreaded. The good news was that the Yant encryption hack was going to be blocked with new security updates, and there would be limits on the potency and types of pharmaceuticals carried by symbioids.

A few interesting back stories about my disappearance came when Gem Towler, my stylist— whom Jessica's and Lauren's aunt called The Red Tower—was arrested for trying to sell off a large number of my personal belongings. The new memorabilia seller she contacted didn't believe her story that I had willed it all to Gem, and she had called the police. Her apartment was raided, and they found boxes of my household goods stacked to the ceiling. This told me that I had too much stuff.

In another odd case, a woman whom I had never met claimed that she and I had been having a torrid, long-term affair. She claimed to have a recording of me promising to turn over my entire estate to her if I died. In a case of poor file management, she sent in the recording of her conversation with the person who was creating the bogus recordings instead of sending in the falsified recording. She called up and told them to send back that recording, and she would send the right one. She was angry, commenting to both the media and the police that she though it unfair that her case fell apart only because of a simple file mix-up. She was even more shocked and angry when they arrested her.

Even if that counterfeit recording had been accepted as legitimate, it wouldn't have mattered, as my trust freezes all sales, transfers, and proceeds from my estate for five full years after I am legally ruled dead and for seven years if my body is not found. Terry suggested this when we were building the safe houses, saying that I might need to disappear for a long period of time. That was wise, as we have seen... Extreme wealth makes people crazy, trying both to get it and to keep it.

For about two hours, we watched some of the revelations contained in Joden's media release until I was sick of the story. There would be plenty of days in the future when this would be all that we heard and saw. We were going to have to come out of hiding soon. That would be a horrible circus event. Our media rebirth could wait a day or two while we recovered from our goliath misadventure and the police rounded up the last of those involved in the conspiracy.

"So, what do you think, shall we go for a walk on the beach and maybe a swim?" I asked Lauren.

Lauren nodded and rose to her feet. "That would be nice."

Outside on the veranda, Lauren and I were leaning on the railing as we gazed out over the bright azure sea. We were shaded from the bright direct sunlight by a big white cloth diffuser wing. The water was calm and a delicate breeze floated past us. Maybe we would go sailing later if the wind picked up. We heard Jessica and Curtis leaving the house to go walk on the beach. They waved to us as they left.

As much as I enjoyed being around them, I was glad that they were off on their own, as I wanted to talk with Lauren alone. I wasn't sure how to start.

Lauren was scanning the striking blue horizon with a gentle smile on her face. "It is so beautiful here."

Fighting to gaze only at her face, I said, "Yes, it is...and so are you." Lauren looked down shyly. "Sorry. I didn't mean to embarrass you."

Lauren's expression was anxious, and I could tell that something big was going on. Had my staring and comments offended her? Combing my fingers through my hair, I tried to think of a way to broach a subject that was eating at me. I needed to act before it was too late.

Studying her gray eyes, I said, "Lauren? I have an important issue to discuss with you. You know that when we come out of hiding, the media is undoubtedly going to say that we are a couple. They expect that of me because of my past. The newsblasters can be trying, prying, and horrible. I am sorry if that implication would embarrass you, and I am sorry for the insane media frenzy that is coming."

"Jessica and I have discussed this. We have an inkling of how the newsblasters are going to go crazy when you rise from the ashes."

"They will be relentless. As I have experience in this, I will help guide and protect the three of you the best I can. Trust me, when they meet you and Jessica, they are going to absolutely flip. Terry's carefully cultivated anonymity is about to be shattered. I hope he can forgive me for that—actually, I hope all of you will be able to forgive me."

Lauren slowly nodded as she analyzed my face. "We understand it was not your plan. Besides, I am sure that we will all be just a small back story as compared to you being alive. Rolland 'The King' Newcastle, the newsblasters' wildest dream has returned from the dead."

Shaking my head, I replied, "I may be a dream for them, but I am done with the wild part." Measuring my words carefully, I said, "But seriously, with your wondrous face and awesome figure, I will be the back story. It will be 'Excuse me, ah...Rolland, isn't it? Can you step aside? We can't see Lauren. Lauren, can we get a swimsuit shoot lined up with you?'"

"I don't think so..." Embarrassed, she looked away. A shy, coy little smile eked out. Her eyes snuck back to seek mine.

She was adorable. "I wish I were exaggerating. The swimsuit request will be the least impolite and invasive thing they will ask of you. When they realize that you two are both beautiful and amazingly smart, it will get even crazier."

Steeling myself, I said, "But this is not what I need to talk to you about. I pray that it is not too quick or too sudden after all that we have gone through, but...Lauren, would you consider being my girlfriend and dating me?"

Lauren's eyes grew wide, and with the sweetest smile she replied, "I would love to."

Stepping over to me, she lifted up on her tiptoes, offering up her soft, wonderful lips. She kissed me so gently that I melted. Wow. I could not think of a more perfect kiss.

Her eyes were welling up with tears, and she smiled so brightly. I heard her whispering, "Please, don't be a dream...don't be a dream."

"It is not a dream, my dear Lauren. I could not be more serious."

Lauren stared up at me, and she let a small shy grin slip. "I have been trying to think of a way to ask you out...without seeming to be just like every other girl who has a crush on you."

My eyes grew wide and I beamed. "Miss DeHavalynd, are you saying that you have a crush on me?" Oh, that sounded egotistical. I was only trying to tease her.

She stared at me with a hint of fear in her eyes as she steadied herself. "Yes, since I was thirteen."

It is still strange to me that people that I have never met could ever have a crush on me. As stupid as this may sound, I often forget that I have been a marketed commodity.

"I hope that I have not been a disappointment to you. I have met a few of my infatuations in the past, and it has almost always been a severe letdown. We are all the same broken and self-absorbed people that you find everywhere. More often we are even more foolish. We just have the help of stylists and media teams to clean us up on a surface level."

Lauren laughed, her eyes twinkling. "Okay, so you didn't show up in a floating carriage pulled by flying pink unicorns to whisk me away, but I will give you points for presentation with the assault mech."

Her face became serious, and she stared up at me with those deep, glistening gray eyes. I was about to speak when she gently placed a soft fingertip on my lips.

She breathed in deeply and exhaled slowly, and her voice trembled as she said, "When I first heard that you were dead, I understood Jessica's mourning and pain when Paul died. I knew it was irrational for me to grieve so much for someone I had never met...but I did. Then, beyond belief, somehow you came back from the dead and showed up at my house. Then, when you made the AA-30s charge the T-37a that almost killed me a second time..."

Lauren was fighting back tears. "At the apartment, I got to know the real you, and I found that I really like who you are, even more than the media's version of you. All the while I kept thinking that you were so completely out of my league. You have everything, and I bring nothing. I feel like I am still that silly little girl with an impossible crush who is about to get her heart broken. Why would you want me? You can have anyone you want. When you show up again in the media, the prettiest and the most aggressive women will come out in herds to try and win your attention. I can't compete with that." Her eyes were seeking and fearing my response.

Astonished, I said, "You say that I can have anyone that I want." Lauren's face fell. "Then I choose you." A hopeful and lovely smile lifted her beautiful face. "My dear Lauren, you have no competition. You are simply the most amazing and remarkable woman I have ever met. You automatically win in every way that matters to me. As we are being so open, let me explain. After I came back to the Lord, I gave Him a detailed and almost impossible list of what I wanted in a mate. I wanted an incredibly smart woman who was beautiful but who didn't focus on her looks first. And she needed to be kind, funny, Godly, thoughtful, and generous to others. Those are just a few of the qualities that I had asked for."

"What about being very busty?" she teased, putting her hands on her hips and pulling her shoulders back.

I laughed and nodded emphatically, impressed with the display. "I was trying not to be a perv and make this a long list of your amazing physical charms, but yes, and very busty."

She grinned broadly. "Good. Because it's how God made me."

I kissed her again and said, "And I love it. He is the ultimate artist and craftsman. He has been extraordinarily generous in the gifts that He gave to you. Here's the deal—you surpass every one of those high standards that I asked for, many times over and in so many other areas that I didn't even think of. You win."

She blushed and impishly asked, "What do I win?"

Gazing into her soft, beautiful gray eyes, I said, "Me. All that I am, and I am sorry for that, but with God's help I will keep changing for the better."

"I gladly accept the prize."

I gave her another kiss. "Lauren, I hope that I am not going to scare you away by saying this, but I have fallen in love with you." Her face was so sweet, and there were tears in her eyes. We kissed again, and I held her close.

Lauren was radiant. "You are such a silly man. Do you really think that telling me that you love me would scare me away after we dealt with assassins, assault mechs, and four rampaging goliaths?" She kissed me again, sending wonderful chills down my spine. "Especially because I feel the same way about you, Rolland...I, too, have fallen in love with the real you."

Amazed and pleased beyond words, I laughed at her endearing forthrightness. "My dear, lovely Lauren. You are spectacularly beautiful inside and out. God is being so amazingly good to me and will be, I hope, to us as a couple for a long time."

Lauren stared into my eyes, and before she kissed me again she said, "Time will tell, my dear Mr. Newcastle, time will tell."

—THE END—

● ● ● ● ● ● ● ● ● ● ● ● ● ● ●

22

A Note from the Author

I didn't seek to hide my Christian faith from readers who were seeking a sci-fi novel. As a person trained in science who was once an atheist and agnostic, I am sensitive to how it felt when people pushed their faith on me. Back then, I would not have given this book a chance. My goal was to create a good, enjoyable read, but I cannot separate my faith from who I am.

Most of the Christ-driven experiences that Lauren, Jessica, and Rolland speak of together happened to me or my wife. I tried to stay true to our experience to keep them as real as possible. No, there is no one chasing me, nor am I a billionaire ex-playboy. I did have that horrible gaping hole in me that nothing could fill, though, and I did try many things seeking to feel whole and to find acceptance. God is the only thing that filled that emptiness.

The Mountain of God and the grass plain experiences happened to me. It was my wife to whom I explained the vision. Even Lauren's instant healing of her hurt was part of my experience and of others that I know. I know it sounds strange and unreal. I can only tell you in all honesty, these happened to me, and they changed my life forever.

I can say without any doubt, Jesus is real. He is not some abstract, made-up fable. He is calling you. No matter what you have or have not done, there is freedom, healing, and forgiveness that He alone can offer as a gift to you. As with any gift or opportunity that you are offered, you have to decide to take it or not. It is that simple. You **do not** have to be pure or free of addictions; you don't need to clean up your life or try harder to be right with God to be able to accept it. No one comes clean to the Lord. We come to Him a total mess.

All you need to do is say, "Lord Jesus, I accept Your life and Your death on the cross as complete payment for my sins, past, present and in the future. I believe that You are the Son of God who died for me and rose on the third day. Please come into my life and my heart and be Lord over me." Your faith doesn't have to be perfect to say this.

You may not be sure about any of that, and that does not matter. You are not expected to know everything or even to feel different. I didn't at first, as I expected fireworks or the heavens to open. If you say it, you are different, forever changed in amazing ways that are beyond our comprehension. I would suggest that you explore a few churches or speak to someone you know who is a Christian and ask them about it. Don't give up or despair. This is good news!

Your great adventure, if you seek it, is about to begin. Welcome to the family. The Father is the best and most loving Father that you could ever hope for. Your new Brother, Jesus, is amazing and powerful beyond words, and the Holy Spirit is a kind and wonderful Teacher. You have graduated into a new and better life.

My prayer for you—come Lord Jesus, come!

David